...ryone LOVE...

...arm ...earted and ...
with such a perfect ending'
Phillipa Ashley

'Perfect escapism!'
Cressida McLaughlin

'Perfect for a winter's evening . . . Loved it!!'
Julie Houston

'A moving, festive, absolutely gorgeous read!
Perfect for curling up with this Christmas'
Samantha Tonge

'A charming love story, that makes you want to curl up in a
cosy cottage [in] front of a roaring fire whilst drinking hot
chocolate. A perfect read in the run up to Christmas'
NetGalley reviewer

'This is a story that will pull at your heartstrings
and I absolutely loved it!'
NetGalley reviewer

'Oh. My. Gosh . . . This is a must-read [for] everyone who wants
to feel cosy and snuggly and get ready for Christmas early'
NetGalley reviewer

'A perfect read for the cosy evenings leading up to Christmas
and for getting you into the Christmas spirit'
NetGalley reviewer

'Loved this book!'
NetGalley reviewer

KATIE GINGER lives by the sea in the south-east of England, and apart from holidays to very hot places where you can sit by a pool and drink cocktails as big as your head, she wouldn't really want to be anywhere else. *The Perfect Christmas Gift* is Katie's eighth novel. She was shortlisted for the Katie Fforde Debut Novel of the Year award for her first novel *The Little Theatre on the Seafront*.

When she's not writing, Katie spends her time with her husband and two kids, and their dogs: Wotsit, the King Charles spaniel, and Skips, the three-legged Romanian rescue dog. (And yes, they are both named after crisps!)

For more about Katie, you can visit her website: www.keginger.com, find her on Facebook: www.facebook.com/KatieGAuthor, follow her on Twitter: @KatieGAuthor or sign up to her newsletter here: http://bit.ly/3gbqMS0

Also by Katie Ginger

The Perfect Christmas Gift

KATIE GINGER

ONE PLACE. MANY STORIES

HQ
An imprint of HarperCollins*Publishers* Ltd
1 London Bridge Street
London SE1 9GF

www.harpercollins.co.uk

HarperCollins*Publishers*
1st Floor, Watermarque Building, Ringsend Road
Dublin 4, Ireland

This paperback edition 2021

1
First published in Great Britain by
HQ, an imprint of HarperCollins*Publishers* Ltd 2021

Copyright © Katie Ginger 2021

Katie Ginger asserts the moral right to be
identified as the author of this work.
A catalogue record for this book is
available from the British Library.

ISBN: 978-0-00-842278-3

To our lovely great-gran Betty and great-grandpa Ernie

Chapter 1

'Amias,' Bella said before biting her lip to stop the laugh escaping. She shouldn't have found it funny, but it was. The boy looked ridiculous and the giggle emerging from his friend was so heart-warming, you couldn't fail to smile, but she pulled in her cheeks and put on her teacher voice. 'Please could you remove the pencils from your nose and ears and give them back to Umar and Richard?'

The nine-year-old boy did as he was told, looking slightly crestfallen. Luckily, Umar and Richard didn't seem to mind their return, given where they'd just been put.

Regaining her composure, she gave the same warning she'd given almost daily since term began. 'Pencils should stay in hands and not be inserted into your body. It's very dangerous, as I've told you before.'

What was it with boys this age and shoving things into every available orifice? She only had to turn her back for two seconds and someone had rammed something somewhere they shouldn't. Especially Amias. The boy was addicted to mischief. Only last week there'd been a slight panic when he'd stuck a marble up his nose. Bella had dislodged it by closing off his other nostril and making him blow his nose as hard as he could. The offending object had shot out at such a speed it rolled across the classroom and ended up under the arts and crafts trays. Half the class had then scuttled out of their seats, following its path to see where it had gone. And then there was the incident with the plastic frog and his inner ear which, quite frankly, didn't bear thinking about. Harrowing was the only way she could describe it. The number

1

of times she'd asked the question *why* only to receive a shrug in reply was mind-boggling.

Amias was what they'd describe at parents' evening as a 'lively' child. If he wasn't sticking things in places they didn't belong on his person, he was doing so on the school premises; shoving toilet paper into the sink or trying to steal it to throw at his friends during breaktime. Every class had a boisterous child like him, and though he could be a handful, on the whole, Bella considered herself lucky. She at least hadn't had to deal with Miss Radcliffe's Year 5 class and a boy they'd nicknamed Lucky Louis on account of his recent fractured wrist, busted lip, and the giant lump on his head, all from his antics on the playground.

Turning back to the board she continued to write out the sum they'd been working on.

'Miss?' Leonie asked, her quiet voice only just audible above the ruckus that had begun as soon as her back was turned.

'Yes, Leonie?' Bella turned back to her class.

'Can I go to the toilet, please?'

'But you've only just got back from break.'

'Yes, but I've drunk a whole bottle of water and now I really need to go.'

'Me too,' said her best friend, Hannah.

Bella absent-mindedly ran her hand over her chin-length blonde hair and tucked it behind her ear. 'Well, Leonie, you can go first and as soon as you're back Hannah can go.' Leonie frowned at the prospect of going all that way on her own as she stood up and pushed her chair under the table. 'Good girl for pushing your chair in. You can move yourself up for that.'

The frown fell away and before she left, Leonie moved herself up the behaviour chart pinned to the wall. Each class had a basic traffic light system, with red and orange being the naughty colours and then moving up through green and silver until you were on top of the gold band, and onto a bright shining star. If you made it onto the star, you earned a reward. Sometimes it was an eraser or a new pencil sharpener, but at this time of year, Bella began cracking out the chocolate. It was amazing how behaviour got so much better as they edged towards Christmas, even with the extreme level of excitement that always brought.

As it was only November, Bella's sweets were tiny chocolate balls in orange and green colours with monster faces on them left over from Halloween, but it wouldn't be long before she could start on the wonderful gold and silver coins. She didn't like the fake bank notes or credit card things you could get these days; they were just odd as far as she was concerned. Bella was all about tradition. It gave structure and meaning to that special time of year, much like a routine does for children, and being a primary school teacher, she knew how much that was needed, even though the children didn't always like it. Christmas traditions were the same for her. She didn't always realise what a comfort they were at the time. Like when she was helping her mum peel a million tonnes of carrots and potatoes on Christmas Eve after volunteering at Bluebell Park all morning. But when she looked back, she wouldn't have been anywhere else.

Her own excitement began to build as she thought of the fun to come. There was nothing quite like Christmas at a primary school. The excitement of the end-of-term play, posting Christmas cards into the little post box made out of cardboard in the corner of the classroom, making decorations during wet play.

As soon as anything remotely festive appeared in the shops she couldn't help but feel that fluttering in her stomach at the prospect of everything her favourite season had to offer: the smell of pine, bright-coloured baubles and twinkling fairy lights, hot chocolates and snuggling down by roaring log fires, her house a mini Santa's grotto.

There was nothing quite like December in Meadowbank. She loved living in the small village, deep in the Kent countryside, and adored the tiny village school where she worked. City schools had large metal fences around them or protective concrete walls, but Meadowbank Primary had a low flint wall that ran all the way around with views over the village green and duck pond to the front, or acres of fields to the back. The children always played in the larger back playground, where the school looked out over farms and meadows. The only traffic they had to worry about were tractors and the occasional duck that had made its way from the duck pond and was hogging the hopscotch. With only fifteen or so children per class, it was a pleasure to teach and nurture the little minds in her care.

'Right, let's try and get this sum sorted out, shall we?' Bella cheered. 'So, don't forget, we start here in the units column. Oliver, can you tell me what eight plus nine is, please?'

Oliver began counting on his fingers and Bella reminded him to try and do it in his head. He was such a good boy. Always playing nicely with the other children, especially Freddie in Miss Radcliffe's class. Freddie and his father Nick were her neighbours in Bramble Cottage.

Last week, Nina told her that Freddie had been far keener to stay in and hand out the books for the next lesson than to go out and play with his friends, of which he had many. Nina had been meaning to have a chat with him about it, but as far as Bella knew she hadn't been able to yet. It can't have been easy for Freddie with his mum leaving six months ago, running off to Bali with another man. It was bound to have an effect.

It had been the talk of the village and, of course, the staffroom. She couldn't understand why anyone in their right mind would leave the man Paige had left behind: Nick Cowley. He looked a bit like a stubbly Henry Cavill and who'd say no to that? Bella would obviously because she was happily in a relationship with Evan. In fact, she'd even go so far as to say blissfully happy. They never argued, never bickered, and agreed on almost everything, even down to what to have for dinner. Evan would sometimes tease her for being so optimistic about everything, but she liked it. It meant he knew her better than anyone. This would be their third Christmas in Lavender Cottage, and she was looking forward to making new memories and traditions with him over the years to come.

Bella was sure that Freddie's mum leaving was the reason for his staying in. This time of year must be especially difficult and she hoped Nina could get to the bottom of it. Bringing her mind back to her classroom, she heard Amias snigger at Oliver's use of his fingers and Bella shot him a warning look. He was skating on very thin ice this week.

'Seventeen, miss.'

She quickly double-checked in her head. 'Brilliant, Oliver, well done. Try and do it in your head though next time. And, Amias – if I see that pencil going anywhere it shouldn't, I'll be moving you down the chart and you're already on orange. If you go down to red, you'll be off to see Mrs White and I can't imagine she'll be happy to see you for the second time this week.'

Leonie returned from the toilet and Hannah made her escape. Another hand shot up.

Bella reverted to her normal cheerful tones. 'Yes, Briony.'

'Can I go to the toilet when Hannah gets back, please?'

Internally, Bella repressed a giggle. Ninety-nine per cent of her time was spent shepherding children to and from the toilet, but she was determined to finish the maths lesson that had been going on for about a million years and teach them at least one useful thing today.

'Yes, of course, sweetheart. Now, Amias, why don't you stop showing Richard your tongue because we've all seen it before, and tell me how you would work out our next sum?'

After much cajoling, including opening the window to wake them up, and downright bribery with the promise of an early story, the maths lesson was finally finished.

Just as they were about to break for a much-needed lunch, Mrs Brody, the Year 1 teacher, knocked on Bella's classroom door. 'Good afternoon, everyone. Good afternoon, Miss Moore.'

'Good afternoon, Mrs Brody,' the children chorused, and Bella felt a swell of pride at their good manners.

'Good afternoon, Mrs Brody. What can I do for you?'

'It's an exciting day, children. I have with me the Christmas play scripts and details of the roles you've been assigned.'

The children began shifting about in their chairs, stamping their feet and all talking at once. The noise level rose about eighty decibels and Bella clapped her hands together in the pattern she'd taught them. Most of them fell instantly silent as they copied her. A few delayed claps followed, and the chatter dissipated. Mrs Brody spoke again.

'I can see you're all excited, but you're going to have to wait until after lunch to learn your parts. Miss Moore will tell you everything you need to know later this afternoon. We agreed all the children would be told at two o'clock, Miss Moore, if you remember.'

'Yes, I remember. Thank you.'

Mrs Brody was planning the play like a military operation and there'd been much anticipation in the staffroom. With a final glance, she adjusted her owl-like spectacles and slid out of the door. Bella just about managed to sort the children out into school dinners and packed lunches before the noise level became too deafening. Grabbing her own packed lunch box, she led them down to the hall. Her stomach bubbled with excitement, as she thought of all the fun this season had to offer: baking with her mum and sister, the village parade, and the new grotto at Bluebell Park. It was going to be a busy one, but Bella wouldn't have it any other way. Life was too short to waste being bored. Not that Amias ever let her be bored at school.

'Amias, carry your lunch box in both hands, please. You don't need to balance it on your head.'

It crashed to the floor, and she helped him gather up his things. Maybe she could be bored for five minutes or so. That didn't seem such a bad idea right now.

* * *

'She's going a bit over the top this year, don't you think?' said Johnny Feker, the Year 6 teacher. He, Bella and Miss Radcliffe, or Nina to her friends, were all stood supervising the playground and musing on Mrs Brody's plans for the play. 'I mean she's even given it a subheading. It's not just called *The Christmas Commotion*. She's added on *A Comical Christmas Catastrophe* underneath. I thought we were just doing a knock-off pantomime. I didn't know we were putting on a sitcom.'

'Surely it's more of a farce or a musical?' asked Nina.

'Do you want me to blow my whistle in your earhole?'

'Oh, sir! But no thank you,' Nina replied, teasingly.

If only Johnny would pluck up the courage to ask Nina out, Bella was sure she'd say yes and there were no rules against getting involved with a colleague. If she were Nina, she'd be sick of waiting by now. He'd been there a year or so and they'd been like this from day one. It made Bella wonder what he was waiting for.

'Will you two cut it out? All this flirting is too much after Amias's lunchtime shenanigans.' Embarrassed, Nina and Johnny stared in opposite directions. Bella missed flirting though. She and Evan had been together for so long they didn't really do it anymore. Flirt, that is. They still did . . . it. Just not quite as often as they once had. Though he'd sometimes look at her with a twinkle in his eye, the days of flirty banter were behind them. It was all part of growing older, she thought ruefully. The next step for them was marriage and kids. She couldn't wait to have children of her own. Even on her worst days at school when the class had been unruly or a bit more of a handful than usual, she was still happy to be working with children and she couldn't wait for Lavender Cottage to be full of giggles and gurgles.

Staring out over the acres of fields that rolled and crested behind the school, she marvelled at how different Meadowbank was with each passing season. The spring brought new life and pretty colours, in the summer the air was awash with the scent of flowers and dancing butterflies, and in the colder months the village became a warm and cosy haven. Where some places felt bleak with the arrival of winter winds and cold chills, the small stone cottages that predominated the village remained welcoming and homely. Chimneys smoked, inviting people in with the prospect of cosy log fires and hot toddies. It was very much a tightknit community and one that had welcomed Johnny to the neighbourhood a year before, though it felt like he'd been there longer. The three of them had immediately hit it off, even though she was thirty-five and Nina and Johnny were both a good few years younger than her. The age difference didn't seem to matter as they all shared the same silly sense of humour and the oddities of their job glued them together.

'What did Amias do this time?' asked Nina, shivering. Her long hair of tight red ringlets poked out from under her hat.

'Somehow he managed to get cheese stuck under his fingernails and I don't mean a little bit. I mean, like an enormous wedge you'd find on a cheeseboard. I had to scrape it out with a dinner knife because it was hurting him. And then he tried to eat it.'

Johnny spluttered.

'The weird thing is, he didn't even have cheese sandwiches for lunch and neither did anyone sat with him. I've no idea where he got it from.' The chill wind whipped around the open space, sending ice down Bella's spine. She pulled up her scarf and tucked her gloved hands inside her pockets. A whistle dangled from her neck though she hadn't yet had to use it. The children were all running around like it was the middle of summer, some of them trying to surreptitiously remove their coats even though it was only five degrees outside. 'But you're right, Johnny. Mrs Brody's certainly stepping up her game this year. Apparently, she wants to buy some weird lighting rig for the school hall, but Mrs White's told her it's not in the budget and she'll have to make do with turning the lights up and down or putting a piece of coloured plastic over them as we've done every other year. I don't think she was that impressed. How was your morning, Johnny?'

It was a well-known fact that Johnny hated teaching Year 6. He much preferred the littler ones but it was customary for them all to swap around each academic year so they had variety and kept up to date with the different Key Stage curriculums. The Year 6s were always more of a handful because they were the big fish in the little pond and thought they ruled the world. Yet, there were still moments when they'd cry or show their innocence and need some reassurance. But that wasn't what bothered Mr Feker.

'Eleven times today they tried to call me Mr Fucker. I wish I could change my name. I've thought about it before, you know. I only haven't because it would break my dad's heart.'

'That's why they all think my first name's Nina,' Nina said sagely. 'If I admitted it was Titania they'd all call me Titty and then I'd have to move to another school. That was my nickname when I was at primary school and I absolutely hated it.'

'I'm not surprised,' Johnny said. 'I like the name Titania.'

'It's from Shakespeare.'

'Oh, look out, Mrs Brody's coming over.'

'Are you three ready to tell your class the parts they've got this afternoon?'

'We are, Mrs Brody,' Bella answered. 'I can't wait. They're going to be so excited.'

Meadowbank Village Primary was such a small school that there were only two Christmas plays a year. One for the tiniest Reception class up to Year 3, and one for Years 4, 5 and 6.

'Now I want us to be practising every day,' Mrs Brody said as if she were talking to her tiny five-year-olds.

'Every day?' Nina asked before immediately shying backwards under Mrs Brody's glower.

'Yes, every day. I want this to be the best one I've – I mean we've – ever done. I've worked hard on that script. I even did an online scriptwriting class in the summer, so I'd know exactly what I'm doing. I've learned all about pacing and the three-act structure and the hero's journey.' Bella bit her lip for the second time that day. It all seemed a bit excessive for a fake pantomime where half the children would be off with colds and the rest would either forget their lines or be too busy fiddling with their costumes to remember when to recite them. Last year, one of the teachers had actually had to step up on stage when one of the angels kept knocking the donkey's ears off. 'This year, I don't want you two and your lackadaisical attitude ruining it.' She pointed between Johnny and Nina.

'They won't, Mrs Brody,' Bella said, protecting them. 'I'll make sure of it.'

Johnny and Nina's attitudes weren't at all lackadaisical. They were just a bit more laid-back than highly strung Mrs Brody. Bella thought them two of the best teachers she'd ever known.

'Good,' Mrs Brody said. 'It's going to be fun, fun, fun for everyone.' She clapped her hands together, beaming.

After pointing once more between Johnny and Nina, Mrs Brody walked off. For a moment, no one spoke in the intimidating silence left in her wake until Johnny blew the air out through his mouth, puffing his cheeks.

'She is actually the most terrifying woman I've ever met. But here's a question. If you were in a pantomime, which end of the pantomime horse would you be?'

'The front of course,' Nina replied.

'Bella?'

'Yeah, me too. For obvious reasons. And because being the other end would put my back out.'

Before they fell into discussing the ins and outs (or fronts and backs) of the pantomime horse, Freddie came up to them and Bella felt her eyebrows pull together.

'Miss Radcliffe?'

'Yes, Freddie.'

'Can I go and set the books out, please?'

'Too cold?' asked Johnny. 'You just need to run around a bit. Want to play some football with me?'

'No, thank you. I don't feel well.'

Bella stepped forwards and put a hand on Freddie's shoulder. His face was so full of sadness her heart almost lurched out of her chest. 'Who were you playing with just now, Freddie? Don't you want to carry on? There isn't long till playtime's over.'

He shook his head. 'I was playing with Amias and Richard, miss.'

'And was everything okay?' asked Nina.

He paused for a moment. 'Yes, miss.'

'What's wrong, Freddie?' Nina leaned down to speak to him.

'My tummy feels funny, and I've got a headache.'

'All right. Don't forget to drink your water bottle through the afternoon, okay? I won't even tell you off if you need the toilet a hundred times.'

Freddie giggled and headed inside. A few minutes later, after checking her watch, Bella blew the whistle for the children to line up. She hoped Freddie wasn't coming down with something. An uneasy feeling nestled in the back of her mind. Should she ask Nina to speak to him? Maybe she could knock next door and speak to Nick. Perhaps she'd mention it all to Evan tonight. He was a brilliant sounding board and always helped her talk things through when she couldn't get her head around them. He'd help her decide on the best course of action.

The end of the day arrived rapidly, the afternoon flying by with talk of the Christmas play and everyone discussing their roles. Soon she'd be at home in her lovely warm cottage with the log fire burning. It was Evan's turn to cook tonight, and she couldn't wait to walk into the homely golden glow from the inglenook and smell the divine aromas emanating from the kitchen.

She let the children go for the final time that week, grateful for the weekend before her.

'Miss Moore? Miss Moore?' Bella checked where the voice was coming from to see Leonie's mum walking towards her. 'I was hoping to have a word with you.'

11

Concern balled in Bella's stomach. Mrs Barnes glanced towards the playground and Bella followed her gaze to see Leonie had gone off to play on the climbing frame. 'Of course. What's the problem?'

'It's about the play.' Mrs Barnes tucked her windswept hair behind her ear and sighed. 'We just can't afford a costume. Kurt lost his job last month and he's been looking every day but hasn't found anything yet. I don't even know how we're going to afford Christmas. I normally save all year round, but we had to get the car fixed so he could go to a job interview and that took everything we had. He didn't even get the job and now we're broke. Is there anything the school can do? Can they change her part so she's a narrator and can wear her own clothes? That would be a bit better.'

'She's a tiger, isn't she?'

Mrs Barnes nodded. 'What's all that about by the way? I didn't think there were many of those in the nativity.'

'Mrs Brody's written us a pantomime. She wants it to be fun and inclusive so some of the parts are a little unusual.'

'That's very nice of her, but I just looked online, and a tiger costume is still a tenner. I know that doesn't sound like much.' She dropped her hands, but Bella could see the pink tinge to her cheeks. She was embarrassed, and Bella felt for her.

'I completely understand. How does Leonie feel about changing parts?'

'She won't want to. She's so excited about being a tiger. I feel terrible doing this to her, but if I don't, she could end up looking like a laughingstock and then her friends would be mean to her.'

'I wouldn't stand for anything like that,' Bella reassured her. 'But I understand what you're saying. Does she have an orange T-shirt and black leggings? We could then do some face paint at school? I'll happily buy a palette to do the kids' faces.'

'She had an orange T-shirt in the summer, but I think she'll have grown out of it by now and her leggings are too small already. I don't know how I'm going to find the money for new clothes on top of everything else.'

Seeing her distress, Bella couldn't help but reach out and take her hand. 'Let me see what we've got in the dressing-up box and if not, I might have something somewhere. If she doesn't want to change parts let's see if we can make it work before I talk to Mrs Brody. Is that okay with you?' Mrs Barnes nodded agreement. 'I'll have a look later before I go home and let you know on Monday.'

'Thank you so much, Miss Moore. It's so stressful at the moment what with December fast approaching.'

'We'll sort something out. Try not to worry.'

Mrs Barnes went off, calling Leonie as she did so. Bella hadn't realised Mrs Barnes was having such troubles. There hadn't been any changes in Leonie's behaviour at school, but it must be so hard for her parents to keep everything normal at home with such worries hanging over them. If only there was something she could do. Evan had told her before she needed a thicker skin but she'd never quite managed to grow one.

Never before had she been so grateful to still live in Meadowbank near to her family and to have Evan by her side. She'd definitely see what she could do to help, just as her family would do for her if ever she were to need it. Fortunately, she never had.

How did she get so lucky?

Chapter 2

Even though it was only five-thirty, the tiny world of Meadowbank lay in darkness. As Bella circled the green to go to the village shop, the duck pond shimmered with silver light from the already risen moon. She nipped into the old-fashioned store for a bottle of wine to go with dinner and as she approached Dairy Lane, she smiled to herself. She was more than ready to kick off her shoes and curl up on the sofa with Evan. His car was parked in its usual spot and she wondered what he'd conjured up for dinner. He was a much better cook than she was. She hoped for something rich and flavourful to fill her grumbling stomach. A thick beef stew and dumplings or sausages and gravy were perfect for a night like this.

As she passed Freddie's house, she thought again about knocking and speaking to Nick, but Nina would surely have a handle on things and from the laughter coming from inside, he was clearly feeling better. Good.

Bella opened the living-room door and stepped back in surprise as Evan charged down the stairs. 'Crikey, Evan, what's up? What's the rush?'

She glanced at the living room. The lights were on, but the house was cold, and no fire burned in the grate. No delicious smells emanated from the kitchen, and she edged further inside. Straddled over two steps, his face had frozen in a mask of panic. He scratched his temple where strands of light brown hair were turning grey. Why was he holding a suitcase?

'Evan?' she asked again, her voice uncertain in the face of his silence. A heaviness began to fill her stomach, driving away the hunger.

'Bella. Ah, umm . . .'

For some reason she laughed. 'Evan, what are you doing with the suitcase? Have you got a work thing?'

He worked as an IT consultant for a firm in nearby Witchbury but he hardly ever worked late at the office or went to conferences. In fact, he normally knocked off at 4 p.m. At least he had done before the last couple of months. He'd also attended more conferences for his 'continuing professional development' lately and Bella had been happy for him to go and improve his prospects. She admired his ambition.

'Have you got another conference?' Why hadn't he messaged her or called to let her know? The heaviness inside her solidified to a stone-like dread.

'No, I – this is awkward. I hoped to . . .' He hesitated as if unsure whether to finish the sentence or not, and he couldn't quite meet her eye. 'I was hoping I'd be gone before you got home.'

'Gone? What do you mean gone?' A chill shot through her, and she longed for the glow of the log fire and its comforting warmth. He'd never looked so serious before. 'Evan?'

He stepped down the last few stairs and placed the suitcase on the floor, then took a piece of paper from the small side table where she normally dumped her keys and handed it to her.

'I left you this to explain everything. I thought it would be best.'

'Explain what? Is it a work thing? Is someone poorly?' She was utterly confused, and it was only on studying his grave face she realised what was happening. Bella's heart plummeted, falling to the pit of her stomach. 'You're – are you? – are you leaving?'

'Bella, I'm sorry.' He dropped his eyes and shook his head.

'This is a joke, right? This can't be real. Evan . . .?' She shook her head as Evan met her gaze for a second then dipped his eyes. 'But . . . why?' She hated how desperate she sounded, but she just couldn't understand. They were happy. A choked cry emerged, and she pressed a hand to her mouth as if she could force the pain back inside.

Evan reached out for her, ducking under the low beam in the

ceiling, but she backed away. He'd moaned at first about buying a small period property, but there weren't actually many other options in Meadowbank. It was almost as if the place had been stopped in time somewhere around the 1900s and apart from a few post-war rebuilds on the very edge of the village, it remained very much how it ever was. Bella loved the period features. The timber frames that ran across the ceilings, the large stone fireplaces and wonky doorways that she'd grown up with, but it all seemed strange now, in this moment.

'Bella, I'm sorry. This isn't easy, but I've met someone else, and we've fallen in—'

'Don't say it,' Bella cried, accidentally screwing up the unread note in her hand. 'Don't. You can't have. I mean – when? How? Who? I – Evan, I don't understand. We're happy. Aren't we?'

His face had taken on a hardness she'd never seen before. It made her feel pathetic and for a second she hated him for it. For doing this to her. His hand reached down to the handle of the suitcase as if he was getting ready to leave regardless of her wanting an explanation.

'I know this is hard, Bella, and I'm sorry for that. Truly sorry.' He didn't look sorry. Not really. 'It was why I wanted to be gone by the time you got back.'

'I got away early,' she replied, her voice small and quiet, like one of the children in class when she was telling them off. 'I thought as it was Friday—'

'I've met someone else,' he announced coldly. 'And we want to be together. I knew that wasn't possible in a small place like this where everyone knows everyone else's business. I didn't want people gossiping about me – about us finishing—'

Very noble, Bella thought gritting her teeth in an attempt to stem the tears falling down her face.

'So I'm moving out. To Witchbury.'

'With her?' Bella asked. Whoever *her* was. 'Are you moving in with her?' He didn't say anything but nodded. 'Who is she?'

16

'Her name's Pepper.'

'Pepper? What kind of a name is that?' Evan didn't answer. 'I mean, Pepper? Really? Who names their child after a vegetable? Or maybe technically it's a fruit, but still.' It was a stupid name. Evan scowled at her reply but unable to stop herself she carried on talking. 'Only a couple of weeks ago you were taking the mickey out of Pepper Potts when we watched *The Avengers*. You said she had a stupid name and we laughed about calling our kids Swede or Parsnip. Was that all just a sham to keep me off the scent?' Finally, the hardness fell away from his eyes and he looked embarrassed. She shook her head as it swirled with anger and hurt. 'I can't believe it. Had you planned to leave me then?'

'Bella, its complicated.'

She couldn't believe they were having this discussion. The coldness of the house bit into her bones and her teeth chattered. Was she in shock? Probably. She'd never seen this coming. Never had any idea he was seeing someone else, let alone that he'd planned to leave her.

Bella knew other couples broke up. It happened all the time. It had happened to her before she and Evan had got together; it had happened to her friends. It even happened to families like Nick Cowley and sweet little Freddie next door. But most of the time there were signs. People saw it coming and said things like: 'That's been on the cards for ages'. You'd only had to see Nick and his wife Paige together to know the relationship was strained. Even in public when they were trying to put on a good show, everyone could see it. Like at parents' evenings and the summer fair. Cracks were visible in the stilted touches and fake smiles they'd presented to the world, but things hadn't been like that between her and Evan. They'd been happy, loved-up, two peas in a pod. Their life together had been good. Perfect.

Well not good enough, clearly, she thought bitterly. Had he really been working late these past months? Had there even been a new project? She didn't always enquire about the details of his workload because she never understood his incessant use of IT terminology. Perhaps she should have done. Maybe then she'd have seen a sign.

'This is why I left you a note.' Evan pointed towards the screwed-up paper in her hand. 'I thought it would explain things better. You know I get tongue-tied under pressure.'

Under pressure? He wasn't under pressure. He was calmly standing there tearing her heart out. She was the one under pressure and didn't she have every right to know more? Evan picked up the case and began to move around her. She thought about blocking the door, forcing him to stay and answer her questions but her mind had gone blank with pain and she couldn't move. How could he be such a coward and try and sneak out without telling her face to face?

'I'll be in touch soon for the rest of my stuff, okay?'

Anger and rage pushed themselves to the forefront of her mind. 'Oh, will you now? Well let's hope I haven't destroyed it all before you get round to it.'

'Please, Bella, don't be silly.'

'Silly?' she squealed. 'Silly? How dare you call me silly.'

Her body convulsed but for all the vehemence in her words, her heart tore apart and she sobbed loudly. There was no lady-like sniffing, no dainty dabbing at her eyes. She wiped fiercely, smearing streaks of mascara across her cheeks as the realisation that her life as she knew it was now over. The man she'd loved and thought one day she'd marry had deceived her. Nothing could hold back the pain that coursed through her veins.

'I'm sorry, Bella. But I can't stay anymore. Read the note. It might explain it all better.'

With a final glance, Evan shuffled sideways like a crab, lugging the suitcase after him, and edged out of the door. Through the pane of glass she watched him walk down the path, climb into his car and drive off.

Bella collapsed onto the stairs. Inside, it was almost as if her heart had stopped beating. Perhaps if she'd been able to grow that thick skin he was always talking about, she wouldn't feel like she was dying. She'd be able to brush off the pain and look on the bright side as she normally did, but what bright side could there possibly be to being dumped? Near Christmas. At thirty-five.

As she sat staring at the back of the front door, she realised he'd taken one of the suitcases they'd bought for their first holiday together. One of the ones that had shipped their clothes into Lavender Cottage: their first home. He'd used something so special to slink off to his new girlfriend's house. He'd have taken his clothes. His mementos. As if she had to see it for herself, Bella charged up the stairs to their bedroom.

As she approached, she almost dropped the note until reflex tightened her fingers around it. The bedroom was a mess, but not just a mess as in dirty pyjamas left on the floor or an unmade bed. Drawers were open and clothes fell over the sides. On the floor, even more had been tossed here and there along with some discarded cosmetics. Had Bella not seen Evan leaving, her first thought would have been that they'd been robbed, but things like that just didn't happen in Meadowbank.

She scanned the room once more, trying to focus through her misted vision. The drawers were open because he'd scooped out all his clothes. His side of the wardrobe hung empty, and the hangers clattered together where his suits had been. For the first time Bella's unwavering optimism could find nothing good to hold on to, nothing positive to think about. She felt herself falling into a deep, dark hole that she wouldn't be able to climb out of.

Evan had left her and worse than that, he'd also cheated. How had he become unhappy enough to do that? The only conclusion she could draw was that for all this time, he must have been pretending a happiness he hadn't felt. But for how long?

Bella sniffed back the pain as she unwrapped the tight ball of paper, but she knew there was nothing he could say in these words that would lessen her pain. Everything he'd said was written down.

Nothing more, nothing less, and unsure what she was supposed to do after such a monumental shock, Bella lay down on the bed among the old, worn-out clothes he'd left behind and cried.

As the house grew colder, Bella shivered. She couldn't stay there forever, sprawled out on the bed, drowning in heartache. Even though all she felt like doing was putting her pyjamas on and sitting in front of the fire, basic human functions needed performing like eating and drinking, and she needed a wee. Though she felt like she'd cried out all the moisture in her body as her mouth was parched and her throat dry and scratchy.

Pulling off her sensible dress and tights, she threw on her warmest pyjamas and dressing gown. It was like being encased in one of her mum's hugs. The thought of telling her family, knowing it would upset them as much as it had her, filled her with dread, but she had to. Someone might have seen Evan leave and news would be travelling around the village. Not in a horrid gossipy sort of way. Only one or two of the villagers were like that. Everyone else would be kind and thoughtful, checking in to see if she was okay, but she wanted her parents to hear the news from her.

Gingerly descending the stairs as if she were an old lady and her limbs unable to support her, Bella made her way to the living room and summoned enough courage to light the fire. Just seeing the flames come to life, filling the room with a warm, orangey hue eased her tense muscles. As the initial shock wore off, she was left with aching limbs but, feeling the warmth grow on her skin, she sighed.

How could it even be possible? It was a cliché to wish it were a dream, but that was strangely how it felt. Like Evan was going to walk back in any second and say it was all a stupid joke. It wouldn't be a very funny joke and she'd probably have some choice words to say to him, but that was preferable to the reality of being thirty-five and newly single when everyone, including your own sister, was settling down and having babies.

Bella pressed a hand to her gurgling stomach. Was she hungry or too upset to eat? Sometimes it was difficult to tell. Her body seemed to crave food no matter what she was feeling, especially in the winter when only rich, gravy-laden stodge would do, but cooking anything was beyond her right now. Leaving the warm living room, she grabbed a tin of beans from the cupboard, poured them into a jug and set them to cook in the microwave. Then, taking the largest glass she owned down from the shelf, she decanted most of a bottle of wine into it. It wasn't that she particularly wanted alcohol. It was just easier than making a cup of tea. All that filling and boiling the kettle, finding the tea bags, milk, sugar, stirring: it all seemed too much effort to her numb mind.

The microwave pinged and she took out the jug and grabbed a spoon from the draining board. The breakfast things were still piled there where she'd washed them up that morning. Evan had sat with her then, eating breakfast before heading off to work. All the while they'd chatted like it was any other day, had he been planning to sneak away?

She replayed the conversation in her head searching for signs. He'd been a little quieter maybe, but he said he'd woken up with a slight headache. She'd thought maybe he was working too hard. A couple of projects had been causing him some stress lately, or so he said. Had those 'projects' been worries about a fancy woman named after a fruit and her desire for him to move in?

Grabbing her first-year-at-university inspired dinner and slumping back on the sofa, Bella watched the flames flicker and dance. She put the television on just to fill the house with noise. Her mind was unable to focus on any one particular thing, swamped as it was, by the tumultuous feelings roiling inside her, but sitting in silence was somehow worse. It seemed to magnify the deep feeling of loss, and grief.

A faint ringing from her pocket shocked her back to life and the beginning bars of her favourite Nineties song 'Groove is in the

Heart' played out. Normally, it never failed to make her smile; this time, though, she could barely see the screen for tears. A part of her hoped it was Evan but even if it was, what would she say to him? And what could he say to her that she'd be willing to hear? Anger surged inside her again, but it was her sister's voice that came down the line as soon as she'd swiped to accept the call.

'My feet are like gigantic boats. Meat boats. They've swollen up so much I can't wear anything other than Crocs and you know how much I bloody hate Crocs. I didn't think there was any excuse for ugly footwear but apparently being seven months pregnant is one. And how am I supposed to wear them in November? My feet are freezing. It's not like I can wear Crocs with socks. There are some lines that just shouldn't be crossed. How can they be swollen and freezing at the same time?'

Bella swallowed, willing the corners of her mouth to lift up, but no matter how much she tried, she couldn't quite manage it.

'Are you there?' Caro asked before launching into a more detailed description of her podiatry ailments. 'I can barely see my toes. They're like dumpy little cocktail sausages attached to a slab of meat. Bella? What's the matter? You're very quiet.'

Taking a breath, Bella managed to squeak out the words 'Evan's left me,' before dissolving into tears again and nearly spilling her jug of beans over the sofa. The line went dead, and Bella slipped the phone into her pocket, knowing exactly what was happening.

Less than five minutes later, her sister stood on the doorstep, and the voices of their mum and dad were audible from just down the lane.

'What happened?' Caro asked, taking her sister in a giant bear hug. It was quite hard for Bella to circle her arms around her sister's bump. Caro released her and rested her hand on her stomach.

She wiped the tears from her cheeks. 'I came home and he was on the stairs, trying to get away before I got back—'

'Oh, my darling girl!' Her mum and dad were hurrying down

the short garden path. 'Oh, my poor sweet darling. Caro phoned. Where is he? Is he here? I've got something to say to that – that . . . Are you eating beans out of a jug?' Cynthia turned to her husband. 'Mungo, she's eating beans out of a jug.'

As her mother bustled past her and into the living room, taking the bean jug as she went, Bella's dad leaned forwards and gave Bella a kiss on the head. 'He's a prick if he's left you, Bella. And if he's a prick, you're better off without him. I know it hurts too much to see that right now, but you'll realise it soon.'

Bella closed the front door behind them. 'He's gone off with some woman named Pepper.'

'Pepper?' The three of them screeched in unison.

A slightly hysterical laugh emerged, and Bella pressed a hand to her lips.

'Well, that's a stupid name,' said her mum.

'Isn't it?' agreed Caro. 'It's like Peppa Pig. Who'd call their child that? No wonder she's got issues.'

'How do you know she's got issues?' Bella asked.

'Umm, hello. She's stolen someone else's boyfriend and she's named after a vegetable.'

'It's a fruit actually.' Why did she keep saying that? It didn't actually help anything and saying it out loud made her seem deranged but still her lips kept moving and sounds emerged. 'It's got seeds in it.'

'Hardly the point, dear,' Cynthia said, taking off her coat and draping it over the sofa. 'Now, sit down and tell us everything.'

She patted the sofa and after Bella squeezed in next to her as she would have done as a little girl, she told them exactly what she'd found when she'd got home.

Her dad was the first to speak. 'That absolute—'

'Now, now, Mungo,' Cynthia replied. 'You're going all splotchy. Remember your blood pressure.'

Mungo took a deep breath. 'I don't think I can actually say what I want to call him out loud. I'll get hit by lightning or

23

dragged down to hell or something, but he better not change his mind and come crawling back. I'll have a few words to say to him if he does.'

Bella felt numb. The events unfurling around her were like something she'd see in a sitcom. She felt detached and like it was all happening to someone else or in a different universe to her usual one. 'I'm going to have to go to bed on my own,' she said suddenly, tears welling in her eyes. 'And I'll be on my own at Christmas too.'

'No you won't,' her mum said. 'You'll be with us.'

'We spend most of the day with Mum and Dad anyway,' offered Caro. Which was true. Though they normally only intended to stay for Christmas morning, once the Moores got together there was no separating them. Especially when the booze was opened. Evan had always found that difficult, but he'd learned to accept it. Was that another thing that had made him leave? Could he not face another Christmas with her family? 'And I need to tidy my bedroom.'

'I won't moan at you if it's messy,' Cynthia joked and Bella explained how Evan had left it. 'Arsehole,' Cynthia declared, crossing her arms over her chest only to release them immediately and hug her daughter.

'Maybe I'll sleep in the spare room tonight. I just can't face it.'

'I think that's a good idea,' Cynthia said, rubbing her back. 'Sleep in the spare room tonight and I'll tidy for you tomorrow. Caro will come up with me in a minute and we'll get you some clothes for the morning, so you don't have to even look at it, and by the time you get home from Bluebell Park I'll have cleaned it all and it'll be good as new. That's if you're still volunteering tomorrow.'

Bella rested her head on her mum's shoulder. At the moment she wanted to stay here, forever protected from the reality of her life by the safety and love her family offered, but she couldn't – wouldn't – let people down and the other option was sitting

24

alone in her cottage all day. 'No. I'll still go. Thanks though, Mum. I love you.'

'We love you too, sweetheart,' her dad said. 'I promise, this won't seem as bad in the morning. It won't be long till my little ray of sunshine is shining again.'

A vision of Miss Havisham only in more comfortable clothes and fleecy slippers popped into Bella's head. She felt a million miles away from her usual self and even the prospect of Christmas had lost its magical glow.

Could what her dad said be true? She didn't think so. If anything, she was sure she was going to feel worse tomorrow. Right now, none of it seemed real. The only thing she knew for sure was that waking up tomorrow without the man she'd loved – that she still loved because feelings didn't get turned off like a light switch just because the other person changed their mind – was going to hurt like hell.

Chapter 3

A knock at the door woke Bella the next morning far earlier than she would have liked. Opening her eyes, realisation dawned that there was no one in the bed with her and that she was in the drabber spare room she'd hoped would one day become a bright, pretty nursery. Forcing back tears, she climbed out of bed and slipped on her big fluffy dressing gown. Her dad had been wrong: it hadn't seemed better this morning. In fact, realising it was real and this would be her life from now on felt like a knife to her heart.

After her family had left last night, which hadn't been until after ten, she'd gone straight to bed, but even with extra blankets over the top of her thick duvet and the heating on, she hadn't been able to get warm. She knew it was shock: her body starting to react to the pain in her heart. Her mind had swiftly followed as the numbness wore off and, stupidly, she'd thought of all the practical things she needed to do: taking his name off the utility bills and buying him out of his half of the property because there was no way she was leaving Lavender Cottage. At least if she cut back on other things, she'd be able to afford the mortgage on her own. They were all things to be thankful for, but they hadn't stopped her shivering in the empty silence of the house as she squeezed her eyes shut, tired of crying.

The knocking continued and Bella grimaced as she glanced at the clock. It was only just seven. She didn't need to be at Bluebell Park until a quarter to nine and was looking forward to at least a small lie-in. Another bang on the door forced her to shout, 'Hang on, I'm just coming,' as she descended the stairs, but the only response was some high-pitched giggling.

Frowning, she opened the door. 'Mum, Caro, what are you doing here?'

'We're taking you on a trip to cheer you up,' her mum answered.

'We talked about it last night after we left,' Caro said, bouncing on her tiptoes which, considering she was enormously pregnant, was no mean feat. 'Luke doesn't mind. He's going to paint the nursery today anyway.'

Bella yawned. It was still dark outside, and the world of Meadowbank lay fast asleep. As she should have been. A few birds twittered and chirped in the hedgerows, and the odd light was on in downstairs windows, but nothing moved apart from the trees. 'I don't understand what you're talking about. My head hurts, my eyes hurt, and I just want to go to back to bed.'

'Rubbish,' Cynthia replied, barging past her and stepping into the house. She immediately began removing her coat. 'We knew today was going to be difficult for you so we decided a nice trip out with two of your favourite people would be just the ticket.'

'But I can't. I'm volunteering at Bluebell Park today.'

Bluebell Park sat on the edge of the village, past the tiny lanes of picturesque, thatched-roof cottages and beyond the outer ring of enormous posh houses suggestive of somewhere Lizzy Bennet would have lived with her brood of sisters. It was a beautiful woodland park complete with a playground and a central area with little wooden huts reminiscent of European Christmas markets. It was run by volunteers, of which Bella was one, and they co-ordinated the hiring of the little huts by various local business. Every weekend, those who visited could buy fresh fruit and vegetables from local farms or other local goodies. At this time of year, one of the huts was always booked out by Annie's Tearoom from the village, providing hot chocolates and snacks, and the others by friends and neighbours who ran crafty sidelines in crochet or jam making.

They were also in the process of erecting a new chalet that would be decorated as Santa's grotto. Every year, old Mr Tomlin with his home-grown bushy white beard donned tiny glasses and a Santa suit, thrilling the children in his role as Father Christmas. Before Bluebell Park had opened, they'd set him up on the village green in a makeshift tent but there never seemed to be enough room with the village Christmas tree and the local church's nativity scene. It also stopped children being able to actually play on it. Even the grumpy ducks objected to the idea and the illusion of a magical, snow-laden workshop was somewhat ruined when they toddled in nibbling the wrapping paper off the fake presents or attacking Mr Tomlin's legs. Moving it to Bluebell Park had been Bella's idea and one everyone was in favour of.

'Don't worry, your dad said he'd cover you there,' her mum said, waving away her concerns.

'Dad?' Bella was now wide awake.

'Yes. Don't look so surprised. He is capable you know. He quite fancies working with Adam to put up the grotto. He said he doesn't know why you haven't asked him to help already. Between you and me, I think he was a tiny bit insulted.'

'I didn't ask because the last time Dad hammered anything, he missed the nail completely and took his fingernail off. Plus, he swore copiously in front of some of my pupils.'

'Oh, yes,' said Cynthia suddenly remembering. 'It went horribly black, and his finger was awfully swollen. He kept moaning and waving it at me like I should be doing something to fix it. What he imagined I could do I've no idea. I did tell him to be careful.' Cynthia brightened, forgetting about her husband's agony. 'Don't worry though. As Adam's a carpenter I'm sure he'll do all the hammering. Your dad will probably just be holding and passing stuff all day. But I might just text Adam and advise him not to let your dad near any *No-nails*. Do you remember the debacle with the picture frame and his middle finger?'

Bella turned to Caro hoping for some support, but Caro was giggling away at the memory and her giant smile and the posh make-up she'd applied told Bella she was as much in favour of this trip has their mum was.

'Come on,' Caro said, ushering her back up the stairs. 'Time to get dressed. We're going Christmas shopping somewhere special.'

Knowing that resistance was futile, Bella did as she was told. Her puffy eyes, sore from crying, struggled to focus as she made it back up the stairs. Her legs felt heavy like someone had removed her bones and replaced them with concrete slabs. Telling herself to find the positives, she didn't know if this was a good idea or a bad one, but she was grateful for her family all the same. Though being at Bluebell Park would take her mind off things, there was every possibility she'd spend the day being asked about Evan and if she was all right, which would invariably bring more tears and additional pain. A day out of the village might be just the thing.

Half an hour later, Caro bellowed from the bottom of the stairs. 'Are you ready yet? What's taking so long? I'm heavily preggers and even I manage to get dressed quicker than this even though I have to wear clothes the size of circus tents and Luke has to put my socks on for me. If you don't hurry up, I'll need another wee.'

'She keeps crying and washing all her make-up off,' Cynthia answered from Bella's spare bedroom.

Bella dabbed at her eyes and sniffed as her mum handed her another tissue. 'Don't worry, I think I'm done now.'

'Good, then let's get going or we'll miss our train. And I know I said I'd clear this today, but I'll do it tomorrow.'

'Thanks, Mum. Where are we going?'

'You'll find out soon enough. Come on.'

After she'd locked the front door behind her, she followed her mum and sister down the small path to Caro's car.

'Oh, this bloody gate has come off its hinges again,' Cynthia moaned. 'You've got to get someone to sort it out, Bella. I'll ask your dad to do it tomorrow.'

'He'll be knackered from a day at the park. Just leave it be, I'll sort it later.' Evan had been promising to fix it since the summer but every weekend there'd been a million and one other things to do. Though sometimes she'd wondered what he did while she was volunteering at Bluebell Park. Shag his fancy woman, probably.

Just as she lifted the broken gate up onto the latch, Nick – Freddie's dad – came out of Bramble Cottage next door to put some rubbish in the bin.

'Bella, hi. You're off out early.'

'Hi, Nick.' She plastered on a smile hoping that if she faked it, she might feel less like her heart had been ripped out, used as a frisbee, and then chomped by an angry dog. 'Freddie still in bed?'

'Yeah. We had a bit of a late night last night. Sorry.'

Despite it all, Bella chuckled. Nick always seemed to think that as she was a teacher, she was continually judging his parenting skills, though the reality couldn't be further from the truth. He'd been doing brilliantly as a single dad. Paige had always been a selfish creature and thought herself far too good for the quiet village Bella loved dearly. She was also delusional thinking she was too good for lovely Nick Cowley. If anything, it was the other way around. He was outrageously good-looking with dark brown, almost black hair and blue eyes. As a landscape gardener, his body had more muscle than most men dreamed of. More than that though, he was kind, and a devoted, if somewhat disorganised, dad.

Freddie appeared at his elbow dressed as a stormtrooper, though his mask and gun were covered in smears of red paint.

'Wow, Freddie, I love your costume,' Bella said. Switching into teacher mode had brought some life back to her voice.

'Thanks, Miss Moore. I'm a stormtrooper, but Dad let me put some red paint on it at Halloween, so I looked more murdery.'

'That's not quite the word I used,' Nick added, placing a hand on his son's shoulder. 'I think I said scary.'

'No you didn't. You definitely said murdery.'

A faint blush appeared on Nick's cheeks and he shook his head. 'Thanks for that, son.'

30

'It's fine,' Bella replied, and for a second, the emotional noise in her head faded away. 'We're all supposed to look a little scary on Halloween.'

With a strange grunt that emanated from somewhere under his mask, Freddie darted back into the house pretending to shoot his gun.

'Listen, Bella, I'm sorry,' Nick said, and Bella inhaled. Was this to be her first conversation about Evan? Had Nick seen him leave? The news was probably all around the village by now. 'I – umm—' Nick continued and feeling tears well in her eyes she knew she had to stem the flood.

'Thanks, Nick, but honestly, I'm fine. I mean, I'm kind of not fine. I had no idea Evan was planning on leaving me, but then you don't do you, I suppose. I'm sure you didn't expect it either, but I'm just taking each day as it comes and – and I'll get over it eventually.' Did she mean that? She wasn't quite sure right now, but words kept tumbling from her mouth. 'Having said that, my heart is kind of breaking, but I hope it'll get less and less every day as I learn to live with it.'

Why was she being so honest with him? Rabbiting on like she was performing some kind of crazy am-dram monologue. Perhaps it was knowing he'd gone through the same thing. An annoying tear trickled from her eye and she dabbed at her face with her big woolly glove. When she looked up, Nick had grown ashen, and his eyes were wide. Bella glanced towards the car, seeing her mum and Caro unsubtly studying the houses on the other side of the lane.

'Oh, look. A duck,' said Caro.

'Yes, lovely,' their mum replied.

'You weren't actually going to say anything were you?' asked Bella.

'No. Sorry. I was going to say I'm sorry that Freddie said murdery.'

'Oh.'

'Yeah.' He pushed his hands further into his pockets and stared at the ground.

'So, you didn't know . . .' She pointed to the house as if that explained everything.

Nick shook his head. 'No, sorry.'

Bella closed her eyes slowly, wishing the ground would open and swallow her down into its depths. Why had she done that? She should have known that of all people, Nick Cowley was not going to be talking about his feelings or hers. They were neighbours. It wasn't like they were best friends who confided in each other daily. Christ she was an idiot.

'Right. Well, that's rather embarrassing, isn't it?' Bella gave a small laugh. 'Sorry. I just assumed – you know what this place is like – I just thought—' She shook her head. 'And yet, here I am, still talking. I really should shut up now.'

'I hadn't heard you and Evan had split. I'm sorry.'

Dropping her eyes and running a finger over the top of the small white gate, she said, 'He left me yesterday when I got in from work. He was just on his way . . . out.'

'Wow.' Nick shook his head. 'That's tough.'

'It is.' She summoned courage enough to look at him and an understanding passed between them. As the moment grew awkward, she muttered a quick goodbye and dived into the car. Caro drove away, almost breathless from laughing and Bella stared straight ahead. 'Don't. Say. A. Word.'

'I wouldn't dare,' Caro squealed, like a pig being chased in its pen. 'But I have to say that's probably my favourite embarrassing memory of yours now.'

'Oh shush!'

'Poor boy,' Cynthia added from the front seat. 'He was absolutely terrified.'

Caro pressed a hand to her side. 'Oh God, I'm getting a stitch.'

'But isn't he handsome when he's surprised,' Cynthia continued. 'When his eyes go that wide you can really see how blue they are.

And he's even better-looking with all that grass and mud washed off him. I quite like him dirty as well though. A bit rough and ready and—'

'Mum!' Caro and Bella shouted in horror.

'Stop it!' Caro yelped. 'I've got to calm down before this baby makes an early arrival.'

Bella could still feel the mortification pulsing through her veins as they drove to the nearest train station, but at least it had taken the edge off her heartache for a second.

Once on the train, her crazy mum unpacked some pastries and Bella settled back and watched the scenery pass by.

'Where are we going then?'

Bella had an idea but hadn't heard for sure because every time an announcement was made her mum and sister shoved their hands over her ears and started shouting. Bella hadn't wanted to ruin their surprise.

'We're going to London,' Cynthia said while Caro nodded along excitedly.

Bella allowed a smile to fill her. Every year the three of them made a trip to London to do some special Christmas shopping. In reality, by the time they normally went in early December, they'd already bought their presents. Getting them online and delivered to your door was far less stressful than battling through crowds desperately trying to get things before they sold out. Their trip to London was always more about looking at the pretty lights, soaking up the special Christmassy atmosphere you could only find in the city, and people-watching. They might grab one or two things, but ultimately the trip was about the three of them spending time together. They'd drink too much, giggle too much and get in people's way as they stopped outside wonderfully decorated windows.

What would today be like? Bella wondered. Would it have any of the magic it had before?

'We don't normally do this for ages though. Will there be any decorations up yet?'

'The Covent Garden tree went up yesterday,' Caro replied. 'I checked. We just felt you needed some cheering up after last night's shock and thought we'd bring it forwards. I can't imagine trying to go places in another month's time. It's hard enough moving about now.'

'You don't mind, do you?' Cynthia asked. 'Your dad worried it would be too much too soon but sitting around at home or being at Bluebell Park wasn't going to help any either.'

'I appreciate it,' Bella replied, tearing a piece from a delicious pecan plait and popping it into her mouth. She then sipped from her takeaway coffee, her appetite returning. Her heart was still utterly broken, but her mum was right. Being in Meadowbank today was going to be mentally tough. At least she'd have a day away to process everything that had happened or bury her saddest thoughts under happier memories before she faced everyone in the village. 'Actually, I'm really grateful. Thanks, sis. Thank you, Mum.'

'You're welcome. Now let's eat these up so we've got some energy for trampling those streets and walking our legs off.' Caro looked alarmed at their mother's words. 'Don't worry, we can take lots and lots of coffee breaks.'

The beautiful rolling hills and pastures of Meadowbank, which even in winter kept their verdant shades of green, were soon replaced by the busy station at Witchbury and from then, urban landscapes dominated until the tower blocks and graffiti-ridden bridges of London popped into view.

Bella loved their Christmas visit to the city. It was like entering a different, faster, more exciting world, but she was always happy to come back home again. The train pulled into the slick station at the heart of the metropolis and Bella couldn't deny the small flicker of eagerness trying its best to light inside her.

Her horrible brain wondered what Evan was doing now with Pepper. She sounded like the type to drink a green juice every morning or eat things with chia seeds in she'd made the night before. Maybe she had a tiny, slender frame rather than the rounded hips and bum Bella had. She sounded pretty. Cynthia's excited voice pulled Bella back from the edge of the rabbit hole. Going down that road wasn't going to end well but a dark, meddling voice inside tried to pull her in. She ignored it, enjoying the bustle of the train station.

'Get your tickets ready,' her mum said, waving hers in the air as she trundled forwards.

'Will do, Mum,' she and Caro replied. Then Caro threaded her arm into Bella's. Whatever happened, she was going to ignore the pain in her heart and hope that today would help it to heal it while she wasn't looking.

After a short tube ride, they left the musty heat of the underground and walked up the stairs to the fresh, cold air of Covent Garden. Within minutes they were surrounded by busy shoppers and shop workers scurrying about like ants in a nest. The giant Christmas tree twinkled against the pale November sky and Christmas music permeated the air as an early busker set himself up ready to make some money. His quiet strumming as he gently sang 'Silent Night' almost brought tears and Bella sucked in a breath, determined to soak up the sparkle and glitz of the city at Christmas time.

'Where shall we start?' asked Caro. 'Covent Garden Market or Oxford Street?'

'Covent Garden Market,' said their mum, leading them on. Caro and Bella exchanged glances, surprised she wasn't holding an umbrella up like a tour guide. 'That way we can have another coffee and people-watch. I always love seeing everyone getting started with their day while we're here just to relax and chat. And I need to spend a penny.'

'I thought I was the one who should need the loo all the time?' asked Caro.

'Not at my age, dear. Two children and age mean Tena Lady and—'

35

'Nope,' cried Bella, holding her hands up. 'Whatever you're going to say, don't say it. I don't think I can cope with it today.'

As they passed the giant Christmas tree where the children of tourists were gazing up in wonder, Bella's eyes fell to a lone beggar being chased away from the shop doorway he'd been sleeping in. She didn't blame the waiter who was asking him to leave as kindly as possible, but the reality saddened her. Somehow her brain always erased those sights and the gloomy feelings they stirred from her memories, leaving only the bright lights, Christmas smells and excited atmosphere of London.

Covent Garden Market at Christmas time was one of her favourite places to be in the whole world. There really wasn't anywhere else like it. Yes, London also had the Southbank Christmas market and Winter Wonderland, but for Bella, sitting in the enclosed, glittering space with her mum and sister was just one of those Christmas traditions she loved so much.

Relaxing at their small table, Caro strategically placed so she had enough room for her bump, they cradled their decaf lattes and inhaled the aroma of rich, velvety coffee. Spooning the froth from the top of hers, Bella listened to the growing chatter and the ever-present hum of music. Up above, the arches shone with beautiful golden lights while giant red baubles swung from the ceiling. Though it was cold and none of them had removed their coats, the bustle of the market gave a sense of warmth. Around the edge of the upper floor hung a garland of ivy, and Bella's excitement for Christmas began to grow again, even though hers would be very different this year. She stared down at her coffee.

'You're thinking about him, aren't you?' asked Caro.

'Sorry. I wish I could stop it, but my brain keeps bringing him up.'

'Don't be sorry, my darling,' her mum said, reaching out a hand and laying it gently on top of her own. 'It's only natural. You had one hell of a shock last night, but that's why we brought you here. We wanted you to know that you can still create happy memories even feeling as broken as you are and when you look back in six months' time, you'll only remember today and not all that happened last night.'

'Oh, Mum, don't. I'll cry.' Bella sipped her coffee hoping it would fool her brain into doing something else.

'Too late,' Caro sniffed waving her hands in front of her face, fanning herself. 'Pregnancy hormones are the worst. Don't worry, I'll stop in a minute.'

The three of them burst into peals of laughter as they finished their coffees, and after Cynthia had a quick loo break, Caro too for good measure, they began their wanderings around London.

On Oxford Street, traditional red buses passed under arches of lights brightening the grey winter sky. Every tree was covered in bright white decorations and the intimidating city seemed more magical. The swiftly moving crowds made Christmas seem like it was only moments away, but this was what Bella loved about her visits to the city. The slower pace of Meadowbank suited her far better day to day, but she liked to be reminded of the world outside her door on occasion.

By lunchtime, shopping bags brimming with Christmas gifts covered the floor at their feet as they sat at a restaurant near one of the theatres, munching their way through three enormous Caesar salads. The small table by the window had barely been big enough to hold the giant bowls they'd been delivered in, but they were persevering admirably. Caro most of all.

'I wish I could have had the four-cheese pizza,' she said, manoeuvring a forkful of food into her mouth. 'Do you know the one food I miss most is blue cheese.'

'It wouldn't be Christmas without blue cheese,' Bella added.

'More for us,' teased their mum. 'I got a whole wheel this year.'

Caro groaned.

Bella took a break and stared out of the window. 'There's another one,' she said, nodding to yet another homeless person stooped in a doorway. He shuffled on the spot, moving from foot to foot in the cold wind.

'Why are you counting?' asked Caro. 'It's depressing. You've given them so much money today you shouldn't feel sad. You've helped lots of people—'

'And unfortunately, love,' Cynthia added, 'you can't help everyone.'

'I know,' Bella replied. She took a sip from the glass of prosecco Caro had insisted she and their mum have. 'Evan used to hate me giving them money. He said it encouraged them.'

'Did he?' Cynthia asked frowning. 'I never knew that.' Her mum's disapproval hung in the air.

'Somehow it just never registered before how bad a problem it is.'

'Not in Meadowbank, luckily.'

'No, maybe not there.' The small, picturesque village was, on the surface, affluent, but there were other problems the teachers knew about. She thought of Mrs Barnes and her request for help with Leonie's outfit for the Christmas play. 'One of the mums at school asked me for some help with their kid's costume.'

'Are you talking about little Leonie and Mrs Barnes?' her mum asked.

'How did you—?' Bella remembered herself just in time. 'I couldn't say. It would be breaking confidentiality.'

'Hmm. Well, I feel for her, poor love. They've had a hard time this year, her and Kurt. I could make a costume. What does she need?'

'Oh, Mum, you are kind, but I've got it under control. Not that I'm saying it is Mrs Barnes of course.'

'Of course.'

Bella had found a tiger costume in the school dressing-up box and hoped it would fit. If it didn't, how would Mrs Barnes react to a gift? Would she be happy? Or would pride make it difficult to accept? She didn't want to overstep or hurt anyone's feelings but there must a solution somewhere.

After a slower wander due to their full bellies and heavy shopping bags, they settled comfortably on the train for the journey home. Bella was always as excited to leave London as she was to arrive there. By the time they'd boarded the train, she'd had enough of long queues and everyone being pressed against her on the tube.

Caro snoozed on her shoulder after moaning about the size of her feet and threatening to take her shoes off, and her mum chattered on about the extra presents she'd bought. For so much of the day she hadn't thought about Evan leaving or going home to her empty house. She hadn't thought about living her life without him, because her mum had been right: she'd been busy making memories with her family. Tomorrow though would bring new heartbreak as she felt it all again. If only she could continue to keep it at bay.

Bella turned her mind to the poverty she'd ignored on her previous visits to London. How many people in Meadowbank needed help but were afraid to ask for it? She thought of the huge Christmas tree in Covent Garden and her mum's idea of a gift for Mrs Barnes and something stirred deep inside her brain. A vague idea began to form, crystallising into something more solid as she worked through it. She'd read about giving trees in magazines before. Charities were using them quite a lot now. They were a great way of helping others and were perfect for this time of year.

Could she set one up at Meadowbank?

There were so many other parents throughout the school who for one reason or another were dreading Christmas, and even some children too. In Bella's own class, she couldn't pretend that last term, Sinead's single mum had pulled her out of a school trip to the local castle because she couldn't afford it. What would she be doing for Christmas this year if she couldn't afford a moderately priced educational visit? She must be dreading Christmas too. Oliver's mum and dad had three other children in school all needing costumes. Would they be worried too?

Every teacher at Meadowbank Primary was aware of the food bank vouchers being given out in confidence. The recent harvest festival donations had gone as quickly as they'd come in. Though neighbours helped neighbours in Meadowbank, some people didn't feel they could ask for help and only spoke to the school begrudgingly. Bella firmly believed that if the village knew more of their neighbours' suffering, they'd want to offer some assistance.

For the first time since discovering Evan's note, she felt something other than pain. That familiar drive that forced its way into her brain, egging her on when she had the bit between her teeth, took hold, forcing back the tears that were constantly bubbling just below the surface.

'You two, listen, I've got an idea.'

Caro stopped leaning against the window and sat upright, her eyes sleepy.

'What do you think of me starting a giving tree?' Both looked blank. 'A giving tree. For the village. I fill out a tag for people who need help and someone else takes it and buys the gift. It's like giving to charity only you buy a present instead of donating money.'

If they did something like this in Meadowbank, all those families who were struggling could be helped.

'Oh, darling, what a lovely idea. What made you think of that?'

'Just seeing the situation here and knowing how hard some people are finding things at home.' She didn't mention the slightly selfish reason of wanting to fill her brain with things other than Evan.

'You'll have to be a bit careful,' Caro added, waking up a little. 'Make sure you tread carefully. You can't go around forcing charity onto people who don't want it. There are a few people in the village who won't like it. Seymour Cole for one.'

It was true that Amias's father had some very conservative attitudes, but she was sure the majority of the village would be in favour of the idea.

'I know,' Bella replied. 'And I don't want to insult anyone either. I just think that everyone goes through hard times and there are so many people in the village who'll be happy to help a friend or neighbour. I mean there's Elsie at the library – she'll be more than happy to help. The guys at Bluebell Park, Nina and Johnny and school.'

Cynthia nodded agreement. 'So how will it work?'

Good question. How could she make it work? Obviously, she could work with the school, but some of the older residents had lost loved ones recently, like poor old Winston whose wife had just died, and faced Christmas alone. They'd never had children and though he was close to Elsie, the librarian, would anyone else buy him gifts this year? There were other older people too who had lost their partners and might be feeling lonely at this time of year. It would be nice to make this Christmas extra special for them too.

'If those who wanted to take part filled out a form, each form could have a number that went on a tag to hang on the giving tree. As long as the tag had the form number and a suggested gift, it would be easy to keep track of.'

'And you could include an option for food gifts as well,' Cynthia said. 'We all know the food bank's already running low. You can't give fresh food, but you could definitely give other things to make the season special like Christmas puddings and selection boxes.'

'That's a great idea, Mum.' Bella grinned. They seemed genuinely excited for the idea, just as she was.

In her mind's eye she saw a tree with a mountain of presents underneath and pictured giving a gift to every house in the village. No one would be sad this Christmas if she had anything to do with it. Every family would wake on Christmas morning laughing and smiling, eager for the day to come.

Her heart had felt like a black, heavy weight in her chest since yesterday, but this would surely get her through the festive season. The less time she spent at home, the better, and between work, volunteering at Bluebell Park and running the giving tree, she'd barely have time to think about the life she'd had.

'And, at Bluebell Park, the grotto's going in front of a belt of fir trees to give a Christmassy feel and there's a really large tree to the right that will be perfect for the giving tree. All we need to do is decorate it with some lights and laminate the tags so they don't get wet.'

It must have been fate.

'It sounds wonderful, darling,' Cynthia said, beaming with pride. 'Count me in for anything I can do.'

'And me,' Caro added, adjusting her position in the chair. 'At least until I get so big I can't actually walk and just waddle around like a duck.'

'You're doing that now,' Bella teased and Caro feigned annoyance.

'Watch it or I really will take my shoes off and kick you with my huge meat boat feet.'

Excitement bubbled up in her stomach and the few niggling doubts she'd had faded. This year, Meadowbank village would have a giving tree and everyone's Christmas would be special and filled with joy, even if hers wasn't.

Chapter 4

Nick watched Bella leave and stretched out his sleepy limbs. Behind him, Freddie was shooting his way around the living room, happy as anything, but a strange feeling settled in Nick's stomach.

Poor Bella. He'd had no idea Evan had left. How awful for her. But then again, Evan was a fool. He always had been. Not in an offensive way – he was just one of those guys for whom the grass was always greener on the other side of the fence. The type who was perpetually dissatisfied. If he thought he'd found someone nicer than Bella Moore, then he was even more of an idiot than Nick had taken him to be with his slicked-back hair and expensively tailored suits. Bella was one of the kindest people in the village. Sweet-natured, pretty too, now he came to think about it. Her dark blonde hair had grown over the winter so it framed her face, tucking under her chin in a way that enhanced her features, and her greenish-blue eyes had a compelling warmth to them.

It wouldn't be long before she found someone better, and if Evan couldn't see the amazing person she was then she was better off without him. Still, he'd seen the sadness in her eyes, dulling their usual brightness.

Break-ups were awful.

In fact, awful was putting it mildly for him. At least Bella and Evan didn't have any kids. Steering Freddie through all this had been the toughest job he could ever have imagined. Every word, every decision led to him constantly questioning himself and second-guessing his actions. No matter what he did he always felt like he'd done something wrong.

Every morning when Nick's hand hit the unused pillow next to him, he imagined seeing his wife lying there. The empty side of the bed where Paige had lain was alien to him now. A no-man's land he still didn't venture into. So often the sheets felt cold beneath his fingers and he missed the warmth of her body beside him. Nick wished he didn't, but it was an instinct. She was his wife; the person he'd intended to spend the rest of his life with, only she'd had other plans. Even though the months before she'd left had been filled with bickering, and tension hung in the air at night when they'd climbed into bed together, he still missed her. Missed the good times they'd had before it all went sour.

Pushing the thoughts deep down, he went back inside to check on Freddie who had now abandoned his mask and gun in favour of his iPad. Nick heard the familiar sounds of YouTube and ruffled his hair as he flopped down next to him on the sofa.

'Morning, mate. You all right?'

'Yeah. I'm fine,' Freddie answered without looking up from the screen.

As that was the end of the conversation, Nick gazed around, wondering what they should do today. The house was a tip. Clothes were left on the floor, toys strewn everywhere. There was a carpet under there somewhere, but he hated to think what state that was in. When was the last time he'd hoovered? He couldn't actually remember. Cleaning wasn't exactly a high priority right now and he was barely keeping up with the washing.

It wouldn't be long and they'd be putting up Christmas decorations. They'd need space for the tree and that always meant shifting around the TV unit and settee to make room. The last thing he wanted to do was ruin that day by having to clean the house first. It was going to be hard enough. This would be the first time without Paige, which meant Freddie would miss his mum even more. Nick too knew he'd feel the loss even deeper, but his anger normally kept the pain at bay.

'How long have you been up?' he asked, aware that before he'd seen Bella he'd only just woken and thrown on some clothes.

Freddie shrugged. 'I don't know. An hour. Maybe ten minutes.'

Helpful. Nick scratched his head through a handful of knotty hair. 'Did you sleep well?'

'Yeah.'

Seeing as conversation was coming second to Freddie's favourite YouTuber, Nick went to the kitchen to salvage the cup of tea he'd half made before emptying the bin. The bag had been overflowing and the teabag he'd thrown in had been the last straw, sending it cascading over. Nick sipped his tea and glanced back at his son.

Not too long ago, Freddie had started every day by climbing into bed with him and Paige for a cuddle. Those sleepy moments of them all pressed together, snuggled under the duvet, had been his favourite way to the start the day, even when he and Paige had spent the evening before arguing. The tenderness of his little body between them and his gentle chatter about what had happened at school the previous day were better than any alarm clock. They woke him up in such a peaceful, loving way.

Now, Freddie didn't bother coming in and every morning was a rush of packing snacks for school – thank God for school dinners – finding a packed lunch for himself and ensuring Freddie was at least reasonably presentable in his school uniform. He might be a little rumpled but everything, including his tie, was always there. It was the one thing Nick had been proud of, though he wasn't sure the arguments about ties and blazers were really worth it for such a small badge of honour.

Nick missed those morning cuddles the most. In the early months of Paige's departure, Freddie had stopped slipping into bed and Nick hadn't been sure whether to make him or not. He kept asking him to, but when the boy said no, what could he do? He didn't want to force him, but neither did he want Freddie to pull away and withdraw even further into himself.

It didn't help that Nick knew he'd been more than a little short-tempered at the start of his life as a single father. It wasn't what Freddie had needed from him, but the pressure of paying all the bills on his own, dealing with his own heartache and trying to navigate Freddie through what could only be described as grief, had exhausted him. He'd been continually strung out. Always on edge. How was he supposed to deal with a ten-year-old's feelings when he couldn't deal with his own? Since the first day she'd left he'd felt like he was drowning underneath the pressure and, no matter how much he tried to get it together, he always failed at the first hurdle.

Last night was a prime example. They'd had pizzas again, and Freddie hadn't made it to bed until nearly ten o'clock. Even on a Friday that was far too late for a ten-year-old. Freddie couldn't possibly be getting enough sleep and that was all down to Nick. He was the father; he should be sticking to a routine. With a sigh and sip of nearly cold tea, he chastised himself again. He really had to do a better job.

Nick went to the kitchen and unplugged his phone from the charging cable. Freddie must be hungry by now. Starving. Berating himself yet again for taking such bad care of the son he loved so much, the child he'd longed for and had sworn to protect from the moment he held the tiny pink baby in his arms, he said, 'Let's get you some breakfast, hey, mate?'

'I had cereal.'

'You did?' He couldn't hide the surprise from his voice. How long had he been up? 'When?'

'Don't know. A while ago. You were still asleep, so I got up and made it myself.'

'Oh, mate, you didn't have to do that. You should have woken me up.'

'You were tired. You fell asleep in front of the telly last night.'

Nick scratched his jaw, digging his nail in to distract himself from the pain shooting into his heart. He couldn't fail this boy any more if he upped and left too. In fact, sometimes Nick felt Freddie would be better off living with someone else but no matter how much he failed he couldn't face the idea of not being with him every day. There were always moments among the sea of failures that made it worthwhile. Like last night when they'd sat playing on the PlayStation, eating pizza, Freddie giggling. Even though he'd been worn out, Nick's love had brimmed over because, despite his weariness, he'd made him laugh. He sighed. He'd just have to try harder. Much harder.

Nick walked over and pulled his son into a tight embrace. 'I'm sorry, mate.'

Freddie buried his head into his T-shirt and a muffled 'S'okay' came back. When he pulled away, he peeped up, his brown eyes large.

'What do you want to do today, hey?' Freddie shrugged as Nick ignored the stack of dirty plates littering the coffee table and gazed out of the large window in the living room.

Evan was a selfish prick if he couldn't see what solid gold he had in front of his eyes. Bella had been incredibly kind and supportive of Freddie since Paige had left, and of him too. She'd never probed deeper, as if she sensed he wasn't quite ready to talk, but he knew she kept an eye on Freddie at school and she'd always enquire about him when they ran into each other in the village. Knowing she was in school and around his fragile, wounded son made dropping him off so much easier.

He wondered where her sister and mum were taking her and smiled at the Moore family's reputation. They were known in the village for being fun and well loved. Some of the more conservative members of the village, his parents being two such people, didn't always approve of their raucous behaviour during the annual summer fair, but Nick had always enjoyed being around them. They didn't take themselves too seriously and were more than happy to just have fun. He wished he was more like that. More carefree. Sometimes he felt like all he did was frown and Freddie deserved to be laughing every minute of every day. To be happy.

Remembering the pain he'd felt immediately after his break-up, Nick watched as the wind took Bella's gate from its precarious position on the loose hinge and flung it about. He suddenly had an idea of something he could do to help. It wasn't much, but it was something and those small somethings made a difference when you were down.

'Mate, do you fancy helping me fix Miss Moore's wonky gate? It won't take long, then we can go for a kick-about on the green. What do you reckon?'

Freddie lifted his head from his iPad and Nick anticipated a moan, but none came. 'Okay. Do I have to get dressed?'

'Nah, you can help me in your stormtrooper outfit if you like, but you'll have to put your coat on. It's freezing out there.'

When he and Paige had split up, he'd been offered so much help from those around him he hadn't quite known what to do. Food deliveries arrived, babysitting services were offered so he could get back to dating again, offers to get his shopping in as he was working full-time, but his parents had always said charity begins at home. They weren't the type to give to charity or help out those who needed it. It wasn't that they were bad people, it was just that they'd had difficult upbringings themselves and didn't think relying on others was good for you. That belief had stuck with him for a long time. It still did sometimes. Why then was he feeling this need to help Bella?

Fixing a gate wasn't a big deal, he told himself. It was just saving her a job. Giving her one less thing to think about when simply existing was going to be hard enough for the time being. Maybe it was for the purely selfish reason that he wanted to feel good about himself for once. Plonking his cup down over a dark brown tea stain on the bright white coffee table, he leaned over the edge of Freddie's iPad. 'Come on then. Let's get that done, then I can beat you about twenty-nil at football.'

'Ha! Twenty-nil to me you mean.'

'Yeah, yeah, yeah.' He ruffled his hair and went out the back to grab some tools.

The wind whipped around the trees that dotted the lane,

pitching the ragged branches to and fro. Nick sent a begrudging Freddie back inside to put on his scarf and gloves, even though he argued that he wasn't cold, and his fingers were pink because he'd been squeezing them together. When Freddie came back out, he was holding a stack of papers.

'What's that, mate?'

'It's the Christmas play. I'm a narrator. I've got lots of lines to learn.'

'When did you find that out?' asked Nick as he screwed the loose hinge back into place.

'Yesterday. I told you last night.'

Had he? Nick felt shame rush up his neck and he was back to feeling a failure. How had he missed that? He'd been so tired last night it was all he could do to keep his eyes open. He loved being a self-employed landscape gardener, but it was hard work. The gardening side wore him out physically while the business side used every ounce of his quite limited brainpower. He'd done okay at school, but he wasn't exactly academic and keeping an eye on costs, writing quotes and pricing jobs addled his mind.

'So, a narrator,' Nick said. 'Pleased?'

Freddie nodded bouncing on his toes. 'Yeah. I get to wear my own clothes and at least I'm not a guinea pig. And I don't have to dance.'

'A guinea pig? In the nativity?'

'It's a pantomime this year.'

'That's cool.' Odd, but cool.

Nick had always wanted to go to the pantomime, but his mum and dad had thought it a waste of money and lowbrow. Nick had once been dragged along to *The Nutcracker* and he'd hated every minute of it. At ten he'd had no interest in boring classical music and men in tights prancing around on stage. This sounded much more fun and considering his son was basically doing schoolwork on a Saturday as he read through his script, he couldn't moan.

49

Yet, Freddie had told him all of this last night and he'd already forgotten, which meant he really needed to get his shit together.

He couldn't let the house become any more of a pigsty and if he didn't get those dishes washed, mould would start growing on them. He'd already found an abandoned teacup with fuzzy blue stuff inside. After fixing Bella's gate and their game of football on the green, Freddie could chill with his iPad while Nick cleaned the entire house from top to bottom. Something had to change, and he couldn't keep waiting for it to magically happen on its own. After all, he was going to have to work extra hard to make this Christmas a pleasant one for his son.

Nick had already asked his parents what they were doing, wondering if they could all spend the day together, but they were off to their fancy hotel in Witchbury, so he and Freddie would be at home alone. Given that it was going to take more than just one afternoon's cleaning to make up for the last six months of falling below par, it was time to get started. He owed his son that much.

Chapter 5

Wednesday morning staff meetings weren't always the most fun as they discussed budgets – or the lack thereof – and covering for holidays, but they always perked up when they got to the little projects and clubs the teachers themselves were running. This morning's meeting had been a bit livelier than other ones as Mr Osbourne questioned Mrs Brody's lyrics in one of the songs in the Christmas play.

'You simply can't rhyme "Christmas" with "simple maths",' he moaned.

'Why not?' asked Mrs Brody, feathers clearly ruffled. 'It works perfectly in the song.'

'And that's a point too.' Mr Osbourne's tiny moustache, which made him look like he wasn't really safe to be around children, ruffled. Mrs White had made repeated efforts to get him to remove it, including reverse psychology and subtle hinting, but as yet, none had been successful. 'Do you think the children should be exposed to 'Poker Face' by Lady Gaga?'

'They're not going to hear her lyrics, are they?' Johnny sang the 'ma, ma, ma' bit and Mrs Brody glared at him. 'They're going to hear mine. Look, let me find it on my phone and I'll sing it for you—'

At this Mrs White stepped in, checking her watch with such obviousness she looked like one of the drama club kids. 'That won't be necessary, Mrs Brody. And, Mr Osbourne, thank you for your concern, but I can assure you that Mrs Brody has a wealth of experience in these matters, and I trust her implicitly to consider what's appropriate for the children. Your concern is noted though and it does you credit. Has anyone got anything else?'

Mr Osbourne mumbled something about rhyming 'gingerbread'

with 'sums in your head', which Bella thought was quite clever, and folded his arms over his chest.

Bella had been biding her time to ask about the giving tree, nervous that people would accuse her of sticking her nose in, or thinking it was too much for her after her 'terrible weekend'. Every member of staff this morning had commented on Evan's leaving and how cowardly it was of him trying to do it while she was at work. She was beginning to wonder if it wouldn't have been easier if he had. Their horrified expressions at the mention of the note had made her feel a little more vindicated in her heartache, but their comments on how broken she must be, however well intentioned, were less helpful in the trying not to cry stakes. Bella had forced a smile and sniffed back the tears saying she was fine, even though she clearly wasn't.

It was already eight o'clock and they'd be due on the playground soon. From the staffroom she could see some of the children arriving for Good Morning Club and being shepherded into the school hall by the receptionist for their breakfast.

'Right, that's everything I have on my list,' Mrs White said, wrapping up the meeting. 'Any other business?'

Bella sat up a little straighter. 'Actually, I have something I wanted to ask you all. I'm planning on starting a giving tree at Bluebell Park and I wanted your approval, Mrs White, as it would affect the school, and to hopefully get everyone's support.'

'A what tree?' asked Mr Osbourne. Although he was only his fifties, he was rather old-fashioned, and Bella knew he'd put up the most resistance. 'What's that when it's at home?'

'It's an American idea, I think.' He scoffed but Bella ignored him and carried on. 'It's basically a Christmas tree where we hang tags saying what people need for Christmas – anonymously of course – and then people take the tags, buy the gift and leave it under the tree. It's a wonderful way to help our neighbours and show a bit of goodwill at this time of year. It's just a little different to donating money to a charity.'

'Won't the presents get wet?' asked Mrs Brody.

'I was thinking they can hand them in at Bluebell Park rather than leave them under the tree. I've become aware of a number of families who are struggling financially, and this could really help them this Christmas.' Mrs White's eyes narrowed slightly as she listened, and Bella's voice wavered as her apprehension got the better of her. She believed so fervently in this idea, but did she have the courage to go against Mrs White if she said no? Perhaps she shouldn't have raised it as a question but more a statement of fact. 'I was thinking we could make it for the entire village as I know some of the lonelier older residents could do with a bit of support too. What do you all think?'

'How will it work exactly?' asked Mr Osbourne. Though he clearly wasn't convinced, Bella was grateful he was hearing her out without dismissing the idea straight away.

'And where will it be?' Mrs White readied her pen. 'You said Bluebell Park, didn't you? That would be better I think. I'm not sure the school would be the right place for it.'

'I wanted to put it at the park so people can freely access it. We have to be so careful about strangers entering the school—'

'Not that we have any in Meadowbank, but good thinking.'

'There's a beautiful fir tree right next to the grotto that would be perfect.'

'I know the one,' Nina said.

Mrs White nodded and made a note on her clipboard. 'Where will you get the information from as to who needs what?'

'That's where we all come in. We all know families who need some help from our own classes, and I was thinking we could have a form for people to fill in for themselves or to nominate others. If we have them available here and at Bluebell Park, then people can hand them in to me. Each form will get a number and I'll then create the tags. The tag will have the number on and state generally what's needed. That way it'll all be anonymous, and no one will get embarrassed. Someone then takes a tag, buys the gift and delivers it back to us with the tag attached. I'll coordinate everything. And then, as we get nearer to Christmas, I'll deliver the donations. What do you think, Mrs White?'

The kindly head teacher, who had one of those voices that was never really raised, replied in a calm, considered tone. 'I think it sounds marvellous. During last year's Breakfast with Santa, Mr Tomlin told me lots of the children had asked for such small things like a new winter coat, or new boots so Mummy didn't have to worry about money. It honestly—' She paused, pressing a hand to her chest, and Bella was surprised to see her eyes shining. Mrs White was all business and had such a formidable can-do attitude, she hadn't imagined these things had touched her so deeply. 'It broke my heart.'

Bella nodded sadly. 'When you look at Meadowbank, all you see are the pretty, thatched-roof cottages, the duck pond . . . It all seems so well-off. It's hard to imagine any hardship in such an idyllic place.'

'People don't always notice what's around them. We're all busy with our own lives and we sometimes forget to really look out for others. But I love this idea. We just need to be careful we aren't making people feel embarrassed that they need help. Often, those who need it don't like to ask.'

'I thought we could all talk to the parents in our classes because they're familiar with us and hopefully won't be upset by us asking if they want to participate.'

'I think it's a fabulous idea,' said Nina, who also volunteered at Bluebell Park. 'And Bluebell Park is the perfect place. What better time to do it than now, at Christmas? I had Mr West bringing Vita in without any baking ingredients because he couldn't afford anything else on the weekly shop. Luckily, I'd brought in extra so I could give her some. He was so embarrassed, and I felt so bad about it. He and his wife work so hard, but sometimes there's only so much money to go around, isn't there?'

'I agree,' said Johnny. 'Eddie's mum came to talk to me about uniform for secondary school because she doesn't know how she's going to afford it. They need so much more stuff when they move on, and it all has to have the school logo on. All I could suggest was starting to buy bits here and there as and when she can, but she made the point that he grows so quickly. I also suggested she speak to the school's PTFA. I know most take donations and pass them on. It wasn't an easy conversation. She was really upset. I think it's—'

'I don't like it,' interrupted Mr Osbourne harshly and Bella nervously toyed with the cuffs of her cardigan. 'People won't thank you for it, Bella, and I'd hate to have someone sticking their nose into my business uninvited.'

Bella dropped her eyes. Even though she had expected this response from him, she was feeling so raw from Evan's leaving that every objection felt like a personal attack. Sunday had been hard being alone in the house, knowing Evan wasn't there and was never coming back, and the weekday mornings had been even harder. She still wasn't used to sleeping alone and as workdays brought with them the regular humdrum routine, going through it had only emphasised how different everything was for her now.

Mrs White leapt to Bella's defence. 'I think that's why Bella has suggested we talk to families in our own classes and not others. We get asked about food bank vouchers and spare school uniform all the time, and if there's anyone who's not comfortable talking to their families, I'm happy to have a quiet word. For practicality's sake, if there are siblings in different years, the older child's teacher can have the conversation, but I, for one, am definitely in favour of the idea. What a wonderful lesson to teach our children. Not only that it's okay to ask for help if you need it, but also, the greatest gift we can give at Christmas is charity. Well done, Bella. It's a big thumbs up from me. Now, the school Christmas tree comes next week so we can start getting the children to make decorations during any wet plays. I don't know about you but that's when Christmas really starts for me at school, and I just know it's going to look lovely in the school hall.'

Smiling at her success, Bella stood and they all filed out of the meeting. For the first time that morning, a small piece of her heart filled with something other than sadness and she strode down the corridor humming Lady Gaga to herself, eager for the day to begin.

'Miss Moore, why am I a turtle? Did they have turtles in Bethlehem? I thought Bethlehem was a hot country. Won't the turtles die?'

'I don't think there are any turtles there, Hannah.' She'd have to google it at breaktime. 'But we're doing something a little different this year. Mrs Brody has thought about different pantomimes and mixed them all up with the story of Jesus and Mary going off to Bethlehem. Doesn't that sound fun?'

Bella hoped her voice sounded convincing because it really wasn't that believable in her head. The truth was, the more she read through the script the more she thought it was all a bit . . . odd. Not that Mr Osbourne was right. She didn't see anything wrong with the songs. In fact, she thought Mrs Brody had done a wonderful job, but the scenes were a bit all over the place. One minute Mary and Joseph were on a donkey and the next minute a mixture of animals that had never before been seen in a Christmas play were singing modern hits in a chorus line, all with a bit of thigh-slapping panto flavour thrown in. It would definitely be one the parents didn't forget, but Mrs Brody's enthusiasm always swept them along. Unless you were Nina and Johnny, in which case your abject terror swept you along.

'Amias, give Richard back his script please. It's not yours; you have your own, so I suggest you pick it up and look at it.'

Amias had clearly thought she hadn't noticed him snatch it as she was talking to Hannah, but over the years Bella had perfected that technique teachers and parents often do of predicting events before they happen. Knowing that Amias was getting bored and a little disruptive, she had kept watch from the corner of her eye and, sure enough, as soon as he suspected her attention was elsewhere, he'd taken poor Richard's script and was refusing to give it back, despite being asked nicely. Amias definitely needed to run off some energy at breaktime.

'Desmond, can you recite your line for me, please? Then we'll finish this scene and have afternoon break.'

'But the other kids have already gone out,' moaned Amias.

'Yes, but, Amias, if you hadn't been messing around so much, we'd have got further along. I'm sorry to say you've been a bit silly this afternoon, haven't you?'

Knowing he was about to refute the allegation, Bella hurried Desmond on. He recited his line in that strange way children have of sounding like a robot whilst also placing inflections in entirely the wrong places.

'Why did that angel have to send us all the way to Bethlehem, Mary? It's miles away and there isn't even a McDonald's.'

The children all dissolved into fits of giggles and Bella joined in. Her class could never fail to lift her spirits and actually, the day hadn't been anywhere near as bad as she'd expected. Whether that was because she was still on a high from Mrs White being so supportive of the giving tree, or merely from not having thought about Evan every second, she didn't know. During English she'd forgotten him for a whole twenty minutes as she struggled to remember, and teach, what fronted adverbials were. Then the pain had come back as soon as they'd finished and her class had disappeared for morning break, but it was still a win as far as she was concerned.

Bella checked the clock on the wall and said, 'Let's stop there, shall we, and we can start with your line, Hannah, when we get back inside. Coats on, everyone, please. And hats, scarves and gloves if you've got them. It's very cold out there today.'

The children all rushed outside, and Bella grabbed her whistle from the top drawer of her desk before donning her winter wear. Hurrying behind them, Nina and Johnny were already waiting for her in the most sheltered part of the playground.

'How are your rehearsals going?' asked Johnny, shoving his hands further into his pockets. 'Mine aren't going very well. We managed half a scene before they all started talking about how none of it makes sense. Did you see the line, "Hey, Mary, do you have your library card because I'm totally checking you out?" I mean, what the hell is that all about? Though to be fair I might steal that.'

Nina raised an eyebrow.

'We just did the McDonald's line,' Bella said with a smile. 'It's all a bit mad, but the kids are enjoying it. I think it's nice to do something different. And the kids are loving the modern songs.'

'I should have known you'd find something positive,' Johnny replied. 'You always do.'

'My class got through the whole of the first scene,' said Nina, lifting her chin over the edge of her coat in pride.

'Oooh, get you. Mrs Brody will be very pleased.'

'I hope so. I've got to make up for the Harvest Assembly when we should have been singing 'He's Got the Whole World in His Hands' and I stupidly taught the kids a version I learned at school and sang 'He's Got a Whole Twirl in His Hands'.'

'That was quite funny,' said Bella trying to feel the smile that came to her face.

'Not for me it wasn't. She gave me the evil eye for weeks afterwards.' Nina turned to Bella, her face full of concern. 'How are you holding up?'

'Okay, actually. I nearly cried when we were looking at long division because that was Evan's favourite type of maths problem, but I managed to keep it together.'

Johnny and Nina stared wide-eyed.

'What?' asked Johnny. 'He had a favourite type of maths problem? That's a bit . . . weird, isn't it?'

'No. It's perfectly normal. Thank you.'

'If you say so.'

Bella knew she'd have to tell them the story now so they

didn't think she was crazy or that their relationship had been so incredibly boring they'd ended up with favourite sums to do. Then again, perhaps that was another sign she'd missed? 'One night I was doing some lesson planning and we had this stupid conversation about what our favourite maths problems were and we ended up talking nonsense and being silly. It was lovely.'

'But you've heard nothing from him?' asked Nina. 'No texts or calls?' Bella shook her head unable to say the words out loud. 'Not even a Facebook message?'

Bella sighed. 'It's horrible to think he didn't have the courage to tell me to my face and was trying to sneak out. I'm so stupid. I didn't even know we were in trouble.'

'You're not stupid,' Nina said, rubbing small circles on her back. 'He's clearly evil, and stupid for leaving you. But it was very nice of hunky Nick Cowley to fix your gate, wasn't it?'

The fact that Freddie's dad had fixed her gate while she was in London had been an unexpected surprise. He was normally a private man, and she hadn't really known how to thank him. Dropping in a pack of beer for him and some sweets for Freddie had seemed the best option and she'd done so first thing Sunday. He'd blushed sweetly and mumbled something about it saving her a job before he shuffled away unsure why he'd done it or what else to say.

'Very nice. He's always been so self-contained and—'

'Sexy,' Nina offered quietly so none of the children could hear.

'Is he?' Johnny asked, his head shooting up.

'Yeah, in a rugged, outdoorsy, muscly way that—'

'All right, calm down.' Johnny inconspicuously tried to look at his bicep, then shuffled his feet. Nina noticed too and giggled.

A cacophony of noise drew Bella's eyes forwards as one of the boys from her class came running over, followed swiftly behind by Hannah and Leonie flanking a crying Freddie.

'Miss?' shouted Hannah, looking indignant. 'Amias has just been really mean to Freddie.'

'He ran into him on purpose,' said Leonie crossly. 'Didn't he, Freddie?'

As much as Bella wanted to take over, she felt it was best if Nina led the conversation. As his teacher, he'd probably want her, and Nina bent down in front of him. 'What happened, Freddie? Let me have a look at you. Did you bang your head?' He nodded and pressed his small hand into the back of his head. 'Do you mind if I feel for a lump? I'll be very gentle.' Freddie sniffed as two fat tears slipped from his eyelashes. Nina felt the back of Freddie's head. 'There's a little bit of a lump, but I think you'll be okay.'

A lump was always a good thing. It was when there was no lump they worried more because it could mean the swelling had turned inwards. On those occasions, they'd complete an accident report and call the parent straight away in case they wanted to take them to a doctor. Bella would inevitably spend all night worrying about them. You'd think after ten years as a teacher she'd have got used to it by now.

'Can you tell me what happened, Freddie?' Nina asked again.

Hannah opened her mouth to speak but Bella stopped her. It was important they found out from Freddie first. 'Just hang on a second, Hannah. You can tell us what you saw in a second, okay? We need to hear from Freddie first.'

Hannah nodded and Freddie wiped at his eyes before speaking.

'I was playing tag with Hannah and Leonie and Desmond and Oliver, and I'd tagged Desmond and was running away when Amias ran towards me and pushed me over.'

Bella caught a slight tightening around Nina's eyes. 'Was he playing tag too?' Freddie shook his head. 'Maybe he was playing a chasing game with Umar and Richard and he didn't see you. You know how they like to race about.'

'No, he wasn't, miss. They were stood by the climbing frame watching us and then when he saw I was on my own he ran towards me and pushed me over.'

'I saw it, miss,' said Hannah, unable to contain herself any longer. 'Amias is always picking on Freddie.'

'Is he?' Bella asked. She'd noticed a tendency to tease coming from Amias recently, but she hadn't considered it as being directed at Freddie. It was normally children in her own class that were affected. She'd have to keep a close eye on the situation. Hannah and Leonie were nodding so much their heads appeared detached from their bodies, so they clearly agreed. 'Do you think he is, Freddie?'

Freddie shrugged which did nothing to reassure Bella because shrugging could mean any number of things from a child. It seemed to cover everything from 'I don't know', 'I don't want to', and 'I don't care', to 'I think so', and anything else in between.

'Freddie,' Nina began gently, taking his hand in hers. 'If Amias or anyone else is being silly to you, you must tell us, okay? Then we can get them to stop. Did anyone else see you get pushed over?'

Hannah and Leonie reeled off a list of names and after Nina took Freddie inside to get him a wet paper towel for the back of his head, Bella went about investigating. The results, unfortunately, were inconclusive. As many children saw Amias push Freddie over as saw it as an accident. Sometimes these things weren't clear, and you had to take the child's emotions into account too. Oliver, for example, always thought people were doing things on purpose because he felt so unsettled. Was Freddie maybe a little unsettled too? It wouldn't be surprising given this would be his first Christmas without his mum.

With nothing concrete to go on, Bella spoke to Amias but made sure not to accuse him of something she couldn't prove. His parents were known for going off the deep end if ever their child was accused of misbehaving. When they came in from break, she settled the class reading their scripts and getting ready for the next scene while she spoke to him near the reading table.

'Amias, I understand there was an accident with Freddie today. Can you tell me what happened?'

'Nothing, Miss. He wasn't looking where he was going and ran into me.'

'Really?' He nodded a little too vehemently and crossed his arms over his chest. That was a guilty response if ever she saw one. 'I've heard it was the other way around. Some of the children saw you wait for Freddie to be on his own and then run up and push him over. Did you do that?'

'No!'

'Are you sure?' He nodded. Bella tried to keep eye contact with him though he kept his gaze away from hers. Another sign that he was being less than honest with her. 'Because deliberately pushing him over would be a very mean thing to do. It caused him to bash his head. You wouldn't want that to happen to you, would you? It would be horrible to think someone had pushed you over on purpose, wouldn't it?' Amias agreed but Bella wasn't convinced he really cared all that much. 'Try and be more careful in the playground, okay? Make sure you look where you're going.'

'My dad said accidents happen, miss.'

'That's true. They do. But that doesn't mean we stop paying attention, does it? Now, come on, let's get back to class.'

It seemed there was nothing more she could do except let Amias's parents know at the end of the day and hope it didn't happen again. Nina would be speaking to Nick. If something else did happen and she found out that Amias had done something to Freddie on purpose, the boy would be cutting out paper strips for paper chains from now until New Year.

The end of the day arrived swiftly and after an early Christmas story – Bella loved reading her class *The Night Before Christmas* and they got through it about ten times before December even arrived – they were packed up and ready to go in no time.

Amias's mum was one of the first she spotted when she opened the door to let them out. Luckily, Amias was at the back of the line, which meant she could send off the other children before she spoke to her. Nick wasn't outside Nina's classroom yet but then he was always late. Nina had asked for Bella's advice at the start of the school year because it had got so disappointing for Freddie to be at the front of the queue, get to the door and not see him, and Bella had suggested Nina give him a little task to do so he ended up at the back of the line. By the time that was done, Nick was normally running into the playground, out of breath but wonderfully happy to see his boy. She loved seeing the way his face lit up, his blue eyes crinkling at the corners as he smiled.

'Mrs Cole, can I have a quick word?'

Mrs Cole's mouth tightened, and Bella could see she was already entering defensive mode. 'Of course. Is everything all right?'

Without naming him (because the rules didn't allow it) Bella outlined what Freddie had said in the playground and Amias's response to being asked about it, making it clear that neither boy was in trouble but that it was important for her to know the incident had occurred.

'Well of course he didn't do it on purpose. Why would he?'

'I just wanted to let you know, that's all. And I've advised both boys to make sure they look before they run about.'

'Why should Amias have to pay more attention? He hasn't done anything wrong. If he said it was an accident, it was.'

'Freddie's lying, Mum,' Amias added.

'Freddie? Well there you go. If it's Freddie Cowley we're talking about, he probably is lying. Acting out because his mother left, trying to get Amias in trouble just to get some attention.' Mrs Cole's voice was growing higher and tighter. How could the woman say something like that? It was cruel. 'Maybe he's jealous,' she finished, flicking back her long dark hair.

Bella tried to defuse the situation. 'As I've said, Mrs Cole, no one's in trouble. I just wanted to let you know what had happened. Both boys are fine, no harm done.'

'Hmm.' Her eyes ran up and down the length of Bella's face, assessing her. 'Come on Amias, darling. Let's go home.'

Mrs Cole held out her hand to her son. If Bella wasn't mistaken, he seemed almost triumphant.

The empty playground lay out before her and just as Mrs White was about to lock the small gate that joined the front playground to the back, Nick came running through.

'Sorry, Mrs White,' he called, dodging the gate.

'You're lucky I didn't lock you out, Nick Cowley,' she called after him, but Bella could hear the teasing note in her voice. 'Or maybe I should lock you in.'

'I'm not sure it'd help me learn anything, Mrs White. It didn't when you taught me.'

Nick smiled as he raced to Nina's classroom. The school was so small and the classrooms so close together Bella could hear the conversation from inside the door.

'Sorry, Miss Radcliffe. Sorry, mate. The traffic was awful. Last one again, hey?' He straightened up and Bella could see the embarrassment and pain in his eyes. She wished she could stop it, but a parent's guilt could rarely be so easily assuaged.

'I'm quite glad, actually, Mr Cowley,' Nina said. 'I just need to let you know about something that happened today.' Nick's face clouded with concern. His eyes shot down to Freddie, scanning him and mentally checking him over. They fell on the 'I bumped my head' sticker on the little boy's chest and eventually raised to meet hers. 'Is everything all right?'

'Do you want to come into the classroom? There's no one else here and it saves us freezing outside.'

'Sure.'

For a few minutes Bella couldn't hear anything more and sat at her desk, starting to tidy up. It wasn't until they were leaving again, and he stepped back into the playground, that she heard his voice. Bella leaned back in her chair so she could see him through the still-open glass door. She really should have shut it. It was freezing. But her excuse was that the room smelled vaguely of feet and needed airing.

'And was this other boy okay?' asked Nick as he stepped outside into the cold wind. It whipped his hair up, blowing it over his head and Bella couldn't help but smile as she turned back to her desk. It was so nice of him to ask. Amias's mother hadn't.

'He's fine. And he's assured me it was an accident.'

'These things happen, don't they? Sixty kids in a playground all running around – someone's bound to knock into someone else.'

Bella could tell Nina was grateful for his understanding. Sometimes it was quite difficult telling parents their child had received a bump or bruise, but Nick made it easy and his concern for the other child was admirable. She still harboured her suspicions about what had really happened, but it was no good passing on suspicions to parents; it only freaked them out for no reason and that never ended well.

'Thanks, Miss Radcliffe. Have a good evening.'

Bella turned her attention back to her desk.

'How are you doing?' Nick asked, sticking his head into her classroom and taking her by surprise.

'Me?' She'd thought he'd go straight home, not stop in to speak to her. 'Yes, I'm fine. Well, mostly. Most of the time.' She fiddled with a stack of papers on her desk. 'Especially at school. You know, while I'm here I don't think about things.' She was doing it again. Chuntering on like a lunatic, and even though her brain was telling her to stop, her treacherous mouth kept moving. 'It's the being at home – alone. That bit gets me. But I'm okay. Catching up with my reading actually.'

Nick was nodding but clearly terrified. 'It can take some getting used to.'

He must think she was completely deranged or having a nervous breakdown. She certainly sounded like she was. 'Anyway, I'm going to stop talking and let you get home. Have a lovely evening.'

Freddie tugged impatiently on his dad's hand.

They disappeared into the dimming winter light, and she imagined them going home to a warm fire and a thrown-together dinner. She didn't think Nick was one to plan a week's worth of meals. He'd floundered so badly at first after Paige had left. She'd noticed Freddie had swapped from packed lunches to school dinners because Nick kept forgetting to pack him one and on the days he did remember, the random assortment of food was rather startling. As soon as she'd noticed, she'd started making extra sandwiches for her own lunch and giving them to Freddie on the sly. She hadn't told Mrs White. As lovely as she was, she wouldn't be in favour of something like that. She'd want her to speak to Nick and let him know, but it had been so clear that despite his own anguish he was doing the best he could, she couldn't bring herself to do it. After a while, things had improved on their own and then Nick had made the switch to school dinners, so she hadn't had to.

Bella's thoughts drifted to her having to go home to her own empty house and she gazed at the pile of books that needed marking. If she stayed here, she could also get ahead for the next couple of days by printing out the worksheets she needed. Deep down Bella knew she was doing anything she could to avoid going home but she just wasn't ready.

The urge to call Evan gripped her and though the various warnings she'd given herself resounded in her head; it was as if her fingers had a mind of their own. Sitting at her desk, she took her phone from her bag and found Evan's number. His face smiled out at her from the tiny profile picture. His light brown hair was just visible, and she thought about the times she'd run her hands through it. He suited the flecks of silver that time had given him, and her heart squeezed unpleasantly in her chest that she'd never get to see or feel it again.

Surely she was owed some further explanation? She had questions, so many questions, and if they continued to go unanswered, they'd drive her insane. She deserved that much, didn't she? She deserved to know when exactly he'd started to fall out of love with her. When he'd first become attracted to this other woman and how they'd met. She and Evan had still been having sex, after all. Okay, it was a bit less often than when they first met and sometimes relatively perfunctory, but that was because they were both busy. She still deserved to know when exactly he'd decided to leave her.

For the first time, a surge of anger at the injustice of it all forced her fingers to tap the screen and in a matter of seconds it was ringing. Her wrath was immediately replaced with swirling nerves and renewed heartache, but she refused to hang up. She'd leave a message if she had to. By slinking out of the door while she was in shock, he'd robbed her of the chance to talk about it, to shout and swear and rage at how unfair it all was. If she'd been able to speak, would she have begged him to stay? She didn't think so and she wasn't going to offer to change in the vain hope he might come back, but right now, all she really wanted was the chance to call him names to his face.

The continual ring of the phone only intensified those feelings. She could imagine Evan pulling his phone out and looking at the screen, pausing as he considered whether to answer or not. Everything he did was considered. He was never rash or hot-headed, which went to show that he must have been planning on leaving her for some time. Yet, she'd never seen the signs. Still the phone rang, and Bella chewed her lip attempting to keep her emotions in check. As it clicked through to voicemail, it became clear he wasn't going to pick up. He was a bloody coward.

Bella took a deep breath though her voice remained shaky and left a message. 'Evan, it's Bella.'

She'd hoped he'd know that, but he could have deleted her from his phone. She paused, unsure how to continue and after a couple of strange noises that were neither legible words nor distinct sounds, she said, 'I know you want to move on with Pepper.' Still a ridiculous name but she managed not to say so. 'But we need to talk. You still have some stuff at our house.'

Our house.

'We need to sort out the financials of the cottage and . . . and I think I deserve some answers before we never speak again. Don't you?'

Her voice was getting a tone. The tone she got when she was being passive-aggressively arsey with phone scammers who rang up pretending to be from Microsoft or who told her her mobile phone had been in a car accident.

'You can't keep ignoring me, Evan, or pretending that the last five years didn't happen.'

She hung up before she descended into the name-calling that had been ringing around her head. Bella wiped a tear from her eye and wished she could stop all this bloody crying. In some ways it was to be expected. It had been less than a week since he'd left, but her eyes were sore, and she hated not feeling like her normal positive self. It was as if Evan had stolen a piece of her when he left last week, and she wasn't prepared to let him have it. From now on, she'd save her crying for when she was alone, at home, which she'd have to go to sooner or later.

With a frustrated sigh, she contented herself with the knowledge that tonight she could really start planning the giving tree that would make a real difference to some of the families in Meadowbank.

Chapter 6

'What do you want for dinner then, mate? I think we've got some pasta bake in the cupboard if you fancy that?'

'Okay.'

Freddie threw his backpack onto the sofa and took off his coat, hanging it on the newel post. He was just about to dash up and get changed when Nick called after him, 'Hang on, son. Come and sit down a minute. Want to tell me about this bump today?'

On the short walk home, Nick had been wondering whether to probe more deeply or leave it all alone. Freddie had seemed somewhat subdued, staring at his feet as he trudged alongside Nick, hand in hand. Though being a parent, especially a single one, was challenging at the best of times, those rare moments of calm when they were walking home from school, Freddie's small hand in his, made it all worthwhile. The world and its problems shrank away as Freddie talked about the good handwriting he'd done in English, or the tasks he'd completed in maths. Normally it all came out in a tumble and Nick would often struggle to keep up, trying to place the events Freddie described in the right order. Freddie's mind darted here, there and everywhere as one thought sprang another. Tonight though, Nick had to ask all the questions as Freddie barely spoke. It wasn't like him, and Nick wondered if he had a headache from his fall.

Freddie climbed back down the few stairs and flopped on the sofa. Nick sat down next to him, gently brushing his son's hair back from his forehead. 'Want to tell me what happened?'

'It's Amias. He's just not very nice.'

'Why isn't he nice?'

'He's always being horrible to me.'

Nick felt his muscles stiffen, wanting to protect his son, but he kept his voice calm and reassuring. 'How?'

'He says mean things and he's really annoying.'

How to deal with this? Was making a big deal out of it and getting angry on his behalf going to do any good? He glanced at his gorgeous boy with the long dark eyelashes. As it was the first he'd heard of it, perhaps playing it down was the best option. Miss Radcliffe had said it was an accident and he trusted her to make a good decision. Although she wasn't as experienced as Bella, she was like her in many ways: calm, kind and sensible. He'd never realised before how pretty Bella's eyes lit with emotion. They were a gorgeous green-blue like the sea glass he'd collected as a child on holidays to the coast. When she'd looked up from her desk, surprised to see him, they'd widened and he'd seen the full brilliance of their colour. He nudged the thought away.

'All kids say mean things sometimes, mate. Some adults do too.' The night his wife had left him she'd called him some pretty nasty things. Not swear words, but dull, boring, unexciting. They'd cut to the bone. 'Sometimes you have to just shake it off. If someone's being mean, it's generally because they're unhappy and nothing to do with you.'

'He keeps blocking me in the toilets and won't let me out.'

'Does he?'

Freddie nodded. 'He did it to Oliver too.'

At least if he was doing it to other people, it was less likely to be targeted. That meant he was being silly rather than picking on Freddie. 'And what happened today? What was the accident?'

'It wasn't an accident. I was playing tag and he waited until I was on my own and got off the climbing frame and ran at me then shoved me over. He did this.' Freddie got up and went to the other side of the room then ran back towards the sofa as fast as he could. Just as he got there, he forcefully pushed the air away as if shoving an imaginary opponent. Something wasn't quite adding up here and Nick knew his son wasn't a liar.

'I thought Miss Radcliffe said it was an accident?'

'Amias said it was so he didn't get into trouble and Umar and Richard backed him up because they're scared he'll hurt them too, but it wasn't an accident, Daddy. It was on purpose.'

Daddy. Freddie didn't always call him that anymore. As he was growing older, he'd begun to call him Dad, only falling back to it occasionally. Nick preferred daddy, probably because he didn't have as long to enjoy it. It was the name that made him want to snuggle his boy up and hold him tight, protecting him from all these horrible, selfish people in the world.

How could Paige ever have left him? Her own son. She hadn't called in months and even if she did, Nick wasn't sure she'd ask to speak to Freddie. Did she not miss him? Nick missed Freddie every day when he was at work, which was stupid really because he knew he'd see him in a matter of hours and there'd probably be some moans and groans about dinner, baths, or bedtime. Nick had no idea how a mother, who was supposed to have a stronger instinct to protect their offspring, could think about leaving a child behind.

'So, you don't believe it was an accident?' Nick asked, pushing his thoughts to another track. Freddie shook his head. 'All right, mate. I'll have a word with Miss Radcliffe and ask her to keep an eye out. Now, do you want to get changed and play on the PlayStation while I cook dinner? But you need a shower tonight, okay?'

'Oh, Dad!'

Back to *Dad* again. Nick smiled. 'Yep. We both need one. We both stink.'

'You stink,' Freddie said playfully, shoving his dad in the arm.

'Not as much as you.'

Freddie's normally bright and beaming smile returned, and Nick had a feeling of disaster being averted. A knock at the door drew his attention, but he recognised the outline of the visitors in the glass and opened it with a grin.

Trish, his neighbour, with her husband and Nick's best friend, Len, were stood with their son, Peter. All three of them held various containers or, in Trish's case, a steaming dish of food in oven-gloved hands.

'Fancy some dinner?' asked Trish. 'We thought we'd pop round. Peter said that Freddie had a bash in the playground today and when I saw you were even later back than usual, we thought—'

'She thought,' said Len, pointing a huge baguette at her. 'I was going to leave you alone.'

'*We* thought,' Trish repeated, eyeing Len and emphasising the word, 'that you might like a hand with dinner.'

Nick laughed incredulously and ran a hand over his stubble. He'd been digging the foundations of a new patio today and probably still had mud in his hair. He could definitely feel the dirt beneath his fingertips. 'Come on in.' He moved aside and as soon as Peter had stepped foot in the house, Freddie was up and welcoming him before they began talking about which game they were going to play. Though Peter was a year older, the two of them had played together since they were toddlers.

'Freddie, can you run and get changed quickly, please?' Nick asked. They'd get another day's wear out of that uniform as long as he didn't spill dinner down himself.

Trish had already gone through to the kitchen with Len following. She placed the giant dish down on the counter while she set the oven then placed the pan inside. It smelled meaty and delicious. 'We've got lasagne and salad with some garlic bread if that's okay?'

'That sounds amazing.'

As glad as Nick was for the free dinner, guilt shot through him once more. He and Freddie seemed to exist on a diet of pizza, chicken nuggets and chips, and the odd jar of pasta bake sauce if he was feeling like pushing the boat out. Token vegetables that were easy to cook like frozen carrots or tomatoes and cucumber would be shoved on the plate, but his son never had amazing meals like this. If Nick wasn't careful Freddie was going to turn into one of those odd thirty-year-olds who only ate beige food. Maybe this weekend he'd do a big shop, cook a load of meals and put them in the freezer. He and Freddie could do it together.

'Is it me or is it a bit tidier in here?' Trish asked, looking around.

'I cleaned the whole place on Saturday afternoon. Well, down here at least. I've still got to do upstairs.'

Trish turned to look at him. 'Good. Well done. I'm glad you're getting things sorted a bit more.'

'Why so late home?' asked Len, clearing the kitchen table that was covered with unopened post, the village newsletter and all sorts of detritus.

'You know Freddie bumped his head at playtime? Well Miss Radcliffe just wanted to let me know what had happened.'

Trish turned, her face full of motherly concern. 'Is he okay? Did they give him first aid?'

'They took care of him. She put a wet paper towel on his head as he had a slight bump. I felt for it on the way home but couldn't find anything, so I think it's gone down now. Bella was there too.'

'Ah,' said Len. 'Sexy Miss Moore.'

Trish found a tea towel and hit him with it.

Nick knew Len was only joking, but the costume she'd worn at Halloween had certainly shown a different side to everyone's favourite primary school teacher. Nick had never really noticed her in that way before because he'd been happily married for so long. Or at least, he thought he'd been happily married. Even unhappily married, he hadn't noticed Bella's curvaceous frame or pretty face because he'd always been in love with his wife.

'And wet paper towels!' continued Len opening a bottle of wine and pouring three glasses. 'Where would the world be without wet paper towels. "Got a broken leg, Jimmy? Let's shove a wet paper towel on it. Your arm's hanging off, Maddie? Never fear, a

73

wet paper towel will have that sorted out in no time. Eyes fallen out of their sockets—"'

'We get the idea,' said Trish, sipping her wine after dishing out salad onto each plate. 'I love Bella. She's brilliant. And she doesn't put up with nonsense. She's kind, but firm and fair. I like that in a teacher.'

'Freddie's being weird though,' said Nick quietly, making sure he kept his voice low. The volume in the living room had grown higher as the two boys played a game together. Among the inane chatter they heard giggles and groans in equal measure. 'He was really quiet on the way home and then when we got here, he said Amias keeps being mean to him. Miss Radcliffe said Bella had spoken to him and he swore it was an accident, but Freddie doesn't think it was. I just don't know how much of it is perception and how much is fact. It's hard to tell sometimes.'

'Amias Cole?' asked Trish, glancing at Len.

'Yeah.' Trish's eyes went to Len's again and Nick felt his shoulders tense. 'What?'

Len cleared his throat. 'If he's anything like his dad—'

'Or mum.'

'He probably did do it on purpose.'

Nick's brows drew together as he frowned. 'I'm hardly in the village during the day so I've clearly missed something. What's going on?'

'Seymour Cole is an absolute—'

Trish cleared her throat and nodded towards the living room. Len got the message and reconsidered his sentence. 'He's not a very nice man. Particularly recently. Always out for what he can get, using people then throwing them aside.'

'But doesn't he do something financial in Witchbury? How can he be using people here in the village?'

'Cheated his way to a promotion over poor old Derek in Stone Cottage,' Len said authoritatively. 'And he refused to pay Adam Noble for some carpentry work he did as well. Adam made him a beautiful table, then Seymour said he'd gone "off spec" and he wasn't going to pay for something he didn't ask for. Adam tried to explain that he'd spoken to Mrs Cole because the original table they wanted wouldn't go through any doorways it was so big, so he'd have to make it in two sections and assemble it in the house. She agreed and then when it turned up, Seymour went nuts and said Adam should have asked him not the wife.'

'Ridiculous,' scoffed Trish. '*The wife.* I ask you.'

'What happened in the end?'

'Cheeky bugger tried to get it for free, but Adam refused and stuck to his guns. Seymour shouted for days saying Adam was a crook but Adam's mum and some of the older ladies from the village set him straight in the pub and we haven't seen him since.'

'Cheated on his wife too,' added Trish. 'Saw him with my own two eyes. Not the first time either. There are problems there for sure. And they both think the sun shines out of Amias's behind. That boy can do no wrong and that's no good for a kid. Children need to know there are expectations and boundaries. Telling them they're the best thing since sliced bread gives them an inflated ego.'

'He's nine,' said Nick, defending this other boy, though he wasn't sure why. Perhaps it was because it sounded like his parents were more concerned with themselves than him. Trish and Len weren't gossips so if they'd heard something they must think or know it was true to repeat it to him.

'Yeah, but kids need guidance and Amias doesn't ever get told off. Do you know—' She paused from slicing the baguette into little rounds ready for her homemade garlic butter. Nick's mouth watered anticipating such a delicious meal. He sipped his wine, eager for her to continue her story. He wanted to get the measure of this boy before he spoke to Miss Radcliffe tomorrow. Or maybe he could mention something to Bella. 'And I'm not gossiping, I know this for a fact because his mother told me, that Amias got in a strop on his birthday and threw something at the TV in his room, breaking it.'

'He's got a TV in his room?' asked Nick. 'I wouldn't trust Freddie with a TV in his room. He'd never go to sleep.'

'That's why Peter hasn't got one. And when he broke it, do you know what happened? They bought him a new one. No punishment, no nothing. Just went out and got him a replacement the very next day and it was all "Poor darling got upset".'

'If Peter had broken something like that, he'd have been doing extra chores until he'd paid for a new one,' mumbled Len.

'Quite right, love,' Trish agreed.

Nick tried to take it in but couldn't believe a nine-year-old could act that way. 'Yeah, but being spoiled doesn't mean he's . . .' He didn't want to say the word *bullying* because it stirred up so many difficult feelings. 'Being a bit mean to Freddie.'

'Just be on your guard is all I'm saying,' said Trish. 'Keep an eye on things, maybe talk to Bella – Peter loved her – and if I were you, I'd have a read of the school's anti-bullying policy.'

'That's a bit steep,' said Len.

Nick was grateful for Len's support. He didn't want to think of the word *bullying* in relation to his gorgeous little boy. Bullying hurt, whether it was physical or mental, and it left scars. Scars that sometimes weren't seen for a long time, but never fully healed. They might be forgotten for a while or fade away, but they were always there. Nick had never been bullied himself, but he and Len had gone to school with someone who had. They'd left the village as soon as they could and never came back, and while they were growing up, Nick and Len had seen the lack of confidence, the paranoia. He didn't want that for his son. The thought of his son crying at school, not wanting to go, being scared and upset flashed through his mind and he forced himself to rein his emotions in.

He'd have a quiet word with Miss Radcliffe tomorrow, and maybe Bella too, just to see what she thought. Though he didn't want to add any more stress on her at the moment. But whoever he spoke to, that would be the end of it. All done and dusted, no need to worry.

'I just don't think it hurts to be prepared, that's all,' Trish continued. 'And you want to make sure you're following their procedures. Right, dinner, boys.'

Within seconds they came running out, Freddie's eyes lighting up at the feast before him. Whatever Nick had to do he would protect his boy. After all he'd been through, he deserved a break and Nick was going to make sure he got one.

Chapter 7

Bella thrust her hands deep into the pockets of her coat as she strolled to Bluebell Park. The icy November wind whipped around her face, freezing her cheeks and chilling her fingers through the thick wool of her gloves, but it would have been silly to drive such a short distance.

She exited Dairy Lane and followed the curve of the green and the duck pond before heading up Mill Lane and on towards the posh houses on the outer road. A pale lemon sun snuck out from between light grey clouds. The rain had stayed away, and it was a bright, crisp winter's day. Bella took big deep breaths of the cold air and before long, the playground, nestled in the middle of Bluebell Park between woods and banks of trees, came into view. Soon it would be full of children running around, screaming and giggling as they climbed on the giant wooden climbing frame or swung on the swings but for now, all was quiet.

Bella loved the stillness of the park in the mornings. At half past eight, the sun had only just made it into the sky and a dusky hue spread over the world. It was that special time of day before everyone arrived and the singing of birds was hidden behind chatter. Before long, crowds would meander along the woodland paths and amble in and out of the trees. Not many people saw the park like this. In the middle of their little piece of the countryside, families would soon huddle on the benches, cupping steaming hot drinks in gloved hands to stave off the chill. It always amazed Bella how children didn't feel the extremes of heat and cold as adults did. They were always so busy enjoying the moment to think about it.

Perhaps she should do more of that once she was over this heartbreak. *If* she got over this heartbreak. Bella shook her head. As painful as it was, she knew that eventually, at some distant time in the future, she would be back to her old self. She just had to take each day as it came. Bella eyed the hedges full of birds and the flowerbeds that next season would burst into life and attempted to be cheerful.

She had always been like her mum, the type who preferred to get on with things. She wasn't great at burying her feelings and wore her heart on her sleeve, but she definitely preferred not thinking about her current situation if at all possible and the giving tree had done a great job of that so far. And, at least all trace of Evan had been removed from her cottage thanks to her mum. What was left of Evan's now sat in a box in what had been his side of the wardrobe.

A small smile climbed onto Bella's face at the thought that when she went home tonight Lavender Cottage would feel more like *her* home than a space they had shared together. She needed to feel in control at the moment, and her home had always been her sanctuary. Now she was making it *her* space and that could only be a step in the right direction, even if it was a painful one.

Taking a breath of the crisp clean air, Bella made her way to the largest of the Alpine chalets that served as an information point and general office for the volunteers. A number of them were set up to the side of the children's play area and they reminded Bella of a European Christmas market. The warm memory of a family visit to Bruges when she was fifteen filled her and it was as if the heavy scents of cloves and cinnamon still lingered in her nose. It wouldn't be long before Bluebell Park was just as enchanting with music playing at the grotto and lanterns shimmering a golden glow over the ground.

The coldness of the day matched the weather they'd had on that trip, though the generators at the different market stalls had kept her warm in Bruges. Lots of hot drinks were going to be required today with working on Santa's grotto, but she could already imagine the kids' faces as they stepped inside, eager to ask Santa for the top things on their Christmas lists. Thankful to get out of the wind, Bella yanked the door to the volunteers' hut open.

Normally the thought of their new, exciting grotto would have brought a huge smile to her face, but today a shroud of gloom covered everything, dulling her feelings. She hated Evan for that. For stealing away things that should have been fun or special, but thinking of her trip last week, the glowing lights of London lit her memories and she vowed not to let him take any more. Today, she was going to announce to the volunteers what Bluebell Park would be up to this Christmas and how much it was going to help the village. They'd be as excited as she was and then these miserable feelings would be buried even further.

'Morning, all.'

Their genial conversation died, and she was met with a stony silence. Glancing around at their sympathetic faces it was clear they'd been chatting about her.

'We weren't sure we'd see you today,' said Hazel, a little uncertainly. 'We missed you last week, but we didn't know whether you'd need some more time.'

Hazel was about the same age as her mum and had been one of the first to volunteer at Bluebell Park. She was one of those people who were on every committee and council they could find because she liked to be busy. Unlike Bella's mum who was enjoying her retirement and had spent much of the summer lying on a sun lounger in the back garden, drinking lethal homemade cocktails at unsuitable times of the day.

Bella hung her coat on the rack and took a seat, aware of the nervous glances in her direction. She vowed not to rattle on as she kept doing with Nick Cowley but to keep her answer short and brief. 'I won't lie . . . it's been really tough this week, but I think the best thing I can do is keep busy.' Bella clasped her hands together in her lap. 'Anyway, I've got something to tell you all in a minute, and it's very exciting.'

Nina handed her a cup of tea they'd already got from the chalet next door where Annie's Tearoom was setting up. She flashed a sympathetic smile and Bella had the feeling she'd tried to steer the conversation away from Bella and Evan but had been unsuccessful. Bella gripped the cardboard cup, focusing on the warmth spreading through her fingers rather than everyone's soppy expressions that were threatening to make her cry for the fifty millionth time. Evan had described her as overemotional in his more unthinking moments, but she couldn't help crying at sad things on TV or blubbing at romcoms. It was just who she was.

'I'm so sorry, Bella,' Hazel said. 'But if he can't see how amazing you are, you're better off without him.'

'Definitely,' everyone agreed.

'I still can barely believe it though,' Matilda Finch said bluntly. She didn't do softly-softly. Matilda loved to be in charge, and would no doubt have lots of suggestions for how she could run the giving tree once Bella announced it. 'You both always seemed so happy, but then, you never know what goes on behind closed doors.'

Hazel tutted at Matilda's tactlessness and Bella, ignoring the remark, carried on. 'I thought we were happy too, but there you go. So, this idea I've got—'

'So there were no signs at all?' Matilda continued. 'Nothing you picked up on?'

Bella shook her head. 'Not that I spotted. Anyway—'

'What an evil man,' Hazel said. 'Mrs Granger mentioned she'd seen him putting some bits into his car and driving off, but she didn't think you'd split up. Evil boy.'

Matilda nodded along with Hazel's appraisal.

'How are you feeling today?' Nina asked gently.

'I don't know really. I'm here and dressed and I've brushed my teeth every morning, so I suppose in the grand scheme of things I'm doing all right.'

'Oral hygiene is very important,' added old Mr Whittaker with a firm nod.

That wasn't quite the point she'd been making but Bella carried on regardless. 'I'm getting on with things at least. So—'

'I should imagine,' Matilda started again, 'that in some ways it hasn't quite sunk in yet. That'll happen later I suspect.'

'Agreed,' Hazel added. 'Are you a bit afraid that at any moment it'll hit you again and you'll dissolve into tears?'

Bella tightened her hands around her cup. 'A little, but let's not talk—'

'Bella won't dissolve,' said Nina. 'She's not the dissolving type.'

She tried to think about how lucky she was to have such a huge support network in her life. She had Nina and Johnny at work, her family, and her other friends here who didn't quite pick up on the subtle I-don't-want-to-talk-about-it hints but were still trying to lift her spirits. She may as well finish the conversation before she told them about the giving tree. She was so excited about the idea and wanted it to have lots of impact when she announced it, which it wouldn't if all they were thinking about was Evan. 'I do keep wondering if I should call him again and—'

'Again?' Nina and Hazel chorused. Mr Whittaker solemnly shook his head.

'What? I called him once and left a message. I really want to know what happened to us from his perspective. Why he became so unhappy he went to someone else. Isn't that a good idea?'

Hazel shook her head. 'What can he say that isn't going to make you feel ten times worse? He'll tell you it wasn't you and that things just changed for him—'

'And you probably won't believe him,' Matilda added. 'And you'll spend your time going over every moment of the last few weeks or months trying to find clues. I bet you've already started doing that, haven't you?' Bella stared down at her cup and nodded. Hazel took over again.

'The simple matter is, he's gone. Your heart will heal, though I know it doesn't feel like it right this minute. It's all too raw, but they don't say time heals all wounds for nothing.'

Despite Hazel's advice, Bella was still sorely tempted to call Evan again. It hurt to think he could just cut her out of his life without a word. It hurt even more to think he'd got her message and ignored it. How could the man she'd loved so much ignore her pain like that? The man who'd done that wasn't the one who'd shared her bed and she couldn't marry the two up. Was he acting out of character, or had it always been in his character, but she'd failed to see it?

'He doesn't deserve you,' Mr Whittaker said with a rather angry jab at the air. Considering he wasn't a touchy-feely sort of man, his kind words meant a lot.

Hazel leaned forwards. 'Promise me you won't call him again.' Her serious expression pinned Bella to the spot.

'I promise I'll try. It's honestly the best I can do. Who knows what might happen when I've drunk half a bottle of wine with my mother tonight? And knowing Mum, it'd be better if I call him rather than her.'

Nina patted her arm, and Bella felt the enormity of it all coming back to her. Pulling a tissue from her pocket, she blew her nose. 'Right, so,' she began forcefully. 'I've got something very exciting to talk to you all about today. I've had an amazing idea and I think you're going to like it too. I think we should start a giving tree.'

All the volunteers except for Nina looked to each other in confusion and Bella outlined her idea and the conversations she'd had at the school staff meeting. Without naming names, she gave examples of the help needed in their peaceful little village.

'I had no idea,' said Hazel. 'I mean, life's not easy at the best of times, but I didn't know so many people were in dire straits.'

'Oh, I liked them,' Mr Whittaker said, tapping his foot to a remembered tune. He then started humming something by Status Quo but no one had the heart to correct him.

'And are you sure we should have it here?'

'Definitely. I did think about the green but once we get the village Christmas tree on there and the church's enormous nativity scene there isn't room. The kids still need to use it for running about on, and the tree next to the grotto is perfect. We can keep any donations nice and secure here in the locked huts. Plus, we can have this as the main donation point. Nina heard about this at school but what do you all think? Hazel? Matilda? Mr Whittaker?'

Hazel bashed her hand down on her leg. 'I love the idea. Much better than doing just a toy drive or raffle. This will really help our friends in ways that they actually need. Brilliant, Bella. Just brilliant.'

Bella glowed. 'Mr Whittaker?'

'I like it too. I think it's the spirit of the season speaking. No need for a stiff upper lip and all that sort of thing, we're your friends and we're going to help you. Good. Very good.'

'Exactly,' Bella replied, smiling widely for what felt the first time in ages. 'I kind of knew you'd all be in favour because you have such lovely, generous hearts, so I already printed out the forms. I hope you don't mind.'

'Not at all,' Matilda replied. Though Bella could see she did mind a little bit.

Bella outlined how she wanted the whole thing to work. 'The biggest thing for you guys is of course accepting the donations and making sure they have the tag on them so I know who it's for, and encouraging people to take a tag from the tree in the first place. I thought we could announce it at next week's Christmas launch.'

'I still think November is too early for Christmas,' Mr Whittaker grumbled. 'We've only just had Halloween and Bonfire Night. Did you see that display Mr Cole paid for? Too many fireworks if you ask me. My poor Mitzie can't cope with all the banging and blasting. She hid under the duvet.'

Mitzie was Mr Whittaker's toy poodle and a thoroughly spoiled dog she was too.

'My Petal did the same,' Matilda said, referring to her fluffy fat cat.

84

Hazel nodded furiously. 'Ostentatious I'd call it. But we all know that Mr Cole likes to show everyone how clever he is and how much money he's got. He likes to come across as generous but he's only out for what he can get. The sign he insisted on putting up showing who'd paid for the fireworks was as big as my front window.'

Though Bella always tried to ignore village gossip, she was interested in what they had to say in case it explained some of Amias's recent behaviour. The Coles were rather snooty and not generally well liked in the village, but it seemed the subject was done.

'And don't go moaning about the Christmas launch, Reginald Whittaker,' Hazel said. 'You were democratically outvoted over launch day. People need time to buy for their families. Christmas is expensive and everyone I know starts early. It's only you blokes who leave it till the last minute and you can only get away with that because all us wives and girlfriends and mothers have sorted out everyone else. I'm sure we're starting at the same time as most.'

'London was all lit up last week when I went,' Bella said.

Mr Whittaker harrumphed.

'My husband got me an ironing board cover last Christmas,' Matilda suddenly piped up.

'He didn't?' Hazel gasped. 'I hope you shoved it up his behind.'

'He said it was just a joke present but I'm sure he honestly thought I'd like it. Lunatic.'

'Men are very naïve, dear. My ex-husband once bought me a hamster for Christmas. A hamster! I ask you, do I look like I'd want a hamster for Christmas?'

'Was that what put the tin lid on it?' asked Bella.

'That and his various affairs. Oh, I'm sorry, dear—' She shot a hand out, panicked that she'd upset her.

'It's fine, Hazel. I'm okay.'

Bella was surprised at just how much she meant it. The prospect of the giving tree and the usual fun she had at volunteering were driving away some of the lingering pain.

'Good. I'll take one of those forms now, if you don't mind.' Bella smiled as she handed the first one over. 'Old Mrs Picard's a bit upset because her daughter's off to Scotland for Christmas and they haven't invited her.'

Mrs Picard must have been nigh on a hundred years old, but still participated in all the village events. She had a daughter who worked in Witchbury and claimed it was too much of a drive when she finished work to come and visit her mum, even though Mrs Picard had recently suffered a bad fall. Bella thought it a bit of a feeble excuse and the rest of the village had been checking in on her when they happened to be passing her cottage.

'That's awful.'

'It is. I think it'd be nice for someone else to get her a present too. I was going to pick her up one or two bits so she had some presents to open on Christmas Day, but it wouldn't hurt for someone else to get her something as well. Think how spoiled she'll feel. I'll probably end up inviting her to have dinner with me again. We had quite a nice time last year getting quietly drunk on sherry and watching the Queen's speech.'

'I think that's a wonderful idea, Hazel, and just the thing we want to encourage. Not the drunkenness but the other bit,' she clarified. 'Okay, I'm going to get started on the grotto. I've got so much to do. Nina and Hazel, you're on the information point, aren't you? And, Mr Whittaker, you're on the gift shop, I think. We can all swap around through the day, and make sure you come in here to warm up if you need to. I'm sure someone will cover you if you need a break.' Bella picked up her cup and headed off. 'Have a lovely day, everyone.'

Outside, Bella approached what would by the end of the day be Santa's grotto with mounting excitement. By the time she'd finished, it would be transformed from little more than a plain wooden shed to the epitome of Christmas cheer and fireside cosiness. Unlocking the padlock that swung on the front, she stepped inside. A hook hung from the ceiling for the light that would be powered by a small generator but that wasn't in place yet, so she hung the lantern she'd brought with her.

Her first job was to hang some garlands around the ceiling. She'd also bought a fake cardboard fireplace, which would sit on one wall and opposite it would be Santa's huge wingback chair and some little stools for the children. She could already picture a Christmas tree in one corner surrounded by presents. Fake ones, of course. The real ones would be in a sack next to Santa. That was another job on her list. This week she had to wrap all the colouring books and sets of colouring pencils ready to give out. If there was that to do as well – a job she'd all but forgotten about among her excitement for the giving tree and her life falling apart – there wasn't time to waste.

The decorations they'd purchased were stored in a box in the back corner and Bella set to work hanging a fake ivy and berry garland from each corner of the wooden chalet so it looped gently around the room. Standing back and surveying her efforts, she was aware of the park coming to life. Children now played in the playground and couples ambled along the paths enjoying the countryside. Villagers waved at her and she waved back, sharing morning greetings, and all around, winter heather bloomed from the flowerbeds in deep purples and pinks, adding splashes of colour.

The berry garlands were pretty, but it still felt a bit dark and dreary. She needed to inject that golden glow you saw in Christmas movies. Something that made it feel as cosy as her roaring log fire did in the cottage. Finding some lights, she hung them just below the garland and as soon as she switched on the little battery packs, the place filled with a warm orangey blush. The walls still needed something else though, and Bella made a note to buy some wreaths to hang up. They also needed to do something with the floor. The traditional red Persian rug was rolled up in the corner, but she felt it needed something else to make it extra special. Taking a moment to stand back and survey the scene, she hit on it.

Snow!

Sprinkled at the edges of the room, under the tree and in front of the fireplace it would really add to the magical feel. And more lights. You couldn't go wrong with hundreds of white twinkling fairy lights, and stockings to hang from the fake fire.

Now to get started on the tree. All thoughts of Evan were soon forgotten as she happily worked away crouched down, fiddling with the base of the bushy fake Christmas tree. Standing back, she admired the gorgeous deep green of the leaves. It was a type of green you only saw at this time of year; there was nothing else like it. After a few more hours of work, Bella stood back surveying the almost ready grotto. The children were going to love it.

She'd always found it incredibly exciting to visit Santa's grotto as a child and loved creating that magic now. As she stepped outside, she glanced at the tree that was to become the giving tree. Soon it would be covered in lights and dotted with special gift tags that could change Christmas for the families of Meadowbank. Bella felt a swelling of pride. She'd heard the saying that it takes a village to raise a child; well this year, it was going to take a village to make a Christmas.

Bella smiled, feeling better than she had ever expected to only a week after her break-up. Checking no one could see, she raised her eyes to the sky and crossed her fingers hoping it would last.

Chapter 8

On Wednesday night, Bella settled on the sofa with her mum and sister next to her. Nina curled in the armchair opposite.

'I can't believe I've had so many forms handed in already,' Bella gasped, looking through the stack in her hands. 'It's such an eye-opener. A sad one, but I'm still glad I'm doing it.'

Giving tree forms had gone home in the children's book bags, and many had already been returned. After work tomorrow she'd take a stroll to Bluebell Park and see how many had been handed in there, but so far, more requests had come in than she'd expected.

'What type of things are people asking for?' asked Caro, cutting pieces of Sellotape and handing them to Cynthia who was busy wrapping presents for Santa to hand out to the children. A huge pile of animal colouring books sat next to ones of superheroes. A box full of little packs of colouring pencils was being tackled by Nina over on the armchair.

'It's crazy but it's not what I expected at all. I thought it would be people asking for the latest fancy toy or a new bike, but it's not even close. So far, I've had at least a dozen requests for scarves and gloves or new boots and one for a car seat because the family can't afford one. And when I told the kids about it in assembly this morning, little Sarah from Year R caught up with me, slipped her hand into mine and asked for a huge meal. She said her mum gives her food but sometimes there isn't that much and she's always hungry. It was heart-breaking.' Bella took a deep breath, again experiencing the pain she'd felt then. 'She looked up at me with these big round eyes and I only just managed to hold back tears.'

Evan would probably have hugged her and told her she couldn't fix everyone's problems, but that didn't mean she couldn't try. She'd always thought of him as supportive, though last year he'd not been happy about being kicked out of the cottage so the three of them could wrap the presents for Breakfast with Santa at the school, even though he got to go to the pub. She always organised it for nights when his favourite football team were playing as well, but he always moaned about having to leave and asking why they couldn't do it at Caro's or her mum's. Thoughts of Evan kept trying their best to fly into her brain, but she focused on the people around her and the Christmas music playing quietly in the background.

Her mum had brought some mince pies and Nina had waved a bottle of mulled wine as soon as she'd walked in the door. Caro was on the hot chocolates but kept taking her sister's glass and sniffing it so she could enjoy the rich, winey aroma. While the three of them wrapped the presents for Santa's grotto, Bella was busy making tags for the forms she'd received using her favourite pen and best handwriting. It had quickly become apparent that if she didn't keep up with them every few days, she'd soon fall behind and they hadn't even officially launched the giving tree yet.

'There,' she said finishing another one and holding it up. She'd cut it into a Christmas tree shape and where it had been laminated to protect against the weather, it shone in the light from the fire. 'That's another one done.'

'What's this one for?' asked Nina.

'A food box, and I've listed some suggestions of what people can buy.'

At first, she'd planned to do all this on her own, not wanting anyone else around while she read and cried over some of the forms, but being on her own meant thinking about Evan so her family and friends had rallied round, as they always did. How she wished she had a fortune she could spend on her little village, fixing everyone's problems like a younger, hopefully more attractive, Mrs Christmas.

Nina shook her head. 'It's hard to believe people can't afford food. It's not like the village shop is expensive. I know they do their best to keep their prices as low as possible. In this day and age and with minimum wage, you wouldn't have thought it. It seems so Victorian.'

'It is, but thanks to Bella, we're doing something about it,' Cynthia said.

'Johnny not joining us?' asked Caro, finishing a present and adding it to the pile.

'No, not tonight,' Bella answered, seeing Nina blush. 'I thought it would just be us girls. You always tease him so mercilessly I didn't want to subject him to another attack.'

'Me?' she answered with a twinkle in her eye. 'Never.'

'When is that boy going to ask you out, Nina? That's what I want to know.' Cynthia devoured the last of her mulled wine and held up her glass for a refill. Bella obliged.

'I'd quite like to know that too,' Nina replied. Finding the armchair too awkward to wrap presents in, she moved to the floor, sitting cross-legged. 'I don't know what more I can do. He must know I like him.'

'You both flirt enough,' Bella answered. 'And that's just in school. You used to be even worse when we went to the pub. I don't see how either of you can doubt the other's feelings.'

'Has he asked you to the pub recently?' Caro asked, resting her hands on her bump. They were almost level with her chin.

'Not for a week or so, but we're all busy. You don't think he's gone off me, do you?'

Bella giggled. 'Definitely not. Why would he?'

'I don't know. I told him about that time I ate ten hot dogs on holiday and was sick in the caravan. Maybe that put him off.'

'Definitely, definitely not,' Caro added, grinning. She rubbed her hand over the side of her stomach. 'Ten hot dogs is far too impressive, even if you did bring them all up afterwards.' She winced and moved her hand to her side.

'Baby kicking?'

'Violently. He or she's going to be a football player. Or a thug. Maybe *you* should ask *him* out, Nina? You don't have to wait for him to ask you.'

'I know but it feels a bit weird, doesn't it? I mean, I'm all for feminism, but it takes a whole lot of courage to ask a bloke out. I think blokes can shake off rejection easier than we can, and if he said no and I have to see him every single day at school . . . yuck.'

'You don't have to worry about rejection,' Bella said and a sharp, stabbing pain shot into her chest. Everyone must have heard her voice catch as they all stared at her. She handed her mum a refilled glass and grabbed a mince pie from the plate on the hearth before sitting back down. 'He's clearly nuts about you. You're not worried about Mrs White, are you?'

Nina shook her head. 'I know she'd been fine about it as long as we remain professional at work. I don't know. I just don't know how much longer I'm supposed to hang around. Not that there's any competition here. Eligible bachelors are a bit thin on the ground in Meadowbank.'

'You've got to get in there pretty quick,' said Caro, who had been at school with Luke and married him at the tender age of twenty-two. 'That's what I did. Snagged the best one before anyone else could get him.' She waved her hand in the direction of the mince pies and Nina handed her the plate.

Bella's eyes were drawn to the window. She hadn't closed the curtains even though it was pitch black outside and bright stars dotted the sky. The wind was stronger tonight and though the branches swayed, the gate Nick had mended stayed firmly shut. For a second, she wondered what he and Freddie were up to right now but then drew her gaze back to the room.

It had been ten days since Evan had left. Ten days that had felt like a lifetime and yet no time at all. In the evenings, her mind had been buried under lists for the giving tree and extra lesson planning for school. She'd managed to keep the tears at bay half the time, but when they came, they came thick and fast and unstoppable.

'Maybe I'll have to pluck up the courage to ask him,' Nina replied, her tone resigned as if she was facing a terrible fate.

'Don't sound so glum,' Cynthia interrupted. 'It's not like you're asking him to pull his teeth out, just to go on a date with you. You can't be that bad at dating, surely?'

'I don't know. I once went on a date with a bloke from Witchbury and he spent the whole time telling me he'd worried I was too good for him but was happy to see I wasn't and then listed all the things I had wrong with me, including my hair being too curly.' She stared at the ceiling as if replaying the event. 'It was quite an extensive list.'

Silence fell as Bella, Caro and Cynthia's mouths fell open.

'That did not happen?' Caro asked.

'Oh, it really did.'

'So this is what I've got to look forward to?' Bella joked, but the reality scared her. She might have to develop that thick skin Evan told her about after all.

'Nonsense,' Cynthia said sternly. 'You just need to find a nice man and go to the pub; that's how we did it in the old days. Nice and simple. Easy-peasy.'

Nina smiled fondly at Bella's mum. 'I won't tell you about the time my date took me to McDonald's because that's all he liked to eat.'

'No, don't.' Bella covered her ears. At least she wouldn't be thinking about dating for a long time to come. If ever. She couldn't imagine feeling anything other than pain for a long while yet. She picked up the stack of giving tree forms again. 'Now, anyone know where we can get a real-life pony because that's what Hannah asked me to put on a tag for her today?'

'Sorry, no.' Cynthia turned to Nina. 'You haven't got a date story involving horses have you, Nina?'

'Funny you should say that—'

As Nina began to recite a tale involving a horse-riding lesson, unflattering jodhpurs and the wedgie of a lifetime, Bella relaxed into the comforting atmosphere around her and the peace it gave. She knew it wouldn't be long until everyone left, and her thoughts would run to what life might look like after Christmas when she had nothing to occupy her time or her heart. She pushed down the fear cresting inside and listened intently to Nina's story. It was unlikely but she might, after all, pick up some tips.

Chapter 9

'And so it was that the Angel Gabriel spoke to Mary and Joseph.'

'That's marvellous, Freddie. Well done.' Mrs Brody clapped her hands together. 'You hardly read your script either. Have you been practising at home?' Freddie nodded, his cheeks growing pinker with the praise. It was clear he had as he was reading less like a robot and putting some wonderful expression into his voice. Bella smiled – maybe she'd stop in on her way home and let Nick know how well he was doing. 'Well done you.' Mrs Brody beamed. 'Good job.'

All the children were piled into the main school hall and group rehearsals were now underway. Mrs Brody had given Bella, Nina and Johnny a timetable detailing when they were to be practising in the classroom and when they were all meeting in the main hall. No one dared argue and all three of them were simply moving their other lessons around to fit. When presented with the laminated document, they'd all nodded like terrified children and promised not to forget.

Having got the children to the hall where Mrs Brody had taken over, Johnny had begun to snooze.

'Mary,' blasted George, who was playing the Angel Gabriel, his voice so loud it echoed around the room.

'Jesus Christ—' cried Johnny, shooting upright like someone had poured freezing cold water over him.

'No, Mr Feker, I'm the Angel Gabriel. Jesus is the doll.' George pointed at the rather grubby doll lying in the cardboard box they were using in place of a manger.

Mrs Brody glared at Johnny and he hunched down in his chair. 'Quite right, George. Sorry for interrupting.'

95

A ripple of giggling circulated around the room and Mrs Brody quelled it with the raising of her hand. George, thoroughly enjoying himself, carried on. 'Mary, you are to go to Bethlehem and there you will have a child.'

'A child!' sang the chorus line along the back of the stage.

On the night, they were all going to be in top hats and tails and in an effort to get them used to it, Mrs Brody had scoured the classrooms for any type of headwear. As a result, the girls and boys were now in an assortment of berets, top hats, tiaras and headdresses and a random fez that none of them were particularly keen on wearing.

'And don't forget, children . . .' announced Mrs Brody, darting up onto the stage and standing in front of them. 'Tap, tap, and . . . step – ball – change. Shall we have a go again?' She began tapping her foot in the tap-dancing shoes she'd worn just for the occasion. 'Tap, tap, step – ball – change. Once more. Tap, tap, step – ball – change.'

'Did you know Mrs Brody could tap-dance?' Bella whispered to Nina and Johnny.

'Nope,' Nina replied. 'And I'm not quite sure that's what you call it.'

Johnny smirked. 'She's a woman of many talents.'

Bella chewed her lip. 'I think she's actually pretty good. She's very . . . enthusiastic.'

'She's certainly moving her arms a lot. I just hope she doesn't do her knee in again. She's getting a bit frisky up there.'

Mrs Brody left the stage and began to play the piano. Bella recognised a strange interpretation of 'Living on a Prayer' and concentrated on the length of her fingernails to stop the smile that was more than a little eager to get out. She flicked through her script to find the song. How on earth Mrs Brody had been able to write something that fitted was beyond her. It seems the songwriting course as well as the scriptwriting one was coming in handy. You had to admire her dedication.

The three friends sat at the back of the hall while Mrs Brody carried on with rehearsals for the Christmas play. Bella was glad of the break. Amias had been a terror this morning and he was taking Richard and Umar along with him. She'd eventually had to separate them and had added to her list of jobs for tonight coming up with a new seating plan so she could divide and conquer. None of the children would like it but needs must. Evan would probably have said she should have done it already. He'd sometimes thought she gave the children too many chances, but he didn't know them like she did. Thank God it was Friday.

'I've got another stack of forms for the giving tree in my classroom,' muttered Nina, speaking a bit louder under the cover of music. When Mrs Brody glowered at her, she enthusiastically sang the line 'She's gonna have a baby', where you'd normally sing Bon Jovi's famous chorus. Mrs Brody didn't buy it.

'Brilliant. I'll grab them later.'

The song finished and Amias went up on stage to recite his line. With an air of disdain and in a tone of immense boredom he said, 'But when Mary and Joseph got to Bethlehem, they couldn't find anywhere to stay. There wasn't even a Premier Inn.'

None of the children laughed, clearly not getting the joke, while Mrs Brody chuckled away to herself like a madwoman. Johnny emerged from his hunkered-down position as a turtle pokes its head out of its shell and joined the conversation.

'The giving tree has been a good lesson for some of my Year 6s in understanding not everyone has as much as them. I think Roy has finally learned that having branded crisps and clothes doesn't make him any better than anyone else. Apparently, he's been teasing Megan about having the cheaper brand from the village shop for ages. I had no idea.'

'It's a good lesson for all the kids,' said Nina. 'A tough one, but a good one.'

Bella shot a look to Amias who had returned to his seat on the floor and was messing about. 'I just feel bad about the ones

I can't fulfil. One form asked for a tree because they haven't got one. What am I supposed to do about that? I wasn't going to deliver anything until the Saturday before Christmas and by then it'll be too late. I'm worried about fulfilling requests early and setting a precedent that could cause me problems.'

'I don't mind buying a fake tree and donating it,' said Johnny.

'Oh, Johnny, that's lovely of you,' Nina said, then blushed.

'Do you guys think it'll be okay to deliver a few things early?'

Nina shrugged. 'I don't see why not. It's not that big a deal, is it? If these people are really in need, then an early delivery could make just as much difference as a Christmas Eve one.'

'You're right. I can run this any way I want, can't I?'

'You can. Has anyone started donating things yet?'

'No, but the launch isn't until this weekend.'

'I'll be there anyway but what about you, Johnny?' Nina asked, beginning to colour.

'Count me in,' said Johnny, catching Nina's eye and smiling shyly. Again, Bella wished he'd just pluck up the courage to ask Nina out.

Evan had asked her out after delivering her flowers. A giant bunch of red roses that had filled the house. He still hadn't called her back and she'd thought about trying again at the weekend. She'd even contemplated ringing from someone else's phone hoping he'd pick up to a number he didn't recognise but that went a little bit too far towards nutcase for her liking. She hadn't completely ruled out the idea for the future, but she didn't want to descend into bunny boiler if she could help it.

As she glanced over her flock of children all sitting nicely in a line, she saw Amias shove Richard so hard he fell into Umar who fell into Hannah and on it went like a domino effect. The boys were all laughing but two of the girls further along the line clashed heads and began to cry.

Bella shot a glance to Nina. 'Can you deal with the girls, and I'll deal with Amias?' Nina nodded. Calmly, Bella stood up and went to Amias, crouching down beside him. 'Amias, this isn't the behaviour I expect from you and because of your silliness you've hurt your friends.'

'They're not my friends,' he replied with far more confidence than a nine-year-old should have.

Bella cocked her head. 'Aren't they? Why not?' Amias didn't answer, and Bella didn't press knowing that in front of everyone Amias would clam up. He had today when he'd accidentally bumped into Freddie again.

Freddie had run to her in tears saying that Amias had punched him in the stomach. On questioning, Amias had claimed it was an accident and that he'd been running with his fists in front of him. It was a lame excuse even by his standards and another escalation of behaviour towards Freddie Bella wasn't happy with. Not happy with at all. It also meant another word with the Coles after school, which was never an easy conversation to have. Hopefully this time, they'd see the absurdity in what Amias was claiming and say something to their son, though she didn't hold out much hope. Bella gave him one last gentle warning and fervently wished it would be enough. Any more and she'd have to move him down the chart again, which would put him on red and mean a trip to Mrs White. 'Let's not have any more, okay? Or I'll have to separate you three boys.'

The rehearsal was interrupted by the arrival of the school's Christmas tree. The two burly men who had delivered it brought it in under Mrs White's supervision. Everyone fell silent as they watched the men get it upright and into the stand. As soon as the branches fell into place, the children gasped and whispered in excitement.

Mrs White walked around it, admiringly. 'Isn't this exciting, children? We can start making some Christmas decorations now.'

Finally, the rehearsals finished for the day and the teachers trooped back to the classrooms with their pupils. Racing the ticking of the clock and the gathering crowd of parents outside,

Bella urged the children to get their coats on and grab their belongings ready to go and enjoy the weekend.

Normally, Bella would be just as excited as them and though she had enough activity to keep her occupied tonight, she felt like a piece of her was missing. Every day she told herself the pain would lessen and then woke disappointed to find it hadn't.

'Can you wait with me, please, Amias?' The boy huffed and threw his bag onto the table. His attitude was really getting worse and worse.

Bella sent out all the other children.

'There's my dad, miss,' said Amias after everyone had gone.

'I know, thank you.' Mr Cole came forward. He wasn't usually late, and he shot a look at Nick as he passed that was almost accusing. Apprehension tightened Bella's chest. She didn't enjoy having these sorts of conversations, but it was better to nip Amias's behaviour in the bud now before it became a problem. 'Mr Cole, I wonder if we could have a quick chat?'

'I am running late, Miss Moore. Can't we do this Monday?'

She opened the large glass door wider. 'It really would be better if we could speak now. It'll only take a moment.' Mr Cole stepped through with a huff. 'I'm afraid that Amias is being a little disruptive at the moment, and there was an incident in the playground with another boy. The boy feels that Amias deliberately punched him—'

'I didn't,' Amias roared. 'Freddie's a liar.' Bella had become quite adept at recognising lies over the years and was positive this was one. His voice was too high, and the words spoken with too much vehemence.

Mr Cole put a hand on his son's shoulder. 'If Amias says he didn't, then he didn't. Wasn't it Freddie Cowley who lied about Amias the other day?'

'It is Freddie, but—' Bella knew exactly where this was going and, as she suspected, the same words his wife had spoken would come out of his mouth.

'Well, he's probably lying for attention. Wants people to feel sorry for him.'

'I don't believe that's the case, Mr Cole. This isn't the first incident with this other boy, and I'd just like to nip any problems in the bud.' Bella knew she had to hold firm.

'By accusing my boy of something he didn't do?'

'Not at all. I just want to make you aware of what has happened, and that this other boy feels these things are being done on purpose. Now, I've investigated and with today's incident, Amias said it was an accident but admitted he was running with his fists out, which isn't a natural way to run.'

'So you are accusing my boy?' Mr Cole glowered at her. 'Unbelievable.'

Bella paused, aware that she had to keep a grip on the conversation and not let Mr Cole's bluff and bluster get the better of her. 'Amias has told me he didn't, and I think it's best if we put these things behind us and concentrate on being kind and playing nicely together.'

Mr Cole scoffed. 'Some kids are just weak and attention-seeking.'

Bella ignored him, though she had to press her jaws together to stop herself from saying how wrong he was.

'Anyway,' he continued brightly, as if their whole conversation hadn't taken place. 'I've heard about this giving tree thing you're doing, and I was wondering if you'd like a tree? I'd be happy to donate one and we could have a little sign that says where it came from like we have at the fireworks display every year. What do you think?'

Little sign? Not according to Hazel.

'That's very kind of you, Mr Cole.' He smiled condescendingly. 'But we're actually going to use one of the fir trees growing at Bluebell Park. There's a gorgeous one that's just the right size right next to Santa's grotto. I did have a request from someone for a Christmas tree though, so if you wanted to donate one to a family in need then—'

'If a family is *in need*' – he made air quotes with his fingers – 'then they should be asking for more than a tree. If you ask me, that's taking the piss.'

Bella felt an imperceptible tightening in her shoulders at his swearing in front of Amias. She wasn't judging. Everyone swore at times, but it just didn't seem right to do it on school property. Normally people swore in front of kids when they were angry or upset and couldn't help themselves. Mr Cole was quite calm.

So that was a no, then. Perhaps Hazel's assessment of Mr Cole had been correct. His offer had come from his head rather than his heart, with purely mercenary motives.

'Right, well, if you'd prefer not to, then I completely understand. I'll let you two get off and have a lovely weekend.'

As they marched away it was then she saw the tall, handsome figure lingering by the playground gates and her heart somersaulted in her chest.

It was Evan.

Chapter 10

The steam of Bella's breath hung in the cold afternoon air as Evan closed the gap between them, striding through the empty playground. Dusk had begun to fall over Meadowbank and the sky was heavy with cloud. Where the sun had set, an orange glow lingered low in the sky and above it a patchwork of pink, blue and grey.

Evan's navy peacoat fitted his frame well, and his gloved hands swung by his sides. God she'd loved this man, but he didn't look up and meet her gaze, keeping his eyes on the ground as he came towards her. If he was here in response to her message, she wished he'd waited until she was home. It would be much easier to talk there. Had he come here so she wouldn't make a scene? Quite possibly.

Bella was vaguely aware of Mrs White locking the gates behind him, meaning she would have to send him to the office reception when it was time to leave. She didn't know why such a practical thought occurred to her. Probably her brain trying to cope with his unexpected arrival. Would they be walking out together? A spark of hope flickered but died almost instantly. She didn't know if she could take him back even if that was why he was here. Could she ever trust him again when he'd been so deceitful? That was what hurt the most. The relationship failing hurt like hell but what stung like salt in the wound was knowing he'd looked her in the eye and lied to her.

'Hi,' Evan said in a low, quiet voice as he drew near. They were meeting like strangers, and it cut deeply. She searched for something to say but couldn't think of anything and simply backed into the classroom, letting him in. 'It's freezing out there tonight.'

'It is.' They were reduced to talking about the weather like people at a bus stop. After five years together was this all they could manage? Well, she wasn't going to sit here chatting about the chance of a white Christmas. She had things to do. Things Evan would know about if he hadn't dumped her and gone off with someone named after an animated piglet. When he didn't offer anything more, she said, 'Evan, what are you doing here?'

'I got your message the other day and you were right. We need to talk.' He sat down on one of the tables, his hands resting in his lap. He hadn't taken his gloves or coat off, so he clearly wasn't planning on staying. 'I've just been to the cottage to clear out the last of my things. I posted my key back through the letter box.'

So he wasn't asking to come home or for her to take him back. Not that she really wanted him to after the way he tried to sneak out, but his measured, detached tone only added to her pain. He was like a doctor talking to a patient. As though they hadn't been constantly together for the last five years, lying in each other's arms at night, as though they hadn't been everything to each other.

Evan loosened his scarf a little. 'I hope that's okay.'

'Well, it's not really, is it?' she fired back, her pain emerging as a moment of uninhibited anger.

'Try and stay calm, Bella,' he said, pinching the bridge of his nose.

'Calm? Me?' Had he always been this patronising? She was sure she'd have noticed and had words with him before now if he had been. 'How dare you say that to me! You're the one who just upped and left without a moment's notice. How long had you been planning it?'

Evan showed no emotion. He'd always been the less expressive one in the relationship, but this level of disinterest was unnerving. He seemed cold, as if he'd turned his heart off from her. 'You said you deserved some answers and that's why I'm here. The answer is, I hadn't been planning it for long. This thing with Pepper, it's all moved quite suddenly. I don't really know how it happened or why and I'm sorry I hurt you.'

'I wish I could believe you.' She wasn't being dramatic, only speaking the truth. He'd broken her trust and she didn't know how to tell truth from fiction with him.

'I am sorry, Bella. I really am.'

'You don't sound it. How long has it all been going on? How long have you been sneaking around behind my back?'

'Please don't say sneaking, Bella.'

'Why not? You have been. You've been lying and sneaking and . . .' She couldn't think of another word as her brain clouded. 'Why couldn't you just tell me that things weren't working for you anymore? I need to know how long it's been going on. You owe me that much.'

'Only a couple of months, Bella. I promise.'

'*Only*?' A couple of months might not seem a long time to him but to her it felt like forever. How many lies had he told during that time? How many times had he said he was going to work when he must have been going to see his other woman? 'Last month when you had a work conference in Leeds, you didn't, did you?'

This time Evan dipped his eyes, ashamed of himself. 'No. I'm sorry, Bella.'

'You were seeing her. Oh God.'

She pressed her cold hand to her forehead, grateful for the cooling effect on her skin. The thought of them in a hotel in Leeds, romping it through the weekend, made her stomach roll. Had he kissed Pepper as passionately as he had her at the start of their relationship? Had the sex been better? Was Pepper a better lover? All these thoughts had passed through her head since he'd left but she'd managed to keep them at bay, forcing herself not to go to that dark place where she compared herself to the other woman. Now though, they rocketed through at an unprecedented speed, tearing down her self-esteem. The thought of his dirty weekend in Leeds magnified those feelings till she couldn't distract herself from them.

'I did see her,' he said coldly. 'And that's when we decided we wanted to make a go of it.'

Indignation burned. 'Oh, so until then you weren't entirely sure, and you stuck with me as the consolation prize? I was still in the running but not the odds-on favourite.'

All that deceit.

'Bella, you have to believe me when I say it was never like that. I never meant to hurt you.'

'Yes, you did.' Bella's voice grew louder, unable to control it anymore. It was the only way to release some of the pain. 'Whenever I found out about this it was going to hurt. You should have told me as soon as you started having feelings for someone else. If that wasn't a sign something was wrong with our relationship, then nothing was. Or were you just going to stay with me until you found someone better, whether that was Pepper or someone else?' Evan didn't answer at first. 'You knew you were going to leave me sooner or later, didn't you?'

'No, Bella. I loved you. Very much, but . . .' He studied his shoes. 'I mean – I suppose I did feel sometimes that we were heading in different directions, but—'

'What do you mean?'

Different directions? Was he reciting things he'd read off the internet? Had he googled the ten best ways to dump someone? It all seemed so inhuman.

'It was clear we were starting to want different things.'

That was the first she'd heard of it. 'Like what?'

'I started to feel more and more that I wanted to live in the city, but I knew you'd never want that. Pepper and I love going to the cinema, or to the theatre.'

'I love trips to the theatre,' she responded, feeling the need to defend herself.

'You like a day trip to London but you like coming home from all that and we don't. We want it more.'

We. He was already talking about him and Pepper as a 'we'. The 'we' that used to be her and Evan. It was the ultimate betrayal and the crucial sign that he'd already completely moved on.

'You love being here in Meadowbank, but I was finding it increasingly claustrophobic. You wanted a family and I—'

'You wanted a family too,' she interrupted. 'You just said you weren't ready yet. Not that you never wanted a family.' Or had he just not wanted a family with her? The way he turned to look out into the dark playground gave her the answer and her heart ripped apart again. Swallowing down her tears, all traces of anger buried under her agony, she said, 'Why didn't you say anything? This is all so . . . so out of nowhere.'

'I should have, but there just never seemed to be a good time. When I met Pepper, we were so in sync. I couldn't help developing feelings for her. I didn't choose to. It just happened.'

If what he said was true, there were far more problems in their relationship than she'd ever noticed. People didn't fall out of love for no reason. People changed and as she hadn't, she could only assume Evan had. Though she knew the words were going to hurt, she still had to ask and pushed them past the lump in her throat. 'Do you love her?'

Finally, Evan lifted his head and met her gaze. Was she ready to hear the answer? She wasn't sure but it was coming, whether she was ready or not.

'I do.'

The brightly coloured walls of her classroom swam before her. The strings of artwork criss-crossing the ceiling merged and swirled. The two words she'd always assumed would be said to her at an altar were now being used for the opposite reason. He wasn't binding himself to her for the rest of their lives, he was saying them to justify his walking away, straight into the arms of another woman. How ironic.

'After only a few months? Wow. She must be very special.'

'Don't be like that, Bella.'

'Like what? Annoyed? Heartbroken? Angry?'

'Bitter.'

Her eyes opened wide as she stared at him in horror. When had he become so cruel? He'd never have spoken to her like that before. His guilt was talking. 'I'm entitled to feel however I want to feel, Evan, and you might not like it because it makes you feel like a shit, but that's your problem not mine.'

Evan's eyes scanned the walls behind her and the excerpts of handwriting her class had done. Bella hated that they were doing this here, in the place that had felt like a second home, and she wanted to shout at him to avert his gaze as if he would sully her wonderful children's work.

The fog of torment and sorrow cleared, giving a moment of clarity. If he was unhappy enough to fall in love with Pepper, he'd have fallen in love with someone else sooner or later. Better now than even further down the line with kids in tow. She had the answers she'd been looking for. Whatever Evan said, she still believed there hadn't been any signs because he was hedging his bets, seeing how things worked out with Pepper. If things hadn't worked out, if she hadn't wanted to make a go of it, Bella was sure he'd still be by her side, and she'd be ignorant of how he felt. If he was like that, she really was better off without him.

'I'm sorry things ended this way,' he mumbled, standing up as if the conversation was over. 'As I said, I've taken the rest of my stuff from the cottage. I've left you the pictures of us.'

The fact that he didn't even want to remember their time together stabbed into her already injured body. Was he just going to erase her from his life, like the last five years had never happened? Did he not even want to acknowledge what they'd had when it had been good?

'Later we can talk about the mortgage or we can go through our solicitors. I don't think it's a good idea to discuss it right now. It's all still too painful . . . for both of us.'

Huh, she doubted that. She doubted any modicum of pain he felt was anywhere near the tearing heartache of reading his letter or the resounding sorrow it had caused every day since. It sounded like a tacked-on platitude because her glower had scared him. Did he think she'd launch across the classroom and attack him with the safety scissors?

Unlike Mr Cole she wasn't going to taint her classroom by swearing in it. Bella crossed her arms over her chest. 'Goodbye, Evan. I hope to God I never have to see you again.'

'You won't,' he replied quietly as he left.

She watched him go, knowing they both had meant what they'd said and determined that this would be the last time she cried over the man who didn't seem to care how much he'd torn her life apart.

Chapter 11

Nick watched the huge pot of bolognese sauce bubbling on the stove, proud that he'd made his first attempt at batch cooking. With the log fire kicking out heat and the heating on low to dry the washing he'd just distributed over the radiators, it was verging on tropical in the cottage, but he was up to his elbows in raw chicken and couldn't stop to do anything about it.

Freddie had been distinctly unimpressed when Nick had said this was how they were going to spend their Saturday morning. He'd been hoping they could put up the Christmas decorations early to which Nick had replied with a firm no. Freddie didn't see why not and Nick had struggled to come up with an answer that didn't make him sound like a Grinch. Freddie also didn't see why they couldn't live on pizza and chips for the rest of their lives and Nick had kindly explained that eating that sort of food all the time would definitely shorten how long the rest of their lives would be. Food like that was great as a treat, but you couldn't eat it every day. He'd then gone on to talk about saturated fat, fatty acids and Omega fish oils (to which Freddie had made fake vomiting sounds) but had got muddled up with which ones were which and finished by saying, 'We just need to start eating better, okay? End of.'

'Right, what's next, Freddie?'

His sous chef ran a finger over the list to the second item. 'Curry, but I don't like curry, Dad.'

'You like a korma. That's the sweet one that tastes of coconut.'

'Only sometimes.'

'Well, it'll be nice for a change. Come on, I'll chop the chicken up because you hate touching it and you can open that bag of chopped onion and chuck it in the pot along with all those jars of sauce.'

As Nick watched Freddie drain each jar, he worried he'd miscalculated exactly how much food he was making. He eyed the stack of silver takeaway containers purchased in preparation then surveyed the pot again. There seemed to be more here than he had room for in the freezer. Never mind. Some would last in the fridge for a few days. 'How about after we get this done, we take a trip to Bluebell Park. It's the big grotto reveal at 4 p.m. and I've heard they've gone all out this year. The community choir are going to be singing too.'

'Mrs Hopkins is scary,' Freddie replied, referring to the leader of the choir, while stirring the onions.

'She is a bit,' Nick replied with a laugh, scraping the chopping board clear of the chicken and watching it fall into the pot with a satisfying thud. 'She was just as scary when I was younger. Do you want to go and get changed? We're both covered in food splatters.'

Freddie climbed down from the chair he'd been kneeling on and Nick pulled him into a hug.

'Thanks for your help today, mate. I enjoyed it.'

'Me too.' Though Nick could tell from his tone he hadn't really. 'You'd better wear a different top, Dad. That one stinks.'

'Does it?' Nick sniffed the front, spying the matching food splatters on his jumper. 'Hey! That's onions, not me. I had a shower this morning.' Freddie giggled. 'Let's both get changed and then we'll head off, shall we? This is nearly done. You can have a play in the playground before it all gets started.'

Giving everything one last stir, Nick left it to simmer and raced Freddie up the stairs to change. Bella would be at the park but probably wouldn't have time to talk. They'd hardly seen her recently except for school drop-off and pick-up. Heartbreak was an uncontrollable thing, very much like grief. One minute you were fine and the next it could creep up on you without hurting as much as it had the day it happened. Shaking off the shadow of his own pain, he pulled out some clothes and changed.

After a few reminders to hurry up, Freddie was eventually ready in his thick winter coat and they began the short walk to the park. It was at times like these that Nick remembered how small the village actually was. After walking through three small lanes, lined either side with pretty cottages, they were on the edge of Meadowbank and at the country road. If you went one way, you'd come across the farms that belonged to Amelia Williams, Adam Noble (though he was now living with Amelia at Meadow Farmhouse) and Mr MacMahon with his ever-faithful dog, Bobby. Walk the other way and you came across the posher houses where people like Mr Hoffelmeyer, their crazy local historian, lived. Settled somewhere between them was Bluebell Park.

This giving tree idea was a new one though. He'd never heard of the concept before and at first, he hadn't been sure what to make of it. His father had always taught him charity began at home and it was a lesson he'd found hard to shake off. It had only been necessity that had forced him to seek help from his best friends Len and Trish when he'd been stuck in traffic one day and unable to make it back to pick Freddie up. With no idea how long he was going to be there he'd called his parents first, and after telling him he should have been more organised and checked the traffic through the day, they'd said they couldn't get Freddie as they were out with friends. He'd then had to call Len and Trish and ask them. Afterwards, Trish had insisted they all have dinner together and had rustled up an amazing feast of homemade burgers with big fat chips.

From that day on, he'd found it easier to ask for help when he needed it, but only with them. The fact his marriage had fallen apart wasn't his parents' fault and he didn't want to burden them or anyone else with his problems. He could see the merits of the giving tree but couldn't help but feel that some people would take advantage.

Nick squeezed Freddie's hand then ran his thumb over the smooth baby-soft skin as they strolled along hand in hand. He knew it wouldn't be long until that went the same way as *Daddy*. It would be something only done occasionally and never in front of his friends. He savoured the feeling again. 'So, how are you doing with your lines? Do we need to practise some more?'

'Mrs Brody was really impressed with me the other day.' He beamed. 'I remember most of them. There's only a couple that I need to practise.'

'We can do that tomorrow if you like, before school on Monday.'

'Okay.'

Nick frowned at the way his son, who had always been happy and excited at the prospect of school, dipped his head and focused on his shoes. On Friday, Miss Radcliffe had told him of another accident with Amias Cole and it had been bugging Nick ever since. Was it really an accident? Freddie didn't think so and he got the impression from Bella that she wasn't entirely convinced either. Though she hadn't said as much. She was always very careful in how she spoke about the kids. Very professional. He'd seen her speaking to Mr Cole at the same time Miss Radcliffe had talked to him. As Bella hadn't mentioned anything else, he'd been crossing his fingers that it was all dying down.

Knowing how excited Freddie had been about the new grotto, Nick decided not to press and instead talked to him about all the other things he liked and asked whether he fancied curry for dinner, to which the answer was a resounding no.

As they entered the park, the pathway to the central area, where all the chalets and the playground were, meandered along, dotted with benches. Acres of fields swept away in the distance to one side and Meadowbank wood lay on the other. Lights had been strung from each of the chalets giving Meadowbank its own small, cosy Christmas market.

'Wow, Dad, look at the grotto.' Freddie pointed and Nick followed his gaze.

Bella had done an amazing job of decorating it and if the inside was half as good as the exterior, the kids were in for a treat. A short picket fence encircled the grotto itself and lights and red bells had been strung all along, though the lights were off until the big reveal.

On the ground, leading up to the front door, was a short red runner with long green garlands studded with lights and red bows on either side. A giant wooden sign, artistically crooked and covered in fake snow, stated 'Lapland' and another by the door declared 'Santa's Workshop'. Two small Christmas trees stood either side of the door with presents in shiny red wrapping paper underneath and beside them, a small snowman and reindeer peeped out. A large red ribbon that Mr Tomlin, who always stepped in to play Santa, was going to cut ran around the whole thing, and the lights were all in darkness.

Freddie dropped his hand from Nick's, now other children were around. 'Can I go and play, Dad, please?'

'Of course.' Nick glanced around spying Bella at the impressive Santa's grotto and next to it, the beautiful fir tree she was using as the giving tree. 'I'm going to go and chat to Bella while we wait for the big reveal. I'll be just over there.'

Nick didn't know why he kept feeling the need to check in on Bella. At first, he'd thought it was just empathy for what she was going through, having been through it himself, but lately he wasn't sure. His mind kept finding questions to ask her, things he wanted to talk about. It was odd given that until very recently, he'd been sure he'd never want to talk to a single woman ever again. Nick edged over. Feeling an apprehension he'd never experienced with her before. 'Hi, Bella. How's it going?'

Bella turned around, smiling broadly. A slight twinkle came to her eyes, but it wasn't as bright as it had been before Evan left and Nick felt an unusual surge of anger at the idiot who'd stolen her shine.

'Nick, hey. Where's Freddie?' He nodded towards the playground where Freddie was now hanging upside down from the monkey bars with a friend pushing him in the back like a swing. Bella giggled. 'I see. Boys, hey? Though honestly, girls can be just as much work.'

'I always wanted a girl as well,' he said without thinking and a slight pinch at the corner of Bella's eyes showed her repressed surprise. He scratched the back of his head unsure why he'd just said that. For the last six months he hadn't thought about the future at all but working to get his life together was bringing something back. Not that he was ready for dating yet. Talking to a woman was a far cry from romancing one and he wasn't making very good conversation anyway. 'I don't really know why I said that. I just always fancied one of each I suppose. A little princess as well as my maniac of a boy.'

'He's a good boy,' Bella replied with a fondness he assumed she used for all the children. 'One of the best I'd say, but don't tell anyone I told you so. He's clever, funny and kind.'

'Ah, like me then,' Nick teased.

'Just like you.' Now it was Bella's turn to look like she hadn't intended on saying anything. After looking away, she said, 'Thanks again for fixing my gate. I'd been bugging Evan for ages to do it, but you know how bad he was at DIY.'

The mention of Evan dampened her eyes again and Nick changed the subject, not quite sure how to start a conversation about Freddie and Amias potentially bullying him. Amias didn't seem to be targeting anyone else except with some mild teasing. He was definitely treating Freddie differently, physically. Thinking of it sent that protective urge up his spine and he willed himself to calm down.

Bella though seemed to have read his mind, or perhaps it was just her talking about the one thing they had in common. 'Freddie's been doing really well with his lines for the Christmas play.' Her cheeks began to colour slightly. 'I was going to pop in last night and let you know.'

115

'You were?' The idea filled his chest with a warmth at odds with the cold weather he stood in.

'Mrs Brody was very impressed.'

'Ah, Mrs Brody. Is she still as terrifying as ever?'

Bella laughed. 'Sometimes, but she's very happy with Freddie so I don't think he needs to worry.'

Nick knew this was his chance to say something about Amias, but he hesitated. He didn't want to ruin this day for Bella by talking about something so serious, and though he knew Miss Radcliffe volunteered here too, he valued Bella's opinion and knew she'd be able to give him good advice. It wasn't that he didn't like or trust Miss Radcliffe, he just felt safer talking to Bella as he'd known her for longer. After clearing his throat, he began.

'Umm, Bella, can I just talk to you about Freddie for a minute?'

'Of course.' Her brows pinched together as he outlined his concerns. 'Right, I see.' He could see from her eyes she was digesting the information and making sense of it. 'Amias maintains that these things are accidents, but I still talked to his parents Friday night. I've made it clear that we won't allow behaviour like this. I'll keep an eye on Amias and ask Miss Radcliffe to do the same with Freddie. I mean, I'm sure she's already keeping an eye on things, but if it's okay, I'll mention what you've told me today. I hope that reassures you.' At this last remark she laughed. 'Sorry, that sounded so formal, didn't it? But I promise we're all against teasing and bullying at Meadowbank Primary.'

Nick smiled and the lines on his forehead softened. 'Thank you, Bella. I appreciate it.'

'The other child has been a bit more boisterous recently, which is not an excuse, but—'

'You don't think he's picking on Freddie?' Nick finished.

'I don't. There have been other children, and unfortunately, these things happen sometimes. Part of teaching is helping kids to learn how to behave socially as well as how to add and subtract.

Some kids take a bit more time to learn it than others or they forget and push the boundaries.'

'Thank you. That makes me feel a lot better.' Nick went to walk away and took a step back towards her. He shuffled about on the spot, searching for the words. 'And are you still doing okay? I mean about Evan? You don't need anything . . .' His sentence trailed away into silence.

'Oh, umm, yeah, I'm fine. Doing okay. Thanks for asking.' She looked like she was about to say more, but nothing came.

'The grotto looks great.'

'Doesn't it? I'm so happy with it. I think it looks really magical. I hope the kids like it.' Her face was full of life again. She'd worked hard for the big grotto opening and with everything she'd been through, she deserved to enjoy it.

'I'm sure they will. It's even making me feel Christmassy. Is old Mr Tomlin Santa again?'

'Of course. Could there be another? He has such a gift with the kids. And as he does Breakfast with Santa at the school too, I honestly think they're convinced he's the real deal. He certainly looks it.'

Nick watched the joy radiate from Bella's face as she talked. 'Your family have always loved Christmas, haven't they?'

'Probably a little too much. Mum and Dad are getting started already, in fact, I think Mum started getting ready in October.'

They couldn't be any more different to his own parents who put their tree up on Christmas Eve, somewhat begrudgingly, and took it down on New Year's Eve. On Christmas Day they always went to a restaurant in Witchbury and they'd never joined Nick and Freddie at the pub on Christmas Eve when the whole village descended and sang Christmas carols together. Come to think of it, Paige had never enjoyed having a singsong either. She didn't have a great singing voice and used to get embarrassed. Nick didn't have a great singing voice either. Neither did Dean, the landlord, or half the village, but that didn't stop them all having a good time.

Normally Nick would see his parents on Boxing Day but only for a short buffet lunch. Freddie would be overtired from the excitement and his parents found it hard to cope with his short temper and selective hearing. He could imagine Bella spent almost every minute of the festive period with her family. The Moores were a tightknit unit. The type he'd always hoped he'd have with Paige and Freddie.

'Tell me more about this giving tree then,' he said to brighten the mood.

'I know it's a bit of an unusual idea and I'm a bit nervous some people aren't going to like it.'

'I'm sure everyone will love it.'

'I really hope so. It just embodies the spirit of Christmas. You see, the tree's a bit like a Christmas tree where you can take a tag and buy something for someone in need—'

'Probably cheeky blighters asking for the latest toy because they don't want to buy it themselves,' came a deep voice from over Nick's shoulder. Both Bella and Nick spun but Nick already knew who it was.

'Afternoon, Mr Cole,' Nick said through gritted teeth. He didn't agree with the sentiment and seeing Bella blush made him feel protective towards her. 'I don't think people will take advantage. Most people aren't like that.'

'They will, you just watch them. This whole thing is nonsense.' With one last parting shot, Mr Cole strode away. 'You mark my words, Miss Moore. You'll have people asking for flat-screen TVs and Xboxes before you can say Merry Christmas. People should work hard to help themselves, not rely on charity. Some people need to pick themselves up by their bootstraps and just get on with things.'

When he'd gone, Nick cleared his throat. 'Wow, that's quite a point of view.'

'It is.' Bella's confidence had faded, and her shoulders slumped. 'I'm sure no one else thinks like that.' She glanced up at him, reassured, and he offered a smile in return. 'So we just take a tag and then bring the present here?'

'That's right. There aren't any names on them, only a specific or suggested present. I got the idea after I went to London. I think sometimes we're blind to other people's suffering and we don't always realise what's happening with our friends and neighbours because we're so wrapped up in our own lives. If we can help someone out, why wouldn't we?'

Why wouldn't we indeed? 'What sort of things are people asking for?'

Bella outlined some of the requests and Nick's conscience pricked. These weren't the types of things he'd expected. Asking for clothes for children, or even food hit him like an icy blast of wind. They were basic things everyone deserved. Maybe Bella was right and he, like so many people, had become too wrapped up in their own lives to notice and help others.

After everything had turned upside down and he'd needed help, he was in no position to judge anyone else. He wanted Freddie to know there was nothing wrong in asking for assistance if you needed it and that helping others was a good thing to do.

Bella said a quick goodbye and went back to hanging the last few tags on the tree as Len and Trish joined him.

'Oy, oy. Getting very chatty there, fella.'

'Give over, Len,' Trish said. 'She's our neighbour, of course he's going to talk to her. Has there been anything more with Amias?'

'Freddie told me today about another incident yesterday, so I wanted to ask Miss Moore's advice.' Nick outlined what had happened and why Freddie hadn't mentioned it.

'Do you know,' said Len, 'I'm starting to think he should punch him back. Sometimes that's the only thing that sorts these bullies out.'

'I know what you mean,' said Trish. 'But I'm not sure in primary school that's a good idea. We don't want Freddie getting into trouble.'

Nick nodded his agreement. 'I know this other boy's been out of line and believe me it hurts me as much as it does Freddie, but I can't condone him punching another child.'

'Punch who?' asked Freddie and Nick jumped.

'When did you get here?'

'Just now.'

'You can't have,' Nick replied. 'You were like a ninja! You never move like a ninja. It's normally like a herd of elephants in giant boots stomping around.'

Freddie laughed as Bella's voice boomed through the loudspeaker. Mr Tomlin, dressed as Santa and with a portly, round tummy to match, marched out behind her as Freddie stood close to his dad. It was time to officially unveil Santa's new grotto.

Chapter 12

Bella's hand shook as she gazed out at the assembled crowd, ready to switch on the lights on Santa's new grotto. From the excited faces she'd seen so far, the children liked it and she loved making Christmas magical for them.

Most of Meadowbank had gathered, and she hoped that at least some of those would also take a tag from the giving tree. She'd printed a stack of flyers at school (with Mrs White's permission) and Mr Whittaker and some of the other volunteers were giving them out. If only a quarter of them decided to take part that would mean a huge number of families were going to get some help this Christmas, but her aim was for every single tag to be taken before this whole thing was over. To one side she saw the smiling faces of her family. They'd been so supportive through these last two weeks she had no idea how she'd have made it through without them.

After Evan's surprise appearance at the school gates last night, she'd gone home to find the cottage the same as she'd left it that morning. Evan had found the box of his belongings at the bottom of the wardrobe and at the bottom of it she'd found their photos. Seeing them cast aside like that, memories not worth remembering, Bella had collapsed onto the floor crying until her head ached and her eyes burned with running mascara. Then, she'd picked herself up and gone downstairs.

While she made the tags for the giving tree, listening to Michael Bublé's Christmas album, she'd drunk most of a bottle of wine. The printing and cutting had been soothing, taking her mind off the exchange while it bubbled around in her subconscious. Every Christmas song that tugged at her heartstrings had made her more and more determined to make this Christmas as special as possible for those who might not otherwise have a good one, and eventually, she'd rolled into bed, her tasks completed.

The cold fresh air that blew over the fields and flowers of the park blasted away the cobwebs, and among the gloom of her present situation and the cold, wintry season, she felt a glimmer of hope. Seeing Evan last night had been painful, but it had given her some closure. There were questions she'd never know the answer to, like if Pepper was a better kisser than her or if she were sexier in bed, but they were ones she was probably better off not knowing. Their conversation had at least transported her out of the limbo she'd been stuck in.

Seeing the expectant faces watching her and Santa, she used the loudspeaker Hazel had thrust into her hand to launch their first ever Santa's grotto at Bluebell Park and, of course, the giving tree. She spotted Nina, Johnny lingering by her side. A small fizz of excitement bubbled in the pit of her stomach and without thinking Bella put her hand there, relieved to feel it. It was proof that Evan hadn't, and couldn't, ruin this for her.

'Thank you, everyone, for coming to the launch of Santa's grotto at our wonderful park.' She paused for a round of applause to ripple through. 'Before I let Santa do the honours—'

'Hi, Santa,' a number of children chorused, waving at him. Mr Tomlin waved back.

Bella laughed and it echoed through the loudspeaker, making her cringe. God, did she really sound like that when she laughed? It was like a mouse on helium. She moved the speaker a little further from her mouth. 'I'm sure Santa will be coming to visit you all very soon, children. You've all been good this year, haven't you?' The children nodded and shouted. 'Good. I just wanted to let you know about a new initiative we have this year and it's one that I'm really excited about. It's called a giving tree and it's a way for us all to do something neighbourly and generous this season. To give a little bit of love to our friends.'

She looked behind her and motioned to the beautifully decorated tree. Among the red, laminated tags were strings of outdoor fairy lights and green and red baubles. At the top of the tree sat a bright shining star. It was a beautiful symbol of what the season was about. A beacon of why Christmas was important and as it was next to Santa's grotto, the two complemented each other. Parents who were waiting to take their children in could grab a tag and it helped set the scene perfectly. Bella took a deep breath before continuing with her speech.

'Christmas is for giving, but it's also a time to really open our eyes and see what we can do to help our friends and neighbours. Here at Bluebell Park and at the school you can pick up a form and nominate yourself or a friend to receive a gift this Christmas. There's space to write down something specific or you can keep it a bit more general. Please take one and then hand the forms in to me here, or at the school. I'll be coordinating everything, and all information will be treated in the strictest confidence. Once I receive a form, I'll make a numbered tag and hang it on the tree – there won't be any names on them. All you have to do, is pick a tag and buy that present. When you wrap it and return it, make sure it has the tag on it, so I know who it's for, and I'll give everything out the Saturday before Christmas.'

'So we don't know who we're buying for?' asked one woman.

This time, Bella didn't bother with the loudspeaker feeling a bit silly. 'No. That's the beauty of it. It's just about doing something nice for someone else and helping a neighbour out.'

'But what if I end up buying a present for someone I don't like?'

Bella hadn't anticipated questions being shouted at her during her announcement and stuttered for a response. She'd thought if someone had a question or comment like that, they'd have asked her privately. Then Nick Cowley, of all people, saved her.

'How can there be anyone you don't like, Maggie? You're friends with everyone.'

The woman blushed at the compliment and Bella took the

chance to forge ahead. 'If anyone has any questions, do come and find me but I know we've got a very special guest here waiting to press the magic button and light up his new grotto. And he's got to get back to the North Pole, so we better get on with it. Kids, are you ready?'

All the children cheered and bounced on their toes.

'And all the grown-ups, are you ready?'

Some of the grown-ups cheered or clapped. Mr and Mrs Cole seemed as bored as if they were waiting for a bus, but Bella let her eyes wander to Nick's. Feeling heat rush up her neck, she said, 'Without further ado, Santa, are you ready to cut the ribbon?'

More cheers abounded, echoing in the cold, still afternoon air as Mr Tomlin nodded. She pulled out the scissors she'd brought with her and handed them to him. Mr Tomlin with his real big bushy white beard and fake glasses beamed around and after starting them off counting down from ten, the crowd joined in until they got to zero and the cut ribbon fluttered to the ground. At the same time, Mr Whittaker – who had retreated to the information point and was in charge of the giant generator housing the switch for the lights – flicked it on and every light around the grotto spluttered into life. The community choir started singing and everyone gazed open-mouthed at the festivity surrounding them. Christmas had finally arrived at Meadowbank.

The crowd applauded and milled around the chalets, enjoying the fresh air and beautiful choral music that added to the wonderful festive atmosphere. Bella went to put the loudspeaker away before one of the children found it. She'd learned from experience, after someone had stolen her whistle at school, that these things never end well. She might even treat herself to one of Mrs Bumble's gorgeous, homemade mulled wines to help ward off the chill. The spicy red wine aroma was too tempting to resist, even if it was only four o'clock in the afternoon.

Evan hated her drinking in the day, she realised with a pang. She'd never understood it. It wasn't like she boozed all the time, but sometimes, like now, or in the summer when it was a gorgeous hot day and you'd finished all the housework, there was nothing better than a cold glass of wine in the afternoon sun. It wasn't like she was constantly drinking tequila for breakfast or anything like that. At least he wasn't here to tell her not to, or tut and huff until she gave in and abstained. He always had been a bit of a killjoy.

'Well, that went very well, darling. Well done,' said her mum as she came and joined them. 'And don't worry about Mrs Tyldesley. She's always been that type of woman.'

'What type of woman?' asked Luke, Caro's husband.

'A pernickety one.'

'It's a valid question,' Bella conceded.

'But she didn't have to go shouting it out in front of everyone. She should have shown a little more decorum.'

Caro giggled. 'This coming from the woman who last Christmas wrestled the karaoke mic off Dad and proceeded to sing the whole of 'Show Me Heaven' complete with Eighties air grabs?'

Cynthia pulled the collar of her coat up. 'Dean said I was very good.'

'It was nice of Nick to save you.'

'It was, wasn't it?' Bella replied. 'He deflected her really well.' She didn't quite know why he'd done it, but she appreciated the gesture and the smile he shot her afterwards.

Standing by the stall, chatting with her family, Bella didn't know anyone else was there until a small hand touched her arm. Spinning around she saw it was Freddie. 'Hello, Freddie, are you having a nice time?'

'Yeah. The lights look really pretty and the grotto's awesome. I asked if I could come over and see you.'

'Right, is everything okay?' She led him a little further away so they could talk in peace. Guilt bit at her as she thought about her earlier conversation with Nick.

The little boy glanced over his shoulder, his dark hair the same as his dad's falling into his eyes. 'Can I give you this, Miss

Moore?' He pulled a folded piece of paper from his pocket and held it out to her.

'Of course. What is it?'

'It's one of those forms for the tree thing.' He pointed over his shoulder at the giving tree.

'Oh, right, thank you.' Bella opened it out and began reading, forcing back the familiar sting that signalled tears.

The form had been filled out in Freddie's scrawling hand. His writing was actually very good for a Year 5 boy. Bella often found that boys were the ones who struggled, but he'd done well and seeing some of the words spelt phonetically made her heart throb.

'My dad doesn't get any Christmas presents except sometimes one from Trish or something from Nanny and Grandpa that he doesn't like, but I don't think that's fair. I can't buy them for him. I don't get enough pocket money, but I want him to have a present this Christmas. He's always looking after me and I want him to be looked after too. Dad said the tree is for people who really need stuff and I know Dad doesn't, but I want him to be happy. It's . . .' The boy faltered, then carried on with a maturity that surprised her. 'It's going to be hard for him without Mum.'

'Oh, Freddie, that's so lovely of you. I'm sure someone will be happy to get something nice for your dad. What do you think he'd like?'

'I know I can't ask for a PlayStation game – that'd be too cheeky. And Dad always says we should be grateful for all the games we have, even though some of them are old. I think he'd like a new jumper. The one he always wears has holes in the elbows.' Bella resisted the urge to hug the little boy knowing that if no one else took the tag, she would. 'You won't tell Dad, will you? I want it to be a surprise.'

'I promise I won't. I'll make his tag tonight and make sure someone takes it.'

Freddie's eyes brightened. 'If anyone wants a set of colouring pencils, they can have mine. I got a new set for the start of the school year, but I still have my old ones. We could share them.'

The generosity of children had always shocked Bella. It didn't matter how much or how little they had, they were often the ones happiest to share. How did people forget that as adults? Bella pressed a hand to her lip, affection welling inside. 'I promise if anyone does, I'll let you know. That's very, very kind of you, Freddie. I'm sure your dad would be proud to know he's raised such a kind, caring little boy. But don't worry, I won't say anything about this. It's our secret.' She refolded the paper and put it in her pocket. 'Now, why don't you go and play and enjoy the rest of your Saturday? Do you think your dad might treat you to a hot chocolate to warm up?'

'What's that?' asked Nick coming towards them. Bella stood.

'I was just asking if Freddie was going to get a hot chocolate to warm up. I might have one too.'

'That's a good idea. I'll get them. Whipped cream, Freddie?'

Freddie's eyes lit up at the prospect. 'Yes, please. And marshmallows?'

'And marshmallows. What about you, Bella? Whipped cream and marshmallows?'

'Oh, thanks.' She hadn't realised the invitation extended to her. 'Is there any other way to have a hot chocolate?'

Nick laughed. 'What about a Flake?'

'Of course,' they replied together, and Nick went off to get the hot chocolates from Annie's Tearoom. Freddie and Bella followed along behind. When Nick returned, juggling three large takeaway cups, two of them overflowing with whipped cream and marshmallows, she couldn't resist removing her gloves to pick the marshmallows off the top and scoop the whipped cream with her fingers. Freddie did the same.

'You two are gross,' Nick said, grinning as he sipped his plain and boring drink.

'It's the only way to drink a hot chocolate, isn't it, Freddie?'

127

Freddie nodded and after a few moments he went off to play again, leaving Nick to hold his drink while it cooled.

Nick's bright eyes watched her. She hadn't realised before just how attractive they were. Actually, that was a bit of a fib. She and the other women in the village all knew how attractive Nick Cowley was but she'd never actively thought about it.

'Bella?'

'Yeah?'

He paused. 'Are you sure you're okay? It's just that earlier I thought you were going to say more but . . .'

'Yeah, I—' She hadn't intended on saying anything more as her verbal diarrhoea seemed to get the better of her whenever she was around him. But under his kind gaze she felt she could speak. 'I didn't want to bore you. I feel like I'm always banging on about my broken heart.'

'You won't bore me.'

Sometimes, Nick could look rather stern and forbidding but the small crinkles that formed at the edge of his eyes as he smiled brought character to his face. As he was five years older than her their paths had only ever crossed as neighbours. They hadn't hung out together or really known each other at school. He blew his hot chocolate to cool it.

Bella glanced around her, forming the mass of emotions into something tangible she could explain. 'I think I'm doing okay, but I saw Evan last night at school.' Nick's eyebrows raised a fraction. 'It was tough, but I got some answers. It's been a couple of weeks now and I've got more used to going home to an empty house. Having all this to focus on has kept me busy most evenings so I don't have time to mope. Is it a good idea to just keep busy, hoping the heartbreak will ease off?'

Nick shrugged. 'It worked for me, though I don't know if it's necessarily a good idea. They say you have to deal with your emotions rather than repress them, but sometimes you have to push them down so they're not so overwhelming you can't actually cope.' He suddenly looked up as if he'd been speaking to himself. 'Sorry. That was all a bit maudlin, wasn't it?'

'Not at all. I know exactly what you mean, and I asked the question so . . .' Bella searched for something more to say, finally settling on: 'What do you think of the giving tree then?'

'I think it's a great idea. Which is funny really given I used to think asking for help was a sign of weakness.'

'Did you? If there's ever anything I can do . . .' Bella gripped her drink tighter. His comment had surprised her, and she hated to think of Nick or Freddie struggling with anything. She resolved to keep more of an eye on Amias so she could take one worry off his list.

He smiled, watching the steam from his drink rise into the air and disappear. 'It took a while after Paige left for me to ask for help with Freddie. But thanks. And if you ever need a curry, just ask.'

'A curry?' She laughed. Nick explained how he'd been batch cooking that morning, eager for them to have a better diet. 'It still sounds delicious.'

'I'll drop one round.'

Bella smiled as Mrs Barnes, who had spoken to her about Leonie's costume, interrupted. Nick gave a small smile and went off to find Freddie on the climbing frame. She was sorry to see him go. She'd been enjoying his conversation. The fact that he knew exactly what she was going through had been a surprising bond between them and he'd shown a level of empathy she hadn't credited most men with. Perhaps that was just because Evan could sometimes be a little insensitive. She'd always excused it with tiredness or speaking without thinking but now she wondered if that had been one of the signs she'd been missing.

'Miss Moore, do you have a second?'

'Of course,' she replied. Bella had sent the tiger costume she'd found in the dressing-up box at school home with Leonie to try. Thankfully, it had fitted perfectly. She wondered if there was another problem though as Mrs Barnes wrung her hands together, finding the courage to speak. 'I wanted to ask about these forms. Are you the only one who knows who things are for?'

'That's right. I coordinate everything and the tags all have numbers on, so I know who they're intended for. The information on them is general, not specific. It might say girl's teddy age 3–5 or boy's trainers size 3. I thought that would be the easiest thing to do.'

'I – I was thinking about filling one in. I know you sent one home in the book bags and that you've already helped us out with a costume, but my husband, he doesn't like asking for charity and neither do I, to be honest. It makes me feel ashamed. Like a failure.' Mrs Barnes pulled a tissue from her coat pocket and wiped her nose.

'Oh, Mrs Barnes, please don't feel like that. I never started the giving tree to make people feel bad. This is so that Meadowbank can do what it's always done, which is help out our neighbours. Do you remember when Amelia came back from Paris and got the flu? Everyone took her food baskets and things to help her out. I just wanted to do something a little different at a special time of year. Charity isn't a dirty word and I like to think of it more as help. The same way we'd drop a library book back for a neighbour or buy flowers when we know someone's been poorly.' Mrs Barnes relaxed a little more.

'Okay, I'll talk to Kurt. Thanks, Miss Moore.'

Mrs Barnes left and as she sipped the hot chocolate Nick had bought for her, she hoped he would remember to drop round that curry he mentioned. The thought filled her with warmth as she gazed back at the beautiful giving tree with its magical, glimmering fairy lights, and her fingers caressed the piece of paper in her pocket. She was really proud of Freddie. Probably more than she should have been as just his neighbour, but she couldn't help it. There was something special about him and maybe something special about Nick too. Though she wasn't sure why that thought had crossed her mind so soon after her break-up with Evan.

Chapter 13

Bella left the school, closing the gate that sat in the low flint wall behind her, and hurried across the green. In the evening darkness, the wind tried to steal the forms she'd been given for the giving tree from her hands, and she pushed them into the enormous carrier bag she dragged along.

Only two days after the launch of the giving tree and Meadowbank was already in action, showing its support. The launch of the giving tree and Santa's grotto at Bluebell Park had been just as exciting and well received by the village as Bella had hoped. Every time someone spoke to her about it, she glowed at the praise and loved the positivity with which the village was getting on board with the idea. She was even starting to feel some of her old excitement for Christmas returning.

A number of gifts had been handed in to the school reception and passed on to Bella. She'd nipped out and taken some home at lunchtime, but there were still more to carry, and more forms too. The sheer number of both frightened and pleased her. Thankfully, she'd have help to write and laminate the tags tonight when Nina, Caro and her mum came round again. She just wanted to nip into the village shop for a bottle of wine and some supplies for them all first.

'Hi, Meredith,' Bella said as she entered. 'Do you mind if I pop this bag down while I grab some bits? It's a bit difficult to manoeuvre.'

The shop channelled an old-fashioned vibe and in between the banks of shelves were wicker baskets full of local produce. In the spring and summer months they normally lined the street outside, but now they were indoors full of Christmas essentials like decadent puddings.

'Course not,' Meredith said happily. 'I've got some bits for you too.'

'You do? That's great. Thank you.'

Meredith began to load boxes onto the counter. 'One of them is from me and the others are from Mr Crocket and Mrs Singleton. When I said I was dropping my bits for the giving tree round tonight they asked if I could take theirs too and you popping in will save me a trip.'

'Will they fit in the bag?'

'I think so.'

Bella went to the wine bottles at the back and grabbed a couple, then stopped at the crackers. She was thinking of cheese and wine for nibbles tonight. Her mum would bring mince pies so she didn't need to bother with those. Cynthia was slightly addicted to them and bought them as soon as they appeared in the shop. Bella quite fancied something a little different. Before long she stopped at the till.

'Anything else?' asked Meredith.

'No, thanks. Just these bits.'

'How are you coping, my lovely?'

She was getting used to the question now and Bella summoned some cheerfulness. 'Pretty good actually. The tree's keeping me busy as you can see. How's little Georgie?'

Meredith had recently given birth and Georgie was now about four weeks old but there was no keeping Meredith from the shop she loved so much. It had been her parents' before her, and she was determined to keep it going. Luckily, it didn't seem to be struggling as everyone in the village used it.

'She's a terrible sleeper but we're starting to get her into a routine so I'm sure she'll settle down soon. All the others did.'

The bell over the door tinkled again as Mrs Baxter, an elderly neighbour, walked inside. She had an old-fashioned scarf wrapped over her head and tied under her chin. 'I thought I saw you come in here, Bella. I took one of your tags on Saturday and I've got my present here all wrapped up and ready to go. I stuck the tag on. Was that the right thing to do?'

Bella quickly scanned the beautifully wrapped parcel. The tag from the giving tree had been stuck on top so she knew exactly who it was for. 'It was, Mrs Baxter. Thank you.'

'Oh, it was my pleasure, Bella dear. I'm very lucky with my pension, that it's enough, especially with my mortgage all paid off years ago. It's the least I can do.'

'Well, I can't tell you how much I appreciate your support and I know whoever receives this will too.'

'What can I get for you, Mrs Baxter?' asked Meredith.

'Nothing, dear, I just popped in to give this to Bella. Toodle-oo.'

Mrs Baxter disappeared, and Bella eyed the paper bag of wine and the larger carrier bag of gifts. Meredith followed her gaze.

'Are you going to manage all of this?'

'I think so,' Bella replied, paying. She tucked Mrs Baxter's present under her arm, then picked up the carrier bag and Meredith handed her the other, the wine bottles clanking as she steadied herself. She had no idea how she was going to find her keys, but she should at least make it the short distance up the lane to her front door.

'Here, let me get the door for you.' Meredith darted out from behind the counter and opened the door, wishing her a good night as she left.

Bella made it home just as Caro and her mum arrived. They immediately began taking things off her.

'More donations?' asked Cynthia. 'That's quite a few already.'

'I know. I never expected so much so soon.' Bella rifled in her pocket for the keys and let Caro through first.

Cynthia lugged the huge bag of gifts over the threshold and Bella switched on the lights. After shrugging off her coat she lit a fire and before long the house was warm and cosy.

'I brought wine, and cheese and crackers for nibbles.'

'Yummy,' said Caro. 'I've been craving really strong cheddar lately. Have you got any of the local stuff from the deli?'

'I do.' Bella went to the fridge and began collecting everything together, placing it on a board and taking it into the living room. She went back to open the wine as the doorbell chimed. 'That'll be Nina. Can you let her in, Mum, please?'

Cynthia did and the four of them settled in the living room. After catching up on the day's gossip, they got down to work. Cynthia and Caro wrapped more presents for Santa's grotto, while Nina fired up the laminator and cut out Christmas tree shapes from sheets of red card for the giving tree tags. Bella went through the forms she'd been given so far, completing the spreadsheet she was using to keep track of everything and then filing them in an A4 folder once the tag was completed. As she read another one, she gasped.

'What is it, love?' asked Cynthia, pausing a story about Mungo's new obsession with leaf blowers.

'It's just this form is for nappies and baby milk, and it sounds quite desperate. They're not Christmas presents, are they? They're necessities.' Bella shook her head. 'I know I can't cry over every one, but goodness me. That's a tough one to read.'

'I bet I can guess who that's for and she is rather desperate,' Cynthia said, patting her knee. 'But just think of all the difference you'll make.'

Bella sniffed as she began writing the tag. Once done, she handed it to Nina who laminated it and made a hole in the top for the ribbon to go through.

'I followed your advice, Cynthia,' Nina said. A hint of a blush formed on her cheeks.

'Mum's advice can be a very dangerous thing,' Caro teased. 'I'm not sure you want to go down that road.'

'My advice is always excellent, thank you very much.' Cynthia turned to Nina. 'So which bit of my outstanding guidance did you follow?'

'After the launch of the giving tree, when my stint finished, I subtly suggested to Johnny that the pub was open and I was hungry, and so—'

'You had a date?' Bella cheered, clapping her hands together. This was just the news she needed to cheer her up.

Nina blushed furiously. 'We just went for a quiet drink—'

'Umm hmm.'

'But I don't know if it was a date. I'm not sure Johnny thought it was one.'

Bella laughed. 'What else could he think it was?'

'Did he kiss you?' Caro asked and Nina toyed with her ringlets.

'No. But we sat very close together and a couple of times our fingers touched, and he didn't pull away.'

'How romantic,' Cynthia said dreamily.

'You don't mind that we didn't invite you, do you, Bella? It's just that I wanted to see what would happen if we were alone and you were busy at the park so . . .'

'I don't mind at all. It would have been weird if you'd invited me given what you wanted to find out. As long as it wasn't because I've been so miserable you didn't want me around.'

'You haven't been miserable,' Nina said. 'It's been nice to see you get back to your old self. I mean, you've not been one hundred per cent bright and breezy but more than I'd expect.'

Though the news was reassuring Bella asked, 'Do you think that's a bad thing? Do I seem heartless?'

Caro answered before Nina could. 'God no! You don't seem heartless. I think you're doing the right thing, filling your life with new things and not wallowing over that scumbag. I'm proud of you.'

'Me too,' their mum added. 'I think if I saw Evan now I'd find some exciting new use for your dad's leaf blower.' She loaded a cracker with cheese and popped it in her mouth.

Bella didn't focus on what that new and exciting use might be.

'Don't eat all the cheddar,' Caro scolded. 'I'm not allowed Brie or Stilton so you can at least save me that and the posh chutney.'

Cynthia cut a wedge of cheddar and popped it on a cracker before handing it to her daughter. Caro gave their mum a soppy smile.

'How was Freddie today?' Bella asked Nina quietly so the others wouldn't hear.

She paused from tying the ribbon on the tag they'd just made. 'I'm a bit worried about him actually. He's becoming more and more withdrawn in class and he's not playing as much at breaktimes.'

'I've been keeping an eye on Amias after everything Nick told me. He left him alone today, so I'm hoping that's the end of it.'

'What are you two talking about?' Cynthia asked.

'Just school stuff,' Bella replied.

'Oh, I meant to tell you, Mrs Cole was having a right old ding-dong with Elsie at the library the other day.'

'Elsie? She's the loveliest person in the village,' Caro said. 'What was she supposed to have done?'

'Mrs Cole was accusing her of deliberately miscalculating her library fine.'

'Elsie wouldn't do that. Isn't it all done electronically now anyway?'

Bella nodded. 'What happened in the end?'

'Elsie let her off the fine. She'd had that book for four months but couldn't be bothered to bring it back. Poor Elsie was as red as a beetroot – you know how she gets. I nearly went over and gave Mrs Cole a slap for being so rude to her. She's a good girl, Elsie. Never does any harm to anyone and doesn't deserve that grief.'

As much as Bella wasn't happy with Amias's behaviour recently, she didn't entirely blame him for it. Something had certainly triggered it and she needed to find out what. Perhaps she'd ask Mrs White for some advice about speaking to his parents.

After helping herself to cheese and crackers, Bella looked at the next form. It was the one for Nick that Freddie had handed to her. She'd enjoyed her conversation with Nick at the launch.

He'd revealed more of himself in that short time than in all the years they'd been neighbours. As she typed up the details and wrote the tag, something strange happened to her heart. It seemed to grow in her chest, filling up all the space in her ribcage. She exhaled slowly, thinking it would ease the pressure, but it didn't. It wasn't an unpleasant feeling by any means. In fact, it made her feel quite happy.

Cynthia began to probe Nina for more details of her date with Johnny and Bella listened intently, glad that romance was blossoming for her friend. She took the next form and worked through her process. With so much to get through she couldn't let her thoughts linger on anything, or anyone, else.

Chapter 14

'I'm not sure I can take any more of this,' Johnny said, rubbing his hands over his eyes.

The next day, they were in the school hall rehearsing the Christmas play. They weren't quite at the dress rehearsal stage, but they were getting scarily close, and Mrs Brody had stepped up her mania. The large Christmas tree had now been placed at the back of the hall and was covered in decorations the children had been making during the various wet plays they'd had.

Excitement in the village was almost as high as in school as everyone prepared for the Christmas parade and as it was the end of November, the time was growing ever closer when decorations would be strung up indoors and outside, and the whole of Meadowbank would be transformed into a winter wonderland.

A light drizzle tapped at the windows of the school hall. With wet play this morning and rehearsals for the first part of the afternoon there'd been a lot of sitting around. From her seat at the back, she could see the children getting twitchy and conversations breaking out due to boredom. It was even worse on the stage. The chorus line had shuffled about so much one child had fallen offstage and one of the girls had started an argument with another who was stood in front of her, booting her off the bench she was sitting on. Mrs Brody had not taken kindly to it.

'No, No, No!' she shouted with mounting fury, then as if by magic her placid demeanour returned. 'Come on, children, this is supposed to be fun. You're doing brilliantly with your lines, everyone. Now, Virginia, can you try really hard to remember yours – it's only two words and you say it right after Tom.' Virginia thought hard, but nothing dawned. 'Only two words, sweetie. Any luck? No? It's "Let's go!" Ready, say it with me: let's go.' Virginia mumbled something along those lines and Mrs Brody hid her disappointment well before moving on. 'Let's try the song one more time, okay? And then it'll be breaktime.'

As they broke into their rendition of 'Poker Face' with revised lyrics, Johnny groaned. 'I really can't take this. My lot have been a nightmare today. They made a record with the Mr Fuckers today. Twenty-four attempts. I'm going to go and set out the hoops and bits in the playground. I'll be back in a minute to get my class.'

The song finished and Mrs Brody led the children off the stage and back into their seated lines on the floor. Johnny crashed back through the doors just in time to lead his class away. Nina and Bella went to the ends of their lines and one by one, they asked the children to stand and led them in a decent interpretation of orderliness back to the classrooms.

'Thank God that drizzle has stopped,' said Nina as they took their places on the playground. 'I'm not sure I could have coped with them all indoors again. What's the matter with you today?'

'Nothing,' Johnny grumbled. 'I think I'm getting a cold.'

'Poor lamb.'

Bella giggled. 'Right, it's your turn to patrol the playground, Johnny. Off you go. It'll take your mind off things.'

Johnny sloped off and Nina and Bella shuffled about in silence for a moment, until Freddie came running towards her, his dirty, wet blazer hanging off one shoulder, his tie loose, shirt and jumper skewed and fat tears falling down his face. He was crying so hard his breath came in short, sharp gulps.

Bella's heart rocketed upwards and ricocheted back down. She leapt towards him. 'Freddie, what's happened?'

He was nigh on hyperventilating and Bella had to wait for him to answer. She wrapped her arm around him, aware he was missing his coat. After a moment, Freddie's breathing quietened a little, but the tears were coming fast. As much as she wanted to give him a hug, she knew she shouldn't. It was then she noticed the torn knee of his trousers, wet from the ground and the slightly bloody graze poking through. He must have had a nasty fall, but she hadn't seen it happen. He'd been playing behind the climbing frame the last time she'd spotted him and visibility through the apparatus could be quite difficult with all the children blocking the view.

'What happened, Freddie? Did you fall over?'

Freddie's tears intensified, and he pressed his hand into his eyes, forcing the water out. He was far too little to be that upset and after a few gulps of air, he spoke in stuttered short sentences. 'Amias and Richard – they ran after me and – pulled off my coat then pushed me over – started punching and kicking me in the back.'

Bella went cold as a wave of horror ran over her. How had they all missed it? She glanced at Nina whose wide eyes conveyed as much shock as she was feeling. 'Oh, Freddie, where did this happen? Behind the climbing frame?'

'Behind the toilets.'

That was another blind spot on the playground. One she'd already told Amias to stay away from after he'd blocked all the loos by ramming whole toilet rolls down them. She'd patrolled them only moments before and he hadn't been there. Had he waited for her to go? 'Then what happened?'

'I – I tried to run away but then he grabbed my blazer and punched me in the stomach.' A fury she'd never felt before and had only imagined she'd feel with her own child rose from her stomach. Her chest tightened and she made a concerted effort to control her breathing. Freddie sniffed and wiped his face with the tissue she offered. 'I dodged them and came and found you.'

'Were they both hitting you?' Nina asked, her face white with shock.

Freddie shook his head. 'Just Amias, but Richard pulled off my coat and chased me.'

'I'm so sorry this has happened, Freddie,' Bella said, her voice slightly wobbly. 'It's completely unacceptable.' Frightened by the emotions nearly getting the better of her, she took a breath.

'Why don't you take Freddie inside,' Nina said. 'And I'll go and find his coat.'

Bella agreed and led him into the warmth of the classroom then pulled up a chair for him to sit opposite her. After settling him, she fetched his water bottle from Nina's classroom along with some tissues.

'Where are you hurt, Freddie?'

He pointed to a number of places on his back and legs, and using a wet paper towel she wiped the grit and dirty water from his palms and knee. He'd begun crying again, which wasn't surprising given the ordeal he'd been through. 'And he kept saying things about my mum. He said she didn't love me and that's why she ran off.'

Even when Evan had left, she'd never felt such pain. 'Freddie,' she said calmly, 'I'm going to ask Miss Radcliffe to come and sit with you while I fetch Amias and Richard and take them to Mrs White's office. I'll be right back, okay? Try and drink some water.'

Freddie took his water bottle, and she watched his small hands tremble as he grasped it.

Stomping into the playground, she sent a horrified Nina, who had now found Freddie's coat, in to sit with him. Bella's eyes scanned the playground and fell on Amias. Remaining calm she strode over. As she approached, Richard nudged him and when Amias looked at her, it was clear he knew a whole world of trouble was about to come his way.

'Amias, did you at—' She stopped herself from saying the word *attack*. Although she completely believed Freddie, it was important to hear both sides of the story and labelling the incident as an attack wasn't professional. She began again. 'Amias, did something happen with Freddie?'

'No.'

'Well, Freddie is in the classroom and he's very upset. I'd like you to come inside and talk to me about it.'

'But I haven't done anything.'

'He did, miss,' shouted Hannah, climbing down and running over. One of her bunches had fallen halfway down her head and she tossed it back. 'He and Richard pushed Freddie over and started punching and kicking him.'

'Thank you, Hannah. I appreciate you telling me what you saw. I'll chat to you later so you can tell me everything, okay?' Hannah beamed at the praise from her teacher. 'Anything to say, Amias?' He shrugged. 'Richard?' Richard had the good grace to look at the ground, ashamed. Now he was faced with the consequences of his actions she could tell he was doing his best not to cry. His parents would not be pleased when they heard what he'd done. It was out of character for him too, but Freddie said the extent of his involvement had been in chasing him and pulling off his coat – that was something at least. 'Both of you come with me.'

Bella led them into the classroom and noticed the way Amias sneered at Freddie who was sat with Nina, a pile of tissues in front of him. He still hadn't stopped crying and Nina was doing her best to comfort him. Ever observant, Bella clocked Richard's expression of abject horror when he saw what he'd done. His eyes widened and all the colour drained from his face. But the thing that upset Bella most was the fear radiating off Freddie when he saw Amias. Her blood ran cold. She would not have any child feeling like that in her school.

Within seconds she marched them down the corridor to Mrs White's office.

'Come in,' Mrs White said in her normal cheerful tones after Bella had knocked.

Bella opened the door and ushered both boys inside. Mrs White quietly put down her pen and clasped her hands in front of her on the desk, looking over the edge of her spectacles. 'Is something wrong, Miss Moore?'

'I'm afraid so, Mrs White.'

Bella outlined what had happened, confirming that at least

one witness had backed up Freddie's story and she would continue to investigate though she suspected more children would come forward corroborating Freddie's side of events. She also mentioned the other incidents that had happened recently. Guilt wrapped its ugly hand around her lungs, squeezing the air out. Had she failed Freddie by not picking up on the pattern? There was no denying this was bullying. Amias's comments about Freddie's mum were just horrible. Kids could be cruel, though it was normally unintentional as they learned new social skills, but there was something different about this and it was clear from the comments she'd already had from Mr and Mrs Cole, Amias was parroting things he heard at home.

Mrs White signalled to the two chairs in front of her desk but stood up herself. 'Thank you, Miss Moore. If you'd like to go back and check on Freddie and continue speaking to the other children, I'll speak to Amias and Richard.'

Bella did as she was told, noticing the fear on Richard's face while Amias was petulant. She closed the door behind her and went back to Freddie. He was still upset but slowly calming down and his breathing had returned to normal. About ten minutes later, Mrs White appeared with Richard, who was instructed to sit down. He did, away from Freddie and unable to make eye contact with him. Bella and Nina went to Mrs White.

'Miss Moore, will you speak to Richard's parents at pick-up time, please? And Miss Radcliffe, as Freddie's teacher, sees if he's happy to continue in school. If he's very upset, he can come and work with me in my office, but he may prefer to be with his friends. If he wants to go home, that's fine too. He's had quite a shock, but as it's already half past two, there may not be time for his dad to get here.'

'I'll speak to Freddie and ring Mr Cowley straight away if he wants to go home.'

'Thank you.'

'Is Amias staying in your office?' Bella asked.

'No. I'm afraid I've asked his parents to collect him immediately. I think it would be prudent for him to be excluded from school for one day so we can deal with things.'

'Right.' Bella shot a glance at Nina. She'd never known a child to be excluded for the day and it went to show the seriousness of Amias's actions. Bella had worried she was overreacting, but this proved she wasn't.

Nick would be absolutely devastated to know this had happened to the son he so clearly adored, and as hard as it would be, she wished she rather than Nina could be the one to call him, though her heart stung at the thought of bringing him even more pain.

Chapter 15

Nick only realised he had a voicemail when he stepped out of his truck and checked the time on his phone. The signal between Witchbury and Meadowbank could be a little patchy when you hit one of the valleys, but most of the time it didn't matter. He always called clients back if they left a message and he wasn't a fan of hands-free.

It wasn't until he saw the name *Meadowbank Primary* that his stomach lurched unpleasantly. He'd been worrying every day there'd be another incident, but hopefully Freddie had simply forgotten something: his PE kit or some baking ingredients.

As he listened to Miss Radcliffe's voicemail his hand began to tremble. Heat carried up the back of his neck, instantly warming it from the cold wind hitting it now he was out of the van. There'd been an incident at school involving Freddie and another child. He didn't need her to say who the other child was; he already knew. It could only have been Amias. Amias the spoiled kid who didn't have any boundaries and had clearly decided for whatever reason that he didn't like Freddie. She was asking if he could come and get Freddie now. He'd been very upset by the incident and wanted to go home. The message was left at two forty-five but as he'd suspected he'd have been in one of the dells then. Guilt hit him so forcefully he took a step backwards, leaning against the van.

They'd been doing so well. He was getting his life more organised now, washing clothes every night so there weren't as many dirty ones hanging around the house. He was even loading the dishwasher before bed and emptying it in the mornings. He still had to get on top of dusting and hoovering, but at least he was

145

headed in the right direction. He wouldn't be completely embarrassed to have someone round his house now.

Within seconds any feeling of progress in his fatherly self-esteem had gone, and he felt a failure again. More so than ever before. Freddie had needed him, and he hadn't been there. His poor boy. His sweet, gorgeous boy had been beaten up. In primary school. Nick could barely believe it and he raised his eyes to the dusky blue sky. He couldn't remember anything as bad as this happening when he was younger.

Miss Radcliffe had kept the message brief, her voice strained, not giving any real details, only that it happened at afternoon break. Nick's mind pictured Freddie with a black eye or a bloody nose, his uniform torn and hanging off him like some desperate street urchin. He was being melodramatic. He had to calm down. Until he knew what exactly had happened, getting worked up wasn't going to help anyone. It certainly wasn't going to help Freddie.

It was already ten past three; the children would be coming out of school any minute. Nick shoved his keys back in his pocket and marched straight there. The feelings flooding into his system were stronger than anything he'd ever felt before. Of course he'd been angry at times through his life. Who hadn't? But this . . . this was something else. It was a guttural rage. Fierce and defensive. Some primal instinct to protect his boy that rushed the adrenalin through his veins.

As he raced to the school, Nick realised he was running, rather than walking. The small front gates had only just opened and though the receptionist said hello, Nick couldn't spare the time to speak. He made his way around to the back playground and paced outside the large glass doors to the classroom. He couldn't stand still as his muscles twitched for him to keep moving. The other parents sensed something and asked tentatively if he was okay, but Nick could only mutter vague, non-committal replies. Thank God he'd left a little earlier today. After having worked like a pack horse all afternoon, making the most of a break in the rain, he'd hoped to get Freddie back before it started again. He'd imagined a cosy night in, hail battering the windows while they snuggled by the fire playing games and laughing. He'd been feeling so much more positive, but that was all fading now.

He paced past Bella's classroom and when she saw him, he could tell she was upset too. Her eyes were awash with concern and her cheeks pale. If only he could say he didn't blame her. He knew instinctively it wouldn't be her fault, but he couldn't deny the anger inside. His son had been hurt badly at a place he was supposed to be safe. Still, he didn't blame Bella, he blamed Amias and, more accurately, Amias's parents. Nick's fists tightened again, and he edged away from the other parents as if the anger coming off him might burn them.

Moving back to Miss Radcliffe's class, he saw Freddie sat at the back in his usual seat and his throat thickened. Freddie's eyes were puffy and red from crying, his nose pink, and he was wearing his PE kit, which meant something had happened to his uniform. A glimmer of hope sprang into Freddie's eyes when he spotted Nick there. It could have been happiness at being able to go home on time and forget about this awful day, but it seemed to be more than that: a plea for protection. His son needed him to make this right. To take the pain away and as soon as he was near enough, he'd wrap him in the biggest hug he could. His strong arms would shield his wonderful boy from the world and act as a barricade. He was never letting go.

Miss Radcliffe lined the children up as usual, but Freddie stayed seated. As she led the rest of the class to the door and began sending them out to their parents, chatting to one or two, Mrs White marched into the classroom. That was when Nick knew for sure that whatever had happened was incredibly serious and he wasn't just overreacting. He checked Bella's line for Amias and noted he wasn't there. What did that mean?

Nick glanced at Bella and saw her deep in conversation with Richard's mum. The boy appeared utterly terrified when he saw

147

Nick and his mum's face reddened as Bella, with an unusually stern expression, explained something to her. Richard's mum, taking his hand firmly, marched him away, her eyes on the ground.

Eventually, all the children went home so it was only Nick left, and moving through the door that joined the classrooms, Bella went and stood with Mrs White.

Miss Radcliffe stepped forwards. 'Mr Cowley, I'm so sorry. Please come in and we'll explain everything.'

He pulled the thick woollen hat off his head and scrunched it in his fingers. As soon as he stepped through the door, Freddie launched out of his seat and into his arms, sobbing quietly. 'Hey, mate,' Nick said, rubbing the back of his head, feeling his soft silky hair in his fingers. 'It's okay. I've got you. And we'll get this sorted out, okay? I've got you, little man.'

Freddie lifted his head to stare at his dad, tears running down his cheeks. Nick cupped his face and began to wipe them away with his thumbs, using every ounce of self-control he had to bite back the alarm rising inside him. He studied Freddie's face for cuts and bruises, but he was unharmed.

'Amias pushed me over and kept punching and kicking me.' He buried his head against Nick's stomach and Nick folded himself over, squeezing him tight. 'And he said things about Mum.'

Nick's heart rate sped up. 'Oh, mate. Don't worry about what he said. He doesn't know anything.' He studied Bella, then Miss Radcliffe, then Mrs White. 'What happened?'

Miss Radcliffe went through everything, then Mrs White explained what she and Bella had discovered through their investigation of events. Though she didn't say as much, it was clear to him that Amias had gone for Freddie, pure and simple. He'd waited until Freddie was out of sight of the teachers, chased him and pushed him down onto the cold, wet ground to then punch and kick him. If that wasn't bad enough, when she mentioned the things he'd said about Paige it was like his blood was on fire. It had taken months for Nick to convince Freddie subtly and quietly that his mum had left because she wanted something different but that she loved him all the same. How much damage had Amias done with his cruel, unnecessary words?

Nick's entire body began to shake, and he went to sit down on one of the tiny children's chairs. Freddie sat beside him, closer than he'd ever been before. Nick couldn't say out loud the thoughts running through his head. He wanted to get hold of that boy and question him himself. He didn't believe in smacking children, but he'd love to take away some of his toys and teach him a lesson or two. He wanted to have a word with the parents as well.

'I'm so sorry, Mr Cowley,' said Bella. 'Amias was sent home and won't be allowed in school tomorrow, and Miss Radcliffe has looked after Freddie all afternoon. We got him to pop on his PE kit so he wasn't in wet trousers and I've bagged those up for you. We did ask if he wanted to go and sit in Mrs White's office, but he preferred to stay in class with his friends.'

Miss Radcliffe nodded. 'All the other children have helped look after him too. They've been checking on him and some even fetched his bag and coat and tidied all his things away for him at home time.'

'And of course,' said Mrs White, 'we'll be putting measures in place to make sure this never happens again. If Amias cannot play nicely in the playground with other children, he won't be allowed out and can stay inside with me. I'm going to have a think about other things we need to do, but I thought you might prefer to talk about those at a later date. I'm sure right now you just want to get home with Freddie. Freddie?' Mrs White bent down in front of him, so she was at eye level. 'I'm very proud of you. You did exactly the right thing going straight to a teacher and not hitting back. What Amias has done is very serious and very wrong and I want you to know I won't put up with it.'

Nick stood and tried to smile but he knew it was a pale imitation of one. 'Thanks for looking after him.'

His eyes met Bella's and his throat tightened again at her

sorrowful expression. He had the urge to hug her and tell her it was all right. For a fleeting moment, the thought of holding her sent a shot of happiness through the fog of anger and pain that had wrapped around him since he got the message. Since Paige left, if he was honest.

After a second too long, she tore her eyes away. 'You've done brilliantly today, Freddie. You're a real credit to your dad and this school. Go on home now and have a good night's sleep, and I promise you, I won't let anything else like this happen again. Okay?'

Freddie nodded.

'Come on, mate.' Nick held out his hand and as soon as Freddie slipped his in, he pulled him close and kissed the top of his head. 'Curry or bolognese for dinner?'

'Urgh, Dad! We've eaten that every night. Can't we have pizza?'

Relief washed over him as he heard his son's voice return to normal and he even heard a chuckle from Mrs White and Bella. He wanted to glance over his shoulder and see her smile but didn't dare. He couldn't tell if the feelings inside him were to do with Freddie or not and the thought terrified him. 'Maybe just tonight we can have pizza. I think we've got some in the freezer.'

Nick's feelings tumbled inside as he tried to figure out what to do now. Did he encourage Freddie to talk or just forget it? Right now, he'd do or give anything to see Freddie's normal, wide smile back on his face. Did he encourage him to hit Amias if he tried anything again? That's what Len had suggested but was that right? Mrs White had said how proud she was he hadn't hit back. Surely it would be confusing for Freddie if Nick told him something different. It was all too much to think about. Too painful, too confusing.

Perhaps he should go and see the Coles himself? They'd tell him that somehow Freddie had started it and Amias would be blameless, but he had to end this somehow. He simply had to make it stop.

As Nick drew level with the gate, he couldn't resist glancing behind him to see Bella standing at the doorway watching them go. She busied herself inside as if she hadn't been looking at all and the strange feeling he'd felt earlier returned. This time, he buried it beneath the more forceful, angrier ones. Freddie had to be his priority right now. Now and forever.

Nick closed the front door behind them, grateful for the warmth of the central heating he'd had the rare foresight to set to timer. He'd also put the hot water on and though he was desperate for a hot shower to wash away the traces of anger still lingering in his system, he offered to run Freddie a nice bath while the oven heated up for dinner.

'Do I have to?' Freddie asked in a whiny voice. Nick smiled, grateful for business as usual.

'You need a bath or a shower tonight because you didn't have one last night and I thought that—' He finished hanging his coat and went to his son, bending down so he could look him in the eyes. 'Sometimes you can get a bit of shock after something upsetting happens. You feel all cold and super tired and I thought this might warm you up and help you relax.'

Freddie eyed his dad suspiciously. 'Can I have a really deep one?'

'Sure.'

'With extra bubbles?'

Nick chuckled. 'With extra bubbles.'

After Paige had left, everyone said that Freddie would be fine because children were incredibly resilient, but he hadn't realised his boy would have to put up with so much. Freddie had dealt with his mum leaving brilliantly, but to now have to put up with bullying? It seemed so unfair and yet, here he was grinning and asking for extra bubbles like it was any other day of the week. Perhaps they'd go to Bluebell Park at the weekend. Freddie always seemed at peace there. In fact, Nick had even thought about the two of them volunteering. The giving tree had given him the perfect reason and he wanted to spend time with Freddie away from the house so they could talk and bond. Freddie always spoke more freely when they were there and not sidetracked by technology or toys.

Nick left Freddie getting a drink from the fridge and headed off upstairs to run the bath. When Freddie joined him a few minutes later, Nick kept an eye on him as pulled off his T-shirt checking for bruises. Luckily, none were appearing yet. He was just about to let Freddie jump into the mass of bubbles when the doorbell rang.

'Don't get in the bath yet, mate, okay? Wait till I'm back.'

'But I'm cold.'

'Pop your dressing gown on then.'

'Dad, I'm not a baby.'

'You're my baby,' he answered with a grin. He knew it was silly. Freddie was ten years old and had bathed without supervision before, but today was different.

Nick raced down the stairs somehow hoping it was Bella, then chased the thought from his mind. The fleeting time she'd been in his brain caused a smile to pull at his lips until he opened the front door.

'I want a word with you,' Seymour Cole shouted, pointing his finger at Nick. His bald head was pink with cold and his flabby jowls tremored as he spoke. 'And your son.'

Nick felt irritation rise. Who did this man think he was coming to his house and demanding to speak to his son? His son was the injured party in all of this, whatever the Coles may choose to believe. Nick kept his voice calm. 'You can have a word with me, but you're not getting anywhere near my son.'

'Your son has lied and now my boy has been excluded from school.'

'For one day, Seymour—'

'The likes of you can call me Mr Cole.' He raised himself up to his full diminutive height and his chest and belly poked out.

Nick's heart palpitated. It seemed to beat far too slowly, and then three times as fast. 'I'll call you whatever the hell I like, and you can leave my son alone. Your son's the bully here.' He wanted to add, *I wonder where he gets that from*, but decided not to. There was no point in making a bad situation worse.

The raised voices had drawn some of their neighbours from their houses. Net curtains ruffled in the windows and some even came to their doorways to watch the spectacle. Others left their homes, pulling cardigans close and crossing arms over chests, resting at their gates or by the small picket fences that lined the gardens. Trish and Len opened their front door and stepped outside. He glanced over at them, and Len gave a small nod to show Nick his support.

'Your son attacked my boy in school, Mr Cole.' He emphasised the *Cole*, showing his disdain for the man's attitude. 'He chased after Freddie when he was out of sight of the teachers, pushed him to the ground, then punched and kicked him.'

Trish gasped, as did many of the neighbours, and her hand shot to her mouth. 'Oh my God! Really? Is he okay?'

Nick nodded among the sea of muttering that now surrounded them. If people were going to talk – and who wouldn't after seeing something like this – he was going to make damn sure they had the facts and didn't apportion any blame to his son. 'Freddie's calmed down now but he was in a right state when I picked him up—'

The rest of the crowd were saying things like 'Poor lamb' and this seemed to anger Seymour Cole even more.

'Faking, no doubt,' interrupted Mr Cole adding a scornful laugh for good measure. Anger urged Nick forwards.

He took a step, straightening his spine and meeting Seymour's eye. But Nick wasn't a violent man. He was rarely even an angry one. Forced by the powerful urge to protect his son he thought about shouting and screaming and defending him to the hilt, but Freddie wasn't a liar, and everyone knew that. Nick wasn't going to give this man any more time than he deserved. Freddie still needed his bath and more than that, he needed a cuddle and some reassurance.

'Go home and look after your son, Mr Cole. I'm going back inside to look after mine.'

Glancing back at the house, Nick became aware of Freddie descending the stairs in his dressing gown. He looked so tiny, more like a toddler than a ten-year-old as he stood there worrying his sleeves. Upon seeing Mr Cole his eyes widened in terror and all Nick wanted to do was close the door and comfort his boy. Nick turned and began to walk away. He was done here. 'It's all right, son. Let's—'

'There he is the little liar. I want a word with you, boy—'

Freddie's eyes filled with tears and Nick immediately spun back. The anger that had been simmering in his stomach erupted into rage. The primal instinct he'd felt earlier erupting as he faced Seymour Cole and his ire.

As angry as Nick was with Amias, children made mistakes and he'd been willing to think Amias would learn something from today. Mrs White was clearly not going to stand for his behaviour even if his parents were. He had some sympathy for the young lad, but Seymour Cole had always been a snide, arrogant man and calling his son a liar was a step too far. Replaying the word in his head in the nanosecond it took for it to register, Nick felt his muscles flex and a burning in his throat.

'What did you say?'

'You heard me.' Seymour lifted his head defiantly, jowls rippling.

'You called my boy a liar? All because you don't want to accept that your son has behaved badly and needs some discipline. Oh, I see. It's easier to try and blame my boy than to face up to your own bad parenting, isn't it? But you're the one who—'

'My bad parenting? I'm a great dad and a great husband.' He scoffed. 'Is it any wonder your wife ran off.'

154

A small explosion happened somewhere at the back of Nick's brain. Yes, his wife had run off and it hurt like hell, but he was doing his best for his boy and, he realised now he was doing a pretty good job. His son was kind, funny, clever, hard-working. He'd never think to hurt another child no matter what they did. He hadn't fought back against Amias partly through shock and partly because he'd been taught that we don't hurt others. His son was someone to be proud of and he told Mr Cole as much.

'I don't know why your boy decided to hurt mine, Seymour, but he better keep away from him in future. Do you hear me?'

'Or what? What are you going to do about it? You don't have the balls to do anything. You didn't have the balls to keep a wife and you haven't got the balls to stay and face me.'

Though Mr Cole continued to sling insults and bluff and bluster, knowing Freddie was waiting, Nick began to walk away. Freddie was his one and only priority and seeing him stood on the stairs in tears, wringing the belt of his dressing gown, he had to go to him. Freddie needed that bath, especially after everything he'd just seen and heard, and he needed a cuddle on the sofa, to eat pizza and play video games while his dad made him laugh. Nick turned his back on Mr Cole and took a step towards the door. A hand on his shoulder pulled him backwards and he spun. A balled fist waved in his face. Spit had formed at the corners of Mr Cole's mouth and the thin white line of spittle grew and shrank as he continued to shout at him.

Feeling threatened by the vehemence of the man's anger and his close proximity, a hint of fear combined with that guttural fury surged inside. His breathing grew heavier and without thinking, Nick pushed him backwards hoping to get some distance between them. Mr Cole stumbled and fell onto his backside. A few people guffawed as a thick, ruddy pinkness flew up his neck and onto his cheeks.

'You all saw that,' he bellowed, staring around the assembled crowd. 'You all saw him push me over.' Just at that moment, Mr

Whittaker went past with Mitzie. 'Did you see that, Mr Whittaker? He pushed me over.'

The old man cast a glance over the tubby, angry man on the ground. 'Don't talk nonsense, Mr Cole. Now get up. You're upsetting my Mitzie.'

The little dog yapped as the crowd giggled. Nick couldn't help but feel that many of them were happy to see Seymour Cole taken down a peg or two.

'You should all be ashamed of yourselves,' shouted Jocelyn Carmichael, coming out of her house a few doors down. 'Brawling in the street like Neanderthals. What do you think you're doing? You're grown men.'

She was right, and Nick turned his eyes to his son, embarrassed at what his boy had just seen, even though he'd acted in self-defence.

'He assaulted me,' shouted Mr Cole.

'Rubbish,' Trish screeched back. 'You're a liar, Seymour Cole.'

Len joined in. 'You started it by putting your hands on him.' Trish took hold of his arm, stopping him leaping over the small wall that separated their properties. 'Don't try and pin this one on anyone else.'

Mr Cole continued to remonstrate. 'Unnecessary force, that's what it is! And I'm pretty sure if it weren't for the crowd, you'd have hit me. I'm calling the police.'

'You put your hands on him first,' shouted Trish. 'We're all witnesses. He was walking away.'

Nick had never been more grateful for his support network, and he realised how right Bella was about the giving tree. Everyone deserved the same support he was getting from his friends and neighbours, but as grateful as he was, their words had no effect on Mr Cole.

'You're a thug, Nick Cowley.' He scrambled up to standing and brushed the back of his coat before heading home. Noises carried on the wind as he continued to chunter to himself.

Just as he said these words, Nick's eyes fell on Bella, pausing at the edge of the crowd, her face aghast. She stared between Mr Cole and Nick, knowing full well what the altercation had been about.

Nick's rage subsided as he suddenly realised the thoughts he'd been having about her had edged towards romantic. Disappointment at himself bit deep as his eyes roved to hers and he closed the front door. God only knew what she thought of him now.

Chapter 16

A few days later, Bella took a moment to enjoy the twinkling fairy lights surrounding Santa's grotto. If she put aside her worries over Freddie she was, on the whole, feeling more hopeful about Christmas than she had ever expected. Against a rather stark grey sky the lights glittered and shimmered, brightening even the darkest of moods and her mood had been dark since Tuesday.

Amias hadn't been allowed in school on Wednesday but when he'd come back on Thursday, she'd felt the tension in the air between him and Freddie and seen the fear in Freddie's eyes at playtime. The Coles hadn't liked Amias's punishment or that he was only allowed to play outside for a shorter time than the rest of the children, but the things he'd said and done were too severe to ignore and Mrs White had stood her ground. It was clear that his actions had had a profound effect on Freddie who now played as near to the teachers as was humanly possible while still joining in with his friends. He was frightened, and she was determined that before the school broke up for Christmas, she would have him feeling safe and secure and playing as he normally would, running around, tagging his friends or climbing on the apparatus.

Seeing Mr Cole shouting at Nick with poor little Freddie in the background had confirmed that he was one of the most horrid men in the village, but of course she hadn't let that affect her dealings with Amias. The school was there to teach and hopefully Amias had learned that he couldn't treat people like that. She was planning on catching up with him in a few days to ensure it and to allow him to play as normal with the other children if he'd shown some remorse.

The cold fresh air stung her nose as she took a deep breath. At least it didn't carry the smell of manure, which was a hazard of living in the country. Instead, it was clear and crisp. Bluebell Park had become her own enchanted hideaway from the difficult feelings she'd been experiencing but recent events had pushed all thoughts of Evan and heartbreak from her mind. Although the park was an important part of the village, the way they'd transformed it for Christmas gave the place a special atmosphere.

Today she'd focus on the giving tree and wrapping the donations she'd received that hadn't already been gift-wrapped or tagged. She didn't mind – she absolutely loved wrapping presents and people were busy. She was just grateful they'd taken a tag and made a donation in the first place.

'Morning, Mr Tomlin,' she called as he marched along to the grotto.

The red of his Santa trousers was just visible between his huge duvet-like coat and big black boots. He waved and opened the door to be welcomed by her usual crew of Saturday volunteers. She swiftly followed, eager to escape the freezing, still air they'd been greeted with this morning. The frost that had made the ground twinkle when she left the cottage was fading and with any luck it would warm up a little more before the children arrived to visit Santa.

Inside, the volunteers' hut had been looking like a second Santa's grotto from the pile of donations already made and she had more tags to hang on the tree today too. The village of Meadowbank was being far more generous than even she had hoped for and with any luck any new tags would be gone before long too. Bella waited a moment before removing her coat. 'Gosh that's parky out there today. How are you, Mr Tomlin? We'll have to make sure we get those little heaters on in a minute, so it warms up a bit for you.'

Mr Tomlin coughed before replying. 'Thank you, most appreciated.'

'Are you all right?' asked Hazel, leaning towards him. 'You look a bit pale today.'

'Well, to be honest, I feel a little bit under the weather, but I'm sure I'll survive. I wouldn't want to let all my lovely children down.'

'We'll keep you stocked up with hot chocolates and cakes, don't you worry,' Bella said, but she hoped he wasn't going to come down with anything. Not only was he lovely, but he was also the only Santa they had. Of course they had a fake beard that had come with the costume, but Mr Tomlin resembled the real thing so much he'd be difficult to replace, and they were going to be busy. The Christmas fun was ramping up and everyone was feeling it. The choir were coming back today and would be there most weekends, raising money for a local charity. It added such a wonderful touch to those visiting to hear people singing Christmas carols. It was even better when they joined in too.

'Is everyone ready for another exciting day?' Bella asked.

'Are you on drugs?' asked Mr Whittaker.

'You are *very* cheerful,' added Hazel.

Perhaps she'd been overdoing the enthusiasm.

Matilda dropped her magazine into her lap. 'I expected you to be in the doldrums still. Weren't you and Evan together for five years? You can't get over that in a few weeks.'

'No, you can't,' Bella replied, internally rolling her eyes at the reminder, though she was getting on admirably in her opinion. Every day it felt like a little piece of her fell back into place. She was feeling more positive and able to look on the bright side, taking day-to-day problems in her stride and the situation with Amias and Freddie had taken up so much of her thoughts there wasn't room for anything else. 'And no, Mr Whittaker, I'm not on drugs—'

'Shame,' he replied. 'I was going to ask you to get me some. Dr Gladstone keeps refusing to prescribe me any.'

'That's because you've only got mild arthritis,' Hazel added. 'You don't need them. You just need to turn your heating up and keep a bit warmer. If you weren't such a scrooge about your bills, your joints wouldn't hurt so much. Oh, and take a cod liver oil. I swear by it.'

'I'd rather eat—'

Fearful of what he was going to say, Bella interrupted and moved the conversation on. 'I haven't taken any drugs, I'm just excited and can't wait to get started wrapping all the donations we've been given. Where are they by the way?' she asked, pointing to the corner where they'd been the day before. Yesterday, when she'd dropped off the last few that had been presented to her at school, she brought them here and the pile had covered nearly the whole wall.

'I moved them,' said Mr Whittaker.

'I suppose there were quite a few of them. Where did you put them?'

'In the equipment shed at the back. They nearly fell down the other day and we could barely move in here.'

'Well, I'd better head off then,' she said with a smile. 'I've got lots to collect from the back of the car and we need to get everything open. I can hear some kids arriving already.'

'Have you tried Mrs Bumble's mulled cider yet?' asked Nina, who'd been rather quiet so far this morning.

'Not yet. Is it good?' Nina rubbed her forehead and made a groaning sound. 'Have a drink with Johnny, did you?'

'Not this time. I just got carried away watching *Call the Midwife*. I'm supposed to be on the information point today, but does anyone mind swapping with me? I think my head's going to explode.'

'I'll swap with you for a bit,' said Mr Whittaker. 'But what you need is a nice bacon sandwich—'

Nina crumpled over. 'Urgh.'

'Nonsense, it'll sort you out a treat. I can smell Annie's cooking it now.' He inhaled deeply. 'Delicious.'

The aroma was appetising, and Bella's stomach rumbled. She

hadn't bothered having breakfast before she came out. Normally she was a firm believer in the most important meal of the day but since Evan had left, she'd let the habit fall. In the first week it was because of a continual queasiness present from the minute she woke up, single at thirty-five, but the nausea hadn't been as strong over the last week or so. In fact, some mornings she'd woken up so eager to deliver more forms, put up posters or simply get to work that she'd forgotten about eating. Maybe it was time to get back to her old habit, especially as now she could eat what she wanted and didn't have to worry about Evan. There were certain things he didn't like and would therefore never touch, like smoked salmon, even for her.

'I might grab one on my way,' Bella said, placing a hand on her stomach as if to feel the emptiness. 'I'm famished.'

'Good to see you eating,' said Mr Whittaker. 'We don't want you wasting away. Oh, and don't forget your torch.' He handed her a huge LED lamp that was so bright it could have been used on a lighthouse.

'Umm, excuse me,' said Matilda. 'Are we not even going to talk about Seymour Cole and Nick Cowley having a fight? I've heard all sorts about it. Someone said Nick had a kitchen knife and then someone else told me he had knuckledusters while Seymour had a gun. Honestly. I mean, where does one even buy knuckledusters?'

'On eBay,' said Mr Whittaker knowingly and they all fell silent. Bella didn't want to think about how he might know that. 'Anyway, that's nonsense.'

'I never believed any of them,' Matilda continued in a voice that said she very much had. 'We all know Seymour will have started it. Nick's a lovely fellow.'

'Oh, he is,' added Hazel. 'He cut my grass for free the last time he did it because I'd forgotten to get the cash to pay him. He wouldn't even let me drop it in later. Silly boy.'

'I heard it was about their kids,' said Matilda, looking at Bella.

'I'm not saying anything,' Bella replied.

'Me neither,' mumbled Nina.

'Well,' Mr Whittaker announced, crossing his arms over his chest. 'I can tell you that Nick Cowley did not hit him. I saw it all. I was walking Mitzie, and that foul man Cole tried to get me to side with him. I just ignored him.'

Bella hadn't believed that Nick had hit him but couldn't stop the relief flooding through her knowing for a fact he hadn't.

'Perhaps we'd better get started,' Bella said before they could gossip any more. She knew none of it was meant horribly. People were always going to talk about something like that. She, Nina and Johnny had dissected it after school the next day and the consensus of opinion was that Nick was far too nice to wallop Seymour Cole no matter how much he wanted to. Bella had agreed and thinking of him had brought a warmth to her chest.

As it filled her again now, she headed off to grab a bacon sandwich and make her way to her little Christmas workshop. Bella quite liked the idea of having a little place all to herself and decided to decorate it with some bits and pieces from her house. She was going to be spending a lot of time there after all and she might as well make it cosy.

Opening the door, she moved further in. One end held a workbench, and Mr Whittaker had stacked the presents in the opposite corner. It was fairly small, but she was sure she'd be able to manage. At least it would heat up quickly. After stashing the wrapping paper and Sellotape she'd brought with her, she took the first present from the pile and went to the workbench, eager to begin her work. Fastening a pretty bow and the tag while humming 'Driving Home for Christmas', Bella admired her handiwork before starting a new pile at the opposite end of the shed to the unwrapped ones.

Last night, Bella had noticed three forms from the same family when she went through the ones she'd been given so far. The family in question were known for being cheeky to say the least, and Bella hoped it was just a mistake, but knowing the Foxes as

163

she did, she wouldn't have been surprised if they were trying to pull a fast one. Compared to some of the other items she'd had requests for, there was something off about them too. One had been for a new TV (though they had noted they didn't mind a small one), another had been for a hair dryer and the other had been for a goose to feed fifteen. Firstly, she didn't know if gooses grew that big and secondly, surely turkey would have been fine. Whichever way you looked at it, that was a lot of leftovers for a family of four even with both sets of in-laws round for Christmas.

One thing Bella had never expected was for people to try and cheat the system to such an extent. Had she been naïve? Perhaps a little. She'd always thought the best of people rather than the worst and had been brought up not to judge others' circumstances. She didn't want genuine cases to lose out while greedy people gained. The whole point of the giving tree was to give and not just receive, but was there any way she could actually police it? She'd have to rely on everyone having a good conscience and doing the right thing.

Bella continued her wrapping, singing along as she went. Every time she folded a corner of wrapping paper or fastened a bow, she felt a surge of happiness imagining the person's face when they opened the present on Christmas Day. A little while later, her cheerful humming stopped abruptly as she took the next donation. It was in a thick cardboard box with 'heavy' written on the side, yet she lifted it with ease. Too much ease. She read the number scribbled on the box and grabbed her file of completed forms. Searching through she found the corresponding form and read what the present should have been. It should have been a pair of boy's trainers and a winter coat. So why was it so light? Knowing there was nothing fragile inside she gave it a little shake. Nothing moved inside the box. In fact, it made no sound at all. Grabbing the scissors, she sliced through the Sellotape, holding it closed.

Folding back the lid she found . . . nothing. The box was empty.

'Huh! Why would you do that?' she said into the emptiness of the shed. 'Why would you give us an empty box? Suppose I'd given this to the Morgans, hey?' She raised her eyes to heaven. 'Whoever took this tag I hope you get soggy stuffing on Christmas Day.'

Bella put the box down and calmed herself with a deep breath. Perhaps whoever had given it had unexpected financial difficulties and were too embarrassed to say so. 'Think positive,' she told herself. 'It may not be someone playing a silly joke.'

'Are you talking to yourself?' Bella spun as Nick's voice carried through the open door. She glanced at her watch, realising it was mid-morning already. 'You know that's the first sign of madness, right?'

'I have been told that, but quite frankly, I don't believe them. I think all the best people talk to themselves, and it hasn't stopped me yet. Hi, Freddie.'

'Hi, Miss Moore.'

'What are you two doing here? I didn't think anyone would find me all the way back here.'

'Nina told us where you were. Is everything okay?' asked Nick, frowning in concern.

'Yes, fine,' she trilled. She sounded like a manic canary and she lowered the pitch of her voice. 'Someone just donated an empty box.'

'An empty box? That's horrible.'

'I'm hoping it's just a mistake. Anyway, I've got a lot more presents to wrap. Which is great, but you know . . . Lots to do.' She realised how that might sound. 'Not that I want you to go – either of you. Feel free to stay. I'm always happy for company.' Now she sounded like a crazy old spinster desperate to talk to someone. 'Not that I'm lonely. I'm not. There's lots to do with the giving tree. Oh crumbs.'

'Look, Dad. There's that football I wanted. The blue and green one.' Freddie dived around Bella and into the shed, picking it up in both hands and stared at it like it was the most precious thing in the world. 'Urgh, what's the smell?'

'What smell?' Bella followed him inside and rifled through the donations until she found the offending package. It was another small box. A fairly heavy one this time and incredibly smelly.

'Wow,' said Nick, grimacing. 'What the heck is that? And, Freddie, put that ball back please. I don't think you should be playing with it.'

Bella screwed her nose up as she pulled the box out from under the pile and took it to the workbench. 'It smells like feet and vomit. I better have a look inside.' She searched everywhere for a number. Whoever had handed it in hadn't put the number on but at least she could still figure out who it was for from the contents. Once she knew what it was, she could go through the enormous pile of forms to find the right one, then add the number to the box.

'It's going to be worse when you open it,' Nick said.

Bella held her nose and Freddie giggled, doing the same. 'Okay, I'm going in.' She slid the scissors over the tape and lifted the flaps of the box to find a sea of packing cardboard. Digging through the mass she gasped as she uncovered the tiny smelly contents. 'It's posh cheese.'

'Did someone actually request posh cheese?' Nick asked with a laugh.

'Not that I recall and I'm the only one who's made up the tags. That must be why it didn't have a number on.'

'So,' said Nick. 'Someone's seen the idea for a giving tree but rather than take a tag, they've just decided to send a package of posh cheese? That's a bit odd, isn't it?'

'It's the thought that counts, I suppose. I mean, it's a bonkers thought, but it'll still be a nice gift for someone. I'm sure we can find a good home for it, but I think this one might be past its best.' Bella reached in and pulled out a brie-like cheese that didn't look like it should have been blue but was now threaded with purple-blue lines. It certainly shouldn't have been flattened into a disc.

'Urgh, that's gross,' Freddie cried edging away.

Bella held it in her fingertips. 'Trouble is, I've got nowhere to put it.'

Nick stepped forwards to gallantly take it from her. 'I'll walk it to the bin for you, if you like.'

'Are you sure?'

'Yeah, we want to help. That's actually what we came here for, isn't it, mate?' Freddie ambled over to his dad's side and Nick ruffled his hair. 'What did you want to ask Bella?'

Freddie's eyes were wide and earnest. 'Can we do some volunteering too?'

'Volunteering? Here?' At first, she'd thought she'd misheard. Nick had always been a rather self-contained man and knowing how busy he was she was more than a little surprised.

Freddie nodded and Nick stepped in to explain further. 'Hang on, let me get rid of this stinky cheese first.' He dumped it in the nearest bin then jogged back. Bella couldn't help but admire his broad frame. 'Freddie's always loved the park and we thought it'd be a good way to spend some time together too. At home we just sit around on the PlayStation. Not all day, obviously,' he added quickly, clearly worrying she would disapprove. 'We just thought getting out and doing something else would be really nice.'

'We're always happy to have volunteers,' Bella replied. 'We tend to get more in the summer than the winter months. Most people are afraid of the cold. What sort of thing did you want to do?'

'How about we help you now?'

The idea of spending the day with Nick Cowley in a small room where she'd probably bump into him was too much. 'Me? No, no that's fine.'

'Please, Miss?' Freddie asked. 'I like wrapping presents. It's my favourite bit of Christmas.'

'It is? It's mine too,' she replied in a whisper.

'Dad said I was really good at wrapping Mum's presents last

year.' A shadow of sadness passed over his face and Nick squeezed his shoulder. How could she say no after that?

'If you're going to help me, Freddie, then I think you better call me Bella while we're here. I can just be Miss Moore at school, okay?'

Freddie nodded, though he didn't look convinced.

'Shall we get started with some more wrapping then?'

'Sure,' Nick replied as Freddie bounced up and down.

'So, here's what I think we do.' Bella led them inside. It was a tight, cramped space and she was shoulder to shoulder with Nick. His bodily warmth seemed to seep through his jacket into her arm, hitting like a bolt of electricity. 'If you guys wrap the present and hand it to me, I'll finish it off with a tag and a bow. I need to make sure I get the number on the tag, so I know who to deliver it to. You guys can't know that. It's confidential.'

'What does confidential mean?' asked Freddie.

'It means no one else is allowed to know.'

'Oh. Cool.'

They began working together as a small assembly line and the care with which Freddie and Nick chose the paper based on the present and who they thought it was for was touching. A silence fell on them as the dynamic between them all changed. She wasn't Miss Moore anymore, she was Bella, friend and neighbour. Did they feel the strangeness of it as much as she did? They didn't seem to but unable to work in silence she found some Christmas music on her phone. Freddie's face lit up as the cheerful songs rang out from the tiny speaker.

'How's work at the moment?' she asked Nick, needing to fill the silence but unsure what else to say. It was the most unimaginative conversation opener ever used, but she had to start somewhere. 'You seem really busy.'

'Yeah, it doesn't stop just because it's winter. It slows down a bit, especially at this time of year, in terms of big jobs anyway, but a lot of my regulars still want their garden maintenance. That's what pays the bills.'

'Do you like it? Being a landscaper, I mean.'

'Yeah, I do. I love that I get to do a bit of garden design as well as work outdoors. I don't think I'd last very long in an office.' She pictured him in a suit and her heart fluttered, though he was just as attractive in the thick checked shirt and jeans he was wearing now. 'Did you always want to be a teacher?'

'Pretty much. I've always loved kids and it seemed the most suitable career.'

'Do you think you'll teach me next year, Miss Moore?'

'Bella,' corrected Nick.

Freddie tutted. 'I'm not sure I'll ever get used to that.'

Bella and Nick broke into peals of laughter at his serious, grown-up response.

'I don't know, Freddie. We don't get told which year group we're teaching next until the end of the school year. Gosh, you and your dad are some of the best elves. I think Santa would be very pleased.'

After more time singing along to the Christmas music and wrapping presents, Nick spoke. 'You really love Christmas, don't you?'

'I do. It's always been a magical time with my family. I mean, there's always way too much food and way too much booze, and my mum and dad get ridiculously overexcited, but without all of that, every time I think of Christmas, all I remember is laughter.'

'That sounds . . .' Bella waited as he found the right word. For a second, she hoped he wasn't going to say silly or childish, but deep down she knew those words wouldn't cross his mind. 'Special. Magical.' Checking to make sure Freddie was occupied, he said, 'My Christmases were fun, but kind of . . . reserved. My parents aren't big on Christmas.'

She nodded. 'Not everyone is, but I've always loved it. It's my favourite time of the year, and I want it to be wonderful for other people too. You can't have a magical Christmas if all you're doing is worrying about money.'

'It must make it very hard. Sometimes I forget how lucky I am that I can pay the bills.'

'I think we all do. I still need to sort all that stuff out with Evan, but . . .' She let the sentence die, not wanting to think about it any further.

Freddie suddenly thrust a present under their noses. 'Look what I did, Miss – I mean –Bella.'

'Great job, Freddie! You really are the best elf in the whole of Meadowbank.'

'Maybe even the world,' added Nick.

The day passed in a blur of activity as they finished off the presents. They then worked together to make up some food boxes from the donations they'd been given. The final job was to place the new tags on the giving tree as more requests had come in.

Nick was just lifting Freddie up as they placed the final few onto the tree. 'There've been so many more requests than I expected,' he said sadly.

'I know, but, as my mum says, just remember what a difference you're making.'

'Us? This was your idea.'

'Yeah, but you're helping to turn it from an idea into reality.'

'I suppose we are, aren't we?'

She nodded and almost melted as his face filled with pride.

'I'm hungry, Daddy. Are we nearly finished?'

'We are,' Bella said as she hung the last tag on the tree. 'I'm hungry too.'

'Would you . . .' Nick scratched the back of his head. 'Would you like to come round for dinner? We were going to have a go at making pizzas, weren't we, Freddie?'

Bella checked Freddie's face to make sure he was in favour of the idea. Not only was he smiling, he was bouncing on his toes too. 'You should definitely come, Bella. We've got loads to go on top like sausage and stringy cheese. Not the stuff you used to put in my sandwiches—'

'He means mozzarella – wait, what?'

Bella's skin grew clammy. She hadn't ever really intended for

Nick to find out about that and opened her mouth, searching for the words, but Freddie spoke first.

'When Mum first left, Bella used to bring me in a sandwich because you sometimes forgot to make me one.'

Nick stared at her, but he seemed more concerned or embarrassed than upset. 'Did you?'

'I just wanted to help out,' she said with a shake of her head. She hoped he wasn't cross or insulted and hiding it. 'I didn't mean to offend.'

'I'm – I'm not offended. I . . . Thanks.' She swallowed, grateful that he wasn't going to report her to Mrs White, which is what Mr Cole would have done. 'That was nice of you. Good job I switched to school dinners though. This one's always hungry. He'd have been eating your lunch too.'

When Nick looked at her, something fizzed in the air between them, and she dropped her eyes to see Freddie staring up at her. 'I call it stringy cheese too,' Bella said to Freddie with a wink.

'And we've got tomato sauce too. It's from a jar but it's the really nice stuff they sell at the deli. And Dad bought salad, which is gross, but he said I have to eat some if we're having pizza.'

The idea of spending time with Nick and Freddie made her heart spin. 'If you're sure you've got enough, I'd love to. That'd be great.'

Nick lowered Freddie to the floor. 'Do you want to go and play on the climbing frame before it gets dark?'

But Freddie didn't move, instead, he stared ahead, and Bella followed his gaze to see a police car arriving. Two police officers exited and searched around. They spoke to Hazel at the information point who sent them in Bella's direction.

Fear tightened her stomach and her mind played through a number of terrifying scenarios. Had something happened to her mum and dad? To Caro? To the baby?

'Mr Cowley?' the taller of the two called.

Nick's jaw set firm. 'That's me.'

'Can we speak to you please?'

'Of course. Freddie, why don't you go and play?'

He shook his head until Bella encouraged him. Reluctantly, he moved away, glancing over his shoulder all the while.

'Is everything all right?'

'I'm afraid not, sir. You'd better tell us what happened with Seymour Cole because he wants us to arrest you for assault.'

Chapter 17

'But he attacked me. He—'

'We just want to ask you a few questions at this stage, Mr Cowley. We're still gathering information about what happened and talking to witnesses.'

'Can we just go over here?' Nick signalled away from Bella as heat prickled his skin. Freddie was playing on the swings, though he continued to watch what was happening. Bella made her way towards him, and Freddie left the swing to talk to her. Her face was calm and placid, understanding, and Nick knew she was comforting him, letting him know everything would be all right. She was a pretty amazing woman – friend – neighbour – he definitely meant neighbour.

When they were nearer the trees and away from the crowd, the taller policeman pulled out a notebook and began asking questions. 'So can you tell me what happened on Tuesday, Mr Cowley?'

'There's not much to say, really. There was an incident at school involving our two boys. Bella – I mean – Miss Moore over there will be able to tell you more about that. She dealt with it along with Mrs White, the headmistress, and Miss Radcliffe, my son's class teacher. But the upshot is, Mr Cole's boy attacked mine and got himself excluded from school for the day.' Nick ran his hand over his jaw. 'Then just after I'd got Freddie home, Mr Cole turns up on my doorstep shouting his mouth off, calling my son a liar.'

'So you hit him?' the smaller, rounder one said. From his smug grin, Nick had the feeling he lived his life as if he were in some kind of police drama and not patrolling the tiniest village in England and its even smaller neighbours.

'Hit? No! Is that what he's saying? That I hit him?' The policeman gave no answer, just watched Nick as he went on. 'He got in my face and when I went to walk away, he pulled me back by my shoulder. I spun around and he was waving his fist in my face. I did push him away and he fell on his arse, but—'

'I can imagine Mr Cole didn't like that very much,' the taller officer said. A wry smile threatened the corner of his mouth and Nick wondered if they felt the same way about Mr Cole as the rest of the village did.

'He seemed embarrassed. I would have been if I'd ended up with wet trousers in front of the village, but I swear, I never hit him. He started shouting something about unnecessary force, but I honestly just shoved him to get him away from me.' A thought suddenly occurred to him. 'Mr Whittaker was there. He's the old man over there by the flowerbed. He was walking his dog at the time and saw it all. You could talk to him. He'll back me up.'

'You never hit him at all?' the shorter one asked. He sounded slightly disappointed now. 'You never made any motion to strike that Mr Cole could misconstrue?' Suddenly brightening, he was very pleased with the word *misconstrue*, and Nick wondered how long he'd been waiting to say that sentence.

'No, definitely not. I swear I didn't hit him. My neighbours saw everything. Trish and Len Banks at Pond Cottage. Talk to them, they'll back me up. And there were some other people from the village around, but I can't remember who right now. Sorry. Mrs Carmichael came out of her house and told us to stop acting like idiots. I don't know how much she saw but you could talk to her too.'

'Right, thank you, Mr Cowley.' The taller one scribbled in his notebook, Nick hoped making a note of Trish and Len's address.

'What happens now?' Fear bubbled in his stomach.

The officer cleared his throat. 'Well, although you didn't hit him, you have admitted to pushing him, which means he could still press charges for assault—'

'But I only pushed him.'

'I'm afraid that still counts.'

'As assault?'

The policeman nodded. 'Common assault can be a difficult charge.' If Nick had known that before he'd never had laid a finger on him at all. He'd never even have opened the door.

Seeing the shock on his face, the policeman softened his tone, but the impact of his words echoed around Nick's brain. 'If it goes to court and you're found guilty it could mean up to six months in prison.'

'Six months?' Nick's heart stopped beating. 'But I've got a son. I can't go to prison. And I run my own business. If I don't work, I don't get paid. I'd lose everything.'

The heat of embarrassment that had warmed his face fell away to be replaced by a chill down his spine. This couldn't happen. He'd done nothing wrong.

'We'll talk to the witnesses and to Mr Cole again, but it would be easier for everyone if you could apologise and get him to drop the charges.'

'Apologise?' The word left a bitter taste in his mouth. Not because he didn't like apologising. He'd happily apologise if he'd done something wrong, but he hadn't done anything except for stand up for his boy. Why should he be the one to apologise? But he didn't say so to the two policemen standing in front of him. Instead, he nodded his understanding and they left. Once they'd climbed back into their car, Freddie and Bella came over.

'What was that, Daddy? What did the policemen want? Are you in trouble?'

The fear etched on his son's face made him sick to his stomach. What would happen to him if he ended up in jail for six months? Who would Freddie live with? His mum and dad would take him in, but Nick didn't want to scupper their plans. They always went to Spain in the new year and didn't come back till spring. For some reason his mind went to Bella and the type of mother she'd be. She'd be perfect for him – for Freddie – he corrected himself. An attraction he hadn't felt in a long time inched inside. Like the door to his heart had opened a fraction and something had snuck in or escaped out, he wasn't quite sure which.

'It was nothing, son. They just had a few questions about something.'

'Is it to do with work?'

'Yes, mate. Nothing for you to worry about.' He ruffled his son's hair and Freddie went back off to play.

'Was it about Mr Cole?' Bella asked. 'The . . . altercation you had?'

Nick ran his foot through the leaves spread on the ground around his feet. 'I don't know what you saw, Bella, but I promise you, I didn't do anything except push him away when he got in my face. No matter what he might say, I didn't hit him, I didn't threaten him. I was trying to walk away when he pulled me back and—'

'I know,' Bella said quickly. 'I . . . How can I put this?' He watched her face as she raised her eyes to the sky, thinking about how to tactfully word whatever it was. Her wish not to speak ill of people made him want to smile even though she was talking about Seymour Cole and everyone hated him. 'I know what Mr Cole can be like and I know what you're like. I know you'd never hit anyone.'

Relief washed over Nick like a wave crashing to shore. 'He called Freddie a liar. Said he'd made it up to get Amias into trouble.'

'I wish I could say I can't believe it, but I can. Well, I can assure you that wasn't the case. We investigated fully and have witnesses who saw everything. Freddie didn't lie about a single thing. Every action the school took was justified and right.'

For a moment, Nick's anger got the better of him. 'The Coles have always been that sort of family. Entitled. Thinking they're so much better than everyone else. And now I could end up going to prison.'

'Prison?' Bella's pretty, dark eyes had frozen in fright.

He shouldn't have said anything. He should have just dealt with it himself. He still wasn't used to relying on people or taking them into his confidence. Why was he suddenly doing it now? He knew why. It was because he trusted her. Her unfailing optimism and love of Christmas cheered up even the darkest of moods and there was a warmth to her that radiated out, touching everyone around her, though she didn't seem to notice it herself.

Nick explained about Seymour Cole pressing charges and Bella flushed.

'But that's preposterous. What about Freddie? What about you? We have to do something.' She thrust her hand into her hair. 'This is all my fault.'

'What? How do you figure that?' He reached out and placed a hand on her shoulder, sending a tingling through his fingers.

'If I'd have kept a closer eye at school and stopped Amias getting to Freddie . . .'

'This is not your fault,' Nick said firmly. She kept her eyes down and he wanted to reach out and gently lift her chin but fear of how he'd feel if he touched her prevented him. 'Don't worry. I'll figure something out. Maybe I'll just apologise if it means this doesn't get any nastier. Though I'd like to think right is on my side.'

He wished he could believe that would actually help but life wasn't like that.

'If you don't want to come for dinner anymore, I completely understand.' He hoped his voice didn't ring with the disappointment he felt inside. He'd been looking forward to spending more time with her. Perhaps looking forward to it more than he'd realised.

'No, I'd like to. That's if you're sure?' she asked quietly. 'I don't want to be a pain. If you'd prefer to be alone with Freddie after what's happened, then I—'

'We'd love you to come,' he said quickly before he lost his nerve. 'Really. If you don't come, I'll dwell on it all evening, and

I need someone to read the recipe out to me. I've never made pizza dough before. Have you?'

'Can't say I have,' Bella replied with a laugh. 'But how hard can it be? I doubt it's as hard as getting a class full of nine-year-olds to decorate cookies without spraying icing all over themselves and the person next to them.'

'Now, that does sound like hard work. I can just about cope with one kid; a class of twenty would drive me mad.'

'Some would say I am already. Running the giving tree with everything else that's going on.'

'Or just a lovely person.'

She looked up to meet his gaze, a blush gathering on the apples of her cheeks. Nick felt a flash of vulnerability.

'Do you have a chef's hat?' she asked out of nowhere and he laughed.

'I've got two, actually. One for me and one for Freddie but you can borrow mine. I'm not sure it would suit me anyway.' She looked at him as if imagining the hat on his head and the way she smiled caused him to falter. 'And we've got mushrooms, pineapple and fresh tomatoes depending what you want on your pizza.'

'I'm not sure I'd want all of that together, but I can't wait,' Bella replied, and Nick found that he couldn't either, even with the threat of prison hanging over him.

Was it possible his heart wasn't quite as broken as he'd led himself to believe?

Chapter 18

Nick's cottage was the exact opposite of her own. Where hers was neat and tidy, Nick's was messy and more like a boy's den, though she could see that the kitchen was clean and orderly, and the washing machine had a load sitting in front of it waiting to go on.

Her parents' help in moving on from Evan had been invaluable, but Nick had been self-reliant through his struggles. Wiping all trace of Evan from the house had been just what she'd needed. It must have been so much harder for Nick. Where she could throw all the photos of Evan into a box and hide it, if he did that, he was losing pictures of Freddie too. Being forced to live with the face of the woman who broke your heart must have been torturous. No wonder Nick had floundered for a while. But she'd noticed lately that Freddie was wearing beautifully cleaned school uniform and unrumpled shirts, and Nick too had seemed more together.

'Freddie, can you go and wash your hands, please?' Nick said. 'Bella, did you want tea, coffee or wine?'

'Wine would be lovely, thank you. White if you have it.'

'Daddy, can I play on the PlayStation, please?'

'Of course you can, mate, if you've washed your hands. I think you've earned it today, don't you, Bella?' He glanced up at her from under dark lashes and her stomach flipped over. The easy gesture as they all gathered in his kitchen made her feel a little less self-conscious. Though they'd been neighbours for years she hadn't made it further than the front step to borrow teabags and walking over the threshold had sent nerves shooting into her stomach.

'You definitely have, Freddie. You've worked so hard today. Thank you for everything you've done.'

'Look at this, Bella. This is my favourite game.' Freddie began telling her all about it, pulling her over to the sofa and getting her to sit beside him. He didn't stop talking for about ten minutes and even then, only paused long enough for Nick to bring her over a glass of wine.

'Make yourself comfortable, Bella. I'm just going to clear some room in the kitchen and then we can start making the pizzas.'

'Fab, I'm starving.'

'Me too,' Nick replied, giving another almost shy smile.

Bella stared at her wine for a second, willing her chest to stop knotting. Was it wrong to feel like this so soon after her break-up? So much had changed for her since then and since Evan's visit to the school. He'd become a different person without her realising it and now he was gone she could do as she pleased. It had been a long time since Evan had smiled at her in the way Nick had. It had been even longer since Evan had kissed her in a passionate, tear all your clothes off way. They'd been growing apart so slowly she hadn't really realised it before now.

'I nearly killed him!' shouted Freddie, leaping in the air and flopping back onto the sofa.

'Calm down, mate,' Nick called out from the kitchen. 'Sorry,' he said to Bella. 'He just gets a bit carried away. It's not really a violent game. It's only Lego.'

'It's fine.' Bella chuckled, standing up from the sofa and coming to join him in the kitchen. 'Honestly, please don't think of me as Miss Moore. I'm not going to tell him or you off. This is your house and I'm very grateful to be asked in for dinner.'

'It's lovely to have you here.'

The rich colour of his blue eyes seemed to pierce her soul and the moment became thick and heavy. The butterflies dancing low in her stomach filled her with excitement and apprehension. Something was definitely happening here between them but what exactly was it and what could it be? Were either of them ready?

'Shall we get started then?' said Nick. 'This dough needs to prove for an hour before we can make the pizzas. I should have got us some nibbles. Olives or something.'

'I'm more than happy with a packet of crisps if you've got some of those.'

'Those we've definitely got. Freddie, can you grab out some crisps, please?'

Freddie leapt over the sofa and yanked open a cupboard, pulling out a large multipack of crisps. 'What flavour do you like, Bella?'

'Are you all going to moan if I say prawn cocktail?'

'Urgh,' Nick and Freddie said in unison.

Bella rolled her eyes. 'I always get that. I can't help it.'

Nick held up a hand while Freddie made fake vomiting noises. 'Sorry, Bella, but they are the worst flavour crisps in the whole world. No one in their right mind likes prawn cocktail.'

Right now, she didn't think she was in her right mind for a whole host of reasons. 'Well, I do. And it never hurts to be different, does it?'

'Right,' said Nick, placing the chef's hat on Freddie's head. 'Shall we get started then?'

'Wait!' Bella cried, grabbing her phone. 'We need Christmas music.'

'Will it make any difference if I say no?'

'None whatsoever.'

'Do you have an advent calendar in class, Bella?' Freddie asked. 'We do. Look, I've got mine already.' He ran to the furthest worktop in the kitchen and showed Bella a chocolate one the village shop had been stocking since the start of November.

'We definitely do, Freddie. It wouldn't be Christmas without an advent calendar.'

The memory of making the pizzas that Saturday night was one that would stay with Bella forever – she was sure of it. It rivalled her own memories of cooking with her family at Christmas time because all she could remember was laughter. Freddie's high-pitched giggle, which only came out when he was exquisitely

181

happy, danced around the kitchen. Seeing Nick forget the worry that Mr Cole had forced upon him had also lifted her spirits. He didn't deserve it. If only there was something she could do.

Her mind ran through different possibilities until it hit on an idea. There was something she could do, but would it get her into trouble at school? Possibly. At the moment, being with Nick and Freddie made it worth the risk.

While the dough proved, Nick sent Freddie up for a shower and he prepared the toppings. Bella sat at the breakfast bar at the end of the kitchen counter, eating crisps out of the bowl Nick had sweetly emptied them into. He topped up her wine glass.

'Sorry we haven't got any fancy appetisers or something nicer.'

'Hey, prawn cocktail crisps are good enough for me. My mum gets them in especially every year because I'm the only Moore who likes them.'

'I remember that year your mum and dad started a Christmas can-can around the village on Christmas Eve.'

'When they fell out of the pub on Christmas Eve you mean?'

He grinned. 'Don't remind me. Caro and I were mortified.'

'You shouldn't be – they're fun.'

She moved her elbow, accidentally knocking over a photograph of Freddie, Paige and Nick that had sat at the corner of the counter. 'Sorry! I'm so sorry.'

'Don't worry.' Nick took the photo and stood it up on the windowsill. 'I'm always knocking it over too.'

'Is it hard having her picture around?' she asked. 'I've hidden everything with Evan in, but you can't do that, can you?'

'No. It wouldn't be fair on Freddie. He needs to see what his mum looks like. I don't want him to forget and as I don't know when she's coming back . . . She could look completely different by the time she gets here.'

Was he fully over her, she wondered? She shook the thought from her head. 'Freddie's such a great kid. You've done an amazing job guiding him through all this. He's still such a happy boy.'

'I don't know how.' Nick leaned back against the counter and crossed his arms over his chest. His glass of wine dangled from one hand and he took a sip. She felt so easy in his company, but nervous too, not wanting to make a mistake and spoil it all. 'I just plod along day to day, but I have tried to get a bit more organised recently. I just feel like whatever I do, it's never enough or not right.'

'I think every parent feels like that. I know every teacher does.'

'Are you spending Christmas with your family?'

Bella nodded as she drank. 'It's just what we do. We all pile into Mum and Dad's and spend the day there drinking and eating too much. We'll probably play some board games in the afternoon or go for a walk to sober up, then it's back for cheese and wine in the evenings. Evan used to hate it.'

'Why? It sounds perfect.'

'Hate it might be a little harsh,' she admitted. 'At first, he used to join in as much as everyone else, but the last couple of years he's tried to get away. He said it was because I was always volunteering at Bluebell Park on Christmas Eve and he wanted time just the two of us. I understood but I just love being with my family at this time of year. It may sound silly coming from a thirty-five-year-old woman but as I get older, I realise I don't know how much longer I'll have them around for. Not fit and able like this, and I want to make the most of it.'

'And he couldn't understand that?'

'Not always. He didn't see his folks till New Year and even then, he wasn't that bothered about it. I've been thinking about it a lot lately, and I've realised that there were quite a few times when we were growing apart and changing in different ways that I never picked up on. Do you know what I mean?'

'That's generally how it goes,' he said with a smile. 'You don't realise what's happening until it's done.'

'Last year he made me feel so guilty about spending Christmas Day with my family we left at five o'clock.'

'That must have been before the cheese and wine,' Nick replied with a wicked grin.

'It was. Can you imagine? Who leaves before cheese and wine? And you know what my mum's like – the cheese board was more like a cheese shelf. I'm sure she'd bought everything the deli sold.'

Nick laughed and she savoured the sound of the throaty rumble that started somewhere deep inside him.

There'd been other things too that she'd slowly been piecing together. She loved doing her charity work, which Evan would sometimes moan about. Apparently, it was unfair that he didn't get to see her all day on a Saturday unless he was off to play golf with his mates, then he didn't mind. They'd begun to disagree about what to watch. She loved re-watching old programmes that had made her laugh while he only ever wanted to watch new things, particularly shows that were doing the rounds as the best thing since sliced bread. Bella wasn't always interested in what was good if it was about something that would make her sad. She just wanted to be entertained, made to laugh. Evan hadn't laughed much in the last few months. Perhaps it was even longer than that.

'Are you okay? You've gone very quiet,' Nick said, topping up her glass.

'I'm fine,' she replied and then admitted what she'd been thinking about.

'I did that too. After Paige left, I suddenly found a million and one things that weren't right with our relationship. I wrote them all down once.'

'You did?'

He nodded. 'I just couldn't accept it had really been that bad and then one night when I'd got Freddie to bed, I just thought, I'm going to write it down. I needed to make it real somehow and the only way I could think of was to see it on paper with my own eyes. It wasn't a great moment, but it helped in the long run. It helped me take her off her pedestal and see things for how they really were.'

'It doesn't make it any less painful though, does it?' she asked quietly.

'No, it doesn't. I found that I could cope with her leaving me, but I couldn't fathom how she'd leave Freddie. It was just so wrong to me. I don't care what happens, I could never leave him or not see him.' Nick took another drink as if he'd spoken more openly than intended and needed time to compose himself. 'Thanks for helping with Freddie's lunch when it all first happened. I had no idea.'

'I know I shouldn't have. I should have spoken to you about it. Mrs White would go mad if she knew what I'd done, but you were just so busy trying to deal with everything. You held it all together so well for Freddie, I couldn't bring myself to add more worries. It just seemed easier to make a little extra and bring it in just in case. It didn't happen every day. To be honest, I don't know how you managed to cope without falling apart.'

'You think I coped well?'

'Yes,' she said with a laugh. 'You did amazingly well.'

'Thanks. I mean – I'm okay now. More than okay, I think, but it took a while to get here.'

Their eyes met and she felt a lump form in her throat. She wondered what it would be like to feel his lips on hers. An image of the passion that had been so lacking in her relationship with Evan flashed into her brain and she felt her muscles contract.

Freddie chose that moment to come tumbling into the kitchen in his most Christmassy pyjamas. Bella guessed they were from last year given that they finished well above his ankles. His face, pink from the steam of the shower, resembled a particularly naughty cherub and his wild hair stuck up in all directions.

She'd always wanted moments like this: imagined them with her own children. Would that happen for her now? She was already thirty-five and everything she read said her biological clock was ticking. She was aware of wrinkles forming on her forehead and lines around her eyes. Evan had been putting her off for ages, saying he wanted to get married first, but in reality, he hadn't wanted to marry her or start a family. If only he'd been honest, it could have been far less painful. She buried the sting of his betrayal under another sip of wine.

'Do you like my pyjamas, Bella? Look, they've got Christmassy dinosaurs on them.'

'They're gorgeous, Freddie. I've got some with Christmassy llamas on them.'

'Really?'

She nodded.

'Who's ready for pizza then?' Nick asked with a flourish. 'And after dinner, mate, you can have an hour calm downtime before bed, okay?'

'Will you read me a bedtime story, Bella? Please?'

Nick seemed so shocked by the suggestion he almost dropped the bowl of dough he was retrieving from the back of the cooker where it had proved. Bella froze too. She wanted to say yes. She loved reading stories to the kids, especially at the end of the school day and she'd always looked forward to doing that with her own children one day but without knowing how Nick felt about it, she couldn't just agree. She turned to him.

'Sorry, the bowls a bit slippery from the olive oil.'

Freddie looked between them as if sensing something was up.

'Umm,' Bella stuttered. 'If your dad doesn't mind.'

Nick relaxed, a warm smile filling his face. 'No objections from me,' he replied, dividing the dough into three equal balls. 'But I warn you, it won't be the gentle stories you read at school. He loves to end the day with his enormous book of superhero tales.'

'Spider-Man's my favourite,' Freddie replied stealing some cheese. 'And I can do his moves. I can show you on the apparatus on Monday.'

'That sounds good to me,' Bella said. She'd never wanted to read a story quite so much in her life.

'Are you going to the Christmas parade next week?' Nick asked, pressing the dough into three round discs.

The Christmas parade was a Meadowbank institution and one that the whole village turned out for. Some houses had started adorning their gardens with Christmas decorations already, or putting up their Christmas trees, but by next weekend every single house would be lit to the hilt and the whole village would sparkle and shine like a winter wonderland. Everything seemed different resplendent in golden Christmas lights, and she couldn't help but feel like a tourist in her hometown.

'I never miss it,' she replied.

'We could all go together couldn't we, Daddy?'

When Nick agreed and glanced at her to make sure he hadn't signed her up to something she didn't want, she had the sensation of floating. It was entirely possible she'd drunk too much on an empty stomach, but she wasn't convinced that was it. She felt strangely at home in Nick and Freddie's company, and she wanted to hold on to this feeling forever. But was it possible to get over a heartbreak so quickly? She'd never thought so before, and always criticised TV programmes or films when it happened on screen. It all seemed too unrealistic, but she couldn't deny the way she was feeling right now. She wanted to explore what this thing was between her and Nick. It felt important, constant, pure.

Wouldn't it be stupid to ignore something so special because she'd arbitrarily decided she should be heartbroken for longer? Especially as, when she compared the way she felt now to everything she'd believed her relationship with Evan to be, she realised it had never even come close.

'I'd like that very much, Freddie,' she said quietly and pressed her feet into the floor to make sure this was all perfectly and wonderfully real.

Chapter 19

The next day, Bella knocked on Mr Cole's door and stepped back. She'd never been so nervous in all her life and wasn't sure who she wanted to answer more: him or Mrs Cole. Either was a daunting prospect but given that it was Mr Cole she needed to speak to, it was probably better that he answered so she could get this over and done with.

Last night, after dinner with Freddie and Nick, she'd gone home and followed Nick's unwitting advice. The list she'd made of all the things that had been going wrong with her and Evan's relationship was far longer than she'd expected and went further back in time. How had she missed so much? They were all things she'd put down to off days or bad moods but even that provided a startling realisation. They must have been having far more off days than good ones. The list was now safely tucked away in her handbag. She wanted to show it to Caro and see what she thought. There was every possibility she'd think she was crazy, but Bella was willing to take the risk given how much it had helped her and seeing it all written down had unexpectedly strengthened her resolve to help Nick as much as possible.

The Coles lived in one of the larger houses on the outer circle of Meadowbank. The houses were so big that 'just down' really meant at least half a mile further on, but Bella was happy for the exercise. Last night's pizza had been delicious and very filling, and she could wander back through Meadowbank wood and the fields to get to her mum and dad's house with enough appetite built up for her Sunday roast. All along the outer road, the houses were set back down gravel drives that you normally entered through large wooden or cast-iron gates.

She had no idea how Mr Cole was going to react to her request or what the consequences of it might be, but she knew she had to try. She'd run through a number of terrifying scenarios but whenever she thought of Nick's face and his horror when the police had arrived, she knew it was worth the risk.

On the other side of the door, the clopping of shoes on the floor hastened towards her and she readied herself for Mrs Cole only to find it was Seymour in a pair of shiny Cuban heels designed to add an inch to his below-average height. When she lifted her eyes, she saw his shirt buttons had been done up wrong, but not wanting to dwell on what he might have been up to, she said, 'Hello, Mr Cole.'

'Miss Moore,' he barked in surprise. 'What are you doing here?'

'I was hoping to speak to you. May I come in?'

Mr Cole checked over his shoulder. 'Oh, well, umm—' He half closed the door again. 'My wife isn't here I'm afraid. She's visiting her mother with Amias.'

'That's no problem. It was actually you I wanted to see.'

'Right. Can't you come back later? Or my wife could talk to you at school tomorrow?'

'It is rather urgent, and I really was hoping to speak outside of school. I'm not trying to be difficult, but if you could spare me a few minutes, I don't think it'll take long.'

She felt like a dodgy door-to-door salesman as she waited in silence for him to open up. After another glance behind, Mr Cole reluctantly opened the door and let her in.

'This way, Miss Moore.' He led her through a large pristine hallway into an enormous living room with two sofas placed opposite each other in the centre.

The Coles employed one of the local ladies as a cleaner and clearly worked her to the bone. There wasn't an area in the room that didn't glisten or gleam in the winter sun bursting through the large windows. He sat on one sofa and motioned for her to sit on the other. 'What can I do for you?'

Gathering her courage, she clasped her hands in her lap. 'I

was hoping to speak to you about the incident between yourself and Mr Cowley.'

His flabby jowls reddened and wobbled as he shook his head. 'That's none of your concern, Miss Moore. Or the school's.'

'I'm not here in an official capacity. I'm here as a friend and neighbour of—' She was going to say Nick's but didn't think that level of familiarity would actually help matters. 'Of both of you. I wondered if there was any way we could sort this whole thing out without the involvement of the police.'

'The police are already involved.'

'Yes, I know, but—'

'How do you know?'

'They spoke to him at Bluebell Park yesterday. I was there.'

This seemed to amuse Mr Cole. 'Good. Hopefully it embarrassed him as much as he *tried* to humiliate me.' He stressed the word *tried*. 'Anyway, there's nothing more to say. The police are dealing with it.' He stood and motioned to the living-room door.

Bella stood too, determined to keep trying until he forcibly removed her from the premises. 'Mr Cole, it isn't good for anyone to go down this road. It's more stress on you and your family, and stress on Mr Cowley and his son. If he does go to prison, his son will lose a father.'

'That's tough luck. His mother shouldn't have run off.'

Hearing him say something so cruel stiffened her resolve. 'No, she shouldn't, but that's neither Freddie's nor Nick's fault. He didn't hit you, Mr Cole, and you did put your hands on him first. I'm sure the police will take that into account.' Though she knew she was risking at the very least, a big telling-off and, at worst, the sack, she added, 'You were waving your fist in his face, which I'm told could also be classed as assault.'

'What? What nonsense.'

'I'm afraid it isn't.' She'd only got that information this morning from some random solicitor's webpage, so she hoped it was true. It had certainly rattled him more than anything else she'd said.

'I'm happy to wait for the police's decision. Now, if there's nothing else.'

Just as she was about to leave, the living-room door opened and she feared the arrival of Mrs Cole, but instead a rather voluptuous blonde-haired lady who was very much not Mr Cole's wife slipped through the gap in the door wearing nothing but a black lace negligee. It was the type of nightwear no one actually sleeps in and is only bought at the beginning of relationships for naughty weekends away. She wondered if Pepper had worn something like this during that weekend in Leeds but found the pain didn't stab anywhere near as harshly as it had before.

'Where's my big beasty-boy? I – oh—'

With a cry of alarm, the blonde spun on the spot and scampered back out of the room. Bella's eyes widened as she made sense of the scene and slowly, she turned back to Mr Cole.

'Ah, now, Miss Moore. It's not what it looks like. That's— She's—'

In her head, Bella gave thanks. Though she was reticent about taking advantage of the situation she wanted to relieve Nick's worries. 'It's not for me to say anything, Mr Cole, but clearly should I be asked by the police about your character I would feel it my duty to mention . . .' She let the implication hang in the air and looked towards the door so he knew exactly what she meant. 'And as Mr Cowley's next-door neighbour and a witness, I'm sure they'll be speaking to me soon. Of course, if you dropped the charges, they wouldn't need to speak to me at all, but that's entirely your decision.'

The excitement pulsing through her veins made her feel more alive than she had in ages. Mr Cole's face grew so red she was sure the top of his head was about to fly off and hit the fake and rather ugly chandelier dangling from the ceiling.

'Miss Moore—' His voice was steely but heavy with embarrassment.

'I'll see myself out, Mr Cole, as you're rather, umm . . . busy.'

Bella left, holding her head up high but as soon as she left the living room she virtually ran to the front door and outside before he could catch up with her. Her heart pounded up into her throat. She couldn't wait to tell her parents about what she'd just done. Or Nick.

'You said what?' Caro couldn't stop grinning while her dad chuckled away. Their mum was stirring the gravy, sipping wine and laughing like a drain.

'I can't believe I did it,' Bella said breathlessly. Her heart had beaten a techno dance tune since she closed the Coles' front door behind her and marched to her parents' house. The cold, fresh air and pale winter sky had cleansed her skin of the embarrassment the awkward situation had caused. She'd heard rumours of his affairs of course. Who in the village hadn't? But she hadn't ever imagined she'd walk in on him having one. That woman must have been cold, wearing such a flimsy, see-through nightdress. It was absolutely freezing today.

Bella sipped her small glass of wine as her dad carved the beef. 'Dirty bugger. I've never understood these men who go elsewhere when they've got a cracker at home. Oops, sorry, my darling.' He waved the electric carving knife towards Bella, and even though she was a fair distance away, she flinched.

'Dad, don't mess about with that thing. And I'm actually feeling okay about things at the moment. The time I spend moping is becoming less and less.' Her mum and dad shared a sly glance. 'Why are you looking like that? And please start looking where you're cutting before you slice your own fingers off. Why are you glaring at each other?'

'We're not,' her mum replied in a thoroughly unconvincing way.

'Yes, you are. Spill.'

It was Caro's turn to join in now. 'They're looking like that because we all know where you spent yesterday evening and who you spent most of the day with too.'

'I have to say you have wonderful taste, darling,' Cynthia said. 'He is rather hot.'

'Mum! Stop it. Dad's here.'

'Oh, darling, your dad knows when someone's handsome or not, and it's not like I'm going to run off with him, is it?'

'It's fine, sweetheart,' her dad said. 'I think we all recognise that Nick's an exceptionally good-looking chap.'

Bella pretended her body had grown warm from the heat of the kitchen and not the conversation. 'My friendship with Nick is nothing more than that at the moment. Just a friendship.'

'Ha!' Caro shouted, making Luke jump. 'You said at the moment. So does that mean you'd like to get all smoochy-smoochy kissy time with him?'

'How old are you?' she asked Caro teasingly. Knowing the pinkness of her cheeks were a giveaway for any lie she told, she may as well admit it. 'I really like him, but I don't know if I'm ready. I don't know if he's ready.'

'I'm not sure he'd like all of us,' said Cynthia. 'I mean we've already got the Christmas decorations up outdoors.'

'Took me half an hour with the foot pump to get that inflatable snowman up,' Mungo interjected. 'And I think the bugger needs a top-up today.'

'I worry we'd be too much for him.'

'You wouldn't. He's really—' All eyes focused on her. 'Really—'

'Really what?' Luke asked with a grin.

'Really nice. He's like you, Luke, except much better-looking.'

'Ouch,' Caro replied. 'She got you there.'

'Yeah,' Mungo joined in. 'Let's hope the baby has got Caro's looks and your umm . . .'

'Brains?' Luke offered. 'Brawn? Sense of humour? Anything?'

'Cheerful disposition,' Mungo answered, and everyone sat down to eat still laughing.

Luke had fitted into the family so seamlessly and Bella hadn't noticed until now how Evan had always been a little apart from the rest of them. It wasn't that he hadn't been welcomed. Her family couldn't help but welcome people in, but Evan had always held something of himself back. She'd always believed it was shyness, but she'd begun to wonder recently if it was because he didn't entirely approve of the unremitting good time they always had. Maybe even a hint of jealousy was mixed in there too. She had no fear that Nick and Freddie would be welcomed into the family if that ever were to happen.

What was she even thinking about? They'd had a nice evening together as neighbours. One. Nothing more. Nothing had happened. Nothing was even close to happening. It was more than a little presumptuous on her part, but she couldn't stop herself imagining. As she sat eating her dinner, the scene before her played out with two extra guests and her heart skipped. At one point she had to pretend Luke had been especially funny so that no one thought she was insane for grinning like a lunatic at a roast potato.

The plates were cleared, and she and her sister washed up while everyone else had gone to the living room.

'When are you and Nick seeing each other again?' Caro asked.

'I'll probably see him at drop-off and pick-up but the next time we'll get to speak will be at Bluebell Park next weekend. He and Freddie have started volunteering.'

'Have they now? I wonder why?'

'Don't look like that,' Bella said, handing Caro a soapy plate. 'Nick thought it'd be good for Freddie after the whole thing in school.'

Caro tutted. 'I still can't believe that little toad did that.'

'Amias isn't a little toad,' Bella said. 'Something's got to be going on for him to act like that.' He'd always been a bit excitable in class and a bit of a tease to the other kids, but this was something else. She was worried about him, and with his dad's antics his behaviour was probably related to that.

'You're too nice, Bella. You've always been far too nice about people. When this one arrives' – she patted her bump – 'I hope they never do anything like that.'

'I'm sure they won't with you as a mum.'

'I'll threaten them with living with Luke's parents if they do.' Caro began stacking some plates away in the cupboard.

Bella tried to say her next words easily, playing them in her head first. 'Oh, and I'm seeing Nick and Freddie at the Christmas parade as well, but we probably would have anyway. So it's not like a . . . thing or anything.'

Caro straightened up and leaned against the side to catch her breath. 'You mean like a date-like thing? How many dates will that be?'

'They're not dates, Caro, they're just meetings. Run-ins. Neighbours doing something together like the way this whole village does stuff together. Are you sure you don't want to sit down? I can do this.'

'I'm fine. Don't try and change the subject, and of course it's just neighbourliness, darling. You keep telling yourself that. Then again, I'm not sure they class as dates if there are kids around.'

'Exactly.' Bella paused as soap suds slid from her fingers. 'Caro, I can't fall for anyone yet, can I? It's far too soon.'

'Who says?'

'I don't know, but don't you think it is?'

'Not if that's what your heart is telling you. Think about me and Luke. We got together a week after I split from Terry the Turd.'

'Yeah, but you were with Terry for a few months. Evan and I were together for five years. It doesn't seem right somehow.'

'That's for your heart to decide, really. You can't tell it what it can and can't feel.'

Bella had to admit that her feelings for Nick were growing stronger. She looked forward to seeing him every day and Freddie was just a wonderful, sweet little boy. He was special. They both were. 'Nick mentioned he made a list after Paige left. He said he found it hard to understand where things had gone wrong, so he listed all the things they'd fought about.'

Caro scrunched up her face. 'Bit mental but carry on.'

'I thought it was a good idea.' Bella scowled. 'I couldn't put my finger on what had gone wrong with me and Evan. I mean, I thought of one or two times where we seemed to be going off in different directions, but that was it. So last night I did it too. I made a list and it really helped me solidify a few things.'

Caro let out a breath and placed a hand on her bump.

'Caro? What's wrong? Caro? Shit. Have you got a contraction? What's happening? How far along are you again? Is it okay if the baby comes now? It's not, is it? Shit. Shall I call Mum? Mum!'

Cynthia shot into the kitchen.

'What?' Bella asked as Caro's face changed into a grin.

'It's indigestion, you lunatic, that's all. Calm down. Jesus, I'm glad you're a teacher and not a midwife.'

So was Bella. After everything she'd seen that day and Caro's words, she couldn't handle anything else. With a tut their mum went back to the living room and Caro stopped drying the dishes and sat down at the kitchen table.

'So what did you figure out?'

'Just that things hadn't been great for a while and I just didn't really notice. I was so wrapped up in our comfortable routine I didn't see how unspectacular it was and for ages there'd been so many things we didn't agree on, opinions of his that had changed. I think we'd got to a point in our lives where we wanted different things and he saw it before I did.'

'He still shouldn't have left you the way he did, trying to sneak out leaving you a Dear John and a ransacked bedroom.'

'No, he shouldn't, but then Evan was nowhere near as perfect as I made him out to be.'

'And Nick Cowley?' Caro asked with a mischievous glint in her eye.

'I don't know about perfect, but he's a pretty good specimen of what a man should be.'

Caro rubbed her bump. 'Then I don't think it matters what your head says, Bella. Your heart's clearly telling you all you need to know.'

For once Bella was happy to admit that her little sister may well be right.

Chapter 20

The week passed in a blur of smiling activity for Bella as she came closer to understanding her feelings for Nick. Pantomime rehearsals were stepping up a gear as showtime grew ever nearer, which meant Mrs Brody was a bundle of highly strung nerves. Wednesday's staff meeting had been unusually exciting after the latest rehearsal had been even more of a shambles than the first. Voices had been raised (Mr Osbourne's and Mrs Brody's) and criticisms voiced (Mr Osbourne again, though vehemently denied by Mrs Brody). Mrs White had refereed events wonderfully while Bella, Johnny and Nina sat silently spectating. It seemed that some of the children weren't bothering to learn their learns and those who had, had forgotten them already. They were still having trouble with the new rendition of 'Poker Face' and most of the time the children fudged their way through the bits they couldn't remember and sung extra loudly on the bits they could to make up for it.

For Bella, it was a huge relief that things between Freddie and Amias had quietened down, though she was unsure if he was just turning his attention to someone else. He'd been teasing poor little Hannah and two times this week he'd been on red on the behaviour chart and off to Mrs White's office. Something was definitely going on and knowing that his father was having an affair, Bella wondered if he'd picked up on something at home. She resolved to have a chat with him this week and see if he'd open up to her.

Most of all though, she couldn't stop thinking about Nick and longed for pick-up time each day when she might see him and the possibility of a conversation, albeit a brief one, lingered in the air. As the clock ticked around to three-fifteen, she fidgeted and flittered like a teenager. She hadn't yet told him about her encounter with Mr Cole because it wasn't something to discuss in a few minutes at the end of the school day and though she'd thought about knocking on his door and going in, the right time had never come. She and Nick had been like ships passing in the night with the hours of work needed on the giving tree. She was busier than ever, exactly what she'd hoped for when she'd started this whole thing, but it had meant she couldn't just drop in and mention in passing something so important.

More and more donations were flooding in and now Saturday morning had come, she was looking forward to seeing Nick and Freddie as they came to volunteer for a few hours.

On this particular Saturday, something magical floated in the air. Knowing that it was the Christmas parade that evening and that the village lights and church's nativity scene would be revealed, it felt like Christmas was almost here.

Bella stood in her little hut now decorated with tinsel and fairy lights, going through the forms and preparing more tags for the giving tree. Still in her hat, scarf and big winter coat, she shivered. There wasn't any heating in the little hut, and she hoped her nose wasn't turning red from the cold. The number of forms had reduced from the initial rush of requests, but she was glad they were still coming in and that the tags were being taken and wishes fulfilled. In general, there seemed to be an air of joy in the village. Whether that was down to the season or her work with the tree she didn't know, but it was lovely to see everyone so happy.

Picking up the next form in the pile, she read through, scowling. Surely this was made up. She'd never heard of a Mrs Vi Brator. Had she? She searched her mind. Bella thought she knew everyone in the village, but maybe she didn't. Perhaps they were new, but the address wasn't familiar either. As she was running through all the people she knew in her mind, Nick and Freddie entered the hut.

'Morning.'

'Hi, Bella,' Freddie said, shaking off his coat despite the freezing temperature.

'Everything all right?' asked Nick.

Bella frowned. As she moved past the personal details to the actual request, heat rocketed up her back. Mrs Vi Brator was requesting an intimate pleasure device 'strong enough to make your teeth rattle'. Finally, she got the joke. 'Very funny. Idiot.'

'What's that?' Nick asked. 'Are you sure you're okay? You've gone all pink.'

Looking up and seeing Nick's handsome face, her skin prickled. 'Yes,' she shouted far louder than was necessary. 'It's nothing. I'm fine. It's absolutely nothing.' She hid the form behind her back and Nick narrowed his eyes suspiciously. Bella then scrunched the form into a ball and threw it to the corner of the desk out of the way.

'Okay.' Nick hesitated as he pointed to some presents. 'Shall we get started wrapping?'

'Yes, please.' Bella edged over, taking her file with her, but as she read the next form, she couldn't stop herself speaking out loud. 'Here's another one,' she declared. Someone had clearly been playing silly buggers. 'Listen to this—'

'Whoa!' Nick held up his hands to stop her. 'I thought these forms were confidential.'

'Real ones are but these are just nonsense. Listen, Mr Al Coholic would like a bath full of booze and . . .' she flipped to the next one '. . . Mrs Moore-On would like an encyclopaedia.' Despite herself, she began to chuckle.

'Someone's had far too much time on their hands.' Nick laughed as he started cutting wrapping paper with Freddie. 'Was that another one of them?'

She glanced at where he was pointing and absent-mindedly replied that it was as she went through, weeding out the nonsense from the real requests. It wasn't until Nick grabbed it and unfurled the paper that she realised her mistake.

'No, don't read that it's – it's—' She tried to grab the paper from his hand, but he held it aloft. As she reached up, her body pressed into his and desire fired through her. From the way Nick had stared down at her, she'd thought he'd felt it too. With her body on fire, she backed away.

As Nick read, his eyes widened, and a mischievous grin spread over his face. 'It really is, isn't it?'

Freddie asked, 'What is it, Dad?'

'Nothing, mate. Just someone being silly and asking for silly things.'

'Like what?'

'Never you mind.'

Bella was just about to organise the day's tasks when Nina ran into the hut, breathing heavily as if she'd run all the way here. 'Gosh, Nina, what's wrong?'

'It's Mr Tomlin. He's called in sick. Says he's not well.'

Nick edged over. 'He was a bit peaky when I saw him in the village shop yesterday.'

'Then we've got no—' Bella stopped herself from saying it in front of Freddie. She moved Nina away and after asking Freddie to start choosing the wrapping paper for the next present Nick joined them too. 'We've got no Santa.'

'What are we going to do?' asked Nina. 'Mr Whittaker's not coming in till later. He's got to take Mitzie to the vet. She ate something yesterday that's upset her tummy. I'll spare you the precise details he gave me about what he came down to this morning. To be honest, it's put me off ever getting a dog.'

'He's probably been feeding her people food again. He's been told it's too rich for her, but he does spoil that dog.'

Nina checked her watch. 'The grotto opens in ten minutes and children are already starting to arrive. What are we going to do?'

They couldn't disappoint all those children and they didn't have any other old men to take the part. Sadly, a Mrs Santa just wasn't going to cut it and she didn't trust her dad not to say something inappropriate, so he was out. 'Wait!' Bella declared. They didn't have an old man to take the part, but they did have a young one right there. She turned to Nick.

'Why are you looking at me like . . . Oh no! No! No. No. No. No. No.' He shook his head then leaned in and whispered, 'What about Freddie?'

'He can stay with me and help wrap the donations,' Bella replied, crossing her arms over her chest. 'Don't worry. I'll look after him.'

'Or he could come to the information point with me,' Nina said. 'It'd give him a change and I've got a secret stash of chocolate buttons there.'

'We all know about your secret stash,' Bella replied. 'Why do you think it never goes down?'

'Oh.' Nina pushed her hair back from her face. 'I never realised that actually.'

'You just thought you'd had the same bag of chocolate buttons for the three weeks?'

'Maybe.'

Bella smiled at her friend, then turned back to Nick. 'Anyway, there's no one else.'

'But I'm not jolly.'

'Of course you are. You're perfectly jolly. You just need to deepen your voice a little.'

'What's wrong with my voice?'

'Nothing.' She panicked now, thinking she'd upset him. 'Nothing. It's just not old-mannish. It's more young-mannish . . .' She searched for more descriptive words. 'Kind of . . . gruff and sexy-ish. No, not sexy, just umm . . .' Nick's gaze stopped on her while Nina giggled. Why did she keep doing this? Why was she unable to speak to him without embarrassing herself? Bella hurried on, her heart palpitating. 'It's just not like a jolly old man. Know what I mean? You have to help us.'

After staring at her for a second too long he pulled his eyes away and let out a deep, heavy sigh. 'Fine. Let me just tell Freddie I'm helping somewhere else for a bit.'

'Brilliant,' said Nina. 'We'll get you kitted out in no time.'

'Why do I have a feeling I'm going to regret this?'

'It's only for the morning. We'll get Mr Whittaker to take over this afternoon,' Bella called out after him.

Nick spun and walked backwards. 'You owe me, Bella. You owe me big time.'

'I promise I'll make it up to you,' she replied, and as her body replayed the feeling of being pressed against him, she let her thoughts wander to exactly how she could do that and how wonderful that might be.

As lunchtime neared, Bella and Freddie made their way to the volunteers' hut in the centre of Bluebell Park. They'd spent the whole morning talking about how excited they were for Christmas, and she was pleased to see that despite missing his mum he was still able to enjoy the season. What a little trouper. They were both particularly excited for the Christmas parade and seeing the village become a magical Christmas fairyland.

'You stay in here with Hazel, Freddie, and I'll go fetch us a sandwich and find your dad. I'm sure he's finished helping Nina by now. Don't move though, okay? You must stay in here.'

'I will,' he replied and as Hazel nodded her understanding through the open door, Bella made her way to the grotto.

Only a couple of children remained in the queue and Bella edged her way inside. As she stared at the scene before her, at the magic she'd created, pride filled her. The sparkling fairy lights, fake snow, piles of presents under the twinkling tree and large chair with a wonderfully cheerful Santa perched in it, made her feel like a child. A little girl was sitting on the chair next to Nick, listing all the things she wanted for Christmas, counting them off on her fingers as she went.

'And I'd like a unicorn and a new bike with streamers on the handlebars and a basket to put the cat in.'

'The cat?' Nick's voice almost slipped, and he lowered it again. Bella muffled her laugh. 'Well, have you been a good girl this year?'

The little girl nodded. 'I have, haven't I, Mummy?'

The Mum tipped her head from side to side. 'Well . . . I'm not sure . . .' The little girl's face froze and the mum laughed. 'Yes, she has, Santa. She's been very good.'

Nick leaned in and winked. 'I knew that already.' The little girl giggled, pressing her hand to her mouth. 'I think you're definitely on the nice list, but I need you to go to bed early on Christmas Eve so that I can leave you something special under the tree. Is that a deal?'

'Deal,' she declared.

'In that case, here's a little something for being such a good girl so far this year.' He took a gift from the large sack next to him and handed it to her and she danced out of the grotto.

Bella couldn't tear herself away as he dealt with the last few children and then closed the grotto door behind them. He was so kind and caring. So gentle and thoughtful.

Pulling off his hat, Nick said, 'I'm absolutely roasting in this.' He went to tug off the beard, but the elastic had stuck behind his ears. Feeling the need to be near him again, Bella reached out and unhinged it, easing it down. Nick reached up too and his fingers reasted on hers. He looked down at her, a little flushed from the heat of the Santa suit, with eyes bright and clear. She wished he would kiss her and for a second his eyes dropped to her lips and his head tilted a fraction. He drew nearer. Was he thinking about it too? Time seemed to stretch out before them but was over all too soon as he cleared his throat and inched away.

Bella stepped back and he finished removing the fake beard and jacket that he'd worn over his jumper. 'Thank you for helping us out,' Bella said. 'Sounds like you did a brilliant job.'

'No problem. It was fun actually.'

'Mr Whittaker's back now so he'll take over this afternoon and

204

Nina's going to call in on Mr Tomlin tonight. Hopefully he'll be back tomorrow.'

'Okay. Where's Freddie?'

'He's in the volunteers' hut with Hazel having some lunch. I thought you two might want to head off and spend some time together as you've been doing this all morning.'

'Only if you're sure? We don't mind sticking around.'

As he'd decided not to kiss her, she needed some space. She didn't know whether to be happy that it had appeared he'd wanted to or sad that it didn't happen. She kept her voice level. 'It's fine. You guys should go. You've done so much for us already.'

'Okay, then. I did promise him a games tournament before the parade tonight. Are you still coming? Tonight, I mean.'

A spark of hope reignited. 'Yeah, definitely. I wouldn't miss it.'

'See you at seven then?'

She nodded. 'Seven. Meet you at the gate.'

As happy as she was, confusion flooded her senses. Nick removed the large red trousers from over his jeans and Bella felt the need to turn away. He was still getting changed after all and the idea of him undressing was doing unnerving things to her body. She'd almost forgotten what desire was with Evan. That had been another thing that had died without her realising. They still had sex, but it was all rather automatic, squeezed in at the end of a day because they felt it was something they should do, but she'd buried any concerns under the idea that they still probably had more sex than any of their friends.

Nick stopped in front of her and handed her the Santa costume. 'So, I'll see you later.' She nodded, unable to speak as emotions swirled and whispered in her head.

Nick closed the door, and Bella flopped down into Santa's chair. Was she too old to ask Santa for something on her Christmas list? Whether it was too soon after her break-up or not, she was definitely falling for Nick Cowley and a tiny part of her brain was convinced he had feelings for her too.

Chapter 21

'Why are you getting changed, Dad?'

'Because I want to look nice,' Nick said without thinking. Then added, 'And I don't want to get cold.'

'But you'll be wearing your coat. You don't need to look nice underneath.'

Nick smiled. You couldn't fault his logic. It was a logic he'd shared not so long ago, but he wanted to make an effort. To feel good when he saw Bella. 'I'm almost done. Are you ready?' Freddie nodded. 'You need to wash your face – you've got dinner all round your chops.'

Freddie wiped with his sleeve and managed to remove most of it. It would do. Bella wouldn't mind. She was so easy-going, so happy. She'd been like a fresh winter wind bursting into his house and blowing all the cobwebs and dust away. She'd certainly done that to his heart. He thought of the moment her body had pressed against his in the shed. That had been special enough but when she'd helped get the beard off in the grotto, he felt something so strong it nearly knocked him over. His chest had set on fire and he'd longed to reach out and hold her, to wrap his hands around her waist and pull her close. Her lips called out to be kissed and the idea of that hadn't left him all day. Even when he'd been playing games with Freddie this afternoon, his mind had wandered, picturing what it would be like, imagining the feelings inside him.

From his window he could see Bella walking down the path to the front door. 'Come on, mate. It's time.'

The two of them raced downstairs and Freddie rushed to pull

on his trainers and grab his coat. Nick opened the front door, letting in a cold, icy blast as he pulled on his own coat. 'Hey, sorry we're running late.'

'I don't think you are,' Bella replied, checking her watch. 'I might be a little early. I'm always early for things. Just one of those people.'

'We're almost ready. Freddie, have you got your hat, scarf and gloves?'

'Yes, Dad.' Freddie joined her and placed his hand inside Bella's, walking down the path and chatting about the things they'd done that day.

He wanted to find it heart-warming and to smile, but a sharp pain stabbed inside, pushing away the warmth the scene brought. Paige should have been the one holding Freddie's hand, taking him to the Christmas parade. She should be here with her son. So many times he'd done things with Freddie wishing she was there. He knew Bella would never try and take her place, and he loved that Freddie liked her so much, but at times it still made him angry that Paige had left Freddie as easily as she'd left him. But he had to push those thoughts from his mind before they ruined his evening. He couldn't undo what Paige had done, but he could look to the future.

They made their way to the green to see the nativity scene in place and the large Christmas tree beside it. The duck pond stood quiet and empty beside it although some of the ducks had taken refuge by the manger. It had all but frozen over the other day, and the ducks hunkered down under the rushes. The village Christmas tree still stood in darkness, but some of the decorations sparkled in the light from the old Victorian-style streetlamps and the moon and stars shone brightly above them. It was a cloudless night, and no doubt a frost would glitter the streets by morning.

'Do you mind if we stand near my folks?' Bella asked. 'I mean, you might want to stand near yours.'

'I'll catch up with them later if they're here. They don't always come to watch.'

'They don't? Why not?'

'They're not bothered about this sort of thing. They think Christmas is a bit over-commercialised.'

'Oh.' She raised her eyebrows in surprise.

'That shocks you, doesn't it? It shocked Paige too.' As soon as he mentioned her name Bella dropped her eyes to the ground and he kicked himself. Literally. When no one was looking he bashed one foot against the other. What idiot brings up their ex-wife? Well, wife because he was technically still married. He hadn't got around to sorting out divorce papers because it was something he felt he should tell her in person. Only he didn't know where exactly she was. His anger erupted again, and he pushed it down, eager to enjoy the night. 'Let's go and stand with your folks.'

They ambled over and Nick didn't fail to notice the grin Caro gave Bella. 'Hi, Mr and Mrs Moore. Caro, Luke. You guys okay?'

'Nick,' Mungo said slapping his hand on his shoulder and giving it a squeeze. 'And young Freddie. How are you, young man?'

'Fine, thanks.'

'No, you're not,' announced Cynthia, placing her hands on her hips. 'You've got nothing to eat or drink. Come on, let's find you something yummy. Annie's Tearoom is open just down the lane. Is it all right if I take him to get a hot chocolate and a cookie, Nick?'

'Yeah, sure,' he replied, a little surprised at the warm welcome, though knowing the Moores he shouldn't have been. 'Here let me give you some money.'

'Nonsense. No, no, no.' Cynthia waved one hand at him while the other was held out to Freddie. Without hesitation Freddie trotted off with Cynthia, grinning at the prospect of treats.

Mungo chuckled. 'I think our grandchild is going to be in trouble or we will be when Caro keeps telling us off for spoiling them.'

'That's what grandparents are for, isn't it?'

He and Mungo talked about gardening and work while Bella and Caro caught up. Being with Bella's family felt so natural, and he wasn't the least bit embarrassed that every one of the Moore family were in some kind of Christmassy outfit. A Santa hat adorned Mungo's head while Cynthia wore a red bobble hat complete with antlers he suspected she'd knitted herself.

Bella finished her conversation with Caro and stood by his side. 'I see Mum's already kidnapped Freddie. I think she's always been a little disappointed I hadn't provided any grandchildren by now.'

'I can't imagine your parents would ever be disappointed in you, Bella. You're—' He felt suddenly self-conscious over the compliments he wanted to shower on her. 'You're—'

Seeing his evident humiliation, Bella carried on, though the look in her eye told him she knew he was hoping to say something special. 'Poor Freddie, I hope he's okay. Mum can be a little intimidating in her Christmas madness.'

'He'll be fine. The most he'll get from being kidnapped by your mum is a sugar rush or a tummy ache. Who's Santa tonight?'

'Mr Whittaker agreed to stay on as long as I buy him some of Mrs Bumble's mulled wine.'

'Good man. I was worried you might ask me.'

'I couldn't ask you to miss out on doing this with Freddie. Who, by the way, might have more than just a sugar rush.' Bella pointed at Freddie coming back with three enormous cookies and a loaded hot chocolate.

Nick's mouth watered. 'You have to admit that does look good.'

'It does, but I'm not moving until I've seen the parade. This is one of my favourite nights of the year.'

Bella's joy for Christmas couldn't be contained in her grin or in the air of excitement that radiated from her, and Nick found himself smiling too. Last year, he had watched the parade with Freddie and Paige, but Paige had taken no enjoyment in it. She moaned about the naffness of the floats, the lack of build-up and how small-scale everything was in Meadowbank. She'd wanted to go to Winter Wonderland in London, but Nick had never fancied that. The crowds, the noise, the fear of Freddie getting lost. It just wasn't for him, and he wasn't sure if Freddie would enjoy it all that much either. Nick knew he should have seen it for the warning sign it was but hadn't wanted to admit it, much like Bella had talked about the other day. If Nick was honest, he'd been slowly falling out of love with his wife for a long time, but the bond of shared parental responsibility had shrouded it.

'All right, mate?' said Len as he and Trish stopped beside them, crowding in to see the green. Peter scurried through to stand with Freddie.

'Wow, Freddie, where did you get that from?'

Freddie mumbled a reply through a mouthful of white chocolate and cranberry cookie and Peter turned around looking hopefully at Trish.

'After the parade, okay?'

Bella said hello and after a quick chat edged over to her parents to speak to them.

'So,' said Len. 'Here with the delectable Miss Moore, hey?'

'I'm here with you too, mate, and the rest of the village.'

'You two make a good couple – don't they, Trish?'

'They do and I for one am very happy about it. She was far too good for Evan, and you were far too good for Paige. I'm happy for you both. She'll be good for Freddie too.'

'She's very easy to fall in love with,' Len agreed. 'Not as easy as you, my love,' he added under Trish's glare. 'But she's a diamond, and she doesn't know it.'

Not like Paige, thought Nick. Paige had always known she was pretty, and she'd always known how in love with her he was. He'd confused attitude for confidence and Paige had attitude in bucketloads. Bella, on the other hand, had an unassuming confidence. She knew who and what she was, and that confidence made her sexy. She made her way back over to them as the choir arrived on the green. In the silence that descended Nick heard the grass crunch underfoot where it was beginning to frost.

The small community choir that had sung at the grotto

unveiling at Bluebell Park came in long flowing cloaks, holding their hymn sheets. One held a candle-lit lantern on a long crook. It was like something out of Dickens. Though he hadn't actually read any since school.

'It's starting,' Bella said, and Freddie gazed up at her, smiling and content.

Nick's heart felt fit to burst. He'd been dreading this Christmas. Worried because it would be just the two of them. Troubled that Freddie would be sad and wouldn't want to participate, but he was seeing a change in his son too. He'd actually come in for a cuddle this morning. Snuggled into bed and chatting about the games they were to play during their tournament. There was no getting away from the fact that this year would be painful, but there was no reason it couldn't be filled with happy memories too. Ones that would outweigh the sadness.

Further down the lane Nick spotted the Coles and their son Amias. The boy was enjoying the scene just as every other child was. It was almost inconceivable that he could have acted the way he did. Nick still didn't know why Amias had done it. Freddie had said nothing, and he didn't want to ask Bella in case it put her in a difficult position. He thought again about what the policeman said about apologising and asking him to drop the charges, but he hadn't been able to bring himself to do it. Sometimes he felt like he'd rather die than apologise to that supercilious idiot, but he wasn't about to leave his son to someone else's care while he went to prison. He couldn't think about that now though. If the police didn't come and tell him it was all fine in the next few days, he'd have to swallow his pride but until then he'd ignore it and enjoy himself.

Bella must have seen him looking over as she forgot the parade and said, 'Nick, listen I have to tell you—'

He could feel her breath on his ear, sending shivers over his skin. It overloaded his senses. The noise flared as the parade started and the choir began to sing. 'Tell me later, okay?'

The first few notes of 'Deck the Halls' filled the silence, and the lights were switched on in the nativity scene, which sent a few of the sleepy ducks, who had taken shelter there, squawking and quacking away. A second later the tree lit up, casting a magical golden glow over the green. The bright white lights sparkled in the moonlight and reflected off the still water of the duck pond and Meadowbank river. Anticipation mounted in the crowd as everyone in the village gasped. The choir sang a few more traditional songs with everyone joining in and then the Christmas music rang out from the speaker system erected behind the nativity scene. It did look a bit like the singing was coming from a large plastic donkey stood at the side of the tiny barn, but everyone began jiggling along as the first float emerged from the darkness.

Mr Miller's open-top convertible had been covered in tinsel and his wife was dressed as a fairy godmother hanging out of the back. Her large ballgown had been adorned with strings of fairy lights and she waved a light-up wand in the air. She must have been freezing but her smile never faltered. After a short gap, the next float began circling around the green.

Next up was one of the local lad's pick-up trucks. Lights adorned the bumper and an enormous cardboard house, decorated to look like a gingerbread house, stood on the back. His two young children waved at everyone from beside it as the mum, dressed as an elf, threw out packets of sweets. One landed by Mungo's feet, and he picked it up before handing it to Nick with a grin.

More floats came past ranging from decorated work trucks with giant light-up presents, to a vintage car, beautifully decorated with a wreath and Mrs Santa standing up in the back.

As he glanced at Bella's face, he could see how much she was enjoying it, and Freddie too. Every time a new float came past, she bent down to talk to Freddie, and they pointed and laughed at various things, enjoying each and every moment. Nick stepped forwards wanting to be involved. One hand rested on Freddie's shoulder and without thinking the other went to sit on the curve of Bella's waist. She spun to look at him and he worried he'd gone too far, but then she smiled, and he felt alive again.

The final float circled round the furthest side of the green and Nick heard Freddie and Bella gasp in excitement. His jaw dropped open too. He'd never seen anything so magical in the Meadowbank Christmas parade. Adam Noble, the local carpenter, had created a sleigh and it was pulled along by an old shire horse with Mr MacMahon of Spring Farm holding the reins. The sleigh itself had carefully hidden wheels, but it didn't lessen the magic and Freddie was jumping up and down on the spot.

'Dad, look! Look, Dad! It's a horse! Dad!'

'I can see, son,' he replied, laughing. 'Isn't it great?'

You'd have thought he lived in the city and had never seen a horse before, rather than them constantly galloping in the fields all around them.

'Wow,' Bella and Trish said, before staring at each other and laughing.

Amelia Williams, Adam's fiancée, walked behind the sleigh with him, both dressed as elves along with his mum Lynne, who was handing out even more sweets to the little ones. In the sleigh itself, Mr Whittaker, dressed as Santa, waved at the children.

'Wasn't it brilliant?' said Bella, turning back to him once it was finished. Her face had flushed from the excitement and her dark blonde hair framed her face as it poked out from under her hat. She was so radiantly happy, and he wanted to bask in that warmth. Trish, Len and Peter drifted away, leaving him and Freddie with Bella's family. 'And we can go and get our trees next weekend. At least, that's what my family do. We don't like to leave it too late.'

'Can we, Dad?' Freddie asked. 'Can we get a real tree this year?'

'We've always had a fake one,' he explained to Bella. 'Paige hated having to clean up falling needles and she didn't like the smell.'

'Really? I love the smell.'

'The smell of what?' asked her dad coming over.

'We're talking about real Christmas trees and how we always get ours next weekend.'

'It's a Moore family tradition. Would you two like to come along? Come and join the gang for the day?'

'I don't know if they even want a real tree, Dad.' She mouthed the word *sorry* to Nick, but he couldn't think of anything he'd like to do more and seeing Freddie's pleading face had him agreeing in an instant.

'We'd love to. Wouldn't we, son?'

'Yes, please!'

'Brilliant. I'll tell Cynthia there's two more for breakfast on Saturday.'

Bella added, 'We always have a big celebratory breakfast together before we go to Bluebell Park, but you don't have to come to that if you don't want to.'

'Oh, can we, Dad, please?'

Mungo smiled. 'We do always have an excellent breakfast on tree-buying day. There's something for everyone.'

Seymour Cole sauntered past as they made their way back to their house. He cast his eyes over Nick and Bella but didn't speak.

Nick swallowed, holding his head high.

'Nick,' Bella said gently. 'There's something—'

'Aren't you at Bluebell Park next weekend, Bella?' he asked, eager to steer the conversation away from Mr Cole.

'I always have the day off just for this,' she replied a little sadly.

'Then, if it's no trouble, Mungo, it'd be rude not to.' Nick pushed down his worries over Seymour Cole. Seeing him had been like being caught in a snowdrift. He felt frozen and suffocated, but no one needed their evening ruined with him moping. Instead, he held out his hand to Freddie, enjoying the smile he received from his boy. 'Shall we have one more hot chocolate before we go home, mate? I could do with warming up a bit.'

Chapter 22

'You've got another date?' Cynthia asked Nina, and Bella grinned, happy the attention was away from her for a change.

Since Nick had agreed to go Christmas tree shopping with them, her mum and sister had been teasing her mercilessly. The mention of smoochy-smoochy kissy time had been pretty much non-stop and Bella worried Caro would overexcite herself so much the baby might arrive early. When Nick had placed his hand on her waist at the Christmas parade, she'd wanted to move to his side so he could hold her tighter. She'd thought about wrapping her fingers in his but worried it was too big a leap right now, but the feeling it created hadn't left her.

Cynthia had given up all pretence at present wrapping and watched Nina. 'Is it an official date this time?'

Nina's face grew redder and the orange light from the fire made it even brighter. 'I don't know. I think so. How do you know if it's an official date or not?'

Caro took one of the cushions from the sofa and placed it behind her back then wiggled again to get comfortable. 'I think both of you have to use the word to make it count.'

'So we both have to say it's a date?'

'Yeah. It's a bit like summoning a ghost. Don't you have to say its name three times or something to make it appear?'

'Where did you hear that?' Bella giggled.

'I don't know. I read it somewhere.'

'Well, it's not a date. Johnny definitely hasn't said that word.'

'What does he say then?' asked Cynthia.

'He just says "the pub". I'm worried if I use it first, he'll call it off and I'll look like a dick.'

'No you won't,' Bella said. 'And he wouldn't call it off either. You were meant to be together. Did he suggest it this time or was it you again?'

'He did.'

'Then he definitely won't call it off and I think you can class it as a date regardless of whether he calls it that or not.'

'Bella's right,' her mum said. 'You were meant to be together. You can just see it when you're around each other.'

'Like Bella and Nick Cowley,' Caro added, a teasing glint in her eye. Now it was Bella's turn to blush. She hoped Caro wasn't about to start puckering her lips and making kissing noises. She immediately did and Bella told her to stop. 'Things seem to be going very well there though. You have to admit it.'

'Not on purpose,' Bella protested. Though she'd accepted her feelings for Nick, she still wondered what other people would say. 'We just seem to keep seeing each other.' She cut out the Christmas tree shape, moving the card in one hand and scissors in the other.

An influx of toys had been deposited at school as term neared its end, and the four of them were wrapping the last few presents and making tags for the few forms that had been given in that week. The number handed in was declining but with just over two weeks till Christmas Bella needed to make them quickly and get them on the tree if they were to be taken and fulfilled.

'You can't keep away from him,' Caro continued.

That much was true.

'Have you told him about your trip to the Coles' house yet?' asked Cynthia.

Bella stopped work and pushed back her hair. It flopped forward again, and she tucked it behind her ear. 'Not yet. There just hasn't been the right time. If I see him when he comes to pick Freddie up from school, I'm always busy sending my kids out and I don't want to trot over and tell him in front of everyone.

At Bluebell Park we're so busy that sometimes it slips my mind and again, Freddie's always around. It's just one of those conversations I don't want to whisper in front of him and risk Freddie overhearing. As far as he's concerned, the police spoke to Nick about something to do with work. If he hears something about the Coles, it might upset him, and Nick might need time to digest the information anyway.'

'It is quite a big thing,' Nina said. She was sat cross-legged on the floor by the hearth, nibbling a mince pie.

'I've been so busy with all the giving tree stuff that even in the evenings it hasn't seemed right to just pop in and drop a bombshell like that. I mean, I don't even know if it's worked so I might just be getting his hopes up for nothing.'

Bella realised everyone was watching her. She hadn't really been talking to them, more thinking out loud, but at least she hadn't rambled on incoherently like she did in front of Nick.

'You're going to have to tell him soon,' Cynthia said. 'Even if it comes to nothing, I'm sure he'd want to know you did that for him.'

'I don't want to make things weird, or for him to think I was interfering.'

'I'm sure he won't. He's a good lad. I like Nick.'

'More than Evan,' Caro added, and Bella started.

'Really?'

'I don't mean that horribly. We all thought he was nice enough, but he never fully threw himself into our family, did he?'

'No, he didn't.' Having already realised this herself, Bella chose not to dwell.

The time she was spending with Freddie and Nick was more fulfilling than she ever remembered feeling with Evan. Their relationship had become somewhat empty. She supposed they were so busy getting through the day-to-day she hadn't taken a step back and really seen what was in front of her. The way Evan had spoken to her at their meeting still hurt, but she had to admit some of the things he'd said were true. Over a month had gone by, and the excitement of Christmas and the school Christmas play next week had replaced the last remnants of hurt. Now she was left with only bruised memories that were gradually being traded up for happier ones.

Cynthia finished wrapping a present and handed it to Bella to add the tag. They were working the same way she, Nick and Freddie did at the park, and as much as she loved her girl time, she couldn't wait for Saturday and the chance to see him again. This time, they'd be spending the whole day together and he'd be throwing himself into her family's life.

Her mum sat back with a mince pie and a glass of red wine. 'I was surprised Nick and Freddie are joining us on Saturday. I always thought he was more reserved than that, but I like the way he's taking us as we are. What do you think Freddie would like to eat for breakfast?'

Bella smiled. Her mum was so warm and nurturing. 'I'm sure Freddie will eat whatever you make. Your pancakes are always a winner.'

'Then I'll make extra. No stingy portions at your house.'

'I'm going to have the biggest fry-up imaginable,' Caro declared.

Nina picked up another mince pie. 'Stop it, you're making me jealous. And hungry.'

'You can come too if you like.'

'That's okay. I'm already volunteering that day.' She began fiddling with the silver case her mince pie had come in, and the way she averted her eyes told Bella there was more to the refusal than first met the eye.

'What's going on?' she asked.

'Nothing.'

Realisation dawned and a wide grin spread across Bella's face. 'Is Johnny coming up to get a tree? With you? Are you doing it together?'

Nina shuffled about. 'Maybe.'

She, Caro and Cynthia erupted into cheers and laughter.

'Well, that's fabulous news. It's definitely the start of something,' Bella said.

'I think this whole giving tree might be here to stay too,' Cynthia replied. 'With how well it's done this year, you won't be able to just forget about it and not do it next year. You've signed yourself up for this for many years to come, I think.'

'Do you really think so?'

She nodded. 'People keep stopping me in the street to tell me how thankful they are to you and how proud I must be. Which I am. You've always been a generous and caring girl, but this has taken it to the next level.'

'Well I couldn't have done it without you all, so I'm very grateful.'

Caro rested her hands on top of her bump. 'It's been fun. Even if my back aches from bending over wrapping presents for the grotto. But it was lovely to see the kids up there waiting in line all excited and jumping about. Christmas has definitely been extra special this year.'

As the fire crackled in the huge inglenook, Bella let the warmth wash over her. The cottage felt so her own now it was almost as if Evan had never been there. She hadn't redecorated or even changed her furnishings, but the atmosphere had transformed. It had always felt homely but now it felt like her nest. A safe and cosy sanctuary.

'Do you really think people will want to keep doing it?' Bella asked, pulling her mind back to the conversation.

'Of course they will. Everyone's loved getting involved.'

The thought that in years to come, people would be carrying on the tradition she'd started filled her with such a strong sense of pride she was sure it radiated from every pore. The parade and Christmas tree on the green were a huge part of Meadowbank life and brought the community together in a spectacular way. Could she hope that the giving tree would one day be a part of village tradition too?

It seemed too much to hope for. But so far, this Christmas had given her far more than she ever imagined it could, and the special day hadn't even arrived yet.

Chapter 23

'What about this one?' asked Nick, holding out the tree for Bella to admire.

'Hmm.' She pressed a gloved finger to her lips. 'What do you think, Freddie?'

Freddie shook his head. 'Nah, it's all wonky. Look.' He pointed to one side of the tree where the branches hadn't yet dropped from the netting.

'You need to remember that they'll fall back into their natural position once it's out of the netting and happily in your house.'

Nick spotted her mum and dad having a similar discussion. 'Why didn't your dad bring his car? How is he going to get it home?'

'That's another crazy tradition. Dad and Mum always carry their tree home.'

'Really?' Nick's voice rang with astonishment, and she couldn't blame him.

'Yep. I didn't say we only had good family traditions. Believe me, Caro and I have tried to convince them to stop but they insist. You can call them lunatics, I don't mind.'

'That is a little bit bonkers.'

'I think that one's too bushy,' she declared, having studied the tree. 'What about this one?'

Pulling out another one, Bella asked the man to undo the netting so she could have a proper look at it. The smell of pine filled the air of Bluebell Park, and she kept glancing at Freddie to make sure he was enjoying himself. He giggled like he was in an actual winter wonderland, staring at the trees as if he'd never seen one before. It was cold enough to snow, but none had arrived yet. The addition of the Christmas tree seller made the park seem even more special and Meadowbank residents flocked to buy trees of all different sizes.

Now December was well and truly here, the whole village appeared like something from a Christmas movie. Cottages glittered with icicle lights hanging under eaves and windowsills, and gardens sparkled with decorations. The tree on the green shone over everything, making sure no one forgot what time of year it was, and every child saw it with renewed excitement when they left school each day.

Nick had arrived for breakfast with Freddie, and Bella's nerves had tangled inside her. There was always the worry that her family would be too much for a man who must have been dreading the Christmas season, but Nick had proved her worries groundless. Her parents had welcomed him in as she knew they would, and even better, he'd allowed himself to be a part of it all.

Freddie's eyes had almost bulged out of his head when he'd seen the spread that dominated the kitchen worktops. Pancakes with every conceivable topping were next to various drinks, some of which were far too alcoholic for ten o'clock in the morning. The smell of bacon and sausages perfumed the air from dishes warming in the oven and her mum smiled as she stirred a giant pot of scrambled egg.

'Wow!' Freddie had exclaimed as they'd all gathered around the table and dug in. It was a little cosier with the two extra places, but Bella was pleased to see that Nick and Freddie hadn't minded. Nick had chatted with Luke and her dad, praised her mum, which went down a treat, and best of all, he'd continually glanced at her throughout. Freddie had been a credit to him, showing wonderful manners, except for the one time he tried to stick too much food in his mouth, but Luke had done exactly the same thing every year since he'd joined them, so Nick had nothing to be embarrassed about.

The walk to the park had helped them digest some of the breakfast and she'd gone ahead with Freddie while Nick drove over in his truck. They'd talked a bit about school and he was feeling more settled, which was wonderful to know. He held no grudge against Amias who he felt must be unhappy. It was very astute, and she planned on telling Nick later, if they got a moment alone. She hoped more than anything they would.

Seeing him watch her now, she drew her mind back to the present and the choosing of the tree. Walking around so she could assess it from all angles, she said, 'Yep, I think this is the one. Don't you, Freddie? I think it's perfect.'

'Is it our turn now?'

'It sure is little man,' Nick said, and Freddie began punching the air in joy. Like a rocket he rushed around from tree to tree, pulling at the netting and trying to figure out which one would be best. Bella never had any idea until the netting came off and she could see it open up. Freddie seemed to be making decisions based on how they smelled. She stood by Nick's side, shoulder to shoulder, closer than she would normally stand next to someone, and together they watched him decide.

'I think he's enjoying himself.'

'We've never done this before. It's all new to him.'

Though she didn't want to spoil the moment, she knew she had to tell him about her visit to Mr Cole. Conscious of her mum's advice on Wednesday night and Nick and Mr Cole's silent exchange at the Christmas parade, she said, 'Have you heard from Mr Cole at all?'

'No. I haven't.'

She tensed. If her visit hadn't worked, there was nothing more she could do. She couldn't very well go to the police and say, 'Don't believe him, he's a cheating scumbag.' She supposed she should be lucky Mr Cole hadn't gone straight to Mrs White but how she wished it had worked.

'Thankfully, I haven't heard from the police either,' Nick said with relief. 'I told myself that if I hadn't heard from them by Wednesday, I'd go round and apologise but I couldn't bring myself to do it. I kept putting it off with work and everything.'

'He should be apologising to you. We all saw him start it. Just hang in there, okay? I'm sure everything will be all right.' She really hoped Mr Cole's conscience would make him drop the charges, or at the very least his embarrassment at being caught cheating would force him to. Did he even have a conscience?

'I've never seen him so excited about Christmas,' Nick said, drawing a line under the conversation. She couldn't blame him not wanting to talk about it. 'I mean, he's always loved putting the tree up and decorating it, but this is next-level excitement. I love that your family has made a whole day of it. It makes the whole thing an experience.'

'Apparently my sister and I used to moan that putting the tree up was over too quickly—'

'Moan? You and your sister?' He shook his head. 'I can't believe that.'

'I think they made it up too.' She adjusted her scarf as a gust of wind blew it over her shoulder. 'Anyway, Mum and Dad decided to drag it out further by starting the breakfast thing. And now we have so many decorations for inside the house and out that it really does take a whole day to put everything up.'

A moment's sadness gripped her that she'd be decorating her tree alone this year. Her family had said they'd come round and help, but she'd told them she preferred to do it solo. Part of her wanted to reclaim the event for herself and another wanted to hide in case she got upset. Yet, standing here with Nick, her world felt fuller than it had in a long time and even if she did end up doing it alone, she'd enjoy it too. If Evan couldn't appreciate her and her mad family, he didn't deserve to be a part of it.

'Can we get this one, Dad?'

'It's about eight foot tall, mate.' Nick laughed. 'We won't get it in the house. We'll have to bend it sideways.'

'Oh.' Freddie's head slumped down.

'What about this one?' asked Bella, moving to a particularly fragrant tree that was only six foot in height so with a little off the end it should fit perfectly in their cottage. 'Look, it's got lovely bushy branches and none of the needles are coming off.'

'Can we, Dad? Can we get that one?'

Nick smiled. 'Sure thing, son. We'll need a base for it too.'

'I know where they are.'

Freddie raced off and Nick and Bella followed. Before long, both trees were in the back of his truck and they'd met back up with Bella's family for an apple-pie mulled cider: a new recipe from Annie's that sounded delicious. They huddled together listening to the excited chatter of children queuing at the grotto and the Christmas pop songs playing out of the speaker. Bella glanced at the giving tree, happy to see that nearly all the tags had gone.

She wandered over, eager to see which ones were left and as she reached the tree Freddie joined her.

'Has someone taken my dad's tag yet, Bella?'

She turned the tags, reading each in turn. Every time she'd topped them up, she'd checked to see if it had been taken, but it had still hung from its branch. She supposed it was because it was for a man rather than a child. People were obviously prioritising kids over adults or the elderly, which was fair enough, but her stomach tightened into a knot. Poor Freddie's heart would break if he thought his dad wasn't getting a present. Then an idea struck her. She'd been thinking of getting Nick and Freddie something to say thank you for all their help. Couldn't she take the tag? Before she could change her mind, she said, 'Yep, it's gone. Looks like your dad will be getting a nice gift after all.'

'Yay. Does anyone want my pencils? I've still got them.'

She ruffled his hair. 'Why don't you gather them up and we'll give them as an extra present to someone. What do you say?'

Freddie agreed and headed back to the swings. When he'd

turned, Bella quickly took the tag down from the branch and popped it into her pocket. She knew just what to get Nick and she'd decide on something for Freddie too.

Nick and Freddie drove the trees back and Bella walked home with her family. Caro waddled along discussing Braxton Hicks and how sore her boobs were while her parents just about managed to get the tree to the village with most of its branches intact. Divorce might have been on the cards had either of them had breath left to speak but thankfully they were too exhausted to argue.

Everyone peeled off to their respective homes and Bella found Nick waiting for her at her gate. His smile sent a thrill into her body, warming her up from the inside. The sky had grown dark grey and threatened rain or possibly hail. The temperature was so low that if she hadn't already read the weather forecast, she'd think it might snow.

'Shall we get this inside then?'

Bella found her key and opened the door for him. 'This way.' She led him through to the living room where she'd already positioned the bright red base. Freddie had opted for a gold one, which he'd insisted on holding all the way home. Nick then positioned the tree and Bella and Freddie held it steady while he tightened the screws of the base. Once it was solid and square, she cut off the netting and Freddie stared open-mouthed when the branches fell, splaying out around the thick trunk.

'It looks amazing.'

His eyes were bright and his smile so wide she laughed. 'It looks lovely just like this, doesn't it, but I've got that whole box of decorations to put on it. And I need to water it.'

'I'll do that if you get me a jug,' Nick said, kneeling down on the floor. Bella quickly fetched it for him.

'Do we have to water our tree, Daddy?'

'Yep, every day. So you'll have to remind me.'

'I will. I can do it before school.'

'That'd be really helpful, mate. Thanks. I'm sure together we'll look after it.'

'Who are you going to decorate your tree with, Bella?'

She'd expected his innocent question to send a pain into her heart, but all it did was remind her that at least this time she wouldn't have Evan coming along behind her and moving things up or down a branch. He'd always been a bit pernickety with the tree.

'I'm going to do it on my own,' she replied, cheerfully.

'Because your boyfriend left?'

'Freddie!' Nick exclaimed, his cheeks colouring in embarrassment. 'Bella, I'm sorry.'

'It's fine,' she replied with a chuckle. 'Yes, Freddie, my boyfriend and I split up, so I'll be doing it on my own this year, but I don't mind. I like decorating the tree.'

'We could do it with you.'

Nick glanced at her tentatively. 'Freddie—'

'We could help her so she doesn't feel sad.'

'Oh, Freddie.' Bella's heart filled with affection for the kind little boy in front of her. It had been five weeks now since the split: a week for each year she and Evan had been together. Perhaps Caro was right and the heart didn't work to a timetable. She did want them to stay and the idea of decorating the tree together, drinking hot chocolates and eating the mince pies she'd bought for the occasion would be lovely. Nick hadn't said that they couldn't. And though it was difficult to be sure what his expression meant, she took a chance.

'I'd like that very much, Freddie, but only if you and your dad would like to. I thought you'd want to do your own tree.'

'We can do it after,' Freddie declared. 'Then I get to decorate two trees. This is the best Christmas ever.'

Nick smiled as he shrugged. 'Then I guess that's settled.'

Bella unwrapped her scarf from around her neck and unzipped her coat. 'You'd better take those layers off then and I'll get a fire started.'

'I'll do that if you like,' said Nick, moving to the large wood burner. 'Freddie can help me. Can't you, mate?'

'Shall I make some hot chocolates and get some mince pies or are you both still full from breakfast?'

'I could manage a snack.'

'I don't like mince pies, though,' Freddie said, sneering.

'Do you like snowballs?'

'What are snowballs?'

'What are snowballs? *What are snowballs?* They're only the most delicious things in the world. They're marshmallows covered in chocolate and sprinkled with coconut, so they look like little snowballs. Haven't you had one before?'

Freddie shook his head and abandoned his dad to follow Bella into the kitchen.

With more Christmas music playing, the three of them decorated the tree. Bella let Freddie place things wherever he wanted, grateful for his help, and too quickly the tree was done. It shone with the pale gold lights she loved. Ones that twinkled so beautifully at night with the fire burning beside it. The rest of the decorations were a mixture of red and gold and the star on top nearly touched the ceiling.

'Bella, can I use your toilet, please?' asked Freddie.

'Of course you can. It's up the stairs and to your left.'

'Is that this one?' He waved his right hand in the air.

'No, your other left.'

'Cool.' He ran off and Bella stared at the tree once more.

'Beautiful,' said Nick and when she turned to see him looking straight at her, she wondered if he was talking about her.

Nerves fizzed and sparked in her stomach, and she moved to the fire. Though her body had come over extraordinarily warm, her hands were cold, and she held them in front of the flickering orange flames. Nick did the same and when his broad hands were level with hers, their fingers touched. Excitement ran up her arm and through her veins as Nick wrapped his hand around hers.

Before she knew what was happening, he was turning her towards him, edging closer. The fizzing in her stomach erupted into her chest, filling her lungs with dancing butterflies. She stepped closer. Without saying a word, his lips gently swept hers. It was the softest, most tentative and tender kiss she'd ever experienced. Vulnerable and nervous, gentle and enquiring. They separated by a millimetre, only for her to return the kiss again.

The crackling of the fire and the Christmas music filled the silence around them, but all Bella could hear was the joy pulsing through her body, banging like a drum in her ears. Any doubts she'd had about the timing of their relationship faded. He'd kissed her in the one moment they had together. The one moment Freddie had left the room.

Freddie.

'Freddie!' Nick and Bella dropped each other's hands and she darted back just as footsteps sounded on the creaking old stairs and he ran through the door into the living room.

'Can we do our tree now, Dad?' he shouted, bounding through the door.

Nick pushed his hands into his pockets as if to show nothing had been happening, but a faint blush appeared on his stubbled cheeks. Bella hid the smile that was attempting to get out by biting her lip.

Despite Freddie's arrival and the abrupt end to the kiss, another new, precious memory had formed for her. After all her fears, this Christmas was proving to be rather eventful.

Nick turned his gaze to Freddie as the afternoon twilight fell. The flames glittered in his eyes, brightening them, and Bella stopped herself from begging him to stay. They'd spent hours on her tree, moving pieces up and down, inching the lights forwards or back, but Freddie had shown no impatience. Instead, he'd eaten four snowballs and drunk two hot chocolates, enjoying every moment as much as she had and she was grateful for his patience, especially given the last few minutes.

'Yes, you should definitely go and do your tree. It's getting dark already. Thank you, both.' She tried to read Nick's expression, but it was hard to tell what he was thinking now. The air around them seemed charged as if they had both now recognised the new, exciting start they'd found. Hoping he'd understand her meaning, she said, 'You've made my day more special than I could have hoped for.'

Without any hesitation, Freddie ran forwards and hugged her. She hoped Nick would approve, especially after the kiss, and was relieved to see him smiling. 'Go on, you two. Go get your tree done. I've got some presents to wrap for the giving tree.'

When they'd left, she pulled the tag for Nick from her coat pocket and ran her finger along the edge. For all its lightness, the kiss had been intense, bursting with emotion. Sensual and loving. Unyielding. It spoke of so much more to come, and Bella's heart squeezed at the thought of what might happen now. So many unexpected and happy memories had already formed for her this Christmas, would she be lucky enough to have even more?

Chapter 24

Nick and Freddie set to decorating their tree and if it was possible, Freddie showed even more enthusiasm than he had for Bella's.

Had Nick actually just kissed her? He hadn't planned to, but he'd been swept up in the moment. The Christmas music, the real tree filling the room with the scent of pine, the crackling warmth of the fire. Her fingers had been cold, and he'd been taken by the unexpected urge to warm them in his hands and then before he knew it, he was kissing her. He wouldn't have done it if Freddie had been there of course, but Freddie's short absence had given a rare chance and one he'd felt the need to take. He'd never been so nervous in all his life. For a brief and terrifying second, he'd been worried she might pull away, leap backwards in abject horror. What the hell did he think he was doing? They were just friends. But no. Nothing like that had happened and after that first gentle sweep of her full, soft lips, she'd kissed him too. The world had changed in that second. It had become a happier, brighter place. And then Freddie had returned, running down the stairs like a herd of wildebeest stampeding across the plains.

Realising he hadn't spoken to Freddie for a few moments, Nick said, 'It was nice of you to ask Bella if she wanted help with her tree, mate. That was really kind. I'm proud of you.'

'Thanks, Dad.' Freddie hung a decoration he'd made at school the year before and then stood back to admire it. Deciding it should go somewhere else he took it off the branch and placed it further down. 'I like Bella. She's nice.'

I like her too. Nick's heart gave a double beat. He did like her, a lot. He wouldn't have kissed her if he hadn't. But was Freddie ready to have someone new in his life? Though it had only been six months since Paige had left, the marriage had been over for a long time and while Nick was beginning to feel ready for a new relationship, he had no idea if Freddie was. How did he even talk about that sort of thing with a ten-year-old?

'She is nice, isn't she?' was the best he could come up with to test the waters. 'It was nice of you to hug her. I think that meant a lot to her.'

'Thanks. I like Miss Moore – I mean, Bella – because she stopped Amias bullying me. He hasn't teased me at all since he . . .' Freddie didn't finish, but Nick knew what he meant, and he wrapped his arm around him as they placed more decorations on the tree.

Should he ask about Paige? Was it best to encourage him to talk or leave it and see if he said anything? Knowing that he'd kept some things quiet about Amias's teasing before the big incident, Nick decided to ask. It was better Freddie knew he could talk about her and how he was feeling.

'Are you okay about Mum not being here? Do you miss her?'

Freddie nodded but kept his gaze on the tree. His lip quivered and a tear rolled slowly down his cheek. Nick pulled him in tight. 'Oh, mate, come here.' He lifted him up into his arms. 'Gosh you're getting big, little man. It's okay to miss your mum, my boy. And it's okay to cry.'

'Do you miss her too?'

'Sometimes.'

Freddie buried his head into his dad's shoulder. 'I wish she hadn't gone.'

'Me too, mate.' But he meant it more for Freddie than himself.

'Do you think she'll send me a present?'

In that moment Nick hated her again. Freddie shouldn't be worrying about his mum remembering to send him a Christmas present. She should be here with him, wiping his tears and decorating the house. He didn't have an answer. Nick wondered whether to buy something then address it to Freddie from Paige, but he couldn't lie to his boy. They had a special bond, and he didn't want to risk it being ruined as he tried to cover for her, but he wouldn't paint her as the villain either. They'd both grown apart and he was partly responsible for that too. What she'd done in running off was awful, but he didn't want Freddie to hate her. He stuttered the best response he could think of.

'I don't know, mate. I hope so. I know she loves you very much and I'm sure she'll send something if she can. Now, I know that you're still probably full of those snowballs not to mention that crazy breakfast, but shall we get this tree done and have some dinner?'

Freddie wiped his eyes and Nick plopped him on the floor before turning up the Christmas music, hoping it would help his son forget the pain. He'd made a fire in his own burner and the cottage was warm and cosy as it transformed to their own magical Christmas grotto. He had been worried the real tree would need more decorations being bigger than the fake one in the loft, but in fact it needed less. Nick and Freddie both enjoyed seeing the lush green of the branches behind the decorations and when it was finished, some baubles and tinsel still lay in the box.

'What shall we do with these, Dad?'

'Well, I was thinking we could put our old fake tree up in your room. What do you think?'

'A tree in my room? Yes, please.'

'Let's get the rest of the stuff up and then I'll get it out of the loft.'

They danced around, hanging decorations across the ceiling from corner to corner. Tinsel lay on each windowsill and the selection of cuddly Christmas teddies, dancing Santas and singing snowmen that he and Paige had collected every year since Freddie was born were given pride of place in front of the fire. Freddie grabbed his favourite one, a battery-operated bear that read *The Night Before Christmas* and he snuggled on the sofa with it.

'Is that one going in your room as usual?'

'Yeah. He's my favourite. He reads me to sleep.'

'Come on then, let's get this tree out of the loft. Then I'm having a sit-down. I don't know about you, but my feet are killing me.'

Nick's foot had only just landed on the bottom step when there was a knock at the door. He opened it and the skin around his eyes tightened as he took in the sight before him. His hand gripped the doorknob for support. This was worse than Seymour Cole. It was worse than the police. Nick shook his head, disbelievingly.

'Paige.'

'Mum!' Freddie's voice was barely more than a whisper. 'Mum, you're back.'

A suitcase stood beside her, battered and bruised from its travels. Nick couldn't help but stare at it, then up at Paige. Her skin was deeply tanned, and her blonde hair had lightened to streaks of white from the sun. She must have been cold in the long floaty skirt she was wearing. He'd half expected to see sandals on her feet, but they were encased in cowboy boots.

'Hi, Nick.' Her voice was softer than he ever remembered it being and he couldn't help the way his heart melted as Freddie threw himself at her. Her arms wrapped around him, clinging on to him as though she wished she'd never let him go. Could he hope that was how she felt?

Was it possible she was back for good?

Chapter 25

'I've missed you so much, Mum.' Freddie sobbed into her chest, and she ran her hand through his hair, holding him close.

'I've missed you too, darling.'

Had she? Had she really? Nick knew he should be grateful she was back in time for Christmas, at least he presumed she was staying judging by the suitcase, but he couldn't stop the anger forcing its way up through his body, pushing through every muscle and bone. He wanted to shout and scream and bellow and swear and challenge her on all the decisions she'd made that meant leaving him and Freddie behind.

'Can I come in?'

I don't know, are you staying or are you going to break my boy's heart again? He forced the words back and stood aside. 'Sure.'

'Thanks.'

Freddie let Paige go enough for her to walk in but clung on tight to her waist. Nick could see the taut skin of his white knuckles as he laced his fingers around her. Nick picked up the suitcase and brought it inside.

'We did the tree today, Mum. You just missed it. We've got a real one. Look.' Freddie whirled around, as excited as he had been that morning when they'd picked it.

'Wow. It looks great. What made you get a real one?'

'We fancied a change,' Nick replied tersely. He placed the suitcase down behind the sofa and went to the kitchen to make a cup of tea. He didn't know what else to do or what to say. Every thought running through his head was accusatory or angry and he didn't want to expose Freddie to that. It was better he kept himself busy.

'Bella always gets a real tree,' Freddie said. 'So we got one too. I love it. Don't you, Mummy?'

He'd gone straight back to calling her Mummy and it hurt. He didn't want Freddie to be angry with his mum. He wanted him to be happy to see her, to hold her and cuddle her. He didn't want him to hold on to the hurt the same way he was, but in some small way it felt like a betrayal. Nick shook the thought away. He was projecting his own grown-up feelings. This must be confusing enough for Freddie.

'Bella next door?' Paige asked, turning to Nick. Was there something in her voice? A tone? An insinuation? He told himself to calm down.

'Yes.' Nick filled the kettle and flicked it on. The kiss flashed through his mind again. All his feelings of excitement and joy were fading fast and confusion took its place. 'She's helped sort out some stuff at school.'

'Right.' Paige turned her gaze back to Freddie and squeezed him again, but didn't ask any more about it. Freddie pulled her on to the sofa.

Nick busied himself with finding the cups. Didn't she want to know what had been happening? Didn't she care what he'd meant? She'd missed so much: the end-of-term excitement of Moving On Day; certificates and awards. She'd missed the last day of term and the early finish. On previous years, Nick had always cut his day short, and they'd go to Witchbury for a burger, or if the weather was nice, they'd grab a picnic and sit on the green. She'd missed so many things, not all of them major and exciting, most of them were normal day-to-day things, but they were just as important, and he couldn't forgive that. His irritation grew again, and he carried on with the tea.

'Are you staying for dinner?' Freddie asked. 'Are you going to stay here again? Can you read me a bedtime story? Can I show you my lightsaber?' Freddie dived off the sofa and ran up to his room to search for it.

'Wow,' said Paige, standing up and turning to face Nick. 'He's grown so much. His face has changed. I've missed him.'

'Have you?' This time Nick couldn't stop it. The words were out of his mouth before he could even think about the consequences.

Paige raised her head, indignant. 'Of course I have. He's my son and I love him.'

That didn't stop you leaving though, did it? Nick clenched his teeth. 'We haven't heard from you in months, Paige, and then you just turn up without a word?'

She dropped her eyes downwards and he noticed that she wasn't wearing her wedding ring. The pain rose again. He hadn't exactly expected her to. She had left after all, but its absence was noticeable.

Freddie came charging back downstairs in his stormtrooper outfit, waving the lightsaber in the air. 'Look, Mum.'

'I've made you some squash, Freddie. You should come and have a drink.'

'Okay. Can I show Mum my game?'

'Of course, mate.' Nick cupped his son's face and ran his thumb over the soft skin of his cheek. He must be a mess of emotions inside. Happy, sad, scared, relieved. He felt similar. There was too much. It was crazy. Freddie gulped down the juice and went back to sitting next to Paige who had retaken her seat.

Nick entered the living room and sat down in the armchair furthest away from her. The conversation was, as Nick had expected, dominated by Freddie, and he didn't blame his son one bit. He had six months of things to catch up on and who knew how much time he had to say it in.

Time ticked on without a word between them and when they spoke it was cold and polite. He had to feed Freddie and that meant either throwing Paige out or asking her to stay. He didn't want to do either. He just wanted her to disappear again so things could go back to how they were a few hours ago. A few hours ago, he was getting his life back, moving forward. He'd connected with someone magically and unexpectedly, and now his life was in tatters again, but if he didn't ask her to stay, what did that say to Freddie?

'Paige, are you joining us for dinner, or do you have plans?'

'No plans,' she replied a little shyly. 'I'd love to stay if that's okay?'

It wasn't, but what else could he do? Freddie stared between them, and Nick smiled to let him know everything was all right.

After a strained dinner of pasta, because that was the only thing Nick could manage to cook without thinking too much, Freddie was eventually packed off to bed.

'Will you be here tomorrow, Mummy? Are you back? Are you staying here again?'

She hesitated then mumbled some answers and when she came down from reading him his story, she sat on the sofa opposite Nick. He'd opened a beer and poured her a glass of wine. It felt like the civilised thing to do but it was a pretence: an attempt at normality.

'So why are you back, Paige? It didn't work out in Bali?' There was an edge to his words he couldn't hide. 'Or had you moved on from Bali?'

'I know you're angry, Nick, and you have every right to be.'

You're damn right I do.

'Things didn't work out. I made a rash decision, and I threw away everything I love.'

She toyed with her fingernails. The nail varnish was chipped and patchy. He didn't know what she'd been doing in Bali or where she'd been living, but he couldn't help wondering if her real reason for returning was the comforts of home rather than the people who occupied it.

'I've missed you and Freddie more than I can say. I've even missed this little place. I'd forgotten how pretty it is here at Christmas. I made the decision yesterday that I wanted to come home and I booked the first flight back—'

'Yesterday?' he interrupted. 'You made the decision yesterday?'

Nick was careful to keep his voice low, knowing Freddie probably wouldn't be asleep yet. But the fact that she'd only made the decision yesterday went to show that she was still the same impulsive person she'd been before. She might have changed her mind but for how long? How long before Meadowbank was too quiet for her again and she left once more, breaking Freddie's heart in the process. Nick knew if he said anything it would escalate into a row and that wasn't what Freddie needed to hear. He'd have to ask Trish to have Freddie so they could talk properly. That was if Trish could be trusted not to murder Paige first. He sipped his beer, letting it ease his burning throat.

'So?' The answer was fired back, and a hardness came over her features.

'So where are you staying?' Paige adjusted the fabric of her long skirt but didn't answer. 'You want to stay here, don't you?'

'This is still my home, Nick.'

'Your home?' Hurt pushed itself to the surface, destroying any semblance of civility. 'You left it the day you left us to go off with some bloke and live somewhere more exotic. To start your life over. That's what you said to me when you left. You can't just come waltzing back now you've changed your mind.'

'I've got nowhere else to go, Nick, and I am Freddie's mum. I want to be with him.'

Nick took three slow, deep breaths. 'You can stay until we figure out what we're going to do from now on.'

'I know what I want to do, Nick. I want to come home to you and Freddie.'

'You just want to wake up tomorrow like the last six months have never happened and play happy families?' He launched upright and paced around the living room.

'I don't want to play happy families, Nick, and that's a bit insulting. I just want us to try again, and I am entitled to be here. My name's on the mortgage too.'

She might technically be entitled to stay, but morally? Nick swigged his beer. A part of him wanted to believe her but how could he after everything she'd done. She stood in front of him, looking him straight in the eye.

'I've got nowhere else to go. I want us to try again. I've realised how much I love you and I've never stopped loving Freddie. I want my old life back.'

'It's not that easy,' he said quietly, turning away and Paige's voice softened.

'It can be. If we want it to be.'

He cursed under his breath as a knock at the door took his attention and he strode over to open it. 'Bella, hi.' Panic washed over him, and he wished with all his heart he could remove Paige from the living room and invite her in instead. 'Is everything okay?'

Bella's eyes focused on the suitcase then lifted to Paige who was watching them both, one hand on her hip the other on her wine glass. He wanted Bella to glance back at him so she could see how much he didn't want this etched on his face. But Bella being Bella, she mustered a smile. 'Paige, you're back.'

'I am,' Paige replied with a coolness that made Nick's blood boil. 'Here to stay.' He shot a glance over his shoulder, then turned to Bella. Pain was so clearly written on her face he wanted to kiss her again but everything they'd had earlier was being snatched away.

'Right. Well, umm, welcome home, Paige.' Her eyes were dulled with sadness. 'I . . . Sorry to disturb you, umm – Freddie left his scarf at mine, so I thought I'd better return it. I didn't know if you were off out tomorrow, and it's supposed to get colder. I'm sorry, I didn't know you had – well I better go. Bye, Nick. Bye, Paige. Nice to umm . . . see you back.'

She pressed the scarf into his hands, and he wanted to hold on to them, feel the warmth of her skin as he had before, but she pulled away, tears in her eyes. Nick closed the door. He wished he could call out to her but had no idea what to say. Paige had retaken her seat.

Here to stay? Was she really?

Bella had slipped away from him now. He could feel it. Could see it in her eyes when she'd seen Paige was back.

Though he wanted Paige to be a part of Freddie's life, was there any way they could try again? Could he ever get over his anger at her abandoning them? Some hurts ran too deep. But as he thought of his son lying asleep upstairs, this didn't seem to be about him and what he wanted. It wasn't even about what he could and couldn't forgive. This was about Freddie. His gorgeous, kind, caring boy who deserved a family: a mother in his life who loved him and could see him every day.

Nick stroked the soft fleecy fabric of the scarf. He'd always promised he'd do everything he could to protect Freddie and make him happy. Was taking Paige back the right thing for his son? It would be the ultimate sacrifice for him because whichever way he looked at it, taking Paige back meant letting Bella go, and it seemed she'd already gone.

Chapter 26

Bella hadn't thought her heart could break twice in the space of two months, but evidently it could.

After leaving Nick's cottage having seen Paige (she hadn't even heard her arrive), she'd spent the rest of the evening crying more than she ever had over Evan. Though nothing of the kind had been said during their short exchange, she felt like her future had been stolen from her. The possibilities that earlier that day had existed so firmly were now rubbed out, leaving her bereft and alone.

'Saw Paige in the village shop yesterday,' said her mum.

They were supposed to be dealing with the last-minute donations that had come in, but there wasn't much wrapping being done. Cynthia was on her second glass of wine, cradling it in her lap, quietly furious. Caro was stretched out on the sofa because sitting up meant the baby pressed on her bladder and she kept needing a wee, or at least, feeling like she did, which in her mind was a form of torture. Nina was occasionally folding paper around the box she was trying to wrap but kept losing interest as they discussed the only topic that had been debated in Meadowbank since Saturday night.

Paige's return hadn't escaped anyone's attention and if it had, the way she was waltzing around like she'd always loved the place and was relieved to be back definitely hadn't. Bella hadn't seen Nick as he'd been working, and Paige had done every drop-off and pick-up at school. Bella had worked hard to ignore the almost smug, triumphant smile that appeared on her face, but it had been difficult. Her eyes were red from crying and there was no hiding the complete desolation her soul had endured.

'I didn't speak to her, of course.'

'You didn't ignore her, did you?' Bella asked. The last thing she needed was more gossip and her mum had been more than a little annoyed since Bella had told her what had happened. The list of swear words she'd come out to describe Paige had been really quite impressive and even her dad had been shocked by a few of them.

'No,' Cynthia replied emphatically. 'I just ducked to the back of the shop until she'd gone, but it took everything I had not to walk up to her and give her a slap. And I didn't need to blank her because Lynne Noble did that for me. After her husband left her with young Adam, she's not got the patience for people who abandon their children for any length of time and quite rightly so if you ask me.'

'I'm surprised she didn't say something,' said Caro, smiling. 'She's not exactly backwards in coming forwards.'

'I think her face said it all. Paige kind of scarpered as soon as Lynne walked into the shop and glared at her. As lovely as she is, she can be quite terrifying. But that Paige. Urgh! Bloody woman. Awful. I couldn't stand her before, and I hate her even more now for what she's done to you. And that boy. I mean—'

Before Cynthia could launch into a full-on tirade that would inevitably end up in wine being spilled as she angrily flailed her arms around, Bella asked, 'What was she saying?'

'It's not what she said, it's what she didn't say. She's not saying the words out loud, but she's all but implying that she and Nick are back together. She's coming up with some guff about the break being good for them and both knowing exactly what they want now.'

Bella raised her head, then dropped it down again. She'd been nursing the same glass of wine for an hour. The queasiness had returned every morning, just as it had after Evan had left, only this time it was even fiercer. Why was she surprised? She couldn't compete. Paige was Freddie's mum and though she'd thought Nick wasn't in love with Paige anymore – he'd even said so himself – clearly seeing her again had sparked those old feelings back into life. Any hope that she'd had of being wrong had dwindled slowly over the last three days when he hadn't been round to see her. She could only think that he now considered the kiss to be a mistake. It was over. Over before it had even begun.

'I hate the woman,' said Caro, creeping up onto her elbow so she could take a sip of her hot chocolate. 'I never liked her. Always thinking she was better than the rest of us. Swanning around the village like it was all beneath her. And now . . . now she's just smug. Plain and simple. Smuggy McSmugface. If I see her coming, I walk the other way, but you can't really avoid people in Meadowbank.'

The fire crackled in the grate. It was almost too hot where she was sitting on the floor, and Bella hugged her knees in. 'Do you think Nick told her how close we were getting? Maybe she doesn't have any idea?'

Cynthia held out her hand to her daughter and Bella reached up from her seat on the floor. 'If he hasn't told her, someone else in the village will and if it all played out as you say, I'm sure she must have had an idea when you turned up. You're not great at hiding your emotions, my girl. She'd have seen the shock on your face.'

'And embarrassment.'

'Why were you embarrassed?' asked Nina. She'd given up wrapping altogether and brushed biscuit crumbs from her jumper. 'You've no reason to be.'

'I just feel like I've made a fool of myself.'

'How? You haven't, Bella. Please don't feel like that. You started spending time with a nice, handsome, single man. That that's changed now isn't your fault and you certainly don't have anything to be embarrassed about.'

'Well said, Nina,' Cynthia added with a nod of her head and a tip of her wine glass.

Bella tried to take it all in. The hardest part was that she'd finally reconciled herself to the idea that she could fall in love again this quickly after Evan. To do that, only to find it wasn't to be seemed an especially cruel twist of fate.

'How's Freddie been in your class?' she asked, not wanting to dwell on that particular aspect too much.

'He's been happy, but you can't really blame him. I think he's still quite uncertain. He's been a little quiet at times and I think he's worried what people will say.'

'He must be a mess of emotions.'

'I'm sure Nick's doing his best to keep him level and calm,' said Cynthia. 'But I'd like to know why he hasn't been round to see you so you can talk about everything that's happened. He owes you that much.'

Bella thought so too, but she knew Nick well enough now to understand that he was the type of man who had to get his head around things before he could reach out to anyone else. It had taken him a long time to ask even his best friends for help with childcare. She couldn't expect him to come round until he knew exactly how he felt and decided what he was going to say. Her spirits sank further. Based on what Paige was saying, his not coming around meant the future he wanted wasn't with her. He'd chosen the mother of his child. His wife.

Cynthia, who still held Bella's hand, gave it a squeeze. 'Shall we wrap these last presents then? You won't have time with the school play tomorrow.'

'It's fine. I'll do them later,' Bella replied. She couldn't muster the energy right now.

After Evan had left, the giving tree had kept her going and it spoke to the depth of her feelings for Nick, that even that couldn't lift her spirits. Bella drank a large mouthful of wine and rested her head against the side of the sofa. She'd really fallen for Nick Cowley and his son, and her life seemed bare and empty without them.

Chapter 27

'Are you okay?' asked Nina, as the children dashed in and out of the toilet for one last wee before showtime. 'Is she going to be here tonight?'

'I imagine so,' Bella replied, tuning back in to Nina's question. 'She'll want to see his play, won't she?'

'Who knows,' Nina replied with a shrug before she took her group back to the classroom.

It was too much to hope that Nick would come alone, or Paige chose not to attend. Freddie would have begged her to be here to see all the hard work he'd put in.

'Are you sure you're okay?' Johnny asked.

'Honestly, I'm fine,' Bella replied, smiling at one of the children as they came out of the toilet so it would look genuine. 'Did you wash your hands?'

'Yes, look.' Johnny held up his hands and wiggled his fingers in the air and one of the children giggled.

'Not you, Mr Feker,' Bella replied in mock annoyance, placing her hands on her hips and tutting. More of the children giggled and for a second her pain receded only to come back ten times stronger when she saw Freddie next in line. He waved and she smiled, trying hard to swallow down the tears threatening to get the better of her.

'Come on then, guys, let's get going. It's nearly showtime.' A moment later, Johnny took some of the children, including Freddie, back to class while Bella waited for Amias to finish. He'd been in there a rather long time.

'Amias?' She knocked on the toilet door. 'Amias, are you okay in

246

there?' The faint sound of sobbing came through the door. 'Amias? Amias, what's wrong? Open the door and come out, please.'

A second later, Amias emerged. The fake beard that had been painted on with face paint had smudged all around his mouth and his eyes were red where he'd rubbed them so fiercely. 'Oh, Amias, what's wrong?'

'I don't want to do it,' he sniffled.

'Do what? The play?' Her nerves unknotted a little. 'Have you got butterflies in your tummy? That's perfectly normal, Amias, but I know you can do it. You've worked hard for this.'

He sniffed again. 'No one likes me.' This time his tears erupted and the shield of mischievousness that had made him seem older, melted away to show just how young and innocent he was.

'That's not true. You've got lots of friends. Richard and Umar are your friends.'

'Richard doesn't like playing with me since we got into trouble, and Umar doesn't want to play with me anymore either.'

'Let's come away from the toilets and sit over here.' She took him to one of the small seats nearby and sat him down. 'Do you think what you did to Freddie has made some of the children a little bit afraid of you?'

He nodded. 'They think I'm going to do it to them too.'

As they still didn't really know why he'd done it, she took the opportunity to ask, hoping it would help her understand a little more. 'Why did you do it, Amias?'

'Because everyone likes Freddie, and no one likes me.'

'Now that's not true. I know lots of children like playing with you, Amias, but sometimes you do tease a bit and I think for some of the children, that can be a little hurtful. What I think we need to do is start some new games, don't you? Perhaps we could start at breaktime tomorrow. You and Freddie and some of the other children can play together. I'm sure he'd be happy to, but perhaps it would be helpful not to tease so much.'

'I only do what my dad does.'

A faint alarm bell began to sound in her head. 'Does he tease you a lot?'

'Not me, my mum.' He began crying again. 'I don't think they love each other anymore.'

'Oh, sweetheart.' She rubbed his arm. 'Why don't we have a chat with Mrs White tomorrow and perhaps she can speak to Mum and Dad and let them know how you're feeling. I know they love you very much and wouldn't want you upset like this.'

After seeing Mr Cole's antics the other day, she could well believe that Amias's parents didn't love each other anymore, but for all their faults, they loved their little boy fiercely. It was why they were so protective of him. This wouldn't be the first time Mrs White had had to speak to parents about apparent difficulties at home and how they were affecting a child, but his admission couldn't be ignored. It was always better to tackle things head on. Not that she'd been brave enough to do that with Nick, but hers was a totally different situation.

'Now, take a deep breath and dry your eyes.' He did as he was told, though his shoulders shook as he did so. 'Shall we get back to class and get you ready to go on? You've worked so hard, Amias, I know everyone will want to see you in the play.'

She held out her hand and Amias took it. When she led him back into class, some of the children stared, surprised to see him so quiet and he tried to hide himself away in the corner. Speaking so she was heard above the din, Bella said, 'Amias is feeling a little nervous, everyone. Can we perhaps help him to feel a bit better?'

'I'm nervous too,' said Leonie in her tiger costume, going over and rubbing his arm like a grown-up would. 'I feel a bit sick actually.'

Nina, Johnny and Bella stared at each other in alarm. Vomiting was the last thing they needed right now, but as Bella knew they would, because children are forgiving and kind, several went over and comforted him, including Freddie, giving him words of encouragement and hugs. Amias's statement explained so much about his recent behaviour. If he was feeling uncertain at home, children often brought their worries into school, and unable to deal with it, he'd lashed out at Freddie. Amias had probably felt a little jealous of Freddie as he had so many friends and a dad who doted on him. She refused to think about Paige and blocked her out of her brain. Looking on now though in the Christmassy classroom, the spirit of the season had won out.

After a final topping up of make-up, straightening of head-dresses, wings and halos, Bella led her class down to the school hall. As she held the door open for them, they filed in and with a roll of her shoulders, she stuck on her teacher smile and followed them inside.

The hall was full of parents and carers sat on the rows of chairs laid out in front of the small stage. A special air of excitement that could only be found at school Christmas plays rang around the room. Parents were excited to see their children perform and, scared that it would all go wrong, crossing everything they had in the hope their children would have fun, and not start crying.

Bella's eyes immediately fell to Nick. His tall frame and broad shoulders were hard to miss. Paige looked tiny next to him, especially given how closely she'd snuggled in. Freddie waved at them both, his hand moving so fast it blurred in Bella's vision. She knew how much his mum's leaving had hurt. Actually, she didn't. She could only imagine that pain. Her mum had always been a stalwart of her life and she couldn't conceive of her upping and leaving for six months only to return again out of the blue. Bella swallowed down her judgement. Nick had never been hers to lay claim to and somehow, she had to get over him.

When he saw her looking over he tried to smile, but it was unclear what it was supposed to convey. Was he sorry that the possibility of love between them had disappeared? Was he sorry Paige was back? How could he be with what it meant for Freddie? She turned her attention back to Mrs White who was welcoming everyone and introducing the play.

Taking her script from beside her and placing it on her lap, she began to follow along, prompting the children when necessary and encouraging them with smiles and thumbs up.

Freddie started them off, reading his line as narrator and his eyes remained on his mum and dad while he did so. All Bella could do was watch from the sidelines as her heart broke.

The first part of the play went surprising well. As the children performed their parts, the parents laughed at the appropriate moments and the 'Poker Face' song went almost perfectly, but as they entered the second act, things began to go a little awry. As well as the usual trips on costumes and trampling of props, baby Jesus was dropped about five times so that by the end the doll's head was becoming decidedly loose until Mary picked him up by the leg, dangling him in the air and it fell off completely.

A couple of the children went off script with additions such as Joseph's, 'We ain't got no money to pay for a room so you'll have to shove us in the stables,' which left little Richard the innkeeper totally confused, and Mrs Brody's smile tacked on with superglue. Mary then made a request to Bella to open all the presents presented to baby Jesus, which Bella had to politely decline. She settled for shaking them vigorously to see if there was anything inside.

Yet still, Bella smiled through it all. The kids' Christmas play was a highlight of her year and all in all it had been a success even though a fight broke out between two of the chorus line, and the donkey decided it was time for a loo break halfway through, shuffling off stage clutching his privates. In hindsight, it might have been an error having the three wise men arrive by scooter as one of them launched across the stage with such force, Mr Osbourne had to catch him at the other end, but overall Mrs Brody had done them all proud.

The children finished with a rendition of 'We Wish You a Merry Christmas' and received a standing ovation. Mrs Brody clutched a bouquet of flowers presented by Mrs White and dabbed at her eyes with a tissue. It was done and the children left the hall with beaming smiles, each teacher leading their class out. Bella couldn't stop herself glancing at Nick one last time as she left the hall and was surprised to see him watching her. She wished now she'd been brave enough to glance at him through the play but had resolutely kept her eyes forwards, knowing if she saw him snuggling up to Paige, there was every chance she'd cry.

As she left the reception area and the children shuffled back down to the classroom, talking loudly and excitedly, she heard a door slam shut and his deep voice carried over the din.

'Bella?'

'I'll take the kids down,' said Nina, hurrying them along before Bella could thank her or follow them.

When Bella turned back, Nick took a tentative step towards her. 'Hello.'

'Hi.' Something passed across his face, and she wondered if her professional tone had hurt him. She hadn't intended to. She just didn't know how to act around him now. Their relationship had grown so much closer, and then rocketed backwards leaving her almost dizzy. 'I just wanted to—' He glanced at the hall door and his hand came out, clearly motioning to Paige whether he meant to or not. 'We haven't had a chance to talk.'

'It's none of my business, Nick.' Though her voice was soft, that seemed to wound him too, but Paige was staying at his house, at *their* home. She was Freddie's mum. His wife. There was nothing Bella could do, and she was, after all, only his neighbour. The kiss had been exceptional, monumental, but without a chance to talk she had no idea what it had meant to him. She'd thought it had meant a future, but everything had halted and their chance had slipped away.

'I just thought . . .' The words tapered into silence.

'You thought?'

Her heart sped up, pounding against her chest. What had he thought? Had he hoped as much as she had that they were starting something special? That a future together was somehow building for them. Had she misread the situation with Paige? Maybe he didn't still love her. She hated how hopeful it made her, knowing that it would mean even deeper pain if she was wrong, which she probably was.

The door swung open again and Seymour Cole came out of the hall. Bella shrank back. 'Ah, Nick, there you are.'

This was not what she needed right now and if he started on Nick again on school grounds, she'd have no option but to intervene.

Seymour glanced towards her, his cheeks colouring as he remembered their last encounter. 'Just wanted to say, no hard feelings, yeah? Better just to forget all about it.' He held out his hand for Nick to shake. Nick eyed it suspiciously like it was all some kind of trick.

He withheld his hand for a moment. 'No police?'

'No police. Silly really. Just – you know how we all get about our kids.' Seymour glanced at Bella again. 'Miss Moore came to see me and we . . . discussed how silly it all was. My fault of course. Apologies.'

Nick glanced between Seymour and her and then shook Seymour's hand. 'My apologies too. I shouldn't have pushed you.'

'All forgotten. All forgotten.' After shaking his hand, Seymour headed back into the hall, leaving them alone once more.

'You spoke to him?' Nick asked her. He sounded shocked. 'When?'

'I just tried to defuse the situation.'

'Bella, I . . . thank you.' The relief on his face was palpable. He reached his hand to the back of his neck, pressing as if to ease the knotted muscles. 'She just turned up, Bella. I didn't know what do. I don't know . . .'

His eyes were kind, sorry, and she didn't want to make this even harder for him. In his position, she'd put her child first too. 'I understand, Nick. It's okay.'

252

Her words were quiet and echoed in the bubble of silence around them. Even though there was nothing but noise on either side of them, the air around them was still. The children could be heard from their classrooms and the parents were chatting and laughing in the hall, yet here they were in a strange kind of reticence.

Nick dropped his eyes. 'I'm sorry, Bella. I'm really sorry.' And he headed back to the hall and his wife.

Chapter 28

'I still can't believe she just turned up like that,' Trish said, placing a huge hunk of roast beef onto a cutting board. She wrapped it in foil and placed the Yorkshire pudding pan into the oven, cranking up the heat. 'The bloody cheek of the woman, after all this time, just turning up like she's been on a long weekend with the girls or something.'

Nick buried his head in his hands, pushing the heels into his eyes. At least Freddie wasn't here. He was having the afternoon with Paige next door while Nick came to Trish and Len's for dinner. He needed some space. Some time to think and he couldn't do that in the house filled with Freddie's happiness and excitement. He couldn't bear being there anymore while Paige suddenly took an interest in everything Freddie had done over the last six months. When Len had knocked on the door an hour ago asking if they wanted to come over, Nick had never agreed to anything as quickly.

Len scoffed loudly. 'When I turned up, she was lounging in the living room like she'd never left.' He poured Nick a large glass of wine. 'You're not going anywhere this afternoon are you, mate?'

'Only to hell and back.'

Len splashed some more wine into his glass.

Nick's head thumped from the lack of sleep he'd experienced all week. Of course he'd offered Paige his bed while he slept on the sofa, but no matter how tired he felt sleep never arrived. Every time he closed his eyes he saw Bella's desolate expression. Had she figured it was the end for them too? Why had Paige had to come back? His future had gone from full of hope to some dreary, post-apocalyptic wasteland. His body had woken up at Bella's kiss and now he was slowly dying again. Shutting down like an out-of-battery robot.

'She keeps saying she's realised what a mistake she made and she's back for good.'

'Huh! I'll believe that when I see it,' Trish said, leaning on the back of Len's chair and grabbing her wine glass for a hefty mouthful. 'She's never been happy living here. Not properly. She's never got involved in anything and I can't see that changing. And the cosy glow of Christmas will wear off and she'll be stuck here in deepest darkest winter when the lanes are muddy quagmires and it rains every school run, and she won't like that one bit. That's when she'll be off again, you mark my words.'

'God, I hope not. It would break Freddie's heart. For Freddie's sake I have to believe what she says.'

'And do you believe you two can be a couple again? Do you actually believe she loves you?'

Nick grabbed a handful of hair and tugged. 'I just don't know. And even if she doesn't love me, Freddie deserves a proper family.'

'There are lots of different types of families these days, Nick,' Len said. 'How long's dinner, love, I'm starving.'

'You're always starving.' After fiddling with pans of steaming veg on the hob, Trish sat down. 'Do you love her enough to try again?'

Nick didn't reply at first. Although he'd told himself he didn't love Paige anymore it felt like a betrayal to Freddie to say it out loud. 'I might have to learn to. Maybe if I try again, it'll happen one day.'

'Rubbish!'

Len's hand shot out. 'Whoa, steady on, love.'

'All right, I'm sorry. It's just seeing her lord it around the village like we're all so lucky to have her here again, has really got my back up. Not to mention that I love you like a brother, Nick, and I hate what she's doing to you and Freddie.' Trish rested her hand on his arm. 'All I'm trying to say is that you deserve to be happy, and what's best for Freddie is a happy mum and dad. He's been mucked around enough. Do you think you could be happy together?'

'I don't know. Possibly.'

'I don't believe you.' Trish released him and sat back, but her voice was still soft. 'I think you do know, and you just don't want to admit it because Paige has always bamboozled you. You've never felt good enough for her.'

'It didn't sound that convincing to me either, mate,' Len added. 'What about that list you made? Doesn't it show you just how bad things had got?'

'Lots of couples try again and make it work.'

'Because they love each other,' Trish said matter-of-factly. 'You don't love Paige and you haven't been in love with her for ages. Don't you think I've noticed that recently you've finally gotten over some of the pain she caused you? You've been getting back to your old self, and I mean the old self before things started to go wrong with your marriage. Not just before she upped and left. You've been so happy. And I hate to be the one to say it, Nick, but I'm not sure Paige really loves you either.'

Nick looked up but didn't know what to say. Deep down her knew that was true, but all he could think about was his lovely boy and that he deserved an easy life. A life where his mum and dad lived at the same address, and he wasn't having to swap between houses.

'And what about Bella?' Len asked with uncharacteristic gentleness.

'What about her?' Nick's voice rang with a defensive edge. 'I'm sorry, mate. But do you not think I've thought about her all the time? We were at the start of something special and now I'm going to have to give it up. You should have seen the pain in her eyes when she saw Paige had come back. And did you know she'd gone to see Mr Cole for me?'

'She's pretty special,' said Len.

Trish sipped her wine. 'I heard from Caro she caught him with another woman and threatened to tell if he didn't drop the charges.'

'Bella?' Nick asked startled. 'Bella did that? For me?'

'Of course she did. She's been falling in love with you, Nick. You and Freddie. She probably did it in a nice way, but Caro would know.'

'At the very least, she's definitely got a soft spot for you, mate,' said Len. 'She wouldn't have kissed you if she hadn't.'

'I'd say it's more than that.'

The kiss had meant so much to him, but love? Could he hope it was something so strong? Nick sat dumbstruck trying to take everything in. He'd known something was growing between them but for her to do something like that for him . . . It was more than anyone had ever done. She loved her job and could have got into a lot of trouble. She'd risked so much . . . for him.

'Poor woman,' whispered Trish and Nick felt wretched. 'Just because Paige is back and wants to be a family doesn't mean you have to go running back to her. Dinner in ten minutes, Peter,' she called out to the living room. 'You can eat in there as a special treat.'

'Trish, it's not that easy. Freddie—'

'It's as easy or hard as you make it, Nick. You just have to be straight with yourself and with Paige. Don't you think you deserve to be happy too?'

He did. He knew he did. The trouble was, Freddie deserved it more and for Freddie to get what he wanted, his mum and dad had to be a couple again. Nick tried to erase the kiss from his mind and force down the feelings he had for Bella. It made him feel almost full, as if they were sitting in his stomach as heavy as rocks. He wasn't sure he'd be able to eat his dinner with how hard it all was. Could he suck up his heartbreak for the sake of his boy? The little pink squirming thing he'd been handed ten years ago and promised he'd do everything he could to keep safe and make happy. He'd have to. Even if it meant breaking his own heart to do it.

Chapter 29

For the last week of term Bella threw herself into work. Her contact with Nick was sparse and Paige seemed to have made herself at home, so Bella found solace at Bluebell Park, finishing the giving tree. She would be sad to see it go, but it had done so much for the village. People often stopped and thanked her, saying what a difference it had made knowing they'd have enough food to eat or gifts for their children. In some ways, it had been her Christmas present to Meadowbank, the village she loved so much.

At school, the end of term always heralded excitement and at Christmas even more so. Apart from a few basic lessons the last week was spent on fun activities with the children; reading Christmas stories and watching festive films. They even had a party in each classroom on the last day of term. The weather had forecast snow, and everyone had their fingers crossed for that rarest of things: a white Christmas.

Bella did her best to regain some of her optimism and whenever she was in company smiled and laughed as if heartbreak wasn't keeping her awake at night or taking over her thoughts during the day. Hers and Nick's steps towards each other had been hesitant but based on solid, heartfelt emotion, so it was crushing to see that Paige had slotted herself into Nick and Freddie's life so seamlessly. As much as she longed to see Nick, it was easier without them running into each other.

Today she'd be making all the deliveries from the giving tree. The culmination of all her hard work. She didn't expect either Nick or Freddie to be volunteering even though it was a Saturday. They probably wanted to spend time as a family as it was the last weekend before Christmas. But to cheer herself up, she'd dressed as an elf and decorated her car with tinsel and lights in as close an approximation of Santa's sleigh as she could manage.

Burying her pain under the pile of presents she was loading into the car, she nipped into the volunteers' hut ensuring she had everything, including a delicious festive spiced latte to see her through until lunchtime.

'Well, that tree of yours was a resounding success, Bella,' said Mr Whittaker. 'You'll be making a lot of people incredibly happy today.'

'I can't believe you've dressed as an elf though,' said Matilda, scowling. She'd thought it a little over the top, but Bella wouldn't be swayed.

Bella peered down at the felt elf shoes complete with bells she'd worn over her ankle boots. Her legs were just about warm in the tights she'd squeezed up over thermal leggings, but she couldn't do without her coat. The sky had taken on that strange grey and orange hue it does when snow is on the way. The air was unusually still and the cold bit through her layers, inching over her skin. Still, she couldn't imagine a better day to deliver presents. The weather was Christmassy, her car was Christmassy, she looked Christmassy, and Meadowbank appeared even more magical in the strange dusky light. As she'd driven to Bluebell Park that morning, lights had sparkled and flashed in the gloom, guiding her way.

The night before Bella had been through everything, double-checking that each form had a corresponding gift and planning her route around the village. All the tags had been taken from the tree and donations made so no one would feel left out. Meadowbank hadn't let her down. And the radio played nothing but Christmas songs, which would undoubtedly lift her spirits if everything else failed to.

'I like my elf costume, Matilda, and you can't be one of Santa's elves and not dress up.'

'But you'll freeze.'

'No, I won't. I'll be in and out of the car all the time anyway. I'll be fine.'

'Well, you best hurry,' said Hazel. 'Snow's on the way.'

'It definitely is,' replied Mr Whittaker, nodding. 'My Mitzie didn't want to go out for a wee this morning. I had to pick her up and take her outside. She only does that when it snows. I gave her a whole sausage for being so brave.'

'You mustn't give that dog people food,' Hazel chided. 'She's getting fat enough as it is.'

'My Mitzie is not fat. She's just . . . poofy. It's all that curly poodle hair.'

Bella giggled. 'You really do pamper that dog, Mr Whittaker.'

'Here,' said Nina, 'I'll load these last bits in while you go and get yourself a hot drink and a snack to take with you.'

Bella gave them all a kiss on the cheek, feeling Mr Whittaker's stubbly whiskers against her skin. 'Thank you all for helping with this. It's so wonderful to know we've made a difference.' Feeling her eyes misting with tears, she said, 'But if it does start coming down with snow, you'll close the park and head home too, won't you? I don't want you being stuck out here or walking back in bad weather. You could trip and fall.'

'We will, we will. We promise,' Mr Whittaker replied. 'Now, be off with you.'

'Bella,' Hazel called, and she paused at the door. 'You've done well with everything you've been through. Very well.'

'Hasn't she just?' said Matilda, leaving her tea and stopping by Bella's side. 'You've been marvellous. You're a real treasure. Not like that Paige. Leaving that poor, lovely man and their poor, lovely boy for six whole months. She's got a nerve if you ask me.'

'More front than Woolworths,' said Mr Whittaker.

'Woolworths hasn't got any front anymore, Mr Whittaker,' Nina said. 'They went out of business years ago.'

'Did they? Well, blow me down.'

Bella left the hut as Mr Whittaker descended into a reminiscence of spending his childhood pocket money in the large Woolworths in Witchbury and after securing her coffee, headed to her car. As she approached, she was surprised to see a truck she recognised, and Nick and Freddie step out of it.

'Hi,' Nick said, edging forwards. His eyes widened as he took her in.

It was the first time she'd seen him since the school Christmas play and her heart beat a fast tattoo as she took him in. Even with his beanie hat pulled down on his head, his hair tufted out underneath and she wanted nothing more than to run her fingers through it. His eyes were penetrating, and his square jaw was covered in stubble as though he hadn't slept for days.

'We're here to volunteer – well, Freddie is. I've – I've got something to do. Is it okay if he comes with you?'

'Oh. Yes – yeah, of course.'

Freddie stared up at him almost fearful and she wondered what was going on. Nick knelt down in front of him. 'You remember what we talked about, mate? It's going to be okay, but you've worked hard on these presents and you deserve to deliver them with Bella. I'll be back soon.'

Freddie nodded, a little subdued compared to how she'd seen him since his mum returned. With a guiding hand from his dad, he walked towards her. She held out her hand for him, and with a final glance at them both, Nick got in his truck and drove away, leaving Bella desperately trying to control her breath.

'Do you want a hot chocolate before we go, Freddie? It's a cold day today. They said we might get snow.'

He brightened a little at the prospect of both. 'Can I have a flake again?'

'I should think so. We're going to need lots of energy.'

'I like your costume, Bella.'

She felt a sudden warmth run up her spine. She'd been so stunned at seeing Nick, she hadn't thought about what an idiot she looked in her elf costume. Brilliant. He was probably thinking he was well shot of her. The rambling lunatic who dressed up as an elf at every available opportunity. But she couldn't do anything about it now. After grabbing a drink for Freddie, an unexpected but not unwelcome addition, they began their deliveries.

The first was to Mrs Barnes. It wasn't strictly on her route, but as she had helped to spark the idea it somehow felt right. Bella exited the car, leaving Freddie in the warm as tiny snowflakes began to fall and she stared at the sky in wonder. Shivering slightly, but unprepared to change out of her outfit, (she wasn't entirely sure she'd be able to get the leggings and tights off without pulling a muscle), she knocked on the door.

'Hi, Mrs Barnes, I have two gifts from Santa for Leonie here.'

'Two?' Mrs Barnes asked.

'One's an extra special gift.'

Bella handed over the small parcel containing pencils and a new pencil case from Freddie. Thinking of Freddie and his kindness filled her heart with love. They'd always come as a package and one she'd accepted whole-heartedly. She knew better than to try and replace his mum, but she had hoped that had hers and Nick's relationship grown, he would at least have become fond of her.

'And here's the other one,' she declared, handing over the beautifully gift-wrapped box. Stepping back, she willed the tears away.

'But I don't know who's bought them?'

'That's the beauty of the tree. Someone has bought this out of love and kindness, but they don't know who for.'

Mrs Barnes's face reddened with appreciation. 'Thank you so much, Bella. I can't tell you what a difference this'll make. We could never have afforded the main present she wanted. We were so worried about disappointing her on Christmas Day.' The tears she'd been holding back began to escape and Bella found herself crying too. If the day was going to go on like this, she'd be a blubbering mess by the end of it.

'Now you've set me off,' joked Bella, wiping her eyes.

Mrs Barnes put the present down and dived forwards, giving her a hug. 'I'm sorry. Hang on before you go.' She darted into the house and came back with two large gingerbread men she and Leonie had clearly baked that morning. Leonie had decorated them with chocolate chip eyes and wiggly iced smiles.

'These look delicious, thank you. They'll definitely keep our energy levels up, especially if the snow continues to fall.'

'Be careful out there,' Mrs Barnes replied, waving as she closed the door.

Despite the snow, excitement kept Bella warm, and they delivered gifts to neighbouring houses and down the nearby lanes. By the time they had finished handing over a huge box containing a hamper stuffed with Christmas food to Mrs Malvern and a beautifully wrapped parcel to Mr Binet, the snow was growing heavier and around the village, chimney smoke drifted into the cold air where fires were being lit inside. Shaking the snow from her hair and brushing down her elf costume, she headed back to the safety of the car. Before she drove to the next house, she held her coffee to warm her fingers and Freddie did the same with his hot chocolate. As soon as she could feel them again, Bella slid the car into gear.

'Right onto the next one,' she said to Freddie with a smile.

More deliveries were made, leaving joyful recipients smiling on their doorsteps. Recently bereaved Winston almost cried when she handed over the stack of books wrapped in red paper and tied with a gold ribbon. He had no idea what they were and was just happy to be thought of, and it brought tears to Bella's eyes to think about him opening his gift in a few days' time. But in just half an hour the ferocity of the snowfall had grown. Tiny, delicate flakes had given way to giant splodges on the windscreen, and she turned the wipers up. Nerves built in her stomach as she focused in the dense white light on the road. Meadowbank had never looked more magical as the snow settled on low flint walls and gates and dressed the hedgerows in a shroud of white.

The Christmas tree on the green was even more beautiful as its bright, shining star glittered under the powdery covering it had already received.

Determined to enjoy the snow, knowing it never lasted long, Bella kept her spirits up by singing along to Christmas songs. Freddie joined in too and as the heating in the car revived her, they continued to enjoy their day.

For the next hour, their deliveries were greeted in the same way each time with hugs and kisses and treats aplenty. When they were delivering gifts to some of the older residents who were facing a lonely Christmas, Freddie joined her. He seemed to relish the unadulterated happiness their deliveries made, his smile being as wide and free as theirs were, and Bella wished she could record each response to show to the person who'd taken the tag. In the car, they talked about school and of course Freddie talked about his mum, but he seemed a little more guarded today and she hoped he wasn't uncomfortable around her. Even though it was hard and painful for her, Bella ensured she met every remark with her usual patience and interest.

'It's like a blizzard out there now,' Bella said after a couple of hours. 'I've never seen anything like it.'

'I think it's awesome,' Freddie replied, his eyes wide with wonder.

So would she if she were inside in the warm looking at it through her front window, but driving around in it was giving her a headache. Her car had never liked the cold and before long, it began to slip and slide on the roads. Even though it was only mid-afternoon, the world seemed dark and small and Bella hoped they'd make it back before too long but the pile of presents on the back seat made that unlikely. She might have to cut the rest of the deliveries short and try again tomorrow. She'd try and get a few more done – the ones on the outer road – and that way she could walk the rest of the presents to their destinations tomorrow if need be.

The next deliveries took her to the outer road of Meadowbank. Where the fields rolled away into the distance, a blanket of white snow covered everything. She stopped to make the next delivery on their list and Freddie came with her. After another jubilant thank you, they ran back to the warmth of the car, and she slid the key into the ignition. She turned it, only to be met with a weary, sluggish groan. Bella tried again, the old engine moaning as it attempted to turn over.

'Oh no. No, no, no.'

'Is it dead?' asked Freddie through a mouthful of Quality Street Mrs Dalloway, the last person, had given him.

'It's certainly not very happy, Freddie. Let's try one more time, shall we?' She turned the key and after a protracted mechanical moan, the car came to life. 'I better not turn it off when we next stop, but I'm sure we'll be fine to finish the deliveries. We don't want to let anyone down, do we?' She looked to Freddie who shook his head.

Bella put the car into gear and slowly moved off. Banks of snow had formed either side of the road and the car scrunched its way over the flakes settling thick and fast on the lane. They'd reached the part of Meadowbank where the houses became even more spaced out with acres of land between them. Bella and Freddie were just singing along to 'Jingle Bell Rock' when without any warning, the car engine died, and all the lights went off. For a second, Bella panicked in the gloom but gathering her senses, she turned on the hazard lights and steered the car to one of the banks.

'Umm, Bella,' Freddie said, pulling his knees up onto the seat and hugging them. 'What's happening?'

'The car's conked out,' she replied more calmly than she felt. 'Let me see if I can get it going again.'

Once again, she turned the key only to hear the engine wheeze and groan. It didn't get anywhere near to turning over and worry began to rise in her throat. Snow built on the windscreen, obscuring her view, and she knew she'd have to find the emergency triangle and set it up if the car didn't start soon. Closing her eyes and praying, she turned the key again, but the engine made no noise at all. Worry changed to anxiety as the hairs on her arms lifted in the cold and she shivered. She glanced at Freddie to see him biting his lip.

'Don't panic, Freddie. One more try and if that doesn't work, I'll call the AA or my dad.'

The car managed a single unhappy chug as if it was puffing out the last of its breath. Internally cursing, she gave it another go for good measure but again, the car did nothing. It almost seemed annoyed at her for trying.

Taking her mobile phone, Bella tried her dad first but as he'd already had a drink, it being three o'clock on a Saturday after-noon, he couldn't help. He offered to walk up with some jump cables, but that would take at least half an hour and she didn't like the idea of him out in this weather. They also both realised that without another car to attach the jump cables to, they'd be pretty useless. Her dad then added after a pause, that he didn't actually own any jump cables to which Bella had let out a high-pitched, hysterical-sounding giggle and internally told herself to calm down.

'It looks like it's the AA, Freddie. They could be a while. Are you warm enough? I think I've got a blanket in the back if you need it.'

'I'm okay for now,' Freddie replied, but the car was rapidly cooling down from the below freezing temperature outside.

'Right. Firstly, I need to get out the emergency triangle. It's pretty dark out there and we don't need anything else happening. You stay here.' She dived out of the car and found it in the boot. Skidding and sliding to the bend in the road, she placed it care-fully so it would be seen clearly and warn other drivers. By the time she made it back to the car, her fingers ached and her teeth chattered. 'It's just a shame we're so far away from everyone,' she said cheerfully as she climbed back in. 'We could walk back to

Mrs Dalloway's but that's going to take at least twenty minutes in this weather and the next house on is about that far too. It's very difficult to walk as it is.'

Bella looked down to see his flashing wellington boots with stormtroopers on the side. As good as they were at keeping out the wet, they weren't great at keeping out the cold. His little toes would freeze within minutes. Plus, she hadn't anticipated any of this when she dressed as an elf that morning. Her black ankle boots covered in green felt with a bell at the end were already smelling unpleasant and drooping from the melting snow covering them. No, they were better off staying in the car.

'You should call my dad.'

Could she? Should she? She probably should as she and his son here were stranded in the snow. If she called the AA, she didn't know how long she'd be sat there, and there were still presents to deliver. But Nick had said he had something important to do. What if she disturbed him? As another flurry came down heavier than the one before and the temperature gauge on the car lowered another degree, she knew she had to.

Her fingers trembled from the cold as well as from emotion, but with a deep breath, Bella picked up her phone and dialled.

Chapter 30

After Nick had dropped Freddie at the park, he'd headed straight home. They could have walked, but there was an urgency in his need to get back. He had to speak to Paige. It wasn't going to be the easiest of conversations, but it was necessary, and it was one he wanted to have before Christmas. He wanted to do right by Freddie and this last week he'd thought long and hard about what that was. Finally, he'd come to a decision, and had never been surer of anything in his life before.

Bella's eyes had opened widely when she'd seen him. She clearly hadn't expected to. It hadn't even registered at the time that she'd been dressed as an elf until he'd got back into the truck and was driving away. She made a cute elf, and he knew that Freddie would be having a great time with her, making Christmas special for other people the way she'd made it special for them against all the odds. But he couldn't think about that now; he had to get this done first.

As he placed the key in the front door, Nick took a breath. The gentle fall of snowflakes made him even more eager to get this over with. He wanted to enjoy the snow with his boy, and with Bella. He wanted to build a snowman in the garden then huddle inside by the roaring fire, just the three of them.

Walking into the living room he saw Paige changing some of the ornaments around on the tree. For some reason it annoyed him. He and Freddie were happy with where everything was. It sparkled and glowed with perfection. She had no right to change it, the same way she had no right to come back after six months and expect things to be exactly the same. He was no longer her devoted husband. He'd always be a devoted dad, but he couldn't bring himself to love Paige the way he once had. Freddie . . . Well, Freddie loved his mum and Nick would never get in the way of that, but after his discussion with Trish and Len, he'd come to realise that putting Freddie first hadn't meant what he thought it had.

'Paige, we need to talk.'

'Where's Freddie?'

'I've taken him to volunteer at Bluebell Park. He and Bella are delivering presents from the giving tree.'

'Ah, Bella.' The snide remark stabbed but he let it slide. This wasn't going to descend into an argument. There were serious things to discuss.

'Yes, Bella. I was hoping to go too, but we need to talk.'

'Fine.' She sat down. 'Let's talk.'

'This—' He stuttered, even though at night while he'd lain on the sofa, he'd rehearsed the speech over and over again. 'It's not working, Paige. I—'

'It's not working because you refuse to act like my husband.' Her words reverberated over the noise of the television, some Christmas cookery show, and she came and sat next to him, taking his hand gently in hers. This time, her voice had lost the spiteful tone it carried only moments earlier. 'If we tried to get along like we used to, things might be different. I still love you, Nick, and I still find you attractive.' She went to brush his hair from his eyes and instinctively he pulled away. 'Don't you find me attractive anymore? Don't you still love me?'

They'd come to the crux of the matter far quicker than he'd expected. Over the last week she'd shown him how she felt about him, touching his hand, rubbing his back, snuggling up to him at the Christmas play, but every time all he could think was that he was betraying Bella and betraying his heart. He didn't love Paige anymore and she'd forgotten the months of loveless marriage they'd endured before she left.

'I'm sorry, Paige,' he said kindly. 'But we can't go back to what we had. Our marriage wasn't great for a long time before you left, and I don't – I'm afraid I don't feel that way about you anymore.' He was trying to be kind, to say things nicely, but anger raged behind her eyes.

'It's Bella, isn't it? You've fallen in love with her.'

'Yes, I have.'

He'd thought about lying, about playing it down, but what was the point? He did love Bella. He hadn't expected to, and he was pretty sure she hadn't either. Not so soon after her split from Evan. But he had no doubt that what they had was real and too good to lose. Her quiet confidence and kind heart had won him over and he was sure that theirs would be a long and happy future. It was a future he wanted more than anything in the world.

Saying the words out loud was freeing. She'd made him a better person, a better dad, a better man. Being around her made him feel complete in a way he hadn't with Paige for a long, long time, even before she walked out of the door.

'You can't forgive me, can you? I know I made a mistake, Nick, but that's what it was. A mistake. I've realised that now and come back. I want to be a part of yours and Freddie's lives.'

'And you can – you will. I'd never stop you seeing Freddie and maybe one day we can be friends again too, but I can't just pretend the last six months didn't happen.'

He didn't bother voicing his concerns over her getting bored and leaving again. It would serve no purpose, though the worry was present in his mind. But he couldn't predict the future, all he could do was make the best future he could for him and Freddie and that future included Bella.

'I can't stand the idea of Freddie calling her Mummy,' she snarled.

Nick bit his lip to keep his temper. 'I'm not sure he ever will, but if he decides to, that's up to him. And you're getting a little ahead of yourself. We haven't even been on a date yet.'

Paige crossed her arms over her chest and gave a scornful laugh. 'I can't believe you're throwing our marriage away over someone you haven't even been on a date with.'

'You threw our marriage away, Paige, when you upped and left six months ago to travel around the world with your new boyfriend.' Her mouth flew open in shock, but he carried on, pulling himself back. 'But that's still beside the point. We both know things were difficult before you left. I'll never stop you seeing Freddie, but I deserve to be happy too. And for that to happen, I need Bella in my life. In Freddie's life. And that's something you're going to have to get used to.'

A thick and heavy silence descended, like a layer of animosity over the room.

'Where will I live?' she fired back a few minutes later.

'I don't know. You'll have to get a job and a flat, I suppose. You might have to go and stay with your parents for a while. I wasn't sure when you'd want to leave, so I spoke to Mrs Dalloway. Her other cottage that she rents out is free over Christmas. She said you can stay there. I've booked it from tonight.'

'Tonight? So you're kicking me out?'

'You can't stay here, Paige. It's too difficult, and the longer it goes on the harder it'll be for Freddie. If you go tonight, he's got a little bit of time to get used to it before Christmas. I've already talked to him, and he understands. It's hard but . . .'

It had been the hardest conversation he'd ever had with his son. Harder than the conversation where he'd explained he didn't know where Paige was or when she was coming back. At least he knew things would soon settle down and that this was the right thing for the future. For them all.

'Talking about Freddie, don't you think he deserves a family?'

Nick had known this argument would come as it was the thing he'd been wrestling with himself. 'He deserves happiness and a happy family, whatever that looks like. No family is perfect, but he'd be better off with us apart and happy than together and miserable.'

'Which is what you'd be?'

There wasn't the slightest hint of understanding in her voice. Paige had always been a selfish woman, but he'd taken it as part of her character and worked around it. Not this time though. She wasn't going to guilt-trip him into staying with her for Freddie's sake. He loved his son, but he was a better father as a happy one. When he compared himself now to how he'd been when Paige had first left, the house a mess and him irritable, he wanted to turn the clock back and do better. He couldn't change what had happened, but he could make better choices now.

'I would be,' he said matter-of-factly and let the words drift in the air.

His phone rang in his pocket, puncturing the silence. Had it been anyone else he wouldn't have answered it, but when he saw it was Bella and noticed the snow falling in heavy swirls outside the window, he accepted the call immediately. Besides, they were done here. There was nothing further to say and the discussion was on the edge of falling into insults. He wasn't prepared to sit there and listen to that. He'd said what he wanted to say and now Paige had to accept it.

The thought of talking to Bella knowing he was free to tell her how he felt sent butterflies into his stomach. He felt giddy. Like a schoolboy talking to his first crush. 'Hey, Bella, everything okay? You've what? Where are you? Right, I'll be there soon.'

'Your new girlfriend has summoned you then?' Paige snarled when the call ended.

'She's broken down delivering the presents from the giving tree and Freddie's with her.'

'Best run along then.'

Nick grabbed his scarf and wrapped it around his neck. Luckily, he still had his boots on from this morning. 'I will, Paige, because it's below freezing out there and with the engine off, she and Freddie have got no way of keeping warm.'

273

Chapter 31

'Your dad's on his way,' Bella said to Freddie. The temperature in the car had dropped considerably and the windows were steaming up from their breath. She'd already wrapped a blanket around him, but still he shivered. 'Do you want my coat?'

'Won't you be cold?'

She shrugged. She'd be freezing but Freddie was more important than her. She'd survive. 'If you're still cold you can have it.' He didn't respond and Bella slipped it from around her shoulders and wiggled in her seat until it freed. She then wrapped it over Freddie, tucking it in at the sides so only his head poked out.

It was a shame she hadn't broken down nearer the centre of the village. Not only would she have been close enough to home she could walk Freddie back, but someone would have undoubtedly delivered her a hot cup of tea, or even towed her car back to her cottage. Here on the outer road though, it was far quieter. There was barely any traffic on the best of days, and they hadn't seen a car yet. The houses were so spaced out that no one could see she was stuck, even if they did wander down to the ends of their ridiculously long driveways. Snow gathered around the tyres, and she worried she wasn't going to get out. Her tyres weren't really designed for this sort of weather. Nothing in Britain was designed for this sort of weather. They'd learned to cope with constant drizzle but that was about it.

'Bella,' Freddie said brightly, and she wondered if they were about to have another game of I-spy. He was surprisingly observant and inventive and she'd lost the last two games. 'Do you like my dad?'

Bella felt herself jerk backwards as if the question had hit her in the chest. 'Yeah,' she replied nonchalantly, as if she were talking about any of her neighbours. 'Of course. Your dad's a lovely man. Everyone in the village likes him.' Now she was going over the top, but she couldn't seem to stop herself. 'I mean, he's the best gardener around and—'

'No, I mean, do you *like* him like him?' Freddie's eyes widened as he waited for the answer. 'Like the way mums and dads like each other. Do you love him?'

What the heck did she say to that? Luckily, Freddie kept talking, meaning she didn't have to answer immediately, and Bella attempted to compose a suitable, non-committal response. What was the point in saying yes, she did like him – love him – but as he was clearly going to be trying again with Paige it all seemed more than a little pointless.

'He's been acting weird since Mum came back.'

'Has he?' It must have been a surprise.

'Yeah. It's like he was when Mum left.'

'It must be very strange for you all, but I'm sure you'll get back to normal soon.' Bella kept her voice bright and breezy, but her heart was screaming that it was all so unfair.

'Dad's been much happier since we started doing the volunteering and stuff.'

'I'm glad. Volunteering is a really good thing to do. Look how happy you've made people today, Freddie.' Nice deflection, she thought.

Freddie examined her from the corner of his eye then transferred his gaze to the steamed-up window where he drew a smiley face. Had he been in Year 6, he'd probably have drawn something far worse.

'How long do you think it'll take your dad to get here? Do you know where he was working? I forgot to ask.'

'He wasn't working today. He was talking to Mum about Christmas.'

'Oh, right.'

That explained a lot. On the plus side it meant he shouldn't be long, but on the downside, her heart tore again. They probably had a lot to sort out. Like who was going to buy what and what time they'd have Christmas dinner.

For the first time, a touch of bitterness crept into Bella's thoughts as she pictured them all sat around the table having Christmas dinner, pulling crackers and wearing silly paper crowns. All she could see was them laughing, Nick and Paige declaring a toast to each other and clinking glasses. But life wasn't always fair – it was the whole reason she'd started the giving tree – and Bella reminded herself she had a lot to be grateful for.

'So do you like my dad?' Freddie asked again.

'Me? Well, I suppose—'

Through the fogged-up windscreen, heavy with snow, a light shone round the bend of the road, growing brighter. Bella rubbed at the window as Nick's truck came to a stop just in front of her car. 'Oh, look, your dad's here.'

In the warmth of her embarrassment, she'd forgotten all about her lack of coat and launched out of the car in her full elf costume, immediately shivering. The snow continued to tumble down, layering her hair and shoulders. She stepped towards Nick, her toes refusing to bend from the cold.

'Where's your coat?' Nick asked, grabbing a blanket from the front seat and wrapping it around her shoulders. She pointed to Freddie in the front of her car. He'd rubbed the window too and his smiling face peered out at them above the pile of snow. 'You must be freezing.'

Feeling Nick's body close to her, his broad chest and strong arms as they pulled the blanket around her, sent warmth into her veins. After waving at his son, he paused, rubbing her arms and staring into her eyes. 'I am a bit chilly.'

'A bit?' He laughed. 'You're something else, you know that? Why didn't you wear something warmer than an elf costume?'

'Because it's Christmas and I'm one of Santa's elves. I bet my nose is so red it matches my cheeks.'

'It's a little pink, but it suits you.'

'I doubt that.'

'You look cute.'

Bella's heart juddered, but she couldn't read anything into it. He was just being kind as she'd kept his son safe. And he wasn't about to tell her she looked like Rudolph with a head-cold, was he?

'What am I going to do with you?' he joked.

It hadn't escaped her notice that his hands were still on her upper arms, holding her as if he didn't want to let go. It was undeniable that there was something special between them, and it hurt anew that they couldn't explore it.

'You go and sit in the car,' Nick said, finally releasing her. 'I'll get Freddie. How many presents have you got left to deliver?'

'Quite a few I'm afraid.'

She stepped into his truck and as well as having the heater on, he'd also brought two hot water bottles. She grabbed one and held it close to her as she watched him carry Freddie over the snow and deposit him in the driver's seat. Once he'd shuffled over, Bella pulled the blanket around him again and put one Nick had brought on his lap. Freddie handed back her coat and she quickly exchanged it for one of the hot water bottles. He cuddled it close, warming his hands and body on it.

Christmas music played from the radio and as stupid as it was, for a moment, Bella didn't want to be anywhere else, even though her hands and toes stung as they warmed up. Nick transferred the last of the presents to the back of the truck and even grabbed Bella's handbag, keys and phone, which she'd completely forgotten about.

When Nick climbed back in, he pulled out a flask and two cups, filling them with homemade hot chocolate. 'Here you go, mate. This'll warm you up. It's not as good as the Bluebell Park stuff but it's better than nothing.'

Freddie blew the drink and sipped it while Nick poured another one and handed it to Bella. 'No whipped cream or marshmallows, I'm afraid.'

'Did you talk to Mum?' Freddie asked, his face suddenly solemn.

Nick matched his tone. 'I did.'

Bella stared out of the window pretending to watch the trees, feeling awkward.

'And is she—'

'We'll talk about it later, son, okay?' Freddie nodded and Nick turned to her. 'Where's our first stop then?'

Finally regaining some feeling in her fingers, she found her list and read out the address.

'We're going to have to leave your car here. I don't think we'll get it out even if I can start it and it's getting dark now. They've said it's going to snow all night.'

'Can we build a snowman tomorrow, Dad?' Freddie asked, bouncing in his seat.

'Definitely, mate. Definitely.'

If only she could join them. Paige would do that now. The perfect family scene. Bella turned away, hoping Nick hadn't seen the tears spring in her eyes.

'Are you okay, Bella?'

'Fine,' she replied, focusing on the rattling sleigh bells playing from the radio. 'Shall we get going?'

After delivering the final present, Nick pulled up in front of their cottages. Paige waited at the front door, smiling as Freddie bounded up to her, but before she ushered him inside, she shot a look at Bella that could only be described as hostile. Bella ignored her and waved goodbye to Freddie.

'Thanks for saving me,' she said to Nick. 'You saved Christmas, actually.'

He chuckled. 'I wouldn't go that far, but it was fun. I enjoyed it.'

She knew she should get out of the car, but it felt too much of a wrench. He was leaning towards her, one hand on the wheel, and she wanted him to inch forward and kiss her again. Just one last time. Just so she could imprint it on her memory and always remember what it was like. What might have been. The air smelled of sweet hot chocolate and his earthy, spicy scent and she dropped her eyes to her bag where shiny red wrapping paper poked out through the gap.

'I've got something for you and Freddie.' She reached into her bag and pulled out two presents.

'For us?' Nick asked, startled.

'The one for you was requested on the giving tree.'

'What?' She nodded. 'Did Freddie . . .?'

She wasn't about to break the confidence, and when she told him so, her reply was all the confirmation he needed. 'And I thought Freddie deserved something for helping. He's been brilliant. I'm afraid I didn't get anything for Paige. I'd got these before she came back. I'm sorry. I hope she won't mind.' He didn't say anything, only nodded. With shaking fingers, she handed them over. 'I hope you like them.'

'I'm sure we will. Thank you.' He spoke so quietly it was as if the words were an effort to get out and she didn't know what to make of it.

'Merry Christmas, Nick,' she whispered, and climbed out of the car, forcing herself not to look back.

Inside her cottage, she leaned against the wall and let her bag fall from her hand. She flicked on the living-room lights and made her way to the Christmas tree. The lights twinkled against the dark sky outside, reflecting off the baubles and decorations around them. Her house smelled of pine, and she took a deep breath in. Hopefully next year would be better and this messy, difficult Christmas forgotten.

A knock at the door startled her. She'd only been home a minute or so. Bella answered it to see Nick on the old stone doorstep. Without saying a word, he stepped forward so his body was tantalisingly close to hers. His strong hands reached up to her face cupping her cheeks and with an intent gaze he pressed his mouth to hers. The gentle touch of his lips filled her body with longing, and she reached her hands to his chest. It was more forceful than their first kiss. More urgent and eager. When it ended, he rested his forehead against hers. She regained her breath, though it fluttered around her chest, and as longing took over, she kissed him once more. The strong sense of connection, of love, consumed every inch of her body and mind and rooted itself deep in her heart.

Nick gently pulled away, breathing as heavily as she was, and he whispered, 'Merry Christmas, Bella.'

The seconds stretched out between them, him still cupping her face, his warm hands breathing life back into her. Was this it? Was this the kiss that said goodbye? She couldn't help but feel it was the full stop on the romance that could have blossomed between them.

'I love you.'

The word resounded around her head. Had she heard right? Was she imagining it? He raised her head a little, kissing her again, a short, sweet kiss and she knew it was real. He loved her and she loved him. Her words were breathy, nothing more than a whisper that faded into the snowy air drifting in from outside. 'I love you, too.'

After a moment, Bella finally found the power to speak again. 'But . . . Paige? Freddie?'

'I don't love her anymore, Bella. I haven't for a long time. She'll always be Freddie's mum and I'll never stop her seeing him, but it's you, Bella. I love you.'

Tears of happiness stung her eyes, and she took in a deep breath, the muscles of her stomach shaking. She didn't know if he'd already opened the present she gave him, but if this was the type of thankyou she got for buying him a jumper, what would she get when she bought him a really good present? As he kissed her again, and desire, love and hope rose like a tidal wave within her, she couldn't wait to find out.

Chapter 32

It was Christmas Eve and Paige stood in the queue with Freddie to take him to see Santa at Bluebell Park grotto.

The snow had continued to fall since the day Bella and Freddie had delivered the presents. The day Nick had given her the most mind-blowing kiss of her life and declared he loved her. The ground was still covered in snow that was being topped up every now and again and there was every hope for another flurry tonight. It seemed a white Christmas was on the cards after all.

All around the park, the sounds of the community choir singing their favourite hymns filled the air. Mr Whittaker had come out from the information point and was singing along with some of the villagers, and Hazel and Matilda were gossiping over a hot drink. Over at the grotto, the sound of sleigh bells and classic Christmas pop rang out from the speakers outside.

Nina and Johnny were there too, hand in hand after he'd finally asked her out under the mistletoe hanging in the pub. Bella couldn't have been happier for them. It seemed love, as well as snow, was in the air at Meadowbank lately.

Nick would shortly join Paige and Freddie to visit Santa, but for now, he and Bella were having a rare moment together. Nick had been busy working up until yesterday and Bella too had been finishing off her duties at the park and school. They'd had a couple of dinners with Freddie, holding hands under the table like lovestruck teenagers, but they'd held back on showing affection, mindful that Freddie was still adjusting to his dad dating and to his mum being back, though she was now living in Mrs Dalloway's cottage until they could find something more permanent.

It was clear from Paige that none of this was what she wanted, and she'd much prefer it to be her who was stealing kisses with Nick, but she was responding to Bella's efforts of politeness, which was all they could ask for. Bella knew that eventually they'd all get used to this new dynamic and the prospect of the future in front of her filled her with joy. She'd never anticipated when Evan left her that she could recover from her heartbreak so quickly, but now she thought about it, their relationship was nothing to what she and Nick had, and they were at the very beginning of their journey. She slipped her hand into his and he ran his thumb in gentle circles over her skin.

'Your hands are cold.'

They were freezing, but she wanted to feel his skin on hers and a glove would have got in the way. Better to be cold. 'I'll warm up,' she replied, angling her head so he could kiss her.

'Will you two stop snogging for one minute?' Caro waddled over, her huge bump barely held within her coat. 'Honestly, you're making me queasy.'

'I think that's more your weird thing about cinnamon.'

Caro harrumphed. 'Honestly, this baby is ruining Christmas.'

'Yes, but next year will be pretty amazing when he or she is running around going crazy.'

'It will,' she replied with a soppy grin at Luke. 'Where's Mum and Dad?'

'Boozing it up at the mulled wine stall. Mrs Bumble's making a killing today. I know you can't drink any but it's like Christmas-spiced rocket fuel.'

'Dad!' Freddie cried, waving madly. 'It's our turn next.'

'Back in a minute, okay?' He kissed Bella on the cheek and headed off.

'So,' Caro said as they sat down on one of the benches. 'Things are going well then?'

'They are.' The biggest of smiles stretched Bella's cheeks.

'Isn't it hard with Paige being around?'

'It's a bit more complicated, but I don't mind.'

'Of course you don't,' Caro replied, nudging her sister. 'It's nice to see you stupidly positive again.'

Just then, her mum and dad came over, extra cups of mulled wine in their hands. 'Here you are, poppet,' Cynthia said, handing one to Bella. 'Merry Christmas, darling.'

'Merry Christmas, Mum.'

'I got one for Nick,' said her dad looking around. 'Where is he?'

'In the grotto.'

'Ah.'

As they waited, they talked about plans for tomorrow. Bella had presumed that Paige would be spending the day with Nick and Freddie and that she might possibly see them on Boxing Day or the day after. Every time she'd tried to talk to Nick about it, he'd been a bit cagey, and she'd suspected that some things were still to be sorted out. As much as Paige could be hostile to her, she didn't want her spending Christmas Day on her own.

'Bella,' shouted one of the villagers coming over. 'Oh, Bella, I'm so glad I found you.'

'Is everything all right, Mrs Picard?'

'I just wanted to say thank you for the gift. I don't know who nominated me, but I'm so looking forward to opening it and then I'm off to Hazel's again this year. I don't think I've looked forward to a Christmas as much in years.'

'I'm so glad to hear it.'

'And my daughter, who's swanned off to Scotland, well, I shall be far too busy to miss her and it's all because of you and your fabulous idea for a giving tree. Thank you, darling. You've made my Christmas.'

Mrs Picard wandered away and Bella sipped her drink.

Since the presents were delivered, Bella couldn't walk down the street without being thanked for organising the giving tree. Even though she couldn't love it more, it filled her with affection for her little village. And although she'd arranged it, it was the people around her – her friends and neighbours in Meadowbank – who'd made it possible. As usual, the village had come together and now everyone was going to have a wonderful Christmas with presents, gifts and more than enough food.

Nick, Paige and Freddie exited the grotto and Freddie ran over showing her his present. He'd been allowed to open it, and he waved the superhero comic book in the air as if it was the best Christmas present he'd ever received. As soon as he reached them, Bella's mum and dad had gathered him up and were getting him to show them pictures and talk them through it. They were going to make exceptional grandparents not just to Caro's baby, but to him too.

'Freddie,' called Nick. 'We've got something to do, haven't we?'

He frowned in confusion, then his face brightened. 'Oh yeah.'

Nick nodded at Paige and she went to walk away, but Cynthia stepped in. 'Paige, my love, you haven't got one of Mrs Bumble's mulled wines. Shall we go and get one? It's pretty much pure alcohol and you could probably pickle something in it, but it doesn't half take the chill off.' She wrapped her arm around her waist and hastened her on.

After Bella had told her mum about the kiss and Nick's declaration of love, an overjoyed Cynthia had accepted Paige as part of their family and was making an effort to include her.

'Bella,' Nick said. 'Have you seen there's a tag hanging on the giving tree?'

A cold chill ran down her spine. Had she missed one? Was someone still desperately waiting for a present, feeling like the village had forgotten them? No one had said anything, but perhaps the tag had been handed in late. Perhaps someone hadn't understood how it worked and hung the tag themselves. Bella told herself to calm down. It was late on Christmas Eve, but if she drove straight to Witchbury she'd be able to buy something, she was sure. Nick took her hand, and they went to investigate.

The red ribbon fluttered in the cold winter wind, and Bella

reached out for it. It wasn't Christmas-tree-shaped as hers had been or laminated, and it had been written by a child. Her throat closed over at the thought that a child might miss out because she hadn't double-checked the tree. Slipping it off the branch, she pulled it towards her, then gasped as she read the words out loud.

'We both love you. Will you please be part of our family and spend Christmas with us? Love Freddie and Nick. What?' Tears sprang to her eyes. She'd never dreamed this could happen so soon. She'd thought maybe one day, years down the line, she'd become part of their special day, but so soon? Her voice wavered as she spoke. 'Really?'

They nodded, smiling broadly, and Freddie wrapped his arms around Bella's waist. She was *something* to him now and the idea filled her with love.

'Paige wants to come over in the morning,' Nick said. 'To see Freddie open his presents, but we were hoping you might come over in the afternoon and have dinner with us? Paige is off to see her parents.'

'Dinner?' In her mind she replayed the scene she'd created with Paige and Nick, only this time inserting herself into it. They'd pull crackers and wear stupid crowns and laugh at the bad jokes and play charades. It would be perfect.

'And then later we could go and see your family for cheese and wine.'

'Do you want to come?' asked Freddie, looking up at her, his voice wavering with nerves.

A tear trickled down her face. 'Yes, please.'

'Yay!' Freddie high-fived his dad. 'Can I go and play on the climbing frame now?'

'Go on,' Nick said, laughing before he turned to Bella. 'Sorry about that. They don't know anything about meaningful moments. I hope he didn't ruin it. The tag was actually his idea. He wanted to make sure someone got you something for Christmas too. We hoped it was a decent present.'

'It's the perfect Christmas present,' Bella said, swallowing down more tears. 'The most perfect Christmas present I could ever have wished for.' Tiny, slight snowflakes began to fall from the pale grey sky overhead. 'This is going to be the most perfect Christmas I've ever had.'

'Us too,' Nick said, moving closer. His arms wrapped around her waist and he kissed her again.

Releasing herself to the moment, Bella realised that out of all the residents of Meadowbank, the giving tree had given her the best Christmas gift of all.

Turn the page for an extract from Katie Ginger's heartwarming Christmas romcom, *Snowflakes at Mistletoe Cottage*

Out now!

Chapter 1

London

Felicity Fenchurch primped and preened in front of the camera, brushing her honey-blonde curls back from her face. The director shouted, 'Action,' and she gave a longing smile, dipped down to pull a tray from the oven, and gazing at the camera from under false eyelashes, pouted.

'There you have it,' Felicity announced, removing her pink oven gloves with a flourish. 'A deliciously decadent fabulous four-cheese lasagne, made with fresh homemade perfect pasta.'

'Cut,' shouted David, and the silent studio erupted into life. 'That's a wrap for the day, everyone. Felicity, darling, that was marvellous as usual. How you manage to look so damn sexy serving cheesy pasta is beyond me.'

Esme Kendrick watched as they exited the studio. As a food technologist, she'd done all the cooking this morning: chopped all the ingredients, grated the different cheeses, made a velvety béchamel sauce. She'd even made the pasta at the crack of dawn before the greedy pigeons had started cooing, getting up in the dark and padding about in the cold kitchen as a wintery wind blustered around the apartment. It was November, and as cold as a penguin's flipper outside, but to Esme November meant nearly Christmas, and there was something different about London at Christmas time. Everyone was a little friendlier, a little kinder, and with parties and celebrations the city was alive with a kind of electricity. After a rushed cup of coffee, she'd made her way to work, with the great strings of Christmas lights swinging above, glittering in the winter gloom. The lasagne, complete with a perfect golden-brown finish, had then been presented to the world as the handiwork of TV goddess, Felicity Fenchurch. In reality, all Felicity had done was smoulder at the camera and mix things in a bowl.

'I'm so nervous,' Esme said to Helena, her best friend and a fellow food technician. 'Why am I so nervous about pitching Grandma's double-layer chocolate chestnut cake to Sasha?'

Helena brushed her dark brown bob behind her ear. 'Oh, I don't know, is it because it's your absolute favourite recipe of your gran's? The one you make every year at Christmas, the one you never, ever stop talking about as soon as summer's over and the weather gets even the slightest bit nippy. The one that—'

'Yeah, maybe it's that,' Esme interrupted playfully. 'Right, wish me luck. See you tomorrow.'

Sasha's office was of the new modern glass variety that looks more like a greenhouse. As their producer, she was scary but fair. Never rude or patronising, not like Felicity, but she was a powerhouse – a confident, composed, I've-achieved-my-dreams-with-effort-and-hard-work kind of woman. The type you look up to and fear all at the same time. The glass wall, with a view onto the corridor, was lined with tall green plastic pot plants designed to make the place seem homely. Esme was just approaching the door and about to knock when she heard voices from inside. Peering through the dusty leaves of a banana plant, Felicity Fenchurch sat purring at Sasha discussing something oddly familiar.

'I know it's a late edition, Sasha, but I really think my granny's triple-layer chocolate chestnut cake will be just the thing. Chestnuts are always big at Christmas and nothing screams indulgence like a chocolate cake. And what makes mine special is the addition of a secret ingredient – maple syrup. And a slightly unorthodox method of chilling the batter before baking. It'll be revolutionary.' Felicity smiled and bright white teeth gleamed in the dull office light.

Esme couldn't believe what she was hearing. These were the same things – the same words – she'd used when describing her recipe to Helena yesterday. Felicity must have overheard them and now she was passing off the recipe as her own. An unpleasant feeling grew in Esme's stomach.

'I'm really not sure,' replied Sasha, in cool professional tones. 'We'll need to drop something else and it'll have to fit into that timeslot. I really don't fancy redoing the entire schedule.'

'Of course. I was going to suggest we drop the chocolate orange tart. It's so last year anyway and with some clever cut shots from David this will be sublime.' She smiled at David who glowed at the compliment. Felicity crossed her long legs and Esme, with heat rushing through her body, spotted the red sole of a Louboutin.

'And,' pitched in David, 'I just love that it's her granny's recipe, don't you? People love sentimental cooking. It'll be a bestseller for sure.'

'Okay then,' replied Sasha, nodding. Her grey hair was cut into an elfin crop and her deceptively youthful face remained passive. 'Fine. We can do it.'

Esme stepped back and leaned against the opposite wall, her legs rubbery and almost giving way. Her whole body shook with rage. Stealing boring old day-to-day recipes, as Felicity had done before, was one thing, but stealing this one was something else. This recipe was the one she used to remember her grandma, the one the whole family ate at Christmas with a toast to Gran first. Esme had thought long and hard about sharing it and it had taken her ages to be able to do it. Only this winter had she finally reached the point where she wanted other people to taste it and feel the sense of love and care it imparted, rather than holding onto it as if she was holding on to the memories of her gran. To hear Felicity passing it off as her own grandma's recipe was low. Esme bit her lip to stop the tears from falling and anger tightened her hands into fists. Should she march in and confront Felicity or let it go? Her heart pounded, her temper causing her brain to freeze. As a strong sense of injustice took over, without thinking, she raised her hand and knocked.

'Come in,' said Sasha in a loud clear voice. 'Oh, Esme, can I help you?'

Esme paused in the doorway, unsure what to say. She couldn't quite believe what she'd heard or that her body seemed to be acting of its own accord. 'Sasha, I . . . The triple-layer chocolate chestnut cake Felicity just told you about – that recipe's not hers, it's mine—'

'I beg your pardon,' Felicity replied, shooting up to standing, her face a picture of shocked indignation, but there was a flicker of fear in her eyes. 'How dare you accuse me of—'

'You must have overheard me talking about it yesterday. You stole it!' Esme turned to Sasha who was also now standing.

'Sasha, I came here tonight to tell you about my grandma's recipe for a double-layer chocolate chestnut cake – to see if we could use it in the Christmas show,' Felicity squeaked in outrage, but Esme ignored her. 'It's from a cookery book that's been handed down through my family. It's got all our favourite recipes in. I wanted to share this one because Gran was – it's so special.'

Felicity sat back down and found a tissue in her bag before pressing it to her nose, pretending to cry. 'How can you say that, Esme? You know it's not true.' In support, David, the director, glowered at Esme.

'Esme,' Sasha began calmly, her face placid. There wasn't even a hint in her eyes that she was shocked or finding this remotely uncomfortable. Esme was. She felt decidedly uncomfortable and she had a horrible sinking feeling she should have thought this through before barging into Sasha's office letting her fiery temper take over. 'Are you saying that Miss Fenchurch has stolen your recipe for a . . . what was it?'

'A double-layer chocolate chestnut cake,' Esme replied as confidently as she could, though her stomach burned. Her eyes were drawn to the deep green scarf Sasha had fastened around her neck. It was floral and pretty, and at odds with her cold, harsh demeanour.

Felicity sobbed. 'Sasha, this is absolutely outrageous. And mine is triple-layer anyway.'

'You've just added one, that's all,' Esme blurted. 'The recipe is the same.'

Sasha glanced from Felicity to Esme, her face expressionless. 'Esme, you've made a very serious accusation here. Are you sure you want to continue with this conversation? Is it possible you've made a mistake and this is purely a coincidence?'

'No,' Esme said, quickly, her voice rising. In the back of her mind something told her to stop and think but it was too late, her mouth was still opening and the words flowing out. 'That recipe was from my grandmother's cookbook. Hers is the only recipe I know of with the addition of maple syrup and a method of chilling the batter.'

'Do you have the recipe book with you, to prove that it's yours? I assume that as you were coming to see me this evening to pitch the idea you brought it.'

'Yes,' said Esme, pulling her bag from her shoulder. This would prove her right. She reached into her bag, fumbling around inside, spilling the contents onto the floor. Her hand trembled as with a sickening dread, she realised she'd left it next to the kettle last night after showing Leo something. Running late this morning, she'd forgotten to re-pack it. Esme raised her eyes to heaven and gave a silent prayer, hoping this wouldn't go against her. From the corner of her eye, she caught Felicity's face. A sly smile spread across her plumped-up lips and she held a tissue to her eyes to hide it.

'Do you have it with you?' asked Sasha. 'It would be useful to have a look at it.'

Esme bit her lip as a flush crept up her neck and into her cheeks. 'I'm afraid I left it at home.'

Felicity scoffed. 'Probably because there is no book. You seem to lie about everything, Miss Kendrick. Is Esme even your real name?'

'Now, now,' interrupted David, putting a hand on Felicity's arm. 'I know you're upset, Felicity, and justifiably so, but let's not get personal.'

'Personal?' she shouted, clutching her chest. 'This is very personal to me, David. That woman is accusing me of lying to the whole world. If this got out, it would be a PR nightmare for me and the studio, and I would be left with no option but to sue. I have to protect my reputation.'

Esme's mouth flew open, irked by Felicity's overacting. 'I'm not the liar here, you are. You did steal it. You overheard me say I was going to pitch it and then you jumped in before I could. You must have been lurking by the coffee machine when you listened in to us chatting.'

'Lurking? How absurd,' laughed Felicity, brushing her hair away from her face so they could see her full shocked expression, but Esme detected a hint of concern in her voice. 'You have no proof of that, do you?'

'Do you have any proof, Esme?' asked Sasha. 'Who were you chatting to?' She was so calm Esme wondered if she was a robot and the scarf hid a central control panel. How could anyone be so numb to another's suffering? Esme chewed her lip, the tears welling in her eyes. She couldn't risk Helena getting into trouble.

'I'd rather not say,' Esme replied, but even she knew it sounded feeble.

'May I suggest,' said David, the colour draining a little from his ruddy cheeks, 'if that's the case, we forget about this whole dreadful business. Esme has no proof and I'm sure that if there are any . . . similarities, as Sasha said, it's simply coincidence.'

Esme's mind whirled around. This wasn't right. Felicity should be apologising to her, not the other way around. 'Do you think we both have grandmas who left us cookery books then, David? Sasha, I know I forgot the book, but you must believe me. I haven't made this up.'

Sasha glanced at Felicity then back to Esme. 'Esme, you've accused a colleague of lying and stealing ideas. This is very serious.'

'It's slander and harassment,' added Felicity who stood up to leave. 'I will not sit here being insulted by this – this – liar any longer. Either sort it out, Sasha, or I walk.' She marched to the door.

'Now, wait a second, Felicity.' Sasha rose from her chair. 'Let's not do anything rash.' She turned to Esme, her face was softer, but her voice remained cold and matter-of-fact. 'Esme, I'm sorry, but without any evidence you need to withdraw your complaint and apologise to Felicity.'

Esme sat frozen, staring wide-eyed and bewildered. Slowly, she shook her head. It wasn't just her being cheated here, her grandma was too, and she wouldn't stand for it. 'No. No, I won't. I know I don't have proof with me. I left the book at home by accident. If you let me go and get it—'

'Absolutely not,' Felicity shouted from the door. 'I mean it, Sasha. Unless this is resolved now, I walk. I don't want to, but I will. I'm not lacking for offers, as you know.'

Sasha hesitated and Esme knew what was going through her brain. Without Felicity and the ratings she brought, the whole network could go down. Her show, *Felicity Fenchurch's Fabulous Feasts*, was the only way they were keeping up with the other channels. 'Esme, I'm sorry,' Sasha continued. 'I think we need to get this sorted out now. I'm very surprised you didn't bring the recipe with you if you were going to pitch it. Felicity could simply have a similar recipe. If you apologise to her, we can put this all behind us.'

Still at the doorway, holding a tissue to her eyes, Felicity's voice was almost childlike as she said, 'Even though this unfounded accusation has damaged our relationship beyond repair, Esme, I'm a professional and if you apologise, I'll try and move on.'

Could she apologise? Could she say she was wrong and back down now? Was she even sure she was right? Esme took a deep breath but her mind was made up. Sometimes you had to be strong and stand up for yourself. It's what her gran had taught her and she wouldn't back down now. The secret ingredient and method were too similar, she wasn't mistaken. Esme's shoulders and neck hurt from the tension, even her legs ached, but she shook her head again. 'I'm sorry, Sasha, but I won't apologise. I'm right.'

'Then I'm afraid I have no choice, Esme. This counts as gross misconduct so it's instant dismissal.' Esme felt the tears spring to her eyes but there was no way she would cry in front of Felicity and David.

'I've been sacked?' Her voice sounded strange where she had to force the words past the ball of anger and hurt lodged in her throat. It didn't seem real. Somehow Esme managed to back out of the room while her whole body sparked with suppressed rage. Visibly shaking, she edged passed Felicity and left.

The glittering Christmas lights of London sparkled in the evening darkness. Giant snowflake lights hung high in the air, twinkling overhead, but Esme barely noticed them through her tears. She walked into someone, mumbled an apology and carried on with her head down. The heavy crowds of tourists bustled around her and snippets of Christmas songs carried on the air from the shops she passed. Instead of enjoying the wonderful Christmas vibe – that special atmosphere of excitement Esme loved most about London at this time of year – she dipped her head and marched on as fast as she could. By the time she reached her and Leo's apartment, tears were flowing freely down her cheeks.

Unbuttoning her heavy winter coat, she hung it on the rack then loosened her scarf, feeling drained and exhausted. Walking into the kitchen, she knew there was only one thing she could do to make herself feel better. Cook. She'd make Leo's favourite meal. A nice thick, juicy steak, rare and pink in the middle, and a proper béarnaise sauce with lots of good French butter and fresh tarragon. She'd even make asparagus roasted with sea salt as a side dish. A small smile crept over Esme's face as she searched the fridge for the ingredients but it was instantly replaced by a frown and cold teardrops on her cheeks. How could things have gone so badly wrong today? She shouldn't have acted on impulse and marched in there. She should have waited and thought about what to do. Now she'd thrown her job away and her heart was filled with regret.

Leo got up from the sofa. 'Esme, you're home.'

'Yep. And I got fired,' Esme replied, matter-of-fact, chopping the butter into small cubes before turning to see his face frozen in panic.

'What?' He looked even more shocked than she'd expected and walked to the window to stare out, gripping the hair at the back of his head. She'd hoped for a hug but as he stayed where he was, she poured two glasses of wine and took them over. When he turned back he reached for his wine, then his dark grey eyes gazed at her with concern.

'What happ—'

Esme bit back tears but took a deep breath. 'Felicity stole my recipe again. One of Grandma's. She must have overheard me talking about it with Helena at lunch yesterday and then decided to pitch it before I could. When I went to Sasha's office this evening, she was there saying it was her family recipe. I was so upset, Leo, and I don't know why, but I went in there and confronted her.'

'You did what?'

'I know, I know.' Esme rubbed her throbbing forehead. 'I don't know why I did it either. Well, I do. I did I because it was the right thing to do. She was even claiming it was from her granny and you know how long I've waited to share this special recipe but couldn't bring myself to do it.'

Finally, Leo reached out to her but didn't pull her into a hug, he touched her hand. He was clearly struggling to process everything she'd said. 'Are you sure you were right? I mean, I know you've said before about her doing this, but couldn't it just be a coincidence? You can be a bit dramatic sometimes.'

Esme wiped a tear from her cheek. Leo was always saying she was being dramatic when she lost her temper or got upset. His clear, decisive mind didn't get her passionate, emotional one, and maybe she was being dramatic, but it didn't stop her being right. 'A coincidence? No. That's what she's claiming but she even said about using maple syrup and chilling the mixture first. She could only've known that if she was ear-wigging.' Esme thrust her hand into her mop of ragged curls. 'It's one thing to steal a recipe but another to steal a grandma. She probably doesn't even have one anymore. I bet she devoured hers like a praying mantis. And she's tried to make it three layers instead of two. It won't work as triple layers, it'll just slide about then fall over, not unless you make the sponge thicker or use something other than double cream as a filling.'

'What are you going to do?' He turned to face her, his expression tense.

Esme feigned a hopefulness she didn't feel. 'I'm sure I'll pick something else up quickly, in a few months; or worst-case scenario, I'll go freelance.' Suddenly, Leo took her hand and led her to the table.

'Esme, can you come and sit down, please? I need to talk to you.' Esme paused. His face was serious as he placed his wine glass down, and her heart thudded in her chest. For the last few months he'd been secretive and she and her friends thought maybe he was going to propose. Was this the moment? Sat on the chair, next to their tiny dining table, he knelt down in front of her and Esme's heart rocketed up into her throat. She took a big breath in and bit the insides of her cheeks to stop herself grinning like a fool.

'Esme, I'm sorry, I should have done this weeks ago, the timing is terrible.' She wanted to shout that it wasn't. It wasn't at all. It was perfect timing. Leo raked a hand through his hair and she watched, hoping his hand would reach into his jacket pocket and pull out a tiny box. 'I know today's been difficult for you and I . . .' He shook his head. 'I should've done this before now.'

Esme bit her lip. She was going to get married!

'I think we should break up,' Leo announced.

Her mouth opened then closed again as she stared at him in disbelief. *What?* What had just happened? Everything fell silent except for the blood pounding in her ears and her short gasps of breath as she tried to control her emotions. Leo's eyes dropped and he stood up.

'I just feel we've become friends more than husband-and-wife material, don't you? And I think it'd be the best thing for both of us if we just moved on. Don't you think so?'

If he'd hoped for some kind of agreement from Esme, he was going to be disappointed. 'But it's nearly Christmas,' she said quietly.

'It's not even mid-November, Esme. It's nowhere near Christmas.' Leo went to the window. His slightly curmudgeonly attitude to Christmas suddenly seemed far less endearing and much more Scrooge-like, and as if to confirm it, he said, 'I can give you a few days to move your stuff out, you don't have to go right now. I'm not a monster.'

Dazed, Esme tried to think but she couldn't, she could only feel – and all she felt was that she had to get out. She stood and placed her wine glass on the table, then went and picked up her handbag from the sofa. As she retrieved her coat from the rack, Leo said, 'Esme, where are you going? We can still have dinner and—'

She closed the door softly behind her.

Esme trudged through the rain to the Singapore Sling, ignoring it soaking her hair and running down her face, mixing with her tears. She'd left her hat and scarf at the flat, but wasn't going back for them. She'd rather get wet. Every fibre of her being felt crushed. As she descended the steps to the cellar bar, leaving the world behind, a drop of rain fell from the sign and trickled down the back of her neck. She wanted to hide. To hibernate below ground and never come out.

After an emergency call to Helena, her friends were with her in half an hour. Esme's heart, pounded and punched by the day's events, felt broken and bruised. When she thought of Leo, the last thread of love snapped and her heart deflated like a burst balloon. She could even picture it in her chest all floppy, sad and wrinkled.

Mark, Lola and Helena gathered around Esme, open-mouthed and with drinks untouched as she told them all the details of her day from hell. Dance music thumped in the background and harsh neon lights lit their usual table in the corner. At least the DJ wasn't playing Christmas songs. The last thing Esme wanted right now was Wham's 'Last Christmas' blasting out while her life hit an all-time low. Having finished, Esme couldn't stop the great sob that emerged in a high-pitched puff of air, making Mark and Helena jump.

'Christ, sweetie,' said Mark, 'you need more than just a drink after all that.'

'I don't think I can stomach one right now.'

'Rubbish,' he replied. 'What you need is an enormous cocktail with a little umbrella in.' His bright blue eyes popped against his dark hair and olive skin. 'And as for that witch, well—'

Esme sobbed.

'And Leo is a complete knob,' said Lola. 'I can't believe after five years together this is how he treats you.'

'What will you do now?' Helena asked sympathetically. Esme simply shrugged. 'Tomorrow you need to go out and register with agencies,' she commanded. Helena was scarily matter-of-fact and dealt with everything with an almost military attitude. Esme watched the bubbles fizz in her glass. She had no idea what life beyond today would look like. She didn't yet know if she'd make it to tomorrow. 'You can stay with us as long as you need to,' Helena added, glancing at Mark as they were housemates.

But Esme didn't fancy sleeping on their sofa for the foreseeable future. And Eric, Lola's other half, worked from home so their spare room had been turned into an office. She let out a giant sigh.

'I'll have to move back home for a bit, won't I? I can't rent in London without a job and I don't know how long it's going to take me to get another one. I haven't got any savings and I can't scrounge off you guys indefinitely.' She leaned forward and rested her head on the table as a raindrop dripped from her soaking wet hair onto her nose.

'It wouldn't be scrounging, you're our friend,' replied Lola. 'If Felicity Fenchurch walked in here right now, I'd punch her on the nose.'

Helena rubbed Esme's back. 'From what you've said, back home isn't exactly—'

'London?' offered Esme. 'No, it's not. I don't know what I'm going to do.'

'Could you freelance and commute in?' asked Mark.

'Too far and too expensive.'

'What about some catering work? You know, weddings and stuff?' suggested Helena.

Esme hesitated. 'Yeah, maybe. But I'd still need a good reference and I don't think I'm going to get one of those now.'

'I know,' said Lola. 'You could write that cookery book you're always talking about.'

Lola had been Esme's best friend since school and knew her inside out. They came from the same town, went to the same university and had moved to London when they'd finished their studies, living together in a grotty two-bedroom flat above a kebab shop. She was also eternally optimistic, which was both helpful and, at times, annoying. 'You need to see this as an opportunity, not a setback. Okay, so you move back home for a bit. Without having to pay stupidly high London rent, and without your time being taken up by Felicity, you could write your cookbook and get it published. This is your chance to focus on it.'

'Do you really think so?' asked Esme, who felt a tiny spark of hope in the darkness of the last few hours.

'Of course you could,' agreed Helena. 'You're the best food tech around. Not only that, you're great at creating recipes too.'

Mark nodded. 'You look at this mess. Felicity thought your recipes were so good she wanted to steal them. And when I think about all the dinner parties where you've cooked for us, OMG! That salmon thing you made when I split up with Andrew? Trust me, it made it all worthwhile.'

Esme smiled and nudged Mark with her shoulder. 'What would I do without you guys?'

'Die of thirst, probably. I'm going to get another round.'

'Where will you stay tonight?' asked Helena, taking Esme's hand. 'I'm sure you don't want to go back to the flat.'

'She's staying with me and Eric, aren't you?' said Lola. 'But you're not borrowing my pants like you did at university.'

'I had an excuse then,' Esme replied. 'I didn't know how to do washing.' But suddenly her face clouded in concern. 'There is one thing.'

'What?' asked Mark, pausing on his way to get more drinks. 'After everything you've been though today, I can't believe there's anything worse to deal with.'

'Oh yes there is,' replied Esme, resting her head on the table and speaking from under her arms. 'I still have to tell my mother.'

'Well, you're on your own there, love,' said Helena, smiling. 'I've met your mum and she is batshit crazy.'

Acknowledgements

I think Christmas stories are my favourites to write, even when they don't always behave, like this book did! My first thank you has to go to my wonderful friend Belinda Missen (read her books please, she's amazing and way funnier than me!) for helping me figure out what wasn't working in the first part of the story and getting it right.

I'd also like to thank the lovely Miss Beck at my children's school for answering my questions about the rules teachers have to stick to when it comes to consoling children. Your knowledge played a huge part in the book and I'm so grateful for your time at the end of the day when I'm sure all you wanted was a sit-down and a cup of tea!

My family have always been there for me, helping me to sort out plot holes and being incredibly supportive so I'd like to thank the Baineses and the Gingers for listening to me harp on and supplying me with wine and cuddles when needed.

Finally, I'd like to thank my agent, Robbie Guillory at the Kate Nash Literary Agency, and my lovely editor Sarah Goodey at HQ Digital. I'm so proud of this book and it wouldn't be anywhere near as good without you two! Sarah, we will definitely make it to cocktails soon. I can feel it! I'd also like to give a shout-out to Helena, my copyeditor. The copyedits are my favourite part of the process because it's like putting on your perfume and a final swipe of lip gloss before you go out. Thank you, Helena!

And of course, thank you a million times to my readers. I never dreamed I'd get to write the phrase 'my readers' and it gives me goose bumps whenever I do. I'm so thankful for each and every book I get to write and it's all because of you! Whether this is the first book you've read, or you've been with me since the beginning, I'm eternally grateful that you chose me and really hope you enjoyed it. You're all superstars and I wouldn't be anywhere without you.

Hello bookworms!

Can you believe it's now Christmas in Meadowbank?

Now, I know I promised you a library story as the second instalment, but we had to switch things around, but don't worry! The library story will be coming to you in spring 2022, which isn't actually that far away, is it?!

If you enjoyed reading about Bella, Nick and Freddie, would you consider leaving a review wherever you got the book from? Reviews really help us to find new readers and I can't tell you how much it means to us to know someone has enjoyed our work. (I think it's being in our own heads so much! It makes us needy!)

If you'd like to keep up to date with my writing news and giveaways I'm running, and receive a FREE short story, you can sign up to my mailing list here: https://bit.ly/3gbqMS0. I send out a newsletter once a month, and only pop into your inbox when I've got something to tell you. I promise I won't bother you all the time!

You can also catch me on all the social media because I love chatting to people! My website is: www.keginger.com and I'm also on Facebook: www.Facebook.com/KatieGAuthor, and Twitter: @KatieGAuthor. If you're an Instagram lover, catch me at: @katie_ginger_author

Hopefully I'll see you again soon, and until then, happy reading, everyone!

Lots of love,

Katie

xxx

Dear Reader,

We hope you enjoyed reading this book. If you did, we'd be so appreciative if you left a review. It really helps us and the author to bring more books like this to you.

Here at HQ Digital we are dedicated to publishing fiction that will keep you turning the pages into the early hours. Don't want to miss a thing? To find out more about our books, promotions, discover exclusive content and enter competitions you can keep in touch in the following ways:

JOIN OUR COMMUNITY:

Sign up to our new email newsletter:
http://smarturl.it/SignUpHQ

Read our new blog www.hqstories.co.uk

🐦 https://twitter.com/HQStories

f www.facebook.com/HQStories

BUDDING WRITER?

We're also looking for authors to join the HQ Digital family!
Find out more here:

https://www.hqstories.co.uk/want-to-write-for-us/

Thanks for reading, from the HQ Digital team

If you enjoyed *The Perfect Christmas Gift*,
then why not try another heartwarming story
from HQ Digital?